NP

Dear Reader,

I'm thrilled to be telling you about *Confessions*. This book is two novels in the continuing ... of Whitefire Lake. You met ... my earlier novel that inclu... Rachelle Tremont in *He's a...* and Turner Brooks in *He's ...*

In *Confessions*, another 2-in-1 volume, you'll meet Nadine Warne, a struggling single mother, and Hayden Garreth Monroe the IV, the richest boy in town, in the first story, *He's the Rich Boy*. Then Carlie Surrett and Ben Powell take center stage in the final book, *He's My Soldier Boy*. Their tales are both heartwarming and intriguing. I think you'll like them.

I remember writing these novels when my children were adolescents. Recently one of my grown sons picked up *He's the Rich Boy* and noted that one of the scenes in the book, the part where Nadine's two not-so-perfect sons arrive home from school, was very reminiscent of his own life. He read the scene aloud and asked me if I'd used events from my life (as well as his and his brother's) for this particular book.

"Uh, not *all* of them," I told him. But the truth of the matter is, yes, those two rambunctious fighting boys, they do "remind" me of my own. Hmmm. I wonder why?

Anyway, enjoy *Confessions!* I've had so much fun going back to Whitefire Lake and being reunited with these characters. I hope you do, too!

If you want to catch up with me and my other books, please visit www.lisajackson.com or "friend" me on Facebook and join the conversation. It can get interesting!

Keep reading,

Lisa Jackson

LISA JACKSON

CONFESSIONS

HARLEQUIN®
entertain, enrich, inspire™

ISBN-13: 978-0-373-77728-0

CONFESSIONS

Copyright © 2012 by Harlequin Books S.A.

The publisher acknowledges the copyright holder of the individual works as follows:

HE'S THE RICH BOY
Copyright © 1993 by Susan Crose

HE'S MY SOLDIER BOY
Copyright © 1994 by Susan Crose

Recycling programs for this product may not exist in your area.

CONTENTS

HE'S THE RICH BOY

PROLOGUE

Whitefire Lake, California
The Present

PROLOGUE

NADINE WARNE RUBBED the kinks from the back of her neck and considered taking a bubble bath to soothe her stiff joints. How long had it been since she'd allowed herself the luxury of an hour soaking in a tub of hot water?

Years.

She simply didn't have the time. With the tiring job of cleaning other people's houses, a smaller business on the side that she was trying to get off the ground while single-parenting two rambunctious preteen boys, there didn't seem to be a minute she could call her own.

"Such is life," she told herself pragmatically.

She carried her mops and pails and boxes of wax and cleansers into the house and stashed them inside the cupboard near the back door of her small cabin. The house wasn't much, but it was paid for and the land it rested on, on the south side of the lake, would be valuable someday. She was counting on it. This small plot of land was her investment for the future—her boys' education, and nothing, not heaven or hell, would take it from her. She'd been robbed of the education promised to her, and ever since then she'd vowed to herself that her children wouldn't have to make that particular sacrifice.

And she wouldn't be as foolish as her father and believe in a rich man's dream. She scowled and refused to think about the wealthy bastard who had swindled her father.

She'd put all her hopes and dreams into this little piece

of real estate. Even though the prime properties were located on the north shore of Whitefire Lake, soon enough there would be no more land for wealthy people to build dream homes and they would have to search elsewhere; most likely on the south side.

Nadine was convinced that there would come a time when water-frontage upon Whitefire Lake would all be worth a pretty penny. At least she hoped so. That was why, when she and her ex-husband, Sam, had divorced, she'd fought like a terrier to keep this old cottage.

She smiled as she reheated a pot of coffee and glanced at the kitchen. Large enough for a table pushed against one wall, the cozy room boasted a few pine cabinets, a small expanse of wooden counter and one window surrounded by red gingham curtains that matched the three place mats stacked beneath the napkin holder and salt and pepper shakers on the table. Not much, but all she could afford.

In addition to the kitchen there was a living room, single bath, one bedroom, a large pantry converted into her sewing room and "office" and a loft with bunk beds for the boys. Not exactly the Ritz, but comfortable enough, and what John and Bobby lacked in creature comforts was surpassed by the fact that they lived practically in the wilderness, with the lake a bare twenty yards from the front porch. Frogs, deer, rabbits, squirrels, raccoons and birds were in abundance. Her children, whether they knew it or not, were far from deprived.

They should be returning soon, she thought, and glanced toward the road. Each day after school they rode their bikes to a neighbor's house where they stayed until Nadine arrived home. John was old enough to protest being "babysat," but both boys were too young to fend for themselves even for a few hours.

Pouring coffee into a mug, she wondered how things

would have worked out if, as she'd hoped, Turner Brooks, a rancher she worked for, had shown her the least bit of interest. She'd been attracted to him for years, even fantasized that he would someday open his eyes and fall in love with her, but it hadn't happened. He'd found his own true love with Heather Leonetti, a beautiful girl from his past, and Nadine had surprised herself in letting go of her dream so easily. Maybe she hadn't really loved him after all. Maybe, after the pain of her divorce, Turner had seemed a safe haven—a no-nonsense cowboy who talked straight and didn't promise her the moon.

Unlike the other men in her life.

Sam, her husband, had been a dreamer who'd spent too many hours drinking to actually make any of his plans come together, and the other man—the one to whom she'd given her heart so many years ago—was a forbidden and bitter thought.

Hayden Garreth Monroe IV. Even his name sounded as if it had been hammered in silver. At one time Hayden had been the richest boy in town, with only the Fitzpatrick boys, his cousins, for rivals to the title. And she'd been silly enough, for a brief period, to think that he cared for her.

Stupid, stupid girl. Well, that was all a long time ago, thank God.

She heard gravel crunching on the drive and knew the boys and their bicycles had arrived. Hershel, the mutt they'd inherited when someone had dumped him as a half-grown pup, yipped excitedly at the back door. With the pounding of quick feet and a few insults hurled at each other, the boys scrambled into the house, Hershel jumping at their heels.

"Shoes!" Nadine said automatically.

"Aw, Mom!" John complained, his face an angry pout as he kicked off a pair of high-tops.

Bobby, her seven-year-old, did the same, black Converse sneakers flying against the wall as he shed the shoes and made a beeline in his stocking feet for the cookie jar.

"Hey, wait a minute!" John ordered, concerned lest he somehow not get as many cookies as his younger brother.

"You both wait a minute," Nadine interjected, grabbing John by his thin shoulders and hugging him. "The least you could do is say hello and tell me how your day went at school."

"Hello," Bobby said cheerily, snatching two peanut-butter cookies before the jar was wrested away from him by John. "I got a B on my spelling test."

"That's great."

"Yeah, well, I got a 'biff,'" John retorted with a touch of defiance as he snagged a couple of cookies for himself.

"A what?"

"He got put up against the wall at recess," Bobby eagerly explained. "By the duty."

"Why?"

"'Cause she said I said a bad word, but I didn't, Mom, honest. It was Katie Osgood. *She* said the *S* word."

"I think I've heard enough. But I don't want to hear that you've been saying *anything* that even brushes upon swearing. Got it?"

"Yeah, sure," John said sullenly, looking at the floor. "Uh, Mrs. Zalinski's gonna call you."

Nadine's lungs tightened at the mention of John's teacher. "Why?"

"'Cause she thinks I was cheating on a test, and I wasn't, Mom, really. Katie Osgood asked to use my pencil and I told her to buzz off and—"

"Stay away from Katie Osgood," Nadine cut in, and John, now that his admission was over, muttered something about Katie being a dweeb and followed Bobby into the living room. Hershel, eyes fixed on the cookies, bounded after the boys, his black-and-white tail wagging wildly.

The phone rang and Nadine sent up a silent prayer for her confrontation with the teacher. John was always having trouble in school. He, more than Bobby, had shown open defiance and anger since her divorce nearly two years before.

"Hello?" she answered as the theme music for the boys' favorite cartoon show filtered in from the living room.

"Mrs. Warne?" The voice was cool and male. *Principal Strand!* Nadine braced herself.

"Yes."

"This is William Bradworth of Smythe, Mills and Bradworth in San Francisco. I represent the estate of Hayden Garreth Monroe III…."

Nadine's heart nearly stopped beating and her stomach curled into a hard knot of disgust. Hayden Garreth Monroe III had been the catalyst who had started the steady decline of her family. She'd only met him once, years before, but the man was brutal—a cutthroat business-man who had stepped on anyone and anything to get what he wanted. Including her father. In Nadine's estimation, Monroe was a criminal. She felt little remorse that he was dead.

"What do you want, Mr. Bradworth?"

"Your name was given to me by Velma Swaggart. I'm looking for a professional to do some housekeeping." At this moment in time, Nadine would gladly have strangled her aunt Velma. Just the name Monroe should have been enough of a clue for Velma to come up with another maid service. "So I'm willing to pay you the going rate to clean the house at 1451 Lakeshore Drive," Bradworth continued, and Nadine held back a hot retort.

Instead she stretched the phone cord taut so that she

could look through the window and across the lake. Far in the distance, on the north shore, surrounded by tall redwood and pine trees, the Monroe summer home sprawled upon an acre of prime lakefront property.

"The job would entail a thorough cleaning and I'd want a report on the repairs needed. If you could find someone in the area to fix up the place, I'd like their names—"

"I'll have to think about it, Mr. Bradworth," she said, deciding not to cut the man off too quickly, though she would have liked to have sent him and his offer packing. But right now, money was tight. Very tight. Aunt Velma knew that she was hungry and Velma had probably swallowed her own pride in giving out Nadine's name.

There was a deep pause on the other end of the line. Obviously Mr. Bradworth wasn't used to being put off. "I'll need an answer by tomorrow afternoon," he said curtly.

"You'll have one," Nadine replied, and silently cursed herself for looking a gift horse in the mouth. Who cared where the money came from? She needed cash to fix up her car, and Christmas was coming.... How would she afford to buy the boys the things they needed? But to take money from old man Monroe's estate? She shuddered as she hung up the phone.

Her eyes clouded as she walked out the back door and along the path that skirted the house and led down to the dock. A stiff, November wind had turned, causing whitecaps to form on the lake's usually smooth surface. She remembered the old legend of the lake, conceived by local Native Americans but whispered by the first white settlers. The story had been passed down from one generation of white men to the next, and she wondered how much of the old myth was true.

Rubbing her arms, she stared across the graying water, unaffected as raindrops began to fall. The Monroe estate.

Empty for nearly thirteen years. A splendid summer home, which Nadine had never had the privilege of visiting, but which had gained notoriety when it was discovered that Jackson Moore and Rachelle Tremont had spent the night in the house on the night that Roy Fitzpatrick was killed. Jackson had been the prime suspect as Roy's killer and Rachelle had been his alibi. She'd ruined her reputation by admitting that they'd been together all night long.

Few had gone back to the house since. Or so the gossip mill of Gold Creek maintained. Nadine had no way of knowing the truth.

She thought for a poignant moment about Hayden, the old man's son. Named for his father, born and raised with a silver spoon stuck firmly between his lips, Hayden Garreth Monroe IV had been more than a rich boy. At least to Nadine. If only for a little while. Until he'd shown his true colors. Until he'd proved himself no different than his father. Until he'd used money to buy off her affections.

Nadine bit her lower lip. She'd been such a fool. Such an innocent, adoring fool!

Her Reeboks creaked on the weathered boards of the dock and the wind blew her hair away from her face. Shivering, she rubbed her arms and stared across the lake to the wealthy homes that dotted the north beach of Lakeshore Drive.

To the west, the Fitzpatrick home was visible through the thicket of trees, and farther east, the roofline of the Monroe summer home peeked through the branches of pine and cedar.

"Damn it all," she whispered, still cursing the day she'd met Hayden.

Meeting him…riding in his boat…thinking she was falling in love with him had seemed so right at the time.

Now she knew her infatuation with Hayden had been a mistake that would remain with her for the rest of her life. She could recall their short time together with a crystal-clear clarity that scared her.

As raindrops drizzled from the sky, she let her mind wander back to that time she'd told herself was forbidden:when she'd been young and naive and ripe for adventure, and Hayden Garreth Monroe IV had shoved his way into her world and turned it upside down....

BOOK ONE

Gold Creek, California
The Past

CHAPTER ONE

"YOU MAKE SURE you pick me up at quittin' time," Nadine's father said as his truck bounced through the gravel lot of Monroe Sawmill, where he worked. He parked in the shade of the barking shed, twisted his wrist and yanked the key from the ignition of his old Ford pickup. The engine shuddered and died, and he handed the key to his daughter.

"I won't be late," Nadine promised.

Her father winked at her. "That's my gal."

Nadine's fingers curled over the collar of her father's dog, Bonanza, who lunged for the door and whined as George Powell climbed out of the cab and walked toward the office where he'd punch in before taking his shift in one of the open sheds. "Hold on a minute," she told the anxious shepherd. "We'll be home soon."

Thinking of the Powells' rented house caused a hard knot to form in her stomach. Home hadn't been the haven it had once been and the chords of discontent in her parents' marriage had, in the past months, become louder. Sometimes Nadine felt as if she were stranded in the middle of a battlefield with nowhere to turn. Every time she opened her mouth to speak, it was as if she were stepping on a verbal and emotional minefield.

Squinting through the dusty windshield, she tried not to think of life back at the house by the river, concentrating instead on the activity in the yard of the mill. Trailer trucks rolled through huge, chain-link gates, bringing in load after load of branchless fir trees, and a gigantic crane moved the loads to the already monstrous piles in the yard. Still other cranes plucked some of the logs from the river, to stack them into piles to dry.

Men in hard hats shouted and gestured as to the placement of each load. One by one the logs were sorted, their bark peeled, and the naked wood squared off before it was finally sawed into rough-cut lumber, which was stacked according to grade and size. Her father had been a sawmill man all his life and had often told her of the process of taking a single tree from the forest and converting it into lumber, plywood, chipboard, bark dust and, in some cases, paper. George Powell was proud of the fact that he came from a long line of sawmill men. His father had worked in this very mill as had his grandfather. As long as there had been Monroe Sawmill Company in Gold Creek, a Powell had been on the payroll.

From the corner of her eye, Nadine saw a car roll into the lot—a sleek navy blue convertible. So shiny that the finish looked wet as it glinted in the sunlight, the Mercedes was visibly out of place in an assemblage of old pickups and dusty cars. The sports car looked like a Thoroughbred sorted into a field of plow horses by mistake.

Nadine slid over to the driver's side of the truck and while petting Bonanza, studied the driver as he stretched out of the leather interior. He was tall, but young— probably not yet twenty—with thick coffee-colored hair that had been ruffled in the wind. His eyes were hidden behind mirrored sunglasses and he slung a leather jacket over his shoulder.

Nadine bit her lip. She didn't have to guess who he was. Hayden Garreth Monroe IV, son of the owner of the mill. She'd seen him years before when she was still a student in Gold Creek Elementary. He'd lived here for a short time, the only son of rich parents. His first cousins were the Fitzpatricks who owned the logging company that supplied most of the trees for this milling operation.

"The Monroes and Fitzpatricks—thick as thieves," her mother had often said. Between the two families they owned just about everything in Gold Creek.

Nadine remembered Hayden as a twelve-year-old boy, not as an angry young man, but now he appeared furious. His strides were stiff and long, his jaw set, his mouth a thin line of determination. He glared straight ahead, not glancing left or right, and he took the two steps to the sawmill's office as if they were one. He stormed into the small company office and the door slammed shut behind him.

Nadine's breath felt hot and caught in her lungs. She pitied whoever was the object of his obvious wrath. Fury seemed to radiate off him like the heat rising off the ground.

Suddenly she wished she knew more about him, but her memories of the Monroes and their only son, "the prince" as her brother Ben had referred to him, were vague.

She was pretty sure that the Monroes had moved to San Francisco about the time Hayden was ready to start high school and they only returned in the summer, to live in their home on the lake. Though Hayden's father still owned this mill, he had several others, as well. He only traveled to Gold Creek a couple of days a week.

Her father had summed it up at dinner one night. "Some job Monroe has, eh?" There had been a mixture of awe and envy in George Powell's voice. "Garreth takes a company helicopter from his office building in the city, whirs over here, strolls into the office about nine o'clock, glances at the books, signs a few checks and is back in the city in time for his afternoon golf game. Rough life."

Nadine had never thought much about the Monroes. They, like the Fitzpatricks, were rich. The rest of the town wasn't. That's just the way things had always been and always would be as far as she could see.

Her fingers, clenched tightly around Bonanza's collar, slowly uncoiled. The dog licked her face, but she barely noticed. She spied her father walking from the office to the main gate of the work yard. He waved before entering one of the sheds. Nadine rammed the pickup into reverse, backed up, then shoved the gearshift into first. The truck lunged forward and started to roll toward the road.

"Hey!" A male voice boomed through the opened windows.

Glancing in the rearview mirror, she slammed on the brakes. Her heart did a silly little flip when she saw Hayden, the prince himself, jogging to catch up with her—probably to tell her that the tailgate of the truck had dropped open again.

In a choking cloud of dust, he opened the door to the passenger side of the Ford and Bonanza growled. "Can you give me a ride into—?" His voice stopped abruptly and Nadine realized he thought she was one of the mill workers. He obviously hadn't expected a girl behind the wheel of the banged-up old pickup.

She glanced at the Mercedes. "Isn't that your car?"

His eyebrows knotted. "Look, I just need a lift. I'm Hayden Monroe." He flipped up his sunglasses and extended a hand.

"Nadine Powell." Self-consciously she reached across Bonanza and shook his hand. His fingers clasped her palm in a strong grip that caused her heart to pound a little.

"Ben and Kevin's little sister," he said, releasing her hand.

For some inexplicable reason, she didn't like to be thought of as a kid. Not by this boy. "That's right."

"Are you going into town?"

She wasn't, but something inside her couldn't admit

it because she knew if she told him the truth he would slam the door of the truck right then and there. She lifted a shoulder. "Uh…sure, climb in. I, uh, just have to stop by the house—it's on the way—and tell my mom what I'm doing."

"If this is a problem—"

"No! Hop in," she said with a smile. She glanced guiltily through the grimy back window and silently prayed that her father wasn't witnessing Hayden sliding into the cab. As the door clicked shut, Bonanza growled again, but reluctantly gave up his seat, inching closer to her. Nadine let out the clutch. With a stomach-jolting lurch, they bounced out of the lot. She only hoped her mother would understand and let her drive Hayden to Gold Creek. These days, Mom wasn't very understanding…. Sometimes she wasn't even rational. And though Dad blamed his wife's moodiness on her "monthly curse" or the strain of raising three headstrong teenagers, Nadine knew differently. She'd overheard enough of her parents' arguments to realize that the problems in their family ran much deeper than her mother's menstrual cycle.

So how would Donna react to her only daughter's request? Nadine's hands felt suddenly sweaty. She could just drive Hayden into town, show up late at home and take the consequences, but she didn't want to risk any more trouble.

"I just have to drop off the dog at the house," she explained, casting him a glance.

"I'm not in a hurry." But the tension in his body claimed otherwise. From the first moment she'd seen him screech into the sawmill yard, he'd looked like a caged tiger ready to pounce. His muscles were coiled, his face strained. He snapped his sunglasses back over his eyes.

"Trouble with your car?" she asked.

"You could say that." He stared out the window, his

lips compressed together as Nadine turned onto the main road into town.

"It's…it's a beautiful car."

He flashed her an unreadable look through his sunglasses. "I told my old man to sell it."

"But—it looked brand-new." The Mercedes didn't even have license plates yet.

"It is."

"I'd kill for a car like that," she said, trying to ease the tension that seemed to thicken between them.

His lips twitched a little. "Would you?" Quickly his head was turned and his attention was focused completely on her. Her hair. Her eyes. Her neck. Nothing seemed to escape his scrutiny and she was suddenly self-conscious of her faded cutoffs and hand-me-down blouse. Holding her chin proudly, she felt sweat collect along her backbone. Her pulse began to throb as he stared at her with an intensity that made her want to squirm.

"I— You know what I mean."

"Well, my old man didn't ask me to 'kill' for it, but close enough…." He rubbed the tight muscles in one of his shoulders.

"What do you mean?"

"You ever met The Third?"

"What?"

"Hayden Garreth Monroe 'The Third.'"

She shook her head. "Not really. But I've seen him a couple of times. At company picnics."

"Oh, right." Nodding, he turned his gaze back to the dusty windshield. "I even went to a couple of those. A long time ago. Anyway, then you know that my father can be—well, let's just call him 'persuasive' for lack of a better word. Whatever The Third wants, he usually gets. One way or another."

"What's that got to do with your car?"

"It comes with a price—not in dollars and cents, but a price nonetheless, and I'm not willing to pay."

"Oh." She wanted to ask more, to find out what he was really thinking, but he fell into brooding silence again and she knew by the sudden censure in his expression that the subject was closed.

The pickup cruised by dry, stubble-filled fields of grass and wildflowers, and Nadine turned onto a county road that wound upward through the hills to the little house by the river. Never before had she been embarrassed of where she lived, but suddenly, with this rich boy in the pickup, she was self-conscious. It was bad enough that he'd had to share the tattered seat of a banged-up twenty-year-old truck with a smelly dog, after riding in the sleek leather interior of a new sports car, but now Hayden would see the sagging front porch, rusted gutters and weed-choked yard.

She pulled up to the carport and said, "I'll just be a minute...." Then, remembering her manners, she added, "Would you like to come in and meet my mom?"

He hesitated, but his polite upbringing got the better of him. "Sure."

As Bonanza streaked across the dry grass, startling robins in the bushes, Nadine led Hayden up the steps to the back porch and through the screen door. "Mom?" she called, as they entered the kitchen.

A pan of apple crisp was cooling on the stove and the small room was filled with the scents of tart apples and cinnamon. Hayden took off his sunglasses, and Nadine was witness to intense blue eyes the shade of the sky just before dusk. Her heart nearly skipped a beat and her voice sounded a little weak and breathless when she pulled her gaze away and again called for her mother. "Are you home?"

"Be right down," Donna shouted from the top of the

stairs. Quick footsteps sounded on the bare boards. "What took you so long? Ben's got the car and I've got groceries to buy and—" Donna, with a basket of laundry balanced on her hip, not a trace of her usual makeup and her hair tied back in a careless ponytail, rounded the corner and stopped short at the sight of her daughter and the boy.

Nadine said quickly, "I'll pick up whatever you need at the market. I have to go into town anyway. I promised Hayden." She motioned toward him. "This is—"

"Hayden Monroe?" her mother guessed, extending her free hand while still managing to hold on to the laundry. She forced a smile that seemed as plastic as the basket she was carrying.

"That's right." He shook her hand firmly.

"This is my mom, Donna Powell."

"Nice to meet you," he said, and her mother's lips tightened at the corners as she drew back her hand.

"You, too."

Nadine was mortified. Her mother was usually warm and happy to meet any of her friends, but despite her smile, Donna Powell exuded a frostiness she usually reserved for her husband.

"You should offer your friend something to drink," she said, her suddenly cold gaze moving to her daughter. "And, yes, you can get the groceries. The list is on the bulletin board and there's a twenty in my purse...." She glanced back at Hayden again, opened her mouth to say something, then changed her mind. "Don't be long, though. I need the eggs for the meat loaf." She set the laundry on the table and tucked an errant lock of hair behind her ear before walking crisply to the kitchen closet where she kept her handbag. From within the folds of her wallet, she pulled out some money and handed the bill to her daughter.

"I'll come right back!" Nadine was grateful to be

leaving. She grabbed a couple of cans of Coke from the refrigerator, then snagged the grocery list as they headed outside. Hayden said goodbye to her mother and paused in the yard to scratch Bonanza behind the ears before he yanked open the passenger side of the pickup and settled into the seat.

Nadine was so nervous, she could barely start the engine. "You'll have to excuse my mom. Usually she's a lot friendlier…but, we, uh, surprised her and—"

"She was fine," he said. Again his blue eyes stared at her, and this time, without the sunglasses, they seemed to pierce right to her soul. She wondered what he thought of their tiny house by the river. Was he laughing at a cottage that must appear to him a symbol of abject poverty? He seemed comfortable enough in the truck, and yet she suspected he was used to riding in BMWs, Ferraris and limousines.

"Hold on to these," she said as she handed him the cans of soda, then backed the truck around, heading into town. She knew she should keep the question to herself, but she'd always been quick with her tongue. Her brother Ben had often accused her of talking before she thought.

"What did you mean about a price you weren't willing to pay—for the Mercedes?"

He flipped open both cans of cola and handed one to her. His gaze was fastened to the view through the windshield—dry, windswept fields. Propping an elbow on the open window, he said, "My father wants to buy my freedom."

"How?"

His lips twisted into a cold smile and he slipped his sunglasses back onto the bridge of his nose. "Many ways," he said before taking a long swallow of his drink. Nadine waited, but Hayden didn't elaborate, didn't explain his cryptic remark as he gazed through the windshield. She noticed his fingers drumming on his knee impatiently. It was as if she didn't exist. She was just providing transportation. She could as well have been a gray-haired man of eighty for all he cared. Disgusted at the thought, she juggled her can of soda, steering wheel and gearshift, driving along the familiar roads of the town where she'd grown up.

"Where do you want me to take you?" she asked as they reached the dip in the road spanned by the railroad trestle. They were in the outskirts of Gold Creek now, and houses, all seeming to have been built from the same three or four floor plans in the late forties, lined the main road.

"Where?" he repeated, as if lost in thought. "How about Anchorage?"

"Alaska?"

"Or Mexico City."

She laughed, thinking he was making a joke, but he didn't even smile. "Don't have that much gas," she quipped.

"I'd buy it." He said the words as if he meant every one of them. But he wasn't serious—he couldn't be. He rubbed a hand across the pickup's old dash with the rattling heater. "How far do you think this truck would get us?"

"Us?" she said, trying to sound casual.

"Mmm."

"Maybe as far as San Jose. Monterey, if we were lucky," she said nervously. He was joking, wasn't he? He had to be.

"Not far enough."

He glanced at her, and through the mirrored glasses, their gazes locked for a second, before he snaked a hand out, grabbed the wheel and helped her stay on the road. "I guess if we wanted to go any farther, we should have just taken the damned Mercedes!"

She grabbed the wheel more tightly in her shaking hands. He was talking like a crazy man, but she was thrilled. She found his rebellious streak fascinating, his irreverence endearing.

Flopping back against the seat, he shoved his dark hair off his face. They drove past the park and hit a red light.

The truck idled, and Nadine slid a glance at her passenger. "Since we don't have the Mercedes and since the truck won't make it past the city limits, I guess you're going to have to tell me where you want to go."

"Where I want to go," he repeated, shaking his head. "Just drop me off at the bus station."

"The bus station?" She almost laughed. The boy who'd given up the keys to a Mercedes was going to buy a ticket on a Greyhound?

"It'll get me where I have to go."

The light turned green and she turned left. "And where's that?"

"Everywhere and nowhere." He fell into dark silence again. The bus station loomed ahead and she pulled into the lot, letting the old truck idle. Hayden finished his Coke, left the empty can on the seat and grabbed his jacket. Digging into the pocket, he pulled out his wallet. "I want to pay you for your trouble—"

"It was no trouble," she said quickly.

"But for your gas and time and—"

"I just gave you a lift. No big deal." She glanced up at his eyes, but saw only her own reflection in his mirrored lenses.

"I want to." He pulled out a ten and started to hand it to her. "Buy yourself something."

"Buy myself something?" she repeated, burning with sudden humiliation. All at once she was aware again of her faded cutoff jeans and gingham shirt and hand-me-down sneakers.

"Yeah. Something nice."

He *pitied* her! The bill was thrust under her nose, but

she ignored it. "I can't be bought, either," she said, shoving the truck into gear. "This was a favor. Nothing more."

"But I'd like for you—"

"*I'd* like for you to get out. Now."

He hesitated, apparently surprised by her change in attitude.

"If you're sure—"

"I'm positive."

Scowling, he jammed the bill back into the wallet. "I guess I owe you one." Lines creased his forehead. "I don't like being in debt to anyone."

"Don't worry about it! You don't owe me anything," she assured him, her temper starting to boil. For a minute, with all his talk about driving away from Gold Creek, she'd thought he'd shown an interest in her, but she'd been wrong. Humiliation burned up her cheeks. What a fool she'd been!

"Thanks for the ride." He opened the door and hopped to the dusty asphalt.

"No problem, prince," she replied, then stepped on the gas before he had a chance to close the door. She didn't care. She had to get away from him. The old truck's tires squealed. Mortified, she reached over and yanked the door shut, then blinked back tears of frustration. What had she been thinking? That a boy like that—a rich boy— would be attracted to her?

"Idiot!" she told her reflection, and hated the tears shining in her eyes and the points of scarlet staining her cheeks. She took a corner too quickly and the truck skidded a little before the balding tires held. "Forget him," she advised herself but knew deep inside that Hayden Monroe wasn't the kind of boy who was easily forgotten.

CHAPTER TWO

NADINE'S MOTHER WAS waiting in the kitchen. Running a stained cloth over the scarred cupboard doors, Donna glanced over her shoulder as Nadine opened the door. She straightened and wiped her hands as Nadine set the sack of groceries on the counter. The scent of furniture polish filled the room, making it hard to breathe.

"Running with a pretty rich crowd, aren't you?"

"I'm not running with any crowd." Nadine dug into the pocket of her cutoffs, found her mother's change and set four dollars and thirty-two cents beside the sack.

"So how'd Hayden Monroe end up in our truck?"

"I was just in the wrong place at the wrong time," Nadine admitted.

"I thought you took your father to the mill."

"I did." As she began to unpack the groceries, she gave her mother a sketchy explanation of how she'd met Hayden. Donna didn't say a word, just listened as she folded her dust rag and hung it inside the cupboard door under the sink.

"And he just left a brand-new Mercedes in the lot of the mill?" She twisted on the tap and washed her hands with liquid dish detergent.

"Yep."

Shaking the excess water from her fingers, she said, "You know, it's best not to mingle with the rich folks. Especially the Monroes."

"I thought the Fitzpatricks were the people to avoid."

"Them, too. They're all related, you know. Sylvia Monroe, Hayden's mother, is Thomas Fitzpatrick's sister. They've had money all their lives—and lots of it. They don't understand how the other half lives. And I'll bet dollars to doughnuts your friend Hayden is just the same."

Nadine thought of the ten-dollar bill Hayden had tried to hand her and her neck felt suddenly hot. But her mother probably didn't notice her embarrassment. Donna was already busy cracking eggs into a bowl of hamburger, bread and onions.

"Thick as thieves, if you ask me."

"You don't know him. He's not—" A swift glance from her mother cut her justification short and she quickly bit her tongue. What did she know about Hayden and why did she feel compelled to defend a boy who had mortified her? She remembered the look on his face as he'd tried to pay for her company. He was clearly surprised that she wouldn't take the money. Her mother was right. All Hayden had ever learned was that anyone who did him a favor expected money in return. People were commodities and could be bought…if the price was right. "He's not like that," she said lamely.

"What he's 'not' is our kind. There have been rumors about him, Nadine, and though I don't believe every piece of gossip I hear in this town, I do know that where there's smoke there's fire."

"What kind of rumors?" Nadine demanded.

"Never mind—"

"You brought it up."

"Okay." Her mother wiped her hands on her apron and turned to face her daughter.

Nadine's heart began to thud and she wished she hadn't asked.

"Hayden Monroe, like his father before him, and his grandfather before him, has a reputation."

"A reputation?"

"With women," her mother said, cheeks flushing slightly as she forced her attention back to her bowl. "I've heard him linked with several girls...one in particular...."

"Who?" Nadine demanded, but her mother shook her head and added a pinch of salt to the meat. "Who?" Nadine repeated.

"I don't think I should spread gossip."

"Then don't accuse him of doing anything wrong!" Nadine said with more vehemence than she had intended.

For a moment there was silence—the same deafening silence that occurred whenever her mother and father were having one of their arguments. Donna's lips pinched as she greased a loaf pan and pressed her concoction into the bottom. "I thought you were going out with Sam."

Nadine wanted to know more about Hayden and his reputation, but she knew that once her mother decided a subject was closed, there was little to do to change her mind. She lifted a shoulder at the mention of Sam Warne. She and he had dated a few times. He was fun to hang out with, but she wasn't serious about him. "We might go over to Coleville and see a movie Friday night."

The ghost of a smile touched her mother's lips. She approved of Sam—a nice boy from a good family in town. His father was employed with Fitzpatrick Logging and his mother came into the library often where Donna worked a few afternoons a week. As far as Donna was concerned, Sam Warne had all the right criteria for a future son-in-law. Sam was good-looking. Sam was middle-class. Sam was only a year older than Nadine. Sam was safe. He probably would make a good husband; but Nadine wasn't planning to marry for a long while. She had high school to finish and college—if not a four-year school, at least a two-year junior college.

Though she couldn't get Hayden from her mind,

Nadine held her tongue. Her curiosity was better left alone, she decided, as she spent the next few hours vacuuming the house and helping her mother weed the garden where strawberries, raspberries, beans and corn grew row by row.

An hour before her father's shift was over, Nadine took a quick shower and combed her red hair until it fell in lustrous waves to the middle of her back. She slipped into a sundress and glossed her lips, thinking she might see Hayden again. Her silly heart raced as she dashed to the pickup with Bonanza leaping behind her. Guiltily she left the dog behind. She couldn't take a chance that he would soil or wrinkle her clothes in his enthusiasm for a ride.

A few minutes before quitting time, Nadine turned the old truck into the lot of the mill. Other workers were arriving for the next shift and men in hard hats gathered near the gates, laughing, smoking or chewing tobacco as they talked and relaxed for a few minutes between shifts.

From the cab of the Ford, Nadine scanned every inch of the parking area, but discovered the sleek Mercedes was gone. Her heart took a nosedive. She looked again, hoping to see signs of the car or Hayden, but was disappointed. Her brows drew together and she felt suddenly foolish in her dress.

"Don't you look nice!" Her father opened the pickup's passenger door. Smelling of sawdust and sweat, he shook out his San Francisco Giants cap, squared it onto his head and climbed into the warm interior. "Goin' out?"

"Nope." She stepped on the throttle. "I just wanted to get cleaned up."

He smiled at her and she felt foolish. "I thought maybe you and Sam had decided to go somewhere."

"Not tonight," she replied, irritated at the mention of Sam. Yes, she dated him, but that was all. Everyone assumed they were going together—even her family.

"Boy, am I glad it's quittin' time," he said, rubbing the kinks from the back of his neck. "Hardly had time for lunch, today." He leaned against the back of the seat and closed his eyes as Nadine drove him home.

It wasn't until later, during dinner, that Hayden's name came up. The Powell family, minus Kevin who was working the swing shift at the mill, was seated around the small table. Over the scrape of forks against plates, the steady rumble of a local anchorman's voice filtered in from the living room. From his chair at the head of the table, George could glance at the television and despite his wife's constant arguments, he watched the news. "It's a man's right," he'd said on more than one occasion, "to know what's goin' on in the world after spending eight hours over that damned green chain."

Donna had always argued, but, in the end, had snapped her mouth shut and smoldered in silence through the evening meal while her husband had either not noticed or chosen to disregard his wife's simmering anger.

But this night, George hardly glanced at the television. "You shoulda seen the fireworks at the mill this afternoon," he told his wife and children. Smothering his plate of meat loaf and potatoes with gravy, he said, "I was just punchin' in when the boss's kid showed up." He took a bite and swallowed quickly. "That boy was madder'n a trapped grizzly, let me tell you. His face was red, his fists were clenched and he demanded to see his father. Dora, the secretary, was fit to be tied. Wouldn't let him in the office, but the old man heard the commotion and he came stormin' out into the reception area. Old Garreth takes one look at Hayden and the kid tosses a set of keys to his father, mutters some choice words not fit to repeat at this table, turns on his heel and marches out. Damn, but he was mad."

"What was it all about?" Ben asked, buttering a slice of bread and looking only mildly interested.

"I didn't stick around to find out. But the kid didn't want his car—a honey of a machine—Mercedes convertible, I think."

"Why not?" Ben asked, suddenly attentive.

"Hayden claimed he was old enough to see who he wanted, do what he wanted when he wanted, with whom he wanted—you know, that same old BS we hear around here. Anyway, the gist of it was that he wasn't going to let Garreth tell him what to do. Said he wasn't about to be... just how'd he put it?" Her father thought for a minute and chewed slowly. "Something to the effect that he couldn't be bought and sold like one of Garreth's racehorses. Then he just flew out of there, leaving me and Dora with our mouths hangin' wide open and old Garreth so mad the veins were bulgin' big as night crawlers in his neck."

"Sounds like Hayden finally got smart," Ben observed as he reached for a platter of corn on the cob. "His old man's been pushing him around for years. It was probably time he stood up to him. Although I, personally, would *never* give up a car like that."

"Maybe you would if the price was too high," Nadine interjected.

"Hell, no! I'd sell the devil my soul just to drive a Mercedes."

"Ben!" Donna shot her son a warning glance before her knowing eyes landed on Nadine again. For a second Nadine thought her mother would tell the family about Hayden's visit, but she couldn't get a word in edgewise.

"I've never seen Garreth so furious," George said. "The old man looked like he was about to explode, and I hightailed it out to the yard and got to work. None of my business anyway, but it looks like Garreth's got his hands full with that one."

Donna shot her daughter a glance. "Nadine gave Hayden a ride into town."

Squirming in her chair, Nadine caught Ben's curious stare. "Is that right?" Ben asked.

Her father's eyes, too, were trained in her direction.

"What'd he say?" Ben wanted to know as he tried to swallow a smile.

"About the same thing that Dad overheard."

Ben snorted. "If you ask me, the whole fight isn't about a car, it's over Wynona Galveston."

"Galveston?" Donna picked up her water glass. "Dr. Galveston's daughter?"

"I think so," Ben replied. "Anyway, I heard something about it from his cousin Roy."

"I wouldn't trust anything Roy Fitzgerald said," Nadine cut in.

Shrugging, Ben said, "All I know is that Roy said Hayden's supposed to be gettin' engaged to her and she's the daughter of a famous heart surgeon or something. Roy was bragging about how rich she was."

"Well it seems Hayden isn't interested." George glanced to the television where the sports scores were being flashed across the screen. Conversation dropped as he listened to news of the Oakland A's and the San Francisco Giants, and Nadine was grateful that the subject of Hayden Monroe had been dropped. She picked up her plate and glass, intending to carry them both into the kitchen, when she caught a warning glance from her mother. *See what I mean,* her mother said silently by lifting her finely arched eyebrows. *Hayden Garreth Monroe IV is way out of your league.*

THE NEXT TIME she saw Hayden was at the lake on Sunday afternoon. Nadine and Ben had taken the small motorboat that Ben had bought doing odd jobs for neighbors to the public boat launch. They spent the afternoon swimming, waterskiing and sunbathing on the beach near the old bait-and-tackle shop on the south side of the lake.

Several kids from school joined them and sat on blankets spread on the rocky beach while drinking soda and listening to the radio.

To avoid a burn, Nadine tossed a white blouse over her one-piece suit and knotted the hem of the blouse under her breasts. She waited for her turn skiing and watched the boats cutting through the smooth water of the lake.

From the corner of her eye she saw Patty Osgood and her brother, Tim, arrive. Patty carried an old blanket and beach basket. A cooler swung from Tim's hand.

"I didn't think we'd make it!" Patty admitted as she plopped next to Nadine and began fiddling with the dial of the radio.

"I wonder how she escaped," Mary Beth Carter whispered into Nadine's ear. "I thought Reverend Osgood preached that 'Sunday is a day of rest.'"

"Maybe he thinks hanging out at the beach is resting," Nadine replied. Though she and Mary Beth were friends, they weren't all that close. Mary Beth had an ear for gossip and an eye for the social ladder at school. She was already trying to break into the clique with Laura Chandler, and as soon as she was accepted by Laura, a cheerleader, and Laura's crowd, Mary Beth would probably leave her other friends in her dust.

Patty found a soft rock station and, humming along to an Olivia Newton-John song, began to smooth suntan oil onto her skin. "Your brother here?" she asked innocently, and Nadine bristled inside. Lately she'd had the feeling that Patty was interested in Ben, and had been searching out Nadine's company just to get close to her brother.

Patty tucked her straight blond hair into a ponytail and took off her blouse to reveal a pink halter top that,

Nadine was sure, would have given the Reverend Osgood the shock of his life.

"He's in the boat," Nadine said, though she suspected that Patty, already scanning the lake, knew precisely where Ben was.

Her pretty lips curved into a smile at the sight of Ben's little launch. "Umm. I wonder if he'd give me a ride."

"Probably." Nadine turned her attention to the water. The day was hot and sunlight glinted on the shifting surface of Whitefire Lake. Several rowboats drifted lazily, as fishermen tried to lure rainbow trout onto their lines. Other, more powerful motorboats, sliced through the water, dragging skiers and creating huge wakes that rippled toward the shore.

A candy-apple-red speedboat careened through the water at a furious pace. Nadine's breath caught in her throat. Hayden was at the helm. Her throat closed in upon itself and she tried to ignore the funny little catch in her heartbeat as she watched him.

Wrapping her arms around her knees and staring at the red boat as it streaked by in a blur, Mary Beth clucked her tongue. "So he's back this summer." Her eyes narrowed a fraction. "I thought he'd never show his face around here again."

"His family comes back every year," Nadine pointed out, wondering why, once again, she felt the need to defend him.

"I know. But after *last* summer, I thought he'd stay away." Mary Beth and Patty exchanged glances.

"Why?" Nadine asked, nudging a rock with her toe.

"Oh, you know. Because of Trish," Patty said with an air of nonchalance.

"Trish?"

"Trish London," Mary Beth hissed, as if saying a dirty word. "You remember. She left school last year."

"She moved to Portland to live with her sister," Nadine said, trying to decipher the silent code between the two girls. Trish London was a girl who was known to be fast and easy with the boys, a girl always on the edge of serious trouble, but Nadine had never heard Trish's name linked with Hayden's. In fact, she was certain that most of the rumors about Trish were gross exaggerations from boys who bragged about sexual deeds they'd only dreamed about. The rumor with Hayden was probably nothing more than malicious gossip.

"You mean you don't know why she left?" Patty asked innocently, though her eyes seemed to glimmer with spiteful glee.

Nadine's guts twisted and she wanted to hold her tongue, but she couldn't suppress her curiosity. "I never thought about it."

"She was pregnant!" Mary Beth said, lifting her chin a fraction. "She went to Portland to have the baby and give it up for adoption without anyone from around here knowing about it."

"But—"

"And the baby was Hayden Monroe's," Patty insisted, a cruel little smile playing upon her lips.

"How do you know?"

"Everybody knows! Hayden's father caught him with Trish in the boathouse last summer. Garreth was furious that his son was with a girl from the wrong side of the tracks and he shipped Hayden back to San Francisco so fast, he didn't even have time to say goodbye to her. Not that he probably wanted to. Anyway, a few weeks later, Trish moved to Portland. Very quick. Without a word to anyone. It doesn't take a genius to figure out what happened." One of Patty's blond eyebrows rose over the top of her sunglasses.

Nadine wasn't convinced. "Just because they were together doesn't mean that—"

Patty waved off her argument while glancing at her reflection in a hand mirror. Frowning slightly, she reached into her beach bag and dragged out a lipstick tube. "Of course it doesn't mean that he's the father. But Tim knows Hayden's cousins, Roy and Brian. The Fitzpatrick boys told Tim that old man Monroe put up a ton of money to keep Trish's family from talking."

"Roy and Brian Fitzpatrick aren't exactly paragons of virtue themselves," Nadine pointed out.

"Believe what you want to, Nadine. But the story's true," Mary Beth added with a self-righteous smile. "And it doesn't surprise me about Trish. She's following in her mother's footsteps and everyone in town knows about Eve London!"

Nadine's stomach turned over. Eve London had earned a reputation as the town whore. With three ex-husbands and several live-in lovers, she'd often been the talk of the town. Trish had grown up in her mother's murky shadow.

Patty touched the corner of her lips where she'd smeared a little lipstick. "But that's old news. I heard that Hayden's about to get engaged to some rich girl from San Francisco. I wonder what she would say if she found out about Trish."

"She'll never know," Mary Beth predicted.

Patty lifted a shoulder. "She's supposed to come and visit Hayden at the summer cabin. There's always the chance that she'll overhear some of the gossip." With a wicked little grin, she reached for the radio again and fiddled with the dial. "I wonder what she'd say if she found out Hayden was a daddy."

"You don't know that—"

"Oh, Nadine, grow up!" Mary Beth interjected. "What

is it with you? Why won't you believe that Hayden Monroe made it with Trish?"

"Maybe Nadine's got a crush on the rich boy," Patty said as she found a country station. Settling back on her blanket, she turned her attention to Nadine. "Is that it?"

"I don't even know him."

"But you'd like to, I'll bet," Mary Beth said. "Not that I blame you. Sexy, handsome and rich. Yeah, I can see myself falling for a guy like him."

Nadine had heard enough. She didn't like the turn of the conversation and she didn't want to believe any of Patty and Mary Beth's gossip. The fact that her own mother had hinted about some sort of scandal revolving around Hayden just a few days before bothered her, but she'd lived in Gold Creek long enough to know that gossip swept like wildfire through the small town. Sometimes it was true, other times it was just people starting rumors to add a little spice to their own boring lives.

Slinging her towel around the back of her neck, she walked to the edge of the dock, plopped down and dangled her feet over the edge until her toes touched the water. The sun was hot, intense rays beating against her scalp, the bleached boards of the deck warm against her rear end. Squinting, she watched as Hayden drove his boat flat-out, the engine screaming, the prow slicing through the water.

Her heart did a funny little somersault as she focused on his dark hair blowing in the wind and his bare chest, lean and muscular. Was the story about Trish London true? Or just a figment of a small town's imagination? And what about his engagement to Wynona Galveston? Her stomach wrenched a little at the thought of Hayden getting married, but she chided herself for her silly fantasies. She'd given him a ride to town. Period. As far as Hayden was concerned, she wasn't even alive.

Ben returned, anchored his boat and hoisted himself onto the dock. "You comin'?" he asked, dabbing his face with the corner of her towel. Nadine shook her head. "Fine. Have it your way." Over the sound of Kenny Rogers's gravelly voice, she heard Ben's retreating footsteps and the low laughter of Patty Osgood. Sliding a glance over her shoulder, Nadine thought she might be sick. Patty's coral lips were curved into a sweet smile and she was leaning on her elbows, coyly thrusting out her chest, which was tanned and slick with oil. Ben sat down beside her and could barely keep his eyes from the plunging neckline of the reverend's daughter's halter top and the heavy breasts confined therein.

Shuddering, Nadine turned her attention back to the lake and the sound of an approaching boat. Her heart nearly stopped when she spied Hayden edging his speedboat closer to the dock.

"I was pretty sure I recognized you," he said, once the boat was idling. He was wearing cutoff jeans that rode low on his hips, exposing a bronzed chest with a sprinkling of dark hair. Sunglasses covered his eyes again and the old cutoffs hid little of his anatomy.

Nadine's throat was suddenly dry as sand.

Throwing a line around one of the pilings, Hayden stepped out and plopped next to her on the edge of the dock. Water beaded in his dark hair and ran down his chest. Nadine's insides seemed to turn to jelly as she stared at him. "I figured I could pay you back for the other day."

Her temper inched upward at the thought of their last conversation. Why had she bothered defending him to her family and friends? He was just as bad as they'd all told her he was. "I thought you understood how I felt about your money."

A sexy grin stretched lazily across his jaw. "I wasn't

talking about cash. How about a ride?" He cocked his head toward the boat.

"I don't think that would be a good idea," she said quickly, though a part of her yearned to take him up on his offer. Alone. With Hayden. Knifing through the water with the wind screaming through her hair. The thought was more than appealing, but she didn't trust him. Despite the fact that she'd fantasized about him daily, she still wasn't sure that being alone with him was the right thing to do.

"Look, I owe you—"

"I told you before you owe me nothing. We're square, okay?"

"Then I'd like you to come with me."

Nadine blew her bangs from her eyes. "Look, prince, you don't have to—"

Suddenly one of his large, warm hands covered hers and her heartbeat jumped. "I want to, Nadine. Come on."

She knew she should resist him, that taking a ride alone with him would be emotionally dangerous. If she didn't heed the warnings of her mother and her classmates, she should at least listen to the erratic, nearly frightened, drum of her heart. But she didn't.

He tugged gently on her arm, helping her to her feet, and before she could come up with a plausible excuse, he was helping her into the boat.

"Hey!"

Ben's voice sounded far in the distance as Hayden yanked off the anchoring rope and opened the throttle. The boat took off with so much force, Nadine was thrown back into her seat and her hair streamed away from her face. From the corner of her eye, she saw Ben, running barefoot along the dock, yelling at the top of his lungs and waving his arms frantically. Served him right for ogling Patty Osgood!

"Nadine! Hey! Wait! Monroe, you bastard..." Ben's voice faded on the wind.

Nadine laughed over the roar of the powerful boat's engine. Turning, she waved back and forced a sweet smile onto her lips. Ben motioned with even more agitation and Patty, left on the blanket, was frowning darkly, probably because Ben's attention had been ripped away from her. Too bad. Nadine laughed again before she slid a glance to the boy...well, man really, standing at the helm. The wind blew his hair, revealing a strong forehead with a thin scar, chiseled cheekbones and a jaw that jutted slightly.

"Where do you want to go?" he shouted over the wind.

She lifted a shoulder and hoped that he couldn't see through her sunglasses to the excitement she knew was gleaming in her eyes. "You're the captain."

His white teeth flashed against his dark skin. "If you don't state a preference, you'll have to accept my decision."

"I do."

He laughed at that and the deep, rumbling sound surprised her. "Hope you're not disappointed."

She considered the rumors she'd heard about him, but dismissed them all. She felt carefree and a little reckless as the boat sliced through the water at a speed fast enough to bring tears to her eyes.

He followed the shoreline, turning back on the path they'd taken. On the south side of the lake, they passed by the old bait-and-tackle shop and the dock where Ben's boat still rocked with the waves. Ben was standing at the dock and his expression was positively murderous. Nadine smiled back at him. They passed the public park and moorage, as well as the old summer camp and chapel. Following the curve of the shoreline, the boat sped along the north bank, the rich side of Whitefire Lake. Nadine caught glimpses of huge mansions nestled discreetly in thickets of pine and oak. Boathouses, patios, tennis courts and swimming pools flashed by. Every so often a private dock fingered into the clear water.

"You probably wonder why I'm driving this—" he said, motioning toward the boat, as if suddenly a little self-conscious.

"It's yours?"

"My father's," he admitted with a grimace, and then, as if guessing her next question, added, "Even though I didn't want the Mercedes, this is different. I can use the boat without having to worry about having any strings attached to it."

"No price to pay?"

"Not yet. But it could still happen." His smile faded. "With my old man you just never know. Everything comes down to dollars and cents with him." As if hearing the anger in his voice, he glanced at her. "Still want to hang out with me?"

"Talking about your father doesn't scare me off."

"It should."

"I've got two older brothers. I don't scare easily," she remarked, though her tongue nearly tripped on the lie. Truth to tell, she was frightened even now. Scared of being alone with him, scared of what she might do.

He laughed and shook his head. "You haven't come up against dear old Dad."

Seemingly convinced that she wasn't going to change her mind, he slowed the boat and edged the prow into a small cove on the north shore. Nadine's heart was thumping so loudly, she thought he could hear its uneven beat. What was she doing here, alone, with a boy she barely knew? A rich boy with a bad reputation? He decelerated the speedboat to a crawl, guiding the craft through a thin inlet that opened to a tree-shaded lagoon. "Ever been here?" he asked, and she shook her head.

She'd never been so close to all the expensive homes on this side of the lake. "Is this on your property?"

"My father's." A line of consternation formed between his brows for a second. "Garreth takes great delight in owning things and people."

"Like you?"

One side of his mouth lifted crookedly. "Well, I'm the one thing he can't buy. At least not anymore. It frustrates the hell out of him."

"And gives you great joy."

His white teeth flashed devilishly. "I do like getting his goat." Taking her hand, he guided her to a stretch of beach where sunlight pierced the canopy of pine boughs and pooled on the glittering sand. "I used to come here as a kid," he admitted, eyeing the berry vines that were beginning to encroach along the forest's edge. "But that was a long time ago, when my father could still buy me."

"You act as if your father's an ogre."

"Isn't he?"

"My dad doesn't think so." Nadine sat on a smooth, bleached boulder and wiggled her toes into the warm sand. "In fact, he thinks your father is a prime example of the American dream."

"By inheriting a sawmill or two?" Hayden snorted. "He just happened to be the son of a wealthy man."

She glanced at him pointedly, but didn't say a word.

"I know, 'like me.' That's what you were thinking, so you might as well say it."

"It's just that I don't see that you have all that much to complain about."

"But, then, you don't know my family, do you?"

She shook her head, her long hair sweeping across her shoulders. And when she looked up, he was staring at her, his feet planted wide apart, his muscles tense. She felt the undercurrent of electricity in the air, as surely as the breeze causing the branches overhead to sway. The air smelled of water and cut cedar, and over the erratic beat of her heart she heard the muted sounds of birds chirping and the distant roar of motorboats.

She swallowed against a cotton-dry throat and licked her lips.

"Do you know why I brought you here?" he asked suddenly.

Oh, God! She couldn't breathe. The air was trapped in her lungs.

"I couldn't stop thinking about you. Since the other day, when you gave me a ride."

She could hardly believe her ears and wanted to pinch herself to make sure that she wasn't dreaming. "You... haven't called."

"I didn't want to call. I didn't want to see you again." He advanced slowly and sat down next to her, his body bare inches away. "I mean, I told myself I didn't."

"Then why did you stop at the dock?" she asked, her blood pulsing wildly.

"Because I saw you again and I couldn't help myself." He dropped his sunglasses into the sand and stared at her with the bluest eyes she'd ever seen. Intense. Electric. Erotic.

She licked her lips, and he let out his breath in a whistle through his teeth.

"Why didn't you want to see me?"

Laughing derisively, he touched her arm. Her skin tingled with a heat so intense, she nearly jerked away as his fingers wrapped around her wrist. "Because it'll only cause trouble."

"I thought you liked trouble."

His gaze sparked a little. "Some kinds."

"But—"

"But not girl trouble." His fingers grazed the inside of

her wrist. "Don't tell me you haven't heard all the stories about me—all the dark tales about my past."

"I...I don't believe everything I hear."

He gazed at her long and hard, and a warmth curled inside her, gently turning over and causing her skin to tingle.

"You had a nickname for me."

"What?"

"Prince."

"Oh." She smiled a trifle nervously. "You deserved it."

"Yeah, I suppose I did," he admitted, but he didn't remove his hand. Like a manacle, the fingers encircling her wrist tightened, only warmly, gently. "What about you?"

"Me?"

"Have you been thinking of me?"

She wanted to lie. She told herself she shouldn't give him an inkling of what she really felt, and yet she despised women who calculated every thought or speech to manipulate men. She tried to yank her hand away, but couldn't.

"Well, have you?"

"Thought about you? Not a whole lot." She forced the words over her tongue.

"Liar."

"Why would I lie?" Instinctively she inched up her chin a fraction and found herself staring into eyes so blue, the sky paled in comparison.

"Because I scare you."

"I already told you I don't scare."

His eyebrow lifted an inch and his fingers moved upward to the sensitive skin on her throat. "You're trembling."

"I'm not scared."

"What, then?"

"Cold," she threw back, refusing to acknowledge that his touch caused her skin to quiver.

Laughter danced in his eyes. "Today. When it's over ninety degrees. You're cold?"

"Yes—"

"Could be you're coming down with something. Chills and a fever," he said, with a slightly wicked grin.

"Could be," she agreed, though she guessed they both knew the reason a blush was stealing up her neck and her flesh tingled all over and her pulse was beating rapidly.

He tugged gently on her arm, pulling her closer, positioning her so that his face was bare inches from hers, his breath warm as it fanned over her cheeks. "Or it could be that you're scared," he said again.

"I'm not—"

Her protest was cut short when his lips settled easily over hers. His mouth was warm and hard and persuasive, and all Nadine's resistance faded as surely as the ripples moving slowly to the shore.

Wrapping strong arms around her waist, he pulled her closer and she gasped as they fell to the ground. His tongue found entrance to her mouth, touching and exploring, flicking against her teeth and gums.

A wanton warmth invaded her blood and she opened her mouth even more, tasting him, feeling him, smelling the scent of lake water on his skin. He was hard and male and virile, calling upon a feminine part of her that readily answered.

Her entire body responded to him. Her breasts seemed to stretch the fabric of her swimsuit, and when his chest rubbed against hers, her nipples grew taut and firm beneath the shiny aquamarine Lycra. Hayden groaned and pulled her so close to him that their bodies lying on the sand were pressed intimately together. Her breasts were crushed against his naked chest and her bare thighs fit snugly against his.

A tremor passed from his body to hers, and when he finally lifted his head, his eyes were fired with a passion she'd never witnessed before.

He kissed her again and this time her lips sought his. Desire scorched them, and she felt his hardness pressing into her abdomen. His fingers moved around her rib cage as his lips stole the breath from her lungs. Gently exploring, inching upward beneath her breasts, his hands caressed her.

Moaning, she moved instinctively closer to him and he cradled one breast in his palm.

Somewhere deep in her mind she knew she should stop him, that if she continued kissing him she'd end up in a kind of trouble she'd never even considered, but her body betrayed her and the light, branding touches of his fingers against her swimsuit convinced her that what they were doing was right.

He reached for the knot of her blouse and quickly untied it, parting the cotton fabric before shifting and pressing hot, wet kisses down her neck and into the cleft of her breasts. She arched against him and a wildness deep inside her turned into a molten beast. Her hands delved into the thick strands of his hair, and he ran his tongue slowly up her breastbone, causing her to shiver in delicious anticipation.

There was a dull roar in her ears, the slamming of her heart against her ribs as his fingers rimmed the neckline of her suit. Her breasts felt full and ached for his touch.

"Damn, Nadine, I knew it would be like this with you," he said, lifting his head. His eyes were glazed and his hair fell over his forehead to cover the scar that cut across one of his dark eyebrows.

She could barely speak. "Like what?"

He smiled, a sexy, boyish smile that touched her heart. "Like there could never be enough."

"Oh." She licked her swollen lips, and he kissed her again, harder this time, with a mounting passion that swept from his body to hers. Rolling her quickly onto her back, he threw one leg between hers and she clung to him, kissing him feverishly, dismissing any thoughts of denial. He rubbed against her and she moaned in a voice she didn't recognize as her own. One hand tangled in her hair while the other scaled her ribs. His lips were everywhere. Kissing her face, her neck, her bare shoulders. And she wanted more. He lowered the strap of her suit and the stretchy fabric gave way, allowing her breast to fall free.

Groaning, he lifted it, touching her nipple with his thumb, while staring at the line that separated tanned skin from the white veined flesh surrounding the rosy tip. "So beautiful," he said, his hot breath causing her nipple to stand erect. He touched the hard bud with his tongue and Nadine arched upward, forcing more of her breast into his eager mouth. Heat exploded in her veins as he began to suck and she moved against him, wanting more of his touch. His free hand curved around her waist and fitted over one of her buttocks.

She moaned low in her throat.

"Oh, Nadine, don't do this to me," he pleaded as he lifted his head and her nipple, suddenly surrounded by air, stiffened with the cold.

"Hayden?" she whispered, and he slammed his eyes closed.

"You don't want this," he said.

"I do—"

"Damn it, Nadine, you don't." His fingers, still molded around her hip, dug into her buttock, and he swore loudly. "I don't!" With a guttural sound, he shoved himself off her and ground his teeth together. "Damn it all, Nadine!"

he muttered, rolling to his knees and shoving his hair away from his face with shaking hands. "We *can't* do this!"

Nadine, suddenly bereft, felt a tide of embarrassment stain her neck. As if coming here and making out had been her idea! "You wanted me to come here with you," she pointed out.

"Look...I didn't mean...oh, hell!" He pounded a fist into the ground, then rolled onto his back, staring up at the sky through the pine branches. The bulge in his jeans was still evident, as were the taut muscles of his jaw. "I wanted to be with you. I just didn't realize that things would get *this* out of hand."

"Don't worry," she said, hoping to hide the irrational disappointment that burrowed deep in her soul. She should be grateful for his self-control. Lord knew hers had fled. Brushing the sand from her skin and the folds of her blouse, she forced a brave smile. "Nothing happened."

"*Yet.* Nothing happened yet. But it wouldn't take long." He sent her a look that fairly sizzled. "Don't try to pretend you didn't feel it."

"I think you should just take me back to the dock," she said, wondering how she could have acted so wantonly. She thought of Trish London and realized that all too easily, she could have been seduced by Hayden. Or was it the other way around? Had she inadvertently started to seduce him? Their newfound relationship was already too complicated and frightening to think about.

"Don't get the wrong idea," Hayden said. "I *liked* what happened between us. It was what I wanted. Or thought I wanted. But..." He opened and closed one fist in frustration. "We should think of the consequences."

The consequences of getting mixed up with a girl from the wrong rung on the social ladder, she thought with a bitter taste rising in her throat. "I don't think we should talk about it."

He shook his head. "And just pretend that what we feel for each other doesn't exist?"

What we feel for each other. Her throat clogged. "I...I don't know. Nothing like this has ever happened to me before!"

"Me, neither," he admitted, and with a shaky smile, drew her into his arms again. She wanted to resist, but when he placed a tender kiss upon her cheek, she melted inside. With a sigh he rested his forehead against hers. "Some mess, eh?"

She almost laughed.

"Come here," he whispered roughly and tilted her chin upward before capturing her lips in a kiss that was sweet and chaste and so tender, it nearly broke Nadine's heart.

"What the hell is this?" Ben's voice boomed through the woods, reverberating through the trees and causing Nadine to jump away from Hayden, but she couldn't go very far. With lightning swiftness he caught her wrist and held her fast. Ben, nearly six feet of towering rage, strode into the clearing. His near-black eyes snapped with anger.

"Ben, don't—" Nadine interjected.

"What the devil are you thinking?" His gaze scraped her up and down, and the lines around the corners of his mouth turned white as he stared at her hair and open shirt. Her suit covered her breasts but one strap was still dangling over her arm.

"Oh, God, Nadine, what're ya doing?"

"I don't see that it's any business of yours!" Nadine tied her blouse beneath her breasts.

"Like hell!"

"You weren't invited, Powell," Hayden said, his fingers still gripping Nadine possessively.

"This is my sister."

"I can handle myself!" Nadine interjected.

"You're only seventeen!"

"That's no reason for you to think you're my keeper!" she shot back.

"Well, it looks like someone has to be!"

"That's enough," Hayden warned, his eyes narrowing.

Every muscle in Hayden tensed, but Ben didn't back down an inch. In fact, he seemed almost glad to have a reason to fight—an enemy he could pinpoint.

His fists curled menacingly. "Take your hands off my sister."

"Oh, stop it!" Nadine said, jerking out of Hayden's grasp.

Hayden's nostrils flared, and he looked more than eager for the fight that was simmering in the air. "Don't let him tell you what to do, Nadine."

"I won't!" Outraged, she marched up to her brother and jabbed a finger at his chest. "Leave me alone, Ben. I can handle myself! I'm a big girl now."

"Who's about to make a big mistake! If she hasn't already." Ben plucked a brittle twig from her hair and twirled it in front of her nose.

"My mistake to make."

"Damn it, Nadine. Use that thick skull of yours."

"And you take your macho, big-brother act somewhere else." So angry she was shaking, she stared Ben down.

"Nadine—"

"I said I can take care of myself."

"You always were too stubborn for your own good!" Mumbling a curse under his breath, he threw a killing glance over his sister's shoulder. "Don't you dare touch her, Monroe. Not so much as a finger—"

"Ben!"

Her brother glared at her, but beneath the rage she noticed a deep regret in his eyes. His words, however, cut like the bite of a whip. "Listen, Nadine, I expect you back at the dock in fifteen minutes. If you're not there, I'm not waiting. You can explain all...this—" he flung his arms wide "—to Mom and Dad."

Swiftly Hayden crossed the short distance and glared at Ben. Heat seemed to rise from his body, and the tension he used to restrain himself was visible in the vein pulsing at his temple. "Don't you ever threaten her," he ordered.

"Just as long as you leave her alone." With a scathing glance cast at the rich boy, Ben muttered a choice blue oath under his breath and turned quickly and disappeared down a path. A few seconds later Nadine heard the sound of his boat's engine grind, then roar away, leaving only a disturbing silence.

"I'm sorry," she said, as Hayden's face turned to stone. "I don't know what got into Ben—"

"I'd better take you home."

"You don't have to."

His jaw tightened. "Ben's right—"

"Ben's *never* right!"

"Look, you're not going to get into any trouble because of me. Come on." Without another word of explanation, he grabbed the mooring ropes and tossed them inside the boat. Nadine had no choice but to follow.

CHAPTER THREE

MIRACLE OF MIRACLES, Ben managed to keep his mouth shut. Nadine didn't know if he was honoring their unwritten code not to tell on each other, or if, because he'd been with Patty Osgood, he was as guilty as she of being with the wrong person. The purple patches on Ben's skin, just below the collar of his shirt, were proof enough of Patty's passion. If the Reverend Harry Osgood ever found out that Patty had been showing off her body and kissing Ben in his boat, there was sure to be fire and brimstone in the service on Sunday.

At dinner, Ben had ample opportunity to let the family know that Nadine had been spending time with Hayden, but he'd studiously avoided talking about waterskiing at the lake. Though several times he cast Nadine a meaningful glance across the table, he never said a word. Not even to their older brother, Kevin, when the subject of the sawmill came up.

"You'd think old man Monroe would provide a Coke machine or something out in the sheds," Kevin said as he pronged a slice of ham with his fork.

Their father, always the defender of Garreth Monroe, scooped macaroni salad onto his plate. "There's soda in the company cafeteria."

"Big deal." Kevin glowered at his father and hunched over his plate, even though their mother had told him often enough to sit up straight but at twenty-two, he was well past paying attention. In Nadine's opinion, Kevin was still a kid in a lot of ways. He liked younger girls, had lost all interest in college when he couldn't play basketball and he seemed restless, though he wouldn't give up living in Gold Creek. "All Monroe cares about is making money!" He reached for the salt shaker.

"And that's what he should be thinking about. Remember, I've got money invested with him."

At the mention of the dollars that had been "invested" with Garreth Monroe, Nadine's mother dropped her fork. The subject was touchy and a topic that was usually avoided during the dinner hour.

"It didn't help much when my basketball scholarship ran out," Kevin pointed out, and George bristled slightly.

He turned his attention to his ham and cut off a bite-size piece with a vengeance. "These things take time. The money'll be there—it's just a matter of being patient."

"Some of us are tired of waiting," Donna said.

"If you ask me, you'll never see that money again. Old man Monroe will find a way to keep it for himself," Kevin predicted.

"It'll pay off."

Nadine noticed a drizzle of sweat near her father's temple.

"Monroe's a bastard."

Donna gasped. "Kevin!"

"I'll hear no talk like that at my table," their father ordered, and the dining room was suddenly silent. Deafeningly quiet. Aside from the drone of the anchorman from the television set in the living room, no one uttered a sound.

A piece of ham seemed to lodge in Nadine's throat. She drank a long swallow from her water glass and met Ben's worried gaze over the rim. Their animosity dissolved instantly and once again they were allies in the war that seemed to be growing daily within the family. A war, Nadine was sure, in which no one would be a victor.

THE NEXT WEEK was the Fourth of July. In celebration, and because of the escalating fire danger in the woods due to dry summer conditions, Fitzpatrick Logging Company and Monroe Sawmill Company were closed. The entire town was on vacation. A fever of excitement swept through the streets of Gold Creek in preparation for a parade led by the mayor, a city-wide barbecue put on by the churches and a dance held in the park.

In addition, the Monroe Sawmill Company picnic was slated for that weekend in the county park on the west shore of Whitefire Lake.

Long before she'd met Hayden, Nadine had planned to spend most of the weekend with Sam. Now, as the celebration approached, she couldn't find any enthusiasm for being with Sam. He was nice enough and he cared about her, but…if she were honest with herself, she knew she'd rather spend her free time with Hayden. Silly girl!

The day of the city barbecue dawned sultry. Thick, gray clouds huddled in the western sky and the air didn't seem to move. The house felt a hundred degrees as Donna baked three strawberry-rhubarb pies to take to the potluck dinner.

Nadine rode into town with her parents, watched the parade, then walked to the park where red, white and blue streamers had been tied around the trunks of the largest trees. Balloons filled with helium floated skyward, while children ran and laughed and adults set up the tables covered with butcher paper. Under a canopy, several women set out platters of corn on the cob, green beans, salads, Jell-O molds and every imaginable cake and pie. Men, sweating and laughing, stood barbecuing chicken and ribs.

There was a festive feel in the atmosphere, and even Nadine, glum because she'd agreed to meet Sam, was caught in the good mood. There was a chance that she would see Hayden at the picnic. She helped her mother serve desserts and watched as children ran in gunnysack and three-legged races. Some adults were caught up in a softball game and most of the teenagers were playing volleyball or sunbathing.

Nadine couldn't help scanning the crowd, searching for Hayden. Though she'd agreed to help pour soda into paper cups, her gaze strayed from her task so often that her hands were sticky near the end of her shift.

Sam showed up in the late afternoon. With a group of boys from school, he approached the soda station and suggested that Nadine find someone to take over her job.

"Can't. I promised that I'd work until seven," she said. "Unless you want to finish my shift and spend the next couple of hours pouring soda."

"Very funny," Sam replied, though he didn't smile.

"This is important to Mom. The proceeds go to the library book fund."

"Big deal."

She felt more than slightly irritated by his attitude. "It is if you're the part-time librarian."

"I suppose." Sam ordered a Coke, then hung around the booth's window while she continued to work. He even helped out when the dinner crowd showed up, but still she resented him. Ever since she'd been with Hayden, her interest in Sam had waned. She still liked him; he'd been her friend for years, but she knew she'd never tingle in anticipation when she saw him, would never feel the powerful surge of emotions that seemed to explode in her every time she looked into Hayden's eyes.

At seven o'clock, she was finally relieved by Thelma Surrett and her fifteen-year-old daughter, Carlie. Thelma worked as a waitress at the ice-cream counter of the Rexall Drugstore and Carlie was a couple of years behind Nadine in school. With raven black hair, round blue eyes and high cheekbones, Carlie was drop-dead gorgeous and had already attracted a lot of male attention. Even Kevin, who was twenty-two, had noticed her.

Nadine quickly showed them the cash box, how to change soda canisters and the portable cupboard in which the extra paper cups were stashed. She offered to work longer and help out, but Thelma waved her aside. "I've spent half my life serving these folks down at the store. I figure Carlie and I can handle a few cups of root beer. You two go on along." She shooed Nadine out of the booth. "Have some fun. Dance."

Sam didn't need any encouragement. Grabbing Nadine's hand, he headed toward the stage where a group of local musicians were tuning up and one of the technicians was trying to eliminate the feedback that screeched from the microphone.

She had no choice but to dance with Sam. She had promised that she'd be with him for all of the celebration, yet she wasn't comfortable in his arms, had trouble laughing at his jokes, avoided his lips when he tried to kiss her.

"Hey, what's wrong?" he asked as he held her close and swayed to the band's rendition of "Yesterday."

"Nothing's wrong," she lied, knowing that Hayden Monroe was at the heart of her discontent.

"Sure." He tried to pull her closer and rather than argue, she let him fold her into a tight embrace. How could she explain that she was falling for another boy—a boy she barely knew, a boy who would probably never look her way again? She closed her eyes and remembered the kisses she and Hayden had shared, the feel of his skin, the way his touch could turn her bones to water....

"That's more like it," Sam whispered against her ear. He kissed her temple and Nadine tensed. She felt like a Judas, dancing with him, holding him when her heart was far away with Hayden Monroe.

As the song ended, she disentangled herself and made an excuse about needing to go to the bathroom. Sam found his friends and she hurried off toward the restrooms, intending to splash cold water on her face and find a way to tell Sam that she wasn't interested in him romantically.

"Having a good time?"

Hayden's voice stopped her short. She whirled, hardly daring to breathe and found him in the thickening shadows, lounging against the rough trunk of a massive cedar tree.

"I'm trying to."

"That your boyfriend?" He cocked his head in Sam's direction, where, along with a few of his friends, Sam was adding to his soda from a bottle hidden in a brown paper bag.

"He's…he's just a friend."

"Looked like more than that to me."

"You were spying on me?"

His teeth showed white in the coming darkness. "Just happened to see you." He stepped out of the shadows, and Nadine's heart lurched at the sight of him—his smooth, disjointed walk, his thick dark hair and blade-thin mouth. His eyes, midnight blue in the gloaming, held hers and the night seemed to close around them. Laughter, music and conversation grew suddenly distant, and the air, still and muggy, became thick. When his gaze shifted to her neck, she knew he could see the tempo of her heartbeat at the base of her throat.

"I'm surprised you're here," she said.

"Command performance."

"Who commanded?"

"The king." When she didn't smile, he explained, "You called me the prince. That would make my father—"

"The king," she said.

"So now I've done my duty."

Her heart dropped. "And now you're leaving."

Smoldering blue eyes held hers. "Want to come along?"

"And go where?"

"Does it matter?"

No! her heart silently screamed, but she knew she couldn't just take off. Not without an explanation to her parents and to Sam. "I can't."

"Why not?" He cocked his head toward the group of boys huddled in the parking lot. "Your boyfriend disapprove?"

"I already told you he's not—" He took hold of her shoulders, pulled her impatiently against him and cut off her explanation with a kiss. Hot and supple, hungry and anxious, his lips molded firmly over hers.

She didn't protest, but sagged against him, her arms encircling his neck. She drank in the smell and taste of him, felt the sweet wet pressure of his tongue as it insistently prodded her teeth apart and explored the dark inner reaches of her mouth.

When he dragged her deeper into the foliage, she followed willingly, her lips still pressed to his, her body beginning to respond in wanton, lusty abandon. His hands spanned her waist, and his lips claimed hers with such passion that her head spun and her body began to ache.

When one hand moved upward to cup her breast, she sighed into his mouth. His thumb brushed in eager circles over her nipples and her bra was suddenly far too tight. He slipped his fingers beneath the hem of her blouse, upward until he touched the webbing of lace that covered her breasts. Groaning, he pushed her back against a tree and she sagged as his fingers probed and plundered, massaged and sculpted the shape of her breast until she felt as if she were on fire. The ache between her thighs began to pulse.

"Why do you do this to me?" he whispered hoarsely, as if he were angry with the world. He still held her breast, but now his body was pressed against hers and he was breathing in deep, trembling gulps of air.

"Do...do what?"

"Torture me."

"I don't—"

"Oh, hell, sure you do! You've got to know it! I'm crazy when I'm around you." With his free hand he reached up and tilted her chin so that she was forced to look into his eyes, then slowly, deliberately, he circled her nipple with his other hand, gently rolling the taut bud in his fingers.

Nadine could barely breathe. Her diaphragm pressed hard against her lungs. His hips were snug against hers and his hardness was forced deep against her midriff. "You're all I've thought about for days," he admitted. "I want you, Nadine," he said simply. "And I can't have you."

She wanted to ask why, but knew the answer deep in her heart. He was the rich kid, the boy who was used to taking anything he wanted, and she was a poor girl whose father worked for his, a nobody, and therefore off-limits.

"Nadine?"

"Oh, God, that's Ben," Nadine said with a gasp as she pushed herself away from him.

"What is it with your brother? Doesn't he trust you?"

She glanced back at Hayden and flipped her hair away from her shoulders. "I think it's you he doesn't trust."

Hayden's eyes narrowed. "He's smarter than I gave him credit for."

She looked back to the dance, the torchlights being lit, the streamers and balloons and Sam, standing a little less steadily, laughing with a group of his friends. Ben was walking crisply along the path leading toward them and if it weren't for the fact that Patty Osgood called out to him, he would have surely discovered his sister with Hayden.

"I want to come with you," Nadine said impulsively, and for a second, the ghost of a smile played upon his lips. He reached for her hand, then dropped it quickly.

"Forget it."

"But you invited me—"

Hayden stared at her so hard, she didn't dare say a word. "I want nothing more in the world than for you to climb into that car and go home with me," he said, shoving a handful of dark hair from his eyes. "But it would only get you into trouble again."

"I don't care."

"Your brother—"

"It's none of his business what I do!" she said indignantly.

"But your parents?"

"They'll never know if we come back quickly."

He hesitated, then let out his breath in a whistle. "You're not making this any easier, you know. Besides, what about your…'friend'?"

"I don't owe him anything."

"You came with him."

"I came with my folks."

"You know what I mean."

She did, of course. But she'd risk hurting Sam's feelings to be with Hayden. "It's okay."

He shook his head, though reluctance shone in his eyes.

"Hayden," she said, her voice throaty, "I want to be with you. Maybe it's a mistake, but if you want to be with me, then—" Impulsively she wound her arms around his neck and he groaned.

"You don't know what you're getting yourself into."

"Tell me."

He squeezed his eyes shut, as if closing out her image would push her from his mind, as well. "Nadine, don't—"

He started to untangle her arms. Startled, she looked into his eyes and he moaned loudly. "I don't want to hurt you."

"You won't," she said. "I won't let you."

"Promise?" His face was so close she saw the tiny lines at the crinkle of his eyelids and inhaled the very essence of him.

"Promise."

His mouth captured hers and he gently tugged, pulling her lower lip into his mouth and touching it with his tongue. Liquid warmth rippled through her blood and her joints suddenly seemed to melt.

Hayden's tongue plundered and explored; his hands were hard and anxious, and she felt him tremble as he finally lifted his head and buried his face in her hair.

"What the hell am I going to do with you?" he ground out, his breath ragged and torn. "Just what the hell am I going to do with you?"

"Trust me."

The smile he flashed her was positively wicked. "I don't think either one of us should trust the other. And I *know* you shouldn't trust me. God, Nadine, I— This isn't going to work."

"I want to be with you," she said desperately.

His eyes searched her face and he smiled a little, though reluctance still shone in his gaze. "Meet me later."

"Nadine?"

Ben's voice again!

She froze. "Later?" she asked Hayden, desperate to see him again. Curse her brother for interrupting them. "But how—"

When he didn't answer, she stepped closer, surprised at her own boldness. She touched him lightly on the shoulder and he closed his eyes and gritted his teeth. "Where?"

"Don't—"

"Where?" she demanded.

He held her close and kissed her, appearing to accept their fate. "At the lake. Tomorrow night," he finally said, then turned and disappeared into the darkness. "In the lagoon where we were before."

Nadine shivered as he left. She rubbed her arms and wondered if she'd have the nerve to meet him again. What did she know about him? He was rich. He'd never known the meaning of want. He didn't have much respect for his father. And she lost all sense of reason when he kissed her.

She was acting like a ninny. She was no better than Patty Osgood or Trish London. But she couldn't help herself. Hell could freeze over and Nadine knew that tomorrow night she'd be waiting for him. *At the lake.*

THE AIR WAS thick and heavy, the sky hazy for the Monroe Sawmill Company picnic. Unlike the day before, all the food and beverages were catered and served by a firm from Coleville. Compliments of Garreth Monroe.

A whole pig roasted upon a spit, and cloth-covered tables were arranged under a huge tent, where salads cooled in trays of crushed ice, and a huge electric freezer was churning homemade ice cream to top fresh strawberry shortcake.

Despite the threat of thunderstorms, the mood of the employees of the sawmill company was carefree. Laughter and conversation floated on the air tinged with the acrid scents of cigarette smoke and sizzling pork slathered in barbecue sauce.

Blankets were spread upon the grass and sunbathers soaked up rays while children splashed in the roped-off area of the lake and older kids swam farther out.

Nadine's entire family attended. Her mother, sipping iced tea, sat at a table and gossiped with other wives of the mill employees. George Powell threw horseshoes with some of his friends. They talked and laughed and sipped from cups of beer drawn from a large keg.

Kevin swam with the younger men he worked with and Ben linked up with Patty Osgood, who had come as a guest of one of the foreman's daughters.

The muggy air was cloying, and sweat collected on Nadine's skin as she sat on a blanket next to Sam. Her eyes, hidden behind dark glasses, continually scanned the crowd for Hayden. She knew she was being foolish, but she couldn't stop herself from searching the groups of people. Surely he would attend. His father was here, glad-handing and acting just like one of the men who worked for him. He pitched horseshoes, downed beer and told off-color jokes with his employees. Dressed in crisp jeans and a polo shirt, he squired his wife, Sylvia Fitzgerald Monroe, through the tents and games. Hayden's mother managed to smile, though no light of laughter lit her cool blue eyes. Her silver-blond hair was coiled into a French braid at the back of her head and the nails of her fingers were painted a dusty shade of rose, the same color as her jumpsuit. A delicate scarf was pinned around her neck and diamonds winked at her earlobes.

Hayden was nowhere in sight.

Nadine tried to hide her disappointment and pretended interest in a game of water volleyball, but she wished she'd catch a glimpse of him.

"You're still mad at me," Sam said, touching her arm.

"I'm not mad."

"Just because I tied one on. It was a stupid thing to do and I'm sorry. It won't happen again. Come on, Nadine, don't hold a couple of drinks against me."

"It was more than a couple."

"I got a little out of hand—"

"You threw up all over the back porch, Sam," she said, irritated. Even her parents had been angry.

"I'm sorry. Forgive me?" he asked.

"Nothing to forgive." She leaned forward and wrapped her arms around her knees. Sam had added liquor to his soda last night, and it was the first time Nadine had ever seen him drunk.

Leaning back on his elbows, Sam adjusted his sunglasses to protect his eyes. He had sobered up since the night before and was suffering with a hangover. His skin was paler than usual and two aspirin hadn't seemed to help to ease the pain of what he called a thundering headache. "Don't tell me. I know," he said, wincing as a ten-year-old boy set off a string of firecrackers against all park and company regulations. The kid was promptly scolded by his mother. "I deserve this." Sam reached for her hand and held it between two of his. "I probably wouldn't have gotten so drunk if you wouldn't have been in such a rotten mood."

"So now it's my fault?" she asked, removing her hand and feeling uneasy.

"What's going on, Nadine? Something's not right—and don't bother trying to deny it."

She couldn't. It was time to be honest with Sam. She owed him that much. "I...I just think we shouldn't see so much of each other," she said in a quick rush of breath.

Sam didn't move a muscle, just continued staring across the lake. "So much of each other?"

"Yes..."

"You want to date other guys?"

"I—"

"Who?" he demanded, suddenly facing her. His face suffused with color while his lips turned white.

"Who what?"

"Who is he?" he asked, his voice low. "There's someone else, isn't there?"

"No one special," she lied.

"Like hell! Dammit, Nadine, where'd you meet him?" he demanded, suddenly furious.

"I just think it's time we saw other people. That's all."

"Why now?" He glanced around, as if he expected one of the boys at the picnic to come up to Nadine and claim her as his own. "It's not like we're going steady or anything."

Nadine tucked a strand of hair around her ear and hoped their conversation didn't carry to other knots of people crowded around the stretch of beach. "In this town, two dates with one person is the same thing as going steady. You and I both know it. People couple up."

"And you don't want to be part of a couple."

She steeled herself. She didn't want to hurt him, but she couldn't live a lie. "Not right now, Sam."

His shoulders slumped as if with an invisible weight, and she felt instantly sorry for him. She liked Sam, she did. But he wanted their relationship to deepen, and he wasn't the boy for her. The sooner he knew it, the better for him, she reasoned, but couldn't help feeling like a heel.

And just who is the boy for you? Hayden Garreth Monroe IV? She frowned and picked up a small stone, skipping it along the surface of the lake and watching the rings of water ripple in perfect circles.

"I guess this is it, then," Sam finally said, his jaw set in stony determination.

"We—"

"Don't say 'we can still be friends,' Nadine, because we can't. At least I can't. Not right away."

"I didn't mean to—"

He waved off her apology, stood and without a look over his shoulder, found his way to a pack of his friends who were hanging out with Joe Knapp, Bobby Kramer, Rachelle Tremont and her younger sister, Heather.

Rachelle was a striking girl with long, mahogany-brown hair, and hazel eyes that were as intelligent as they were beautiful. Heather was blonde and petite, but much more outgoing than her older sister. Though the youngest member of the group, she was the center of several boys' attention, including Sam's as he sidled up to them.

Nadine let out a sigh of relief and wiped the sweat from her forehead. Thunderclouds rolled over the mountains, gray and ominous and burgeoning with rain.

Tossing another stone into the water, Nadine closed her eyes, and silently wished that she'd see Hayden again soon.

Forty-five minutes later, as the pig was being carved, a speedboat jetted toward the dock. Nadine's heart leapt as she recognized Hayden steering the boat inland. But her euphoria was quickly doused as she noticed his passenger—a tall, willowy girl who hopped out of the boat before Hayden could set the moorings.

His date was gorgeous. Her short blond hair was thick and streaked in shades of gold. A white sundress showed off a tan and legs that seemed to go on forever. At five-eight or -nine, she was model-thin and radiant. An effortless smile played upon her full lips as she grabbed hold of the crook of Hayden's arm and made a beeline toward his parents.

Sylvia Monroe embraced her and Hayden's father winked and gave her an affectionate pat on her rump while Hayden glowered and the girl, Wynona Galveston, Nadine guessed, was still linked to Hayden. She said something clever, everyone but Hayden laughed and Garreth herded them into one of the shaded tents.

Nadine felt as if a trailerload of stones had been dumped into her heart. Wretchedly she sat alone on her blanket, pretending interest in the swim races being organized for the children, while inside she was miserable. How could she have thought he cared for her—a simple, not-all-that-pretty country girl—when he was used to such sophisticated beauty? She felt incredibly naive and wretched inside.

Avoiding Hayden, she wished she could think of an excuse to go home. She didn't have a ride, unless her father drove her, and from the looks of him, his face starting to flush with the combination of too much hazy sun and beer, a smile fixed onto his face, she doubted he would want to end the party.

Her mother, too, seemed content to sit and gossip with the other women while fanning herself with her fingers. Ben, with Patty Osgood, was having the time of his life. Even Kevin was laughing and joking with his friends and a few younger kids.

Sam was already gaining the attention of some of the girls, but Nadine didn't care. He deserved someone who could care for him more deeply than she could. As for Hayden, he didn't seem to be having much more fun than she.

She was shoving around the scalloped potatoes on her plate when Ben plopped down beside her at the picnic table. "So, it looks like Lover Boy has found someone new."

She shot him a look meant to convey the message *Drop dead.*

"Dr. Galveston's daughter. Big bucks." He picked up his corn on the cob. "She looks good, too—blonde and sexy."

"Like Patty Osgood."

Ben scowled slightly. "I'm just pointing out that Wynona Galveston has looks and money. Who could want anything else?"

"Grow up," she muttered.

"Maybe you should take that advice." Ben ate a row of corn from his cob, then hooked a finger toward the tent where Garreth Monroe was holding court. "Face it, kid, you'd never fit in—and count yourself lucky for that. If Hayden marries Wynona, I'll bet she'll be miserable."

"Why?"

"If not because of her husband, then look at her father-in-law. He's had more affairs than you can count, and see the way he's all smiles whenever Wynona's around. What do you bet, he's already set his sights on her."

"That's gross. He's old—"

"Enough to be her father," he finished for her. "Or her father-in-law. Doesn't matter. He's a tomcat. Always on the prowl. That whole family is bad news, Nadine. You're better off with someone else."

"Like Sam?" she asked, but to her surprise Ben shook his head.

"Don't limit your options, kid. You could have the best. Don't get me wrong. Sam's a good guy, but...well, if you want to know the truth, he's got his share of problems."

"Is there anyone good enough?" she asked, a little hot under the collar. Where did Ben get off, trying to tell her how to run her life?

"Maybe not."

"How about Tim Osgood?" she said. "Patty's brother?"

Ben's good mood vanished and he dropped his corncob onto his plate. "I was only trying to help."

"Well, I can handle myself."

"Sure you can," he said, unconvinced. "Just don't do anything stupid."

"Nothing you wouldn't do," she replied, and his head snapped up as quickly as if he'd been stung. He started to say something, changed his mind and tore into the rest of his dinner. Nadine couldn't eat another bite. She disposed of the remains of her meal in one of the trash cans and started back to the lake again, but stopped short when she nearly ran into Hayden and Wynona, stuck together like proverbial glue.

"Nadine!" Hayden grabbed hold of her arm for just a second, as if he were afraid she might slip by.

"Hi." Her heart was thumping so fast, she could barely breathe. Surely they could both hear its erratic beat. Was she imagining things or did the tiniest smile touch the corner of his mouth at the sight of her? He made hasty introductions and Wynona, still clinging to his other arm, smiled brightly, as if she really was pleased to meet yet another one of Hayden's father's employee's family members. She had grit; Nadine would give her that much.

Hayden's eyes were hidden by sunglasses again, but Nadine felt the power of his gaze. Somehow she managed to make a few sentences of small talk before spying Mary Beth. "Look, nice to meet you, but I've got to run," she said, hoping to stop the awkward conversation.

"Nice meeting you, too," Wynona sang out as Nadine hurried past them. In the brief seconds Hayden had restrained her, Nadine had felt his fingers tighten possessively against the soft flesh of her upper arm, reminding her that they were supposed to meet.

Or was she just fantasizing? He was with Wynona, for God's sake, and though he didn't appear to be having the time of his life, that was easily enough explained. Considering his feelings for his father, he was probably looking for a way to escape this charade of a celebration.

She rammed her fists into the pockets of her shorts and decided there was only one way to find out how Hayden felt. Tonight. She'd meet him at the lake tonight as they'd planned. If he stood her up, then she'd understand that he was just using her for idle sport.

But if he showed up… Oh, Lord, what would she do then?

CHAPTER FOUR

"DON'T YOU EVER think of the children? Of me?" Donna
Powell's voice carried up the stairs and Nadine squeezed
her eyes shut, wishing she couldn't hear the snatches of
conversation that filtered into her room. Though her door
was closed and she was lying on her bed on the opposite
side of her small room, the argument seemed to pulse
around her, rising like heat to the rafters and ricochet-
ing off the sloped, papered ceilings. She'd waited for two
hours, hoping her parents would climb up the stairs and
go to bed so that she could safely sneak out, but their argument had started a few minutes ago and had quickly
escalated into a horrible fight.

"What about all the promises?" Donna went on. "All
the dreams you've put into the kids' heads?"

Nadine barely dared breathe and put her hands over
her ears, praying that they would stop, that this war that
had been going on for the past few years would just end.
But she knew it wouldn't, and her stomach knotted at
the thought that someday soon her mother would file
for divorce.

"Please, God, no," she whispered, fighting back tears.
The room seemed stuffy and close and she had to get
away. Away from the accusations. Away from the anger.
Away from a house where love had died a long time ago.

To Hayden.

If he would still have her. If he wasn't tied to Wynona
Galveston.

Still lying on the bed, she reached for her denim cutoffs, slung carelessly over the bedpost, and she heard her mother's sobs, broken only by well-worn phrases.

"How could you…everything we ever worked for… the kids…did you ever think once about them?"

Her father's reply was muffled and sounded apologetic. Nadine couldn't just lie on her sagging mattress, staring up at yellowed wallpaper, wondering if this would be the time her parents would wander up the stairs and tell their children that they were splitting up.

Besides, Hayden was waiting for her. He *had* to be.

She slipped out of bed, slid into the cutoffs and found a beat-up pair of Nikes her brother Ben had worn three years ago. Yanking a T-shirt over her head, she silently prayed her mother wouldn't come up and check on her.

As she had when she was still a student at Gold Creek Elementary, she opened the bedroom window and hopped onto the wide sill. The heavy branch of the maple tree was less than a foot away. Nimbly Nadine swung onto the smooth limb, crawled to the trunk and shimmied to the ground.

Though it was late, summer heat was still rising from the earth. The moon was full, but partially obscured by clouds, and far in the distance the lights of Monroe Sawmill winked through the trees. She cast a look over her shoulder at the two-storied frame house her family rented. The only light glowed from the kitchen, and through the gauzy curtains, Nadine saw her mother, shoulders slumped, hips propped against the counter. Her father sat at the table, nursing a beer and scowling as he peeled the label from the bottle. For the first time in her life Nadine thought George Powell looked old.

He'd been cranky ever since they'd returned from the company picnic, and Nadine couldn't help speculating if Hayden's father was to blame. Garreth had cornered

George Powell just before the festivities ended, and instead of seeming buoyed by his employer's attention, George had been tight-mouthed and silent all the way home.

Biting her lip, Nadine turned and started walking through the sultry night, away from the anger, the hatred, the lying and heartache of that little house where once there had been so much love.

Dear God, what had gone wrong? She could still remember her mother and father in their younger years, while she and her two brothers were in elementary school. There had been hope and laughter and songs in their house on Larch Street in Gold Creek. Every Friday night, her mother had laughingly told her children she was "taking the day off." Her father had come home from working the day shift at the mill and the family had eaten sandwiches at the big, round kitchen table. As Mom had cleaned up, Dad had dragged out the cards and taught the kids how to play go fish, rummy, pinochle and even poker. Later in the evening, after the cards had been shoved back into the drawer, Mom had played the piano. The whole family had sat in the living room singing familiar old songs, everything from ragtime and big band music to soft rock. Even their father had joined in, his rich baritone contrasting to Mom's sweet soprano.

So when had it changed? Nadine kept walking. Fast. Her brow puckered and she bit hard on her lower lip. She began to sweat. A few cars passed, but, by instinct, she ducked into the shadows, waiting until the taillights, as two glowing red specks, disappeared in the distance.

Life had been good when the Powell family had lived in town, in their own house—a small ranch with three tiny bedrooms and a family room. It had been small, but cozy. Then, a few years ago, her father had decided that his family should sell their house in town and move to the rented place less than two miles from the lake.

Nadine's feet crunched on the gravel strewn between the asphalt road and the ditch. The night was humid and thick, but she kept walking. Soon she'd be at the lake. It would be cooler near the water. And Hayden. He'd be there. He had to be. She crossed her fingers.

The first indication that something wasn't right in her parents' marriage had happened soon after they'd moved.

Nadine remembered the day vividly. It had been one of those hot, lazy summer Sundays when the whole family had planned to be together. In the past those days had been wonderful. The entire family picnicked in the backyard and feasted on Mom's fried chicken, potato salad, berry pie and watermelon.

But that particular Sunday things had started out wrong. Ben and Kevin had been fighting, wrestling in their room across the hallway, and Ben, in an attempt to restrain his older brother, had thrown a punch that landed through plasterboard separating the boys' room from the staircase.

Dad had been furious and threatened the boys with his belt. Her mother, horrified, had blanched at the size of the hole in the wall and had fought a losing battle with tears. Nadine had stood and stared at the wall, while her father had rounded up the boys, forcing them downstairs. "We may as well go get that firewood today anyway," he'd said to his wife, as he'd herded Ben and Kevin to the pickup.

Mom hadn't said a word, just watched from the back porch as the old truck had rolled backward down the lane. Then, without glancing in her daughter's direction, had said, "You'd better get ready for church, Nadine."

Nadine, staring longingly after the plume of dust in the drive, had been about to protest, but her mother's eyes had narrowed quickly. "Now, don't give me any back talk.

I'm not in the mood. I've got a headache coming on and we're late as it is, so hurry on upstairs!"

Nadine hadn't argued. She'd thrown on her one good dress and had pulled her wild red-brown curls into a ponytail. Her mother had hardly said a word as she'd driven into town. Her thoughts had obviously been miles away, but as she'd parked the old Buick wagon in the church lot, she'd turned her head suddenly and stared at Nadine so intently that Nadine had wiped her cheek, sure there was a smudge on her face.

Donna's eyes had been moist and red. She'd forced a trembling smile and touched Nadine's hair. "Take my advice," she'd said, fighting tears, "be careful who you marry. Don't believe in fairy tales."

Nadine had wanted to ask why, but had known from her mother's expression that the question was better left unspoken. Later, after listening to the Reverend Osgood's blistering sermon on the wages of sin, and catching a few curious looks from Mrs. Nelson, Donna had driven home without bothering to switch on the radio. She'd been so lost in thought, Nadine had been certain that she hadn't even seen the road in front of them.

At home, after changing into faded slacks, Donna had baked a strawberry pie and started frying chicken, but she'd cooked as if with a vengeance, ordering Nadine to fetch her the oil, and the flour and whatever else she'd needed. Worst of all, she hadn't sung. Not one solitary note. As long as Nadine could remember, Mom had sung while she worked in the kitchen. Just as she'd sung in the church choir, she'd sung while she'd hung up the clothes on the back porch, she'd sung with the radio when she drove to her part-time job at the town library and she'd hummed while flipping through magazines and dreaming. Music had always been a part of their lives. But that horrible Sunday, while prodding the sizzling pieces of chicken, Donna's lips had been tightly compressed and deep lines had furrowed her usually smooth brow.

Later, when her father and brothers had returned, Mom's grim expression hadn't changed. The chicken had simmered in the frying pan on the stove, the pies had cooled on the kitchen counter and Donna, frowning, had swept the back porch as if she'd thought her life depended upon it, only looking up when she'd heard the familiar crunch of gravel under the battered old pickup's tires.

The lines around her mouth had become firm and set, but she hadn't stopped sweeping. Nadine, whose job it had been to take the potato peels to the compost pile, had stopped dead in her tracks.

George Powell had seemed to have forgotten his sons' bad behavior. He had whistled as he'd parked the old pickup near the carport. His thick red hair had been wet with sweat, his face flushed. Kevin and Ben had torn out of the cab of the truck and found the hose. After taking long drinks, they'd taken delight in spraying each other and even casting a shot or two in Nadine's direction.

"Smells good," George had told his wife as he'd mounted the stairs and brushed her cheek with his lips. "Lord, am I hungry." He'd tried to wrap his grimy arms around his wife, but she'd sidestepped his embrace.

"Supper'll be ready in an hour."

Rebuffed, Nadine's father had rubbed a sore spot in his back and rotated his neck until it creaked. He'd caught sight of his daughter and winked. "You're the lucky one, gal! You won't have to work with your back, ever!"

"Don't talk nonsense to the children—"

With a wide grin, he'd grabbed hold of his daughter and scooped her into his strong arms. "You, missy, might just be the first woman president."

"I said, 'Don't talk nonsense to the children.'"

"Your ma's no fun," George had whispered into

Nadine's ear before setting her on her feet. "We've all got us a little investment plan."

"With Garreth Monroe," his wife had pointed out, scowling as she'd swept the floor so hard, Nadine had wondered if the broom handle might snap.

"And Thomas Fitzpatrick," her father had defended, wiping the sweat from his ruddy face.

"With the money we had from that house of ours." Her lips had turned white. "Rich people don't make a habit of sharing their wealth."

"Well, you might be surprised." George had ignored his wife's disapproval and managed to wrestle the hose from his sons. "You'll see," he'd told them all with a conspiratorial smile as he'd twisted off the faucet and sauntered into the carport where he kept a case of beer in a rattling old refrigerator. "When you kids are famous lawyers and surgeons, we'll just see. Why, I might even buy your mother a new house or take her on a cruise."

The lines around Donna Powell's mouth had deepened. "That'll be the day," she'd mumbled under her breath, and Nadine had wondered why her mother was so cruel, why she didn't believe in Daddy's dreams. "I've never yet seen a Monroe or a Fitzpatrick doing a favor for anyone."

"Garreth Monroe's my boss. He wouldn't sell me short." George had wrenched the cap off his beer, set his boot on the fender of the family's old Buick and taken a long swallow. "Yes sir," he'd said, squinting at the small backyard. "We'll move out of here…maybe get one of those fancy houses on the lake. How'd ya like that, honey?"

Donna had stopped sweeping for a moment. She'd leaned on the handle of her broom and the lines around her eyes had softened a little. A smile had teased her lips, and Nadine had been taken with how beautiful her mother was when she wasn't worried.

"You'd have fancy dresses and jewelry and you wouldn't have to run around in this rattletrap of a station wagon." He'd kicked on the bumper to add emphasis to his words. "No way. We'd buy ourselves a fancy sports car. A BMW or a Mercedes."

"A Cadillac," she'd said. "One with leather seats, air-conditioning and a sunroof."

"You got it!" George had said.

As if she'd been caught being frivolous, Donna had scowled suddenly and shoved the broom over her head and into the corner of the porch roof, jabbing at a mud-dauber's nest. The wasp had buzzed frantically around its attacker's head, but Donna hadn't given up, she'd just kept poking the worn straw of the broom into the rafters until the dried mud nest had fallen to the floor. Grimacing, Donna had swept the remains, baby wasps, larvae and all under the porch rail and into the rhododendron bushes.

"You'll be the richest woman in three counties," George had predicted as he'd finished his beer.

"That'll be the day," Nadine's mother had muttered, and her voice had rung with such bitter disappointment, Nadine's stomach had tightened into a hot little knot.

"Come on, Kev. Ben, we've got work to do. You two unload the truck and I'll split the wood. Nadine, you can bundle up the kindling."

As Nadine had walked to the back of the woodshed where her father's ax was planted on a scarred stump, she'd glanced over her shoulder at her mother, who had tucked the broom into a corner of the porch and walked stiffly through the screen door.

If only Mom believed she'd thought then as she'd thought oftentimes since. *If only she trusted Dad!*

Five years had gone by since that day. Five years of watching as the happiness the small family had once shared had begun to disintegrate, argument by argument.

But the fighting wasn't the worst part. It was the long, protracted silences Nadine found the most painful, when, for days, her mother wouldn't speak to anyone in the house.

"Don't worry about it," her father had advised his children. "She's just in one of her moods." Or he'd blame his wife's sour disposition on "her time of the month." But Nadine knew that the problems ran much deeper. She was no longer a child, not quite so naive and realized that the root of her mother's discontent had more to do with her husband than her menstrual cycle.

Her father's dreams had begun to fade as, year after year, they still lived in the rented house outside of town. Now, not only did her father still work in the mill, but her oldest brother, Kevin, did, as well. Kevin had dropped out of college and returned to Gold Creek—a fatal mistake in Nadine's opinion. A mistake she'd never make.

She walked so quickly, her legs began to ache. Her skin was damp with perspiration. The forest around the road grew thick, and the only sounds in the night were the thump of her shoes on the pavement and the noise of her own breathing. She thought of Hayden and rubbed her sweaty palms on the front of her cutoffs. Was she on a fool's mission? What if he wasn't waiting for her?

The smell of water carried on the wind, and Nadine hurried unerringly to the sandy shore of Whitefire Lake. She grimaced as she considered the old Indian legend that every now and then was whispered in the streets of Gold Creek and wondered if she should stay here until morning, sip from the lake and hope the God of the Sun would bless her. Her lips twisted when she thought about the reverend and what he would say about her blasphemous thoughts.

Following the shore to a dock, she recognized Ben's boat. Ben had traded a summer's worth of work as a handyman and yard boy for the boat and he paid a moorage to the owner of the dock, the father of a friend of his. Nadine had no qualms about using the craft. She climbed into the boat and rowed, watching as moonlight ribboned the water and fish rose to the calm surface.

There was no cooling breeze off the lake. The waters were still and calm; the only noises were the lap of her oars as they dipped into the water, and the nervous beat of her heart. Somewhere, in the far distant hills, thunder rumbled ominously.

She rowed toward the middle of the lake, and once she'd put a hundred yards between herself and the shore, she started the engine. The old motor coughed and died before roaring to life. With the partially blocked moon as her guide, and help from a powerful flashlight Ben kept in the boat, she steered the craft toward the north shore.

Three times she passed the entrance to the cove before she found the break in the shoreline that led to the lagoon. Her hands were oily on the helm. Turning inland, she steered through the narrow straight and, as the lake widened again, cut the boat's engine. Slinging the mooring rope over her shoulder, she hopped over the side and anchored Ben's craft. If her brother guessed what she was doing, he'd kill her, she thought uneasily, but closed her mind to her family and her problems at home. For now, she had to worry about Hayden. If he didn't show up, she'd try to take Ben's advice and forget him; if he did appear, her life would become even more complicated.

Damned if you do. Damned if you don't. One of her father's favorite sayings suddenly held a lot more meaning.

Listening to the sounds of the night, she recognized the soft hoot of an owl, the rustle of undergrowth as some night creature passed, the sigh of a gust of sudden wind as it shifted and turned, moving the branches overhead.

Nervously she checked the luminous dial of her watch every three minutes.

As the first half hour passed, her reservations grew. How long would she wait? An hour? Two? Until dawn? The first few drops of rain began to fall from the sky.

The snapping of a twig caused her to jump to her feet. Heart pounding in her throat, she whirled, facing the noise. What if it wasn't Hayden? What if his father... or some criminal escaping justice were hiding in the—

"Nadine?"

His voice made her knees go weak. "Over here."

She saw him then. His dark profile emerged from a path between two trees. Relief chased away her apprehension and she walked quickly to him.

"I didn't think you'd come," he said as she approached, and before she could answer, he swept her into his arms and his lips claimed hers with such hunger, she melted inside. She kissed him eagerly, her arms wrapping around him, her heart thundering. He'd come for her!

His kiss was hot and demanding, his tongue anxious as it parted her lips and easily pried her teeth apart. Together they tumbled to the ground, hands and arms holding each other close. "Nadine, Nadine," he whispered hoarsely over and over again.

"I was afraid you wouldn't show up," she whispered, tears suddenly filling her eyes.

"I said I would."

"But you were with—"

"Shh." He kissed her again. More tenderly. "I couldn't have not come here if I'd wanted to," he admitted, sighing as if his fate were sealed and he had no way to change it. "I was afraid you wouldn't be here."

"I told myself I'd wait until dawn."

"And then?"

"Then I'd figure that you didn't want to be with me."

"If you only knew," he whispered against her ear, his fingers twining in her hair.

He touched her chin, cupping her face, his eyes dark as a raindrop slid down his nose. "Nothing could have stopped me from being here. Not God. Not the devil. And not even my father."

She thrilled as his lips found hers again and she kissed him feverishly. He moaned into her mouth as the kiss deepened, touching her very soul. His hands were gentle, but firm, and one of his legs wedged between hers. Her fingers curled over his shoulders and her breath was hot and trapped in her lungs. An uncoiling warmth started deep within her, spinning in hot circles, and caused her to press against him.

His hands found the hem of her T-shirt and explored the firm flesh of her abdomen, searching and probing, moving ever so slightly upward, scaling her ribs. She thought she would go mad with want and her own fingers tugged his shirt free of his jeans and felt the hard muscles of his chest, the light springy hair, the flat nipples that seemed to move beneath her hands. Groaning, he reached into her bra, drawing out breasts that ached for his touch.

Nadine's nipples reacted and she wanted more. He yanked her T-shirt over her head and gazed down at her. Within seconds he'd disposed of the lacy scrap of cloth and was kneading her gently, his tanned hands dark against her white, veined skin, rain beginning to splash against the ground.

She moaned, and when he dipped his head to suckle, a shock wave caused her to buck against him, her hips instinctively pressing against his.

"God, you're beautiful," he said, his breath fanning her wet, taut nipple and causing an ache between her legs. She writhed as his tongue flicked across the hard tip. She wrenched off his shirt and her fingers dug into the sinewy muscles of his shoulders.

He took her hand and placed it on his fly. She reacted as if burned, her arm jerking backward. "It's okay," he insisted, and placed her palm squarely on the apex of his legs again. Her throat felt dry as a barren desert; her heartbeat thundered in her ears. Beneath his jeans, she felt him, hard and anxious. "That's what you do to me," he admitted, and she felt suddenly powerful.

Boldly she nuzzled his chest, her hand still in place against the soft fabric of his pants. She scraped her wet tongue across a nipple buried in downy hair and he made an animal sound.

She knew she was playing with fire, that soon this petting and kissing might get out of hand, but she didn't care. Despite the rain, the night was hot, Hayden was hotter still and she wanted, more than anything, to kiss him forever. With him, her problems disappeared. All that mattered was Hayden.

His arms surrounded her and he found her lips again. Kissing her until she couldn't breathe, crushing her naked breasts against his rock-solid chest, Hayden moved against her. His hardness, still encased in denim, pressed deep into her bare abdomen and he shivered, as if trying to restrain himself.

"I should never have asked you here," he said, breaking off the kiss and breathing hard.

Nadine's heart dropped. "Why?"

"Because I want to make love to you, Nadine." He sighed against her hair and all his muscles grew tight and strident. "Nothing else in my life is working and you're all I think about and I…I want you. In the worst possible way." He said the words as if they were vile.

"Is that so wrong?" Tipping her face up to him, she blinked against the rain.

He laughed, but there was no mirth in the sound. "Not usually, but my intentions aren't noble."

Her heart began to break. "What do you mean?"

Gritting his teeth, he held her at arm's length, his fingers digging into the flesh of her forearms, his eyes gazing deep into hers. "All I think about is making love to you. Here, on the beach, in my boat, in my bed, in some sleazy motel room. It doesn't matter where, but I want you. More than I've ever wanted any girl. It's driving me crazy. Right now, all I want to do is push you onto your back, kiss you until you can't see straight and touch your body in places no one ever has. I want to pry your knees apart with my legs and I want to lie on top of you and make love to you until I can't anymore."

She knew she should be frightened, that his words were meant to scare her, but she wasn't afraid. Even in the darkness she noticed the tortured expression on his face, the lines of self-loathing in the turn of his mouth. The wind lifted his hair from his forehead and blew across Nadine's skin, but rather than cool her lust, the steamy breath of air seemed to further fan the flames of desire.

He rolled off her and sat on the ground, his arms slung over his knees, his muscular back to her. "I'll take you home. Come back to the house and I'll get the car and drive you—"

"I don't want to leave."

His muscles flexed. "Really, Nadine, this isn't right—"

Reaching forward, she traced the outline of one wet muscled shoulder with her finger.

His breath whistled through his teeth. "Don't!"

"I want to."

Whirling, he grabbed her offending hand and held it tight in his. "This could go too far."

"I don't think it will—"

"Of course it will!" He dropped her hand and plowed ten fingers through his hair. "Are you a virgin?"

She felt as if she'd been slapped. "What's that got to do with—"

"Are you a damned virgin?" His hands were suddenly on her shoulders and shaking her.

"Yes, but—"

He swore and shoved himself upright. "Get up."

Suddenly embarrassed, she stood, but couldn't hold her tongue. "Are you?"

"What?"

"Are you a virgin?"

He rounded on her. His eyes were black as the breathless night. "I don't see that it matters."

"You started this."

His mouth tightened. "No."

"Good. Then I don't have to worry about ruining your reputation, do I?" Standing on her tiptoe, she threw her arms around his neck and tilted her head upward. With a groan, he kissed her again, and lightning forked in the sky.

"This is wrong, Nadine."

"Only if you think it is."

He was already lowering himself to his knees, kissing her chin and neck, drawing her down and slowly dragging his wet tongue down her breasts as thunder cracked loudly through the hills. As they kneeled in the pooling moonlight, he cupped her breast and placed his mouth around the nipple. Slowly he drew on the dark bud, and Nadine shuddered to her very core.

"Is this what you want?" he asked.

"Mmm." She couldn't think or answer.

"Oh, Nadine." Every muscle in his body went rigid and he drew in a long, ragged breath. His arms surrounded her again and he held her close, resting his chin upon her head. "I think we'd better take this slow…or at least slower. If it's possible." He found her T-shirt and tossed it to her. "Take me for a ride…in your boat."

"My *brother's* boat," she corrected, feeling slightly wounded. Had she done something wrong? True, she didn't know much about satisfying a man or even turning one on, but she'd thought, from Hayden's response and her own, that everything was right.

She fumbled with her T-shirt, then waded to Ben's boat. Hayden helped her guide the craft to the open water, and once in the middle of the lake, he reached over, turned off the ignition switch and let the boat drift. They kissed in the rain, lips touching as lightning sizzled through the air.

Throwing his jacket over her shoulders, he said, "We've got to get home. This isn't safe."

"I don't care—"

"You will." He guided the boat to the landing and cut the engine again. Helping her out of the boat, he slung an arm around her shoulders. As they walked to the county road, he shoved a lock of wet hair from her cheek. "Aren't you going to ask me about Wynona?"

"Do you want to talk about her?"

"Not particularly."

Nadine wasn't sure she wanted to hear about the other girls in his life and yet she was curious, about everything that touched him. Especially the women.

"She's the one my parents have chosen to be my wife."

Nadine's heart did a free-fall and hit rock bottom. "Your wife?" She was suddenly sick inside. He was going to marry someone else? Oh, God, how could she have behaved as she did? How could *he* have nearly made love to her?

"That's what the old man wants. That's what the car

was all about. He gave me the Mercedes as an 'engagement present.' Trouble is, I'm not engaged."

"Yet."

He touched her arm. "Ever. At least not to Wynona."

"She's pretty."

He snorted. "Do you think so?"

"Mmm." She shivered. What was she doing out here alone with him discussing the physical attributes of the woman he was supposed to marry?

"Well, so does she."

"Does…does she think you're getting married?"

He scowled. "It's hard to know what Wynona thinks, but I have a feeling that she'd do just about anything to get a piece of the old man's fortune. Marrying me would be the easy way."

Nadine's heart shattered into a million pieces. Hayden talked about marriage as if it were a prize with which to bargain. She considered her parents' union and knew that wedded bliss was something straight out of fairy tales. Yet she was enough of a romantic to believe that somewhere true love had to exist. It just had to!

She thought of Hayden kissing Wynona, touching her as he'd caressed Nadine, and her stomach roiled painfully. A question loomed between them and she told herself not to ask it, yet she had to know the truth. "You said you weren't a virgin."

He didn't respond.

"Have you…did you…with Wynona?"

Clearing his throat, he grabbed her arm, causing her to stop walking. "Never."

"But—"

"There was another girl."

"Trish London," Nadine guessed.

"So the word got around." He started walking again, his fingers linked with hers. "Don't believe everything you hear, Nadine. At least in Gold Creek. People like to stretch the truth."

She knew instinctively that the subject was closed.

HAYDEN WALKED HER home. Over her protests, he insisted on seeing that she was safely on her back porch where he kissed her gently, then jogged back toward the road. She watched until he disappeared into the night. After assuring herself that he was really gone, she ran through the drizzle to the tree and climbed to the branch near her window. Carefully, so as not to make any noise, she slipped over the ledge and landed softly on the bare floor.

Letting out her breath, she began yanking off her soaked Nikes, but stopped short when she heard the click of a lighter and watched in horror as her mother, leaning against the bureau, lit a cigarette. The tiny flame gave Donna's face a yellow, haggard appearance, and her lips were pulled into a deep frown as she drew in on the first smoke she'd inhaled in over five years.

Nadine's heart nearly stopped. She was caught. There was no way around it.

"Want to tell me where you've been?" Donna asked, white smoke drifting from her mouth and nostrils as she clicked the lighter shut.

"At the lake."

"With?"

"I went by myself," Nadine said, sidestepping the lie.

"What did you do there?"

"Took a ride in Ben's boat."

"Hmm." Another long, lung-burning drag on the cigarette. The tip glowed red, the only light in the room. The smell of burning tobacco mixed with rainwater. "Where?"

Shrugging, Nadine replied, "I just drove it around."

"Alone?"

Obviously her mother didn't believe her. "I…I over-heard you and Dad. The fight. I…I had to get out." Nadine tossed her sodden hair over her shoulders.

"So you walked nearly two miles in the middle of a thunderstorm and then spent the next three hours cruising around Whitefire Lake in the dark. Is that what you expect me to believe?"

"Yes."

Sighing, her mother rested her forehead in her hand. "Of all my children, Nadine, you've given me the least amount of grief. Kevin…well, he's got his problems. When he couldn't play basketball anymore, he quit school and checked out—thought his life was over and took a job at that damned mill. As for Ben…we all know what a hothead he is. He thinks all problems can be solved with his fists or…in the case of girls, by opening his fly." At Nadine's swift intake of breath, she added, "I hate to admit it, but Ben's girl-crazy. As for you… Oh, Nadine…" Her voice trailed off and she drew long on her cigarette again.

Nadine felt miserable. She'd never intended to dis-appoint her mother.

"So, now, tell me. My guess is that you were meeting a boy. Was it Sam?"

Nadine shook her head wretchedly.

"Then who?"

"I…I can't say."

"Why not? Won't I approve?" When she didn't answer, Donna made a quick waving motion in the air. "Well, no, I suppose I won't. Meeting any boy this late at night is begging for trouble, Nadine." She sat on the edge of Nadine's bed, and the old mattress creaked. "I…I guess I should have told you this a long time ago. Maybe you've already figured it out, but Kevin wasn't premature. I got pregnant and had to marry your father." She worked the fingers of her free hand through her hair. "Oh, don't get me wrong, I probably would've married George anyway. But faced with having a baby, well, I just didn't have any options. So there was no way out. I was stuck." Blinking hard, she added, "I just don't want the same thing to happen to you."

"It won't," Nadine said, though her tongue tripped a bit when she realized how close she'd come to losing her virginity this very night. If Hayden had pushed her, seduced her, she wouldn't have argued the point. Contrarily, she *wanted* to make love to him.

"So who's the boy?"

"Mom, please, don't ask."

Stubbing her cigarette angrily in a dish on the bureau, Donna set her jaw. "Are you going to see him again?"

"I...I don't know."

"I'll make it easy for you. Don't see him again—ever." Her mother stood and advanced on Nadine. "I'll find out, you know. This is one helluva small town and someone will figure out who you've been sneaking around with. The truth will come out, Nadine, so don't protect him. He's probably not worth it."

Nadine's mind spun with thoughts of Ben.... No, he would never rat on her, but Patty Osgood would and so would Mary Beth Carter. A lot of people had seen her climb into Hayden's speedboat at the lake. Her mother was right. It wouldn't be long. But she wouldn't be the person to name him. No. Instead she'd warn him that her mother was on the warpath.

"Well?"

"I can't, Mom."

Her mother's lips drew into a disgusted line. "Well, whoever he is, I hope he's as noble as you are." She walked to the door, but stopped, her hands resting on the knob. "It goes without saying that you're grounded.

For the next two weeks. And if I ever catch you sneaking out of this room again, I'll put a lock on the door and bar the windows."

"Mom—"

"Don't argue with me, Nadine. And believe this," she said, turning, her face a study in determination. "I'll do anything, *anything* I can to prevent you from making the same mistake I did."

She slipped through the door and slammed it, her warning echoing through the room.

"THE BASTARD!" DONNA threw her dish towel into the sink and tears began to run from her eyes. Her husband tried to comfort her, to place his big hands upon her shoulders, but she shrugged him off. "How could you, George? How could you believe Garreth Monroe?"

Nadine reached for the screen door, but let her hand drop as she heard the tail end of the argument. Ben was running up the back steps, Bonanza leaping and barking at his heels. Nadine's finger flew to her mouth. "Shh!" she ordered, but it was too late, her parents both turned and saw them huddled on the porch.

Nadine wanted to drop through the dusty floorboards, but Ben, oblivious to the argument still simmering in the kitchen, yanked open the door.

"You may as well both come in," their father said, and Nadine noticed that his normally ruddy complexion was ashen. He gnawed on his lower lip and his hands fidgeted along the dirty red-and-black elastic of his suspenders. Sawdust was sprinkled in his hair and his broad shoulders looked as if they were weighted by invisible bricks. "As this concerns everyone in the family, we'd better talk it out. Sit down." He kicked a chair away from the dining room table and, without a word, Nadine and Ben slumped into the worn wooden seats. "I'll tell Kevin when he gets home.

"You all know that I've been promisin' everyone in this family a whole lot of money. Education for you kids, a new house and car for your mother…everything." His jaw wobbled slightly, and he paused to clear his throat. No one in the room dared breathe. "Well, it's not gonna happen. The money I gave Mr. Monroe to invest is gone."

"Gone?" Ben cried. "Gone where?"

George shrugged. "The investment didn't pan out."

"What do you mean, 'didn't pan out'?" Ben demanded, and Nadine's stomach squeezed so hard, it hurt. "Where did it go? To old man Monroe's pockets? To pay for one of his mistresses? To send his son to a private school?" Ben's face was flushed, his eyes flashing fire.

"Now, hold on. I knew the investment was risky," their father admitted, and Donna made a small whimpering sound. She leaned against the sink for support. "That's the only way to make money—big money. The bigger the payoff, the riskier the investment."

"*What* investment?"

"Oil wells."

"Oh, God," Donna whispered.

"You mean dry wells?" Ben demanded.

Nadine felt sorry for her father as he nodded curtly and said, "It appears that way."

"But who says so? Monroe?"

"I saw the geological survey," their father replied. "There's nothin' there but an empty hole."

"Oh, it's not empty," Donna said bitterly. "It's filled with every dollar we ever saved! It's filled with the house we used to own, and it's filled with our dreams, George, our damned, beautiful, foolish dreams!" Tears were tracking freely down her face, and Nadine wanted to run anywhere to get away from the awful truth and the doom she saw in her mother's eyes.

"How could you trust a Monroe?" Ben demanded. "Everyone in town knows old Garreth's as greedy and crooked as his brother-in-law. He was in on it, too, wasn't he? I'll bet it was Thomas Fitzpatrick's idea. Monroe doesn't have the brains to pull off a scam like this!"

"It wasn't a scam."

"Like hell!" Ben said, standing and kicking the table.

"Ben!" Donna's back stiffened, but he didn't listen to his mother.

He whirled, and planting his flat hands on the table, glared at Nadine. "Now you know what the Monroes are like, little sister," he snarled. "All of them. Cut from the same cloth. And your precious Hayden is no different than his old man."

"Oh, God," Donna whispered. "Nadine. Not Hayden Monroe!" The lines of her face carved deep into her once beautiful skin, and Ben, realizing what he'd done, gritted his teeth.

Nadine's spine stiffened, and though her eyes burned hot with unshed tears, she wouldn't break down. She cared for Hayden, probably even loved him. And, deep down, he felt the same for her. She knew it.

"He's the boy you were sneaking out with?" Donna demanded.

"Oh, hell," Ben grumbled, apparently sick with himself.

"Who's been sneaking out?" Kevin wanted to know as he shoved open the screen door.

"Nadine. With Hayden Monroe." Donna's condemning stare landed full force on her daughter. Her fingers curled around the edge of the table. "There's just one thing I want to know," she said, her voice trembling, and Nadine braced herself for the blow. "Tell me the truth, Nadine. If you lie I'll find out anyway."

Nadine lifted her gaze to meet her mother's. "What?"

"Are you pregnant?"

"Pregnant?" Kevin repeated, shaking his head. "What's going on here?"

Their father eyed his firstborn. "What're you doing home so early?"

"I'm home for good, Dad," Kevin replied as he flopped into a chair. "I got laid off today."

"Laid off?" Donna said, and Nadine hated the disappointment in her parents' eyes.

"Don't you know? They're cutting back shifts. The newest guys like me got pink slips."

Nadine felt the doom settle over the roof of the little frame house.

"If you ask me," Kevin said, "old man Monroe has lost it. And it's probably because of his son. The kid's gone 'round the bend, I guess."

"Hayden?" Nadine whispered.

"You don't know?" Kevin's eyes scanned everyone in the room. "Hayden Monroe is in the hospital. He wrecked the old man's boat this afternoon and the girl he was with, his fiancée, she's been life-flighted to San Francisco. There's a question whether she'll make it or not."

Nadine's life splintered into a million pieces. "And Hayden…is he…?"

"Oh, he'll be all right. Those Monroes are lucky bastards. The way I hear it, he broke a couple of ribs and tore up his leg, but he'll survive."

Donna was already reaching for the telephone, no doubt to confirm the story. Nadine crouched lower in her chair, her eyes hot with unshed tears.

The kitchen seemed to disappear, but she could still hear her mother's quick questions to a friend of hers who worked at County Hospital. It was true enough; Hayden was lying in the hospital emergency room, in pain, perhaps more seriously hurt than Kevin knew.

She heard the receiver click and slowly raised her eyes to meet her mother's. Donna nodded. "The Galveston girl is critical—crushed pelvis, possible internal injuries, but Hayden Monroe will be fine. There's a question about him ever walking without a limp, but he'll survive."

"He's at County?" Nadine asked, involuntarily reaching for her purse.

"That's right."

She felt her father's hand on her shoulder. "I hate to do this, missy," he said, his voice rasping with regret, "but you're not going anywhere."

"I've got to go...." She felt everyone's eyes on her.

"You're grounded," her father said. "Don't even ask me for how long 'cause I can't begin to tell you. Now you listen hear, young lady. There'll be no more sneaking out. Until Hayden Monroe is transferred to a hospital in San Francisco to be with his own doctors, you aren't going anywhere."

"But—"

"Don't argue with me, Nadine. Believe me, I know best." His faded eyes held hers. "I've learned my lesson about the Monroes the hard way, and I'm not going to stand by and see you get hurt."

Panic surged through her. "I won't—"

"You heard me. That's it. We won't speak of it again. As far as I'm concerned, you're to forget you ever met Hayden Monroe."

BOOK TWO

San Francisco, California
The Present

CHAPTER FIVE

MIST GATHERED OVER the tombstone, and the sod, recently turned, smelled fresh and earthy. Chilled to the bone, Hayden shoved his hands in his pockets. Sleet drizzled past the upturned collar of his old leather jacket and dripped from his bare head and nose.

He stared at the final resting place of his father, strewn with roses and carnations and lilies, and he whispered under his breath, "I hope you got what you deserved, you miserable bastard."

A lump filled his throat and his eyes burned with tears he refused to shed. Hayden Garreth Monroe III had been a pathetic excuse of a father. He'd shown his son no love, nor kind words—only strict discipline and upper-crust values.

From his pocket, Hayden withdrew a leather baseball, autographed by Reggie Jackson, and hurled it into the soil. The ball wedged deeply, nearly buried with the old man. Fitting, Hayden thought bitterly. His father had paid a fortune for that baseball, given it to Hayden and never once played catch with his only son. He'd never had the time, nor the inclination.

"Rest in peace," Hayden muttered, before turning and never once looking over his shoulder.

His old Jeep was idling at the curb, and Hayden slid into the torn driver's seat, wrenching the wheel and gunning the accelerator. Leo, a battle-scarred Lab and his best friend in the world—perhaps his only friend—

was seated in the backseat. "One more stop," Hayden informed the dog. "Then we're history around here."

Driving through the gates of the cemetery, he headed into the city for yet another ordeal—a meeting with William Bradworth, of Smythe, Mills and Bradworth, his father's attorneys.

BRADWORTH'S PRIVATE SUITE fairly reeked of blue blood and big bucks. From the mahogany walls to the leather club chairs situated stiffly around a massive desk, the rooms were meant to invite conversation about money, money and more money. Even the view of San Francisco Bay didn't disturb the Wall Street atmosphere that some high-priced decorator had tried to transfer from East Coast to West.

The phony ambience made Hayden sick.

Shifting restlessly in his chair, he glanced from the balding pate of William Bradworth to the window where sleet was sluicing down the glass and the sky was the color of steel.

Bradworth's voice was a monotone droning on and on. "...so you see, Mr. Monroe, except for the money that's been set aside for your mother, her house, her car and jewelry, you've inherited virtually everything your father owned."

"I thought he cut me out a few years back."

Bradworth cleared his throat. "He did. Later, however, Garreth had a change of heart."

"Big of him," Hayden muttered.

"I think so, yes."

"Well, I don't want it. Not one damned piece of rough-cut lumber, not one red cent of the old man's money, not one stinking oil well. You got that?"

"But you've just been left a fortune—"

"What I've been left, Bradworth, is a ball and chain,

a reminder that my father wanted to control me when he was alive and is still trying to run my life from the grave." Hayden gave a cursory glance to his copy of the last will and testament of Hayden Garreth Monroe III, lying open on the polished desk. He slid the damned document toward his father's arrogant son-of-a-bitch of an attorney. "It won't work."

"But—"

Standing, Hayden planted both of his tanned hands on William Bradworth's desk and leaned forward, his gaze drilling into the bland features of a man who had worked for his father for years. "I didn't want the company when the old man was alive," he said in a calm voice, "and I sure as hell don't want it now."

"I don't see that you have much choice." Always unflappable, Bradworth leaned back in his chair, putting some distance between himself and Hayden's imposing, aggressive stance. Tenting his hands under his chin, like a minister ready to impart marital advice, he suggested, "You can sell the corporation, of course, but that takes time and you'll have to deal with your uncle—"

Hayden grimaced at the mention of Thomas Fitzpatrick.

"Tom owns a considerable amount of shares. Meanwhile the employees will want to keep getting paid and, unless you want to close the doors and put those people on the unemployment rolls, Monroe Sawmill Company will keep turning out thousands of board feet of lumber from the mills."

Hayden's back teeth ground together. Even from the grave, the old man seemed to have him over a barrel. Hayden didn't have much love for Gold Creek, where the oldest and largest of the mills was located, but he didn't hate the people who lived there. Some of them were good, salt-of-the-earth types who'd worked for the corporation for years. Thrown out of work, they'd have no place to turn. A fifty-five-year-old millwright couldn't be expected to go back to school for vocational training. The whole damned town depended upon that mill one way or another. Even the people who worked at Fitzpatrick Logging Company needed a sawmill where they could sell the cut timber. The banks, the shops, the cafés, the taverns, even the churches depended upon the mill to keep the economy of that small town afloat. It was the same with the other small towns around the smaller mills he now owned.

With the feeling that he was slowly drowning, Hayden said, "Look, Bradworth, I know about selling companies. I just got rid of a logging operation in Klamath Falls, Oregon. So there must be some way to get rid of the mills around Gold Creek."

The attorney drew back his lips in what Hayden surmised was supposed to be a smile. "Your Podunk logging operation in Klamath Falls—what did it consist of? A few trucks, maybe a mill or two and some timber? Handling a small-time business is a lot different than running an operation the size of Monroe Sawmill, son."

"Doesn't matter. I just don't want it. I don't care if I ever see a dime of the old man's money."

Bradworth's eyebrows raised a fraction. "So you want to donate the corporation, lock, stock, barrel and green chain to—whom? The homeless? The Cancer Society? Needy children?"

Hayden's lips flattened against his teeth. "That's a start."

"How?"

"You're the attorney—"

"Right. So that's why I'm telling you. We can't go out and donate a wood chipper to the Salvation Army.

You know, most people would jump at a chance to own a company like this."

"I'm not most people."

"Obviously." Bradworth's gaze raked down Hayden's body, taking quick appraisal of his soggy jeans, flannel shirt and battered running shoes. His wet jacket had been cast casually over the back of one of the attorney's stuffed leather chairs. Water dripped onto the expensive burgundy-hued carpet. "As for the charitable organization of your choice, I'm sure the board of directors would be more than happy to take your money—but not in the form of the corporation, so you can sell Monroe Sawmill Company to a rival firm, if there is one that wants it, or raffle it off piece by piece to some corporate raider who'll close up shop and put the employees out of work. Your choice. But for the time being, you are, whether you like it or not, the majority stockholder and CEO of the firm, and the next board meeting is scheduled for January 15." Bradworth glanced meaningfully at his desk calendar. "That's barely two months away. I doubt that anyone will buy the company from you by then." He reached behind him, opened a sleek walnut credenza and pulled out several binders. "These," he said with quiet authority, "are copies of the company books. I suggest you study them. As for the town house in the Heights, here are the keys, along with a key to the Mercedes, BMW and Ferrari. There's also the summer place at—"

"Whitefire Lake," Hayden supplied, thinking of the remote house on the shore, the only place he remembered from his youth with any fondness. He'd enjoyed his few years on the lake and the summers thereafter...until his entire life had been turned inside out. "I know."

Bradworth's lips pursed. "As for the money and company stock, it will just take some time to go through probate and transfer everything to you. I've already started putting things in order—some of the buildings need to be cleaned and repaired, leases need to be transferred. Some of the assets of the corporation are personal and—"

"I don't give a damn!" Lead weight seemed to settle over Hayden's broad shoulders. "This is ludicrous," he remarked, though the attorney probably thought the same. It wasn't a secret that Hayden and his father had never gotten along. But the old man insisted on cursing him, even from the ever-after.

"I couldn't agree with you more," Bradworth admitted as he shoved the will back across the desk. "But there it is. Now, how will I reach you?"

"You can't. Just take care of everything 'til I get back."

"But I'll need to know where you are so I can keep in touch—"

"Don't worry. I'll call you." Grabbing the damned documents, the notebooks and the keys, Hayden snagged his jacket with his other hand and strode over yards of expensive carpet to the door. He paused with his fingers resting lightly on the knob. "What's going to happen to Wynona?" he asked, eyeing the attorney.

"Who?" But the lawyer's face tightened spasmodically and Hayden's stomach turned sour.

"Wynona Galveston," Hayden replied without a trace of bitterness.

"I don't know who—"

"Save it, Bradworth. Just let her know the old man's gone. She'll be interested."

Bradworth cleared his throat. "She's been provided for—"

"Bought off, you mean. Like all the rest." Casting a disgusted glance over his shoulder, he added, "Dear old dad left a helluva mess, didn't he?" Without waiting for a reply, he strode through the door, slammed it shut behind him, and walked quickly through the maze of corridors lighted by recessed bulbs. At each intersection in the labyrinthine hallways, original paintings and sketches in pastoral country scenes graced the walls. The whole effect was reminiscent of an Englishman's club. Brass lamps and oxblood leather chairs, mahogany tables strewn with copies of *Forbes, GQ,* and the like were grouped in intimate circles in the reception area, decorated much as Hayden remembered his father's den. All that was missing was the old man himself and the ever-present, sweet smoky scent of his father's private blend of pipe tobacco.

Strange that he should feel a sense of nostalgia for a man he'd grown up hating. Shoving his arms through the sleeves of his jacket, he rode the elevator to the parking garage where his old Jeep stood waiting. Leo's tail thumped against the backseat as Hayden slid behind the wheel. The dog tried to scramble into the front seat, but Hayden ordered him to stay, and Leo, with a sniff, settled down, head between his legs, liquid-brown eyes staring straight at Hayden. "We're going on a vacation," Hayden told the dog as he glanced in the rearview mirror and fired the engine.

Backing the Jeep out of its parking place, he maneuvered through the garage and into the drizzly light of a wintry San Francisco afternoon. The wet streets were crowded with bustling cars and pedestrians. Holiday lights blinked red and green in the windows of major department stores and bell-ringers stood near the doorways, asking for donations for the needy this holiday season. Slowly traffic inched out of the city. "Whitefire Lake," Hayden said, catching Leo's reflection in the rearview mirror. "Believe me, you're gonna love it there." As if the dog could understand him! God, he was losing it.

Frowning at the reminder of the small town, he flipped

on the radio. He's spent most of his summers at the lake hanging out with his cousins, Roy, Brian and Toni Fitzpatrick. Roy was dead now and Brian's wife had finally proved to be Roy's killer. Hayden scowled. Nope—not many fond memories in Gold Creek.

There had been a girl once. Nadine Powell. She'd been different—or so he'd thought. She'd turned his thinking all around until, like the others, she'd shown her true colors and when offered money to stay away from Garreth's son, she'd eagerly reached out her greedy little fingers.

He grimaced at the thought of her hands and the way they had touched his body. Good God, he'd almost seduced her a couple of times. No doubt that had been what she'd been hoping for. When he thought of the way she could turn him on...

"Hell!" He ground the gears and the Jeep slid a little. The familiar notes of "Santa Claus Is Coming to Town" filled the vehicle's interior. Hayden turned the radio dial to an all-news station. He didn't want any reminders of the holiday season as his memories of Christmas were tangled up in emotions he didn't want to dissect.

Though Garreth had proclaimed Christmas as the one time the family was to spend together, he had, often as not, shown up hours late to a goose that was cold and to barely flickering candles that had burned down to stubs of dripped wax.

Even as the spoiled son of Garreth Monroe, Hayden hadn't wanted to become a man like his father. Though his name promised the same wealth and financial wizardry as that of his predecessors, Hayden had no interest in making money. Hell, he'd already done that with the lousy mill in Oregon.

Maybe, he thought, his mouth thinning in repressed

anger, he should change his name. Wouldn't that tick the old man off?

Except it didn't matter now. Hayden alone was the sole survivor of the Monroe line—no brothers to carry on the tainted Monroe name. The H. G. Monroe lineage was destined to die with him because he'd sworn to himself over and over again, he'd never become another Monroe mogul.

He wouldn't marry and he'd never father children. No one really gave a damn, anyway. He knew that he'd been conceived for the express purpose of carrying on the Monroe line and, had he been born a girl, his mother would have been pressed to produce a male child—an heir.

Female after female would have been born until a boy had finally come along. Fortunately for Sylvia Fitzpatrick Monroe, who really wasn't all that interested in motherhood, she'd come through with a male. Saints be praised, the line would continue! Hayden could imagine the magnums of Dom Pérignon that had been uncorked when his father's manhood had been proved and his son had been delivered into the world to preserve the family name.

What a joke, he thought, as the Jeep bucked up the steep hills of the city before merging onto the freeway heading north. He laid on the horn when an old white sedan tried to swerve into his lane ahead of him. "Idiot," he muttered, and Leo snorted in agreement.

The windshield wipers slapped away the rain and the engine thrummed as Hayden shifted down. Cold air seeped in through the windows that didn't quite close, and rain drizzled down the inside of the glass. Hayden barely noticed. He wasn't about to return to his father's house and take the damned Ferrari.

"Damn you, Garreth," he growled, as if his father

could hear him. "Leave me alone." *The way you did when I was a kid.*

If having a son were such a big deal, why hadn't the old man taken any interest in him until he could read the market quotes in the *Wall Street Journal?*

"Bastard." Hayden had grown up all alone, and that's the way he planned to live the rest of his life. Alone.

He could think of worse company.

HANDS ON HER jean-clad hips, Nadine stood near her idling Chevy and stared at the fortress that protected the Monroe summer home. In all her thirty years—even in the few weeks when she'd been secretly seeing Hayden—she'd never walked through the sturdy wrought-iron gates that led to what was rumored to once have been the fanciest house on the lake, built by a movie star in the late twenties and purchased—or, more likely, stolen—by the thieving Monroe family in the fifties.

Her lips turned down at the corners as she eyed the rock wall that stretched around all fifteen acres of prime lakefront property. Only the uppermost branches of the tallest pines were visible over the eight feet of stacked basalt and mortar.

And now, she was allowed—as a servant, she reminded herself—access to the fabled estate. The code she'd been given by the hotshot attorney in San Francisco worked. She punched out the numbers on a keypad and electronically, with a loud clang and groan, the gates swung inward.

Ironic, she thought, that she should be here, called upon to clean up the old manor, get it ready for its new inhabitant. It seemed that the attorney who had hired her didn't know about her connection to the Monroes. All the better.

She slid behind the wheel of her Nova and disengaged the emergency brake. The little car sprang forward, as if as eager as she to view the mansion owned by the man who had nearly single-handedly ruined her family.

The drive was overgrown with weeds, but still seemed inviting as it curved through a forest of sequoia, oak and pine. Pale winter sun streamed through the leafless branches and spattered the ground with pools of shimmering light.

As she glanced in her rearview mirror, she noticed the huge gate swing closed again, cutting her off from the stretch of road that wound through the hills surrounding Whitefire Lake.

She'd thought often of leaving Gold Creek, but after her shattering experience with Hayden, and what had happened to her as a direct result of her short-lived romance with him, she'd never left again. Her family, or what was left of it, still resided in the town, and she wasn't the kind of woman who would fit into the suburban sprawl or the hectic pace of the city. She'd learned that lesson the hard way. So, after being shipped off to a boarding school her parents could barely afford, she'd returned to Gold Creek and her battered family. Through her parents' divorce, through her eldest brother's death and through a bad marriage, she'd stayed.

She'd even, for a brief period, fancied herself in love with Turner Brooks, a rough-and-tumble cowboy whose house she cleaned on a weekly basis.

Nadine squelched that particular thought. She hadn't let herself think of Turner for several months. He was happily married now, reunited with Heather Tremont, the girl of his dreams. He'd never even known that Nadine had cared about him.

Why was it that she always chose the wrong men?

"Masochist," she reprimanded herself, as the lane curved and suddenly the lake, smooth as glass, stretched for half a mile to the opposite shore. Mountains rose above the calm water, their jagged snowcapped peaks reflected in the mirror that was Whitefire Lake.

Nadine parked and climbed out of her old car. She shoved her hands into her pockets and shivered as a cold breeze rushed across the water and caught in her hair. Rubbing her arms, she stared past the gazebo, private dock and boathouse and tried to see her own little house, situated on the far banks of the lake, but was only able to recognize the public boat landing and bait-and-tackle shop on the opposite shore.

Her small cottage was a far cry from this, the three-storied "cabin" that had once been the Monroe summer home. The manor—for that's what it was, in Nadine's estimation—looked as if it should have been set in a rich section of a New England town. Painted slate gray, with navy blue shutters battened against the wind, it was nestled in a thicket of pines and flanked by overgrown rhododendrons and azaleas.

This was where the Monroes spent their summers, she thought, surprised at her own bitterness—where Hayden had courted Wynona Galveston before the accident that had nearly taken the young socialite's life. He'd never called Nadine, never written. Nadine had told herself that the pain and disappointment were long over, but she'd been wrong. Even now, she remembered her father's face when he'd come home and caught her trying to sneak out and visit Hayden before he was transferred to San Francisco. She'd begged and pleaded until Ben had agreed to take her over to County Hospital while her mother had been working at the library, but George Powell, his shift shortened that day and for many days thereafter, had come home early and caught them. Thin lines of worry had cracked her father's ruddy skin, and anger had smoldered bright in his eyes.

After sending Ben out of the room, he'd rounded on his daughter. "Didn't I tell you to stay away from him?"

"I can't, Dad. I love him."

She'd been banished to her room, only to come down later and find her parents engaged in another argument—a horrid fight she had inadvertently spawned.

"I'll kill that kid," George had sputtered.

"Daddy, you wouldn't—"

He changed tactics. "Well, I'll let him know how I feel about him using my daughter. No one's going to get away with hurting my little girl."

"You think you can stop him?" Donna had interjected bitterly, pinning him with a hateful glare. "Haven't you learned yet that those people have no souls? How could you hurt a man like Hayden Monroe? The way you hurt his father? By giving him everything we ever owned."

"Stop it!" Ben had snarled. "Just stop it!"

At that point Nadine's father had nearly broken down; it was the only time Nadine had seen him blink against tears in his usually humor-flecked eyes.

Now, years later, she saw the irony of the situation. Obviously, because her name was no longer Powell, the attorney who'd paid off her father hadn't recognized her. Instead, he'd offered to hire her at an exorbitant rate to clean the place from stem to stern. "...and I don't care how much time it takes. I want the house to look as good today as it did the day it was built," Bradworth had ordered.

That would take some doing, Nadine thought, eyeing the moss collecting on the weathered shingles of the roof.

She'd almost turned down the job, but at the last minute had changed her mind. This was her chance to get a little of her father's lost fortune back. Besides, anything to do with the Monroes held a grim fascination for her.

And she needed to prove to herself that she didn't give a fig what happened to Hayden.

So now she was here.

"And ready to wreak sweet vengeance," she said sarcastically as she grabbed her mop, bucket and cleaning supplies.

The key she had been sent turned easily in the lock, and the front door, all glass and wood, opened without a sound. She took two steps into the front hall, her eyes adjusting to the darkness. Cloths, which had once been white and now were yellow with age, had been draped over all the furniture and a gritty layer of dust had settled on the floor. Cobwebs dangled from the corners in the ceiling, and along the baseboards mice droppings gave evidence to the fact that she wasn't entirely alone.

"Great. Spiders and mice." The whole place reminded her of a tomb, and a chill inched up her spine.

To dispel the mood, she began throwing open windows, doors and shutters, allowing cool, fresh mountain air to sweep through the musty old rooms. *What a shame,* she thought sadly. French doors off the living room opened to an enclosed sun porch where a piano, now probably ruined, was covered with a huge cloth. Plants, long forgotten, had become dust in pots filled with desert-dry soil.

It looked as if no one had been to the house in years.

Well, that wasn't her problem. She'd already been paid half her fee in advance and spent some of the money on Christmas presents for the boys, as well as paying another installment to the care center where her father resided. The money hadn't gone far. She still had the mortgage to worry about. Soon John would probably need braces and God only knew how long her old car would last. But this job, which would take well over a week, quite possibly two, would stretch out the bills a little. And the thought that she was being paid by Monroe money made the checks seem sweeter still.

Covering her head with a checked bandanna, she decided to work from top to bottom and started on the third floor, scouring bathrooms, polishing fixtures, sweeping up cobwebs and airing out the rooms that had obviously once been servants' quarters. Paneled in the same knotty pine that covered the walls, the ceiling was low and sloped. She bumped her head twice trying to dislodge several wasp's nests, while hoping that the old dried mud didn't contain any living specimens.

As she turned the beds, she checked for mice or rats and was relieved to discover neither.

By one-thirty she'd stripped and waxed the floors and was heading for level two, which was much more extensive than the top floor. Six bedrooms and four baths, including a master suite complete with cedar-lined sauna and sunken marble tub.

Summer home indeed. Most of the citizens of Gold Creek had never seen such lavish accommodations.

In the master bedroom she discovered a radio and, after plugging it in and fiddling with the dial, was able to find a San Francisco channel that played soft rock. Over the sound of rusty pipes and running water, she hummed along with the music, scrubbing the huge tub ferociously.

As she ran her cloth over the brass fixtures, a cool draft tickled the back of her neck.

Suddenly she felt as if a dozen pair of eyes were watching her. Her heart thumped. Her throat closed. She froze for a heart-stopping second. Slowly moving her gaze to the mirror over the basin she saw the reflection of a man—a very big man—glaring at her. Her breath caught for a second, and she braced herself, her mind racing as she recognized Hayden.

Her insides shredded and she could barely breathe.

He looked better than she remembered. The years had given his body bulk—solid muscle that was lean and tough and firm.

"Who the hell are you?" he demanded, his blue eyes harsh. His face was all bladed angles and planes, arrogant slashes that somehow fit together in a handsome, if savage, countenance. His hair was black and thick and there was still a small scar that bisected one of his eyebrows. And he was mad, so damned angry that his normally dark skin had reddened around his neck.

Her heart broke when she realized he didn't remember her. But why would he? He must've been with a hundred girls—maybe two hundred—since they'd last seen each other in the middle of a sultry summer night.

"I was hired to be here," she said, still unmoving. Her voice caught his attention and his eyes flickered with recognition.

"Hired?" he repeated skeptically, but his eyes narrowed and he studied her with such intensity that she nearly trembled. "By whom? Unless things have changed in the past four hours, this—" he motioned broadly with one arm "—is my house."

"I know that, Hayden."

He sucked in his breath and he looked as if he'd seen a ghost. "I'll be damned."

"No doubt." Slowly, never moving her gaze from his reflection in the mirror, she turned off the water. Struggling to her feet, she was aware, as she turned to face him, that the front of her sweater and jeans were wet, her hair hidden, her face devoid of makeup. "What I'm doing is cleaning your bathtub," she said calmly, though she was sure her eyes were spitting fire.

"That much I figured." An old dog, golden and grizzled, sauntered into the room and growled lowly. "Enough, Leo," Hayden commanded, and the retriever obeyed, dropping onto the floor near the duffel bag Hayden had apparently carried inside.

Hayden, satisfied that Leo wouldn't give him any more trouble, swung all his attention back to the small woman who stood like a soldier in front of his tub. He couldn't believe his eyes. "Nadine?"

"In the flesh," she quipped, though she didn't smile.

"Why are *you* here?"

Her jaw slid to one side, as if she found him amusing— some kind of joke. "I was hired by William Bradworth to clean this place and—"

"Bradworth doesn't own it," he cut in, sick to death of the pushy attorney. "I should have been told. Oh, hell!" He shoved his hair from his eyes. "What I meant was—"

"Save it, Hayden," she replied quickly. "I don't care what you meant." Her clear green eyes snapped in anger, but she didn't back down. She looked ridiculous, really. The front of her clothes wet, an old bandanna wrapped around her head. Gloves, much too big, covered her hands and yet…despite the costume, she radiated that certain defiance that had first caught his attention all those years ago. She tipped her little chin upward. "Bradworth paid me to finish the job."

"Consider it done."

"No way. I realize this isn't the way you do things, Hayden, but when I agree to do a job," she assured him, those intense eyes snapping green flames, "I do it. Now, you can stand there and argue with me all day long, but I'm really busy and I'd like to finish this room before I go home."

"You're a maid?" he asked, and saw her cringe slightly.

"Among other things. And right now, I have work to do. If you'll excuse me…" Quickly she leaned over the tub and twisted on the faucets again. Water rushed from the spigot and she swished the last of the scouring soap down the drain.

"What other things?" he asked as she turned off the faucet.

Sliding him a glance that was impossible to read, she explained, "Oh, I have many talents. Scrubbing tubs and waxing floors and setting mousetraps are just a few." She yanked off her gloves, and this time she dropped them into an empty bucket. Bending her head, she untied her bandanna and unleashed a tangled mass of red-brown curls that fell past her shoulders and caused his gut to tighten in memory. "Now, I've got to get home, but I'll be back in the morning."

"You don't have to do any more—"

"Oh, yes I do," she said firmly, and the determined line of her jaw suggested she was carrying a sizable chip on her slim shoulders. "I guess I didn't make myself clear. I never leave a job unfinished—no matter who's paying the bill."

"What's that supposed to mean?"

"Figure it out, Hayden," she said, as if she were harboring a grudge against him—as if *he* had done *her* a severe injustice when she had been the one who had used him.

Seethingly indignant, she grabbed her mops, pails and supplies and walked briskly past him. Her flaming hair swung down her back and her jeans hugged her behind tightly as she bustled out of the room and clomped noisily down the stairs. Hayden was left standing between the bathroom and bedroom to wonder if she was going home to a husband or boyfriend.

He heard the front door click shut and moved to the window, where he saw her load her supplies into a trashed-out old Chevy, slide behind the wheel and then, without so much as a look over her shoulder, tromp on the accelerator. The little car lurched forward, and with a spray of gravel from beneath its tires, disappeared through the trees.

"I'll be damned," he muttered again.

Well, at least she was gone. For the time being. He should be grateful for that. He reached for his duffel bag and a flash of light, a sparkle on the rim of the tub, caught his eye. He moved closer to inspect the glitter and saw the ring that she'd obviously forgotten. Frowning, he walked into the bathroom and picked up the tiny band of gold. A single blue stone winked up at him. Simple and no-nonsense, like the woman who wore it.

He wondered if this were a wedding band or an engagement ring, and told himself it didn't matter. He'd take the damned piece of jewelry back to her and write her a check for services rendered as well as those not rendered. He didn't need a woman hanging around right now, especially not a woman who, with a single scalding look, could set his teeth on edge and his blood on fire.

HAYDEN MONROE! BACK in Gold Creek! Nadine couldn't believe her bad luck. She never should have agreed to work for the bastard, and she had half a mind to wring Aunt Velma's long neck! But she couldn't afford to say no to the sum of money that attorney Bradworth had offered. And she'd never expected to come face-to-handsome-face with Hayden again. She'd known, of course, that someone would be staying in the house, but she thought it was probably going to be rented or sold. She hadn't expected Hayden. The last she'd heard about him, he'd moved to Oregon and was estranged from his father.

Ben had been right about Hayden and his dad. They were both cut from the same cloth—dangerously handsome, extremely wealthy; men who didn't give a good goddamn about anything or anyone. Just money.

That's all they cared about. What was the saying? Fast cars and faster women? Whatever money could buy.

Hands clenched over the steering wheel, she mentally kicked herself. It was all she could do not to take him up on his offer and quit. But, in good conscience, she couldn't tell him to take his job and shove it, as she'd already spent a good part of the money. And she didn't want her two sons to lose out on the best Christmas they'd had in years because of her own stupidity.

"Damn, damn, damn and double damn!" she swore, her little car hugging the corners as she headed back to town. She frowned as she guided the Chevy beneath the railroad trestle bridge that had been a Gold Creek landmark for over a hundred years. Hayden Monroe! As handsome as ever and twice as dangerous. She steered through the side streets of town and stopped at the Safeway store for groceries. Christmas trees were stacked in neat rows near the side entrance, fir and pine trees begging to be taken home, but she didn't succumb. Not yet. Not with the windfall she'd so recently received. Just in case she never finished the job. The trees would go on sale later. She picked up a few groceries, then climbed back into her car again, heading to the south side of Whitefire Lake.

She was irritated at having been caught by Hayden again, and was discouraged by the heady feeling she'd experienced when she'd stared into his blue eyes. But she was over him. She had to be. It had been years. Nearly thirteen years!

She only had to deal with him for a week or two. She rolled her eyes and bit her lower lip. Fourteen days suddenly seemed an eternity.

She had no choice, so she'd just make the best of it and avoid him as much as possible. She would simply grin and bear Hayden Monroe with his sexy smile, knowing eyes and lying tongue until the job was finished.

Then it was *sayonara*.

Veering off the road that circled the lake, she drove down a single lane that served as a driveway to several small cabins built near the shore. She slowed near the garage, a sagging building filled with cut cordwood and gardening supplies, and snapped off the ignition. Grabbing both sacks of groceries and her purse, she stepped onto her gravel drive. "Boys!" she sang out, not really expecting to hear a response as both bikes, usually dropped in the middle of the driveway, were nowhere to be seen and the raucous sound of their voices didn't carry in the cool mountain air. "Boys! I'm home."

Nothing.

Well, it was early. They were probably still pedaling from the sitter's.

Juggling the groceries, she reached into her purse for her keys and opened the screen door, only to find that her sons had, indeed, been home from school. The back door wasn't locked and book bags, sneakers and jackets were strewn over the couch and floor.

She left the groceries on the counter, then headed back outside. "John? Bobby?" she called again, and this time she could hear the sound of gravel crunching and bike wheels spinning.

She was carrying her mops, buckets and cleaning supplies into the house when she heard the sound of tires slamming to a stop.

"You're a liar!" Bobby's voice rang through the house, and Nadine walked to the window in time to see her youngest son, his lower lip thrust out stubbornly, throw a punch at his brother.

John, older than Bobby's seven and a half years by a full eighteen months and taller by nearly four inches,

ducked agilely away from Bobby's wild swing and
managed to step over Bobby's forgotten bike. Wagging
his wheat blond head with the authority of the elder and
wiser sibling, John announced, "*I* don't believe in Santa
Claus!"

"Then you're just stupid."

"And *you're* the liar." John leered at his brother as
Bobby lunged. Sidestepping quickly, John watched as
Bobby landed with an "oof" on the cold ground near
the back door.

Leaning down, John taunted, "Liar, liar, pants on fire,
hang them on—"

"Enough!" Nadine ordered, knowing this exchange
would quickly escalate from an argument and a few wild
punches to a full-fledged wrestling match. "Look, I don't
want to have to send you to your rooms. Bobby, are you
okay?"

"We only got one room," John reminded her.

"You know what I mean—"

"John's makin' fun of me," Bobby wailed indignantly.
A shock of red-blond hair fell over his freckled face as
he looked to Nadine as if for divine intervention. "And I
saw Santa Claus last year, really I did," he said earnestly.

"Tell me another one," John teased, sneering. "There
ain't no such thing as Santa Claus or those stupid elves
or Frosty or Rudolph, neither!"

Bobby blinked hard. "Then you just wait up on Christmas Eve. You'll see. On the roof—"

"And how am I s'posed to get there—fly?" John
hooted, ignoring the sharp look Nadine sent him. "Or
maybe Dancer or Vixen will give me a lift! Boy, are you
dumb! Everything comes from Toys 'R' Us, not some
stupid little workshop and a few lousy elves!"

"I said 'enough!'" Nadine warned, wondering how
she would survive with both boys for the two weeks of

Christmas vacation that loomed ahead. Right now, her sons couldn't get along and Nadine's already busy life had turned into a maelstrom of activity. John and Bobby seemed hell-bent on keeping the excitement and noise level close to the ozone layer and they couldn't be near each other without punching or kicking or wrestling.

"You're not really gonna send us to our room, are you?" Bobby asked, biting on his lower lip worriedly.

"Well, not yet—"

"He's such a dork!" John called over his shoulder as he found his rusty bike propped on the corner of the house. "A dumb little dork!"

"John—"

"Am not!" Bobby screamed.

But John didn't listen. He peddled quickly down the sandy path leading to the lake. His dog, a black-and-white mutt named Hershel, streaked after him.

"I'm not a dork," Bobby said again, as if to convince himself.

"Of course you're not, sweetheart."

"Don't call me that!" He pulled himself up, dusted off his jeans and kicked angrily at the ground. His eyes filled with tears and dirt streaked his face. "John's just a big…a big jerk!"

This time Nadine had to agree, but she kept her opinion to herself, and hugging her youngest son, asked, "Are you okay?"

"Yeah." But his hazel eyes glistened with unshed tears.

"You sure?" Nadine asked, though she suspected little more than his pride had been bruised. "How about a cup of cocoa, with marshmallows and maybe some cookies?"

"You got some at the store?" he asked, brightening a bit.

"Sure did."

He blinked and nodded, sniffling as he tagged after his mother into the house.

Nadine heated two cups of water in the microwave while Bobby climbed into one of the worn chairs at the scratched butcher-block table. When the water was hot, she measured chocolate powder into one cup and said, "And as for Santa Claus, I still believe in him."

"Do you?"

"Mmm-hmm. But Oreos won't do for him. No siree. You and I'll have to bake some special Christmas cookies and leave them on the hearth."

Bobby sent her a look that said he didn't really believe her, but he didn't argue the point, either. "Thanks," he muttered when she handed him a steaming cup and a small plate of Oreos. "John can't help us make the cookies, neither."

"Well, if he has a change of heart—"

"He won't. He's too…too…dumb!"

Nadine blew across her cup, not wanting to condemn her eldest quite yet, but needing to placate Bobby. "Look, honey, I know how tough it can be with John. I'm the youngest, too, you know," she said, thinking of Ben and Kevin. A knot of pain tightened in her chest at the memory of Kevin, the eldest of the Powell siblings, a golden boy who'd once had it all, before his dreams and later his life had been stolen from him. Now there was just her and Ben, she thought sadly, then, seeing her son's expectant face, she forced a grin. "Remember Uncle Ben?" She dunked a tea bag into her cup, and soon the scent of jasmine mingled with the fragrance of chocolate, filling the cozy little kitchen.

"Is he a creep?" Bobby asked, his little jaw thrust forward as he dunked an Oreo into his hot chocolate.

"Ben?" She laughed, her melancholy dissolved as she stared at the hopeful eyes of her son. "Sometimes."

Nadine wished that Ben were still around. He'd be home soon, after ten years in the army and she couldn't wait to have him back in Gold Creek. Ben was the only member of her fractured family to whom she still felt close.

Bobby seemed placated slightly. "Well, John doesn't know anything! I saw Santa Claus and I'm not gonna say I didn't!" he stated with a firm thrust of his little chin. He dropped a handful of marshmallows into his cocoa and watched them slowly melt.

To her son's delight, Nadine broke open an Oreo and ate the white center first, licking the icing from the dark wafer. "And what was Santa doing last year—when you saw him?"

Bobby lifted one shoulder. "Dunno," he muttered. "Prob'ly tryin' to figure out which present was mine." His brow puckered again. "I hope he gives John a lump of coal!"

"I don't think that'll happen," Nadine said as he gulped his cocoa then wiped one grubby hand across his mouth.

"Sure it will. Santa knows when John's lying. He knows everything."

"I think it's God who knows so much," she corrected.

Her son lifted a shoulder as if God and Santa were one and the same, and she didn't see any reason to start another argument. Obviously Bobby's imagination was working overtime. But she loved him for his innocence, his bright eyes and that mind that buzzed with ideas from the moment he woke up until he fell asleep each night.

"Come on, you," she said, touching him fondly on the nose. "You can help me dig out all the Christmas decorations and wrapping paper. I think most of the stuff is in the closet under the stairs—"

"Mom, hey, Mom!" John's voice echoed through the small house.

Bobby rolled his eyes and sighed theatrically. "Oh, great. He's back."

"Hey—there's someone here to see you! Says you left somethin' at his place," John yelled.

Nadine glanced out the window to see John, riding his old bike as if his tail were on fire. Hershel galloped beside him, barking wildly.

Nadine froze for an instant when she recognized the reason for all the commotion. Her back stiffened to steel. Behind the boy and bike, striding purposefully up the path to the house, his angled face a mask of arrogance, was none other than Hayden Garreth Monroe IV.

CHAPTER SIX

BRACING HERSELF, SHE walked onto the front porch, arms crossed over her chest. In his beat-up jacket, flannel shirt and faded jeans that fit snugly around his buttocks and rode low on his hips, he didn't look much like the multimillionaire he'd become overnight. He was still too damned sexy for his own good. Or hers.

"I think you forgot something," he said as he strode up the slight incline to her house. His gait was a little uneven, but that was probably due to the rocky ground rather than the result of his boating accident years before.

"Forgot something?" she repeated, shaking her head. "Believe me, Hayden, I haven't forgotten anything." She glared at him, and all the bitter memories of her youth washed over her in a flood.

His eyes narrowed and his anger was visible in the hard angle of his jaw. Digging into the front pocket of his jeans, he withdrew a ring. Her ring. Instinctively she touched her fingers, assuring herself that the band with its imitation stone was really missing. "Yours?" he asked as he climbed the two long steps of the porch.

"Oh." She felt suddenly foolish. And trapped. He was too close. Too threatening. Too male. Squaring her shoulders, she managed to find her voice. "Thanks. I didn't realize I'd left it." She took the ring from his outstretched hands, careful not to touch him. "You didn't have to go to all this trouble. I would've been back for it tomorrow."

His eyes held hers for a heart-stopping second and her lungs squeezed. Quickly he glanced away. "I wasn't sure you'd be returning."

"I said I would—"

"You've said things before, Nadine," he pointed out and the comment cut her as easily as the bite of a whip. He was insulting her, but why? She'd never done anything to hurt him. Or his family.

"Hey, mister, is that your boat?" John's eyes were round with envy as he stared at the dock where a speedboat—shiny silver with black trim—was rocking on the waves.

"It is now."

"Oh, wow!"

"You like it?"

John was practically drooling. "What's not to like? It's the coolest."

"Is this your son?" Hayden asked.

Was it her imagination or was there a trace of regret in his question? Reluctantly, she made introductions. "Hayden Monroe, my oldest son, John," Nadine introduced, and spying Bobby peeking through the window, waved him outside. Bobby came cautiously through the door. "And this is my baby—"

"Don't call me that," Bobby warned.

"Excuse me." Nadine smiled and rumpled his red-blond hair. "This is my second son. Bobby. Or are you Robert today?" she asked, teasing him.

"Hello, Bobby. John." Hayden shook hands with each of the boys, and Nadine wondered if the shadow that stole across his summer-blue eyes was a tinge of remorse.

"Are you the guy who owns the sawmill?" John asked, and Nadine's polite smile froze on her face.

"For now."

"The whole mill?" Bobby asked, obviously impressed.

Before Hayden could reply, John said, "My dad says that the owner of the place is a goddamned mean son of a—"

"John!" Nadine cried.

"Your dad is right," Hayden replied with a glint in his eye.

John's forehead creased into a frown.

"Hayden just inherited the mill from his father," Nadine guessed, glancing at Hayden for reassurance. "He hasn't owned it all that long. Daddy wasn't talking about him."

"You don't like your dad?" Bobby wanted to know, and Nadine sent up a silent prayer. She didn't want to get involved with Hayden, didn't want her children feeling comfortable with him, didn't want to know anything about his life.

"My dad's gone," Hayden said flatly. Then, as if seeing that the boy was still confused, he added, "We didn't get along all that well. Never saw eye to eye."

"My dad's the greatest!" John said proudly as he threw his mother a defiant look.

Hayden's lips turned down a fraction. "That's how it should be."

Satisfied that he'd made his point, John waved to his brother. "C'mon, Bobby. Let's check out the boat!" John was already running down to the dock.

"Be careful. Don't touch any—"

Hayden's hand clamped over her shoulder and she gasped. "They'll be fine," he said. "No need to overmother them."

"But—"

"I'll wager they know how to handle a boat and what to steer clear of."

"You don't even know my boys," she shot back indignantly.

"Maybe not. But I do know about mothers who are overprotective."

His hand was still resting upon her shoulder, but she shrugged the warm palm away from her. "It's none of your business how I raise my children, Hayden," she said crossly.

"Just a little free advice."

"Then it's worth exactly what I paid for it—nothing."

"Boys need to explore, check things out."

"Is this something you've read or are you talking from experience?"

"I was a boy once."

"I know," she said, her heart thumping unnaturally. "I remember."

His gaze sliced into hers, and though he didn't say a word, the air seemed charged with silent accusations. To her disbelief she realized again that *he* seemed to be holding a grudge against *her*. As if in that faraway other lifetime she'd wronged him! As if he and his father hadn't altered irrevocably the direction of her life! As if he hadn't walked away from her and never so much as cast a glance back over his shoulder! Her insides were shredding, and she bit down on her lip so that she wouldn't start throwing angry accusations his way.

Standing on the porch, being so close to him was awkward. Being near him was uncomfortable. And yet she had to be polite. He was, after all, her boss as well as her ex-husband's employer. She dragged an invitation over her tongue. "If you're not worried about the boys damaging your boat, why don't you come in and have a cup of coffee?"

His dark brow arched. "Your husband won't mind?"

"Not at all," she replied quickly, and decided not to tell him that she was divorced. Not yet.

"A peace offering?"

"We got off on the wrong foot. I think we should try again." The minute the last syllable left her lips, she wished she could call the words back, but she couldn't. Silent, painful memories of their youth stretched between them.

His jaw tightened and he hesitated, glancing back at the boat. Nadine felt like a fool. Of course he wouldn't take her up on her offer. He was just returning her ring and had probably delivered it himself to fire her in person. No doubt the minute she'd left his house, he'd phoned William Bradworth, set the attorney straight in a blistering conversation, managed to find out her address and had jetted across the lake hell-bent to hand over her walking papers. Well, she'd be damned if she'd make it easy for him.

"Okay. You're on." He surprised her by accepting and following her into the small cabin.

She poured coffee into two ceramic mugs, offered cream and sugar, then followed him back outside where she could sit on the porch and watch the boys.

Nadine blew across her cup and sat on the old porch swing. Hayden balanced his hips against the weathered rail, his back to the lake, his long legs crossed at the ankles. The stiff wind ruffled his hair and brought her the scent of him—clean and male, no trace of aftershave or cologne.

"Bradworth said your name's Warne now," he observed. "You married Sam," he said without a trace of emotion.

"That's right."

"I thought he was just a friend."

"He was. Then he got to be a better one." She didn't have to explain anything to Hayden, especially something as difficult and complex as her relationship with Sam. Sam, who had once adored her. Sam, who had wanted to marry her and father her children. Sam, who even early in their marriage had shown signs of being unable to control his alcohol consumption. Nadine had thought she could help him with his problem; he'd denied that there had been a problem at all.

She swallowed a long drink of coffee, feeling the warm liquid slide down her throat. Long ago, Sam had been her friend, Sam had been safe, Sam had been there when Hayden and her family had not. Though their marriage hadn't always been happy, she didn't regret marrying Sam, not when she considered her sons. Even with the trouble John and Bobby gave her, she loved them both with all of her heart. Nothing would ever change that. Sam had given her those precious boys.

She felt Hayden's gaze upon her, and she cradled the warm cup in her fingers as she looked up at him. "What about you, Hayden? I read somewhere you were engaged to marry Wynona."

He snorted. "Didn't happen."

"You never married?"

His eyes turned an angry shade of blue. "Never." He didn't bother to explain and she didn't ask. The less they knew of each other, the better. She had a job to do and their relationship was strictly professional. The fact that she felt nervous around him was easily explained and she'd just have to get over it. Whatever they'd shared long ago had been fleeting and was definitely over.

He drained his cup as the boys tired of their exploration. John ran up the narrow path to the porch. "That's a great boat, Mr. Monroe."

"You think so?"

"Yeah, the best!" Bobby chimed in.

"I bet it goes real fast," John hinted, and Nadine wanted to die.

"You boys had better go inside—" she said.

"Would you like a ride?" Hayden asked suddenly.

Nadine nearly dropped her cup. "No!" she said, her stomach doing a somersault as she sloshed coffee on her hand.

"Would I?" John echoed gleefully. "You know it!"

"Me, too!" Bobby chimed in, jumping up and down.

This, whatever it was, couldn't happen! "Now wait a minute. You have homework and chores and—"

"Aw, Mom, just for a little while?" John asked, some of his earlier belligerence disappearing, his face flushed with anticipation. "Please?"

"Mr. Monroe is a busy man." She glanced at Hayden for help out of this one, but found him grinning at her discomfiture. She wiped her hand on her jeans. "I just don't think it would be such a good idea tonight to—"

"I'm not that busy," Hayden replied. "It's okay with me. If, of course, it's okay with you."

Both boys started begging and pleading at once. Nadine felt her cheeks flush and saw the silent laughter in Hayden's eyes.

"You don't have a great track record with boats," she said, and saw his countenance grow deathly still at the mention of the boat wreck that had nearly taken Wynona Galveston's life.

His skin stretched tight over his face, but he didn't back down and Nadine knew she'd said too much. Deep in her heart, she realized that he wouldn't hurt her children—not intentionally. And yet letting them go with him was difficult. "Do you have life jackets?" she finally asked.

"Life jackets are for babies!" John declared.

"I even have one for you," Hayden replied stonily, and Nadine had to grit her teeth. It wasn't that she wanted to deny the boys a good time, she just didn't want to get involved with Hayden in any way, shape or form.

"I don't have time," she said. "And the boys really should get started on their—"

Bobby's eyes filled with tears. Silently her youngest beseeched her. She didn't know if he was putting on an act or not, but he'd been so unhappy lately, she couldn't find it in her heart to say no to him. "I suppose it would be all right for a little while," she said, caving in and knowing that she was not only treading in dangerous waters by allowing Hayden any insight into her or her family's life, she was diving in wholeheartedly! Bobby, the little con man, was suddenly all smiles. His tears seemed to evaporate into thin air. "Be back before dark," she insisted, still trying to assert her authority. She was, after all, still the mother and therefore still the boss.

"We will!" Her sons were already running back to the dock.

Hayden slowly set his empty cup on the rail. "Thanks for the coffee—I'll bring them back soon," he assured her, but there was no warmth in his voice.

Nadine felt instantly contrite. He was just giving her children a much-needed thrill and a little male attention. "Look, I'm sorry for the crack about the boating accident, it's just that—"

"Don't worry about it," he snapped.

She glanced to her boys, already climbing into the speedboat. "I hope you know what you're getting yourself into."

"It's just a ride. Don't read anything more into it, Nadine," he said, and she felt her cheeks flush. "Believe me, I'm not getting into anything."

THE KIDS WERE rambunctious and excited. They could hardly sit still, and each kept pushing the other out of the way so that he could be in the front and therefore in command. The wind tore at their hair and eyes and they laughed with an uninhibited abandon that surprised Hayden. There had been few times in his childhood when he had felt as carefree as these two rowdy boys. Maybe if he'd had a brother or even a sister to share some of the scrutiny and expectations from his two parents, he would have been able to cut loose a little as a kid and would have avoided the rebellion that had slowly become his guiding force as he'd entered high school and had stuck with him through college.

He glanced over his shoulder and saw that the little house Nadine occupied was far in the distance.

Frowning, he realized she'd changed. She was different from the girl he remembered. She had filled out and matured, her hair had darkened and her hips and breasts were curvier. Her green eyes still snapped with intelligence but her tongue had become sharper over the years, her cynicism surprising. There was a deep-seated bitterness toward him. She seemed to blame him for some injustice she'd suffered at his hand. But what?

He gnawed on his lips and his eyes narrowed. True, he'd never called her after the accident. His parents had made it crystal clear that she wanted nothing to do with him, that she'd only cared about his money. He hadn't trusted them of course, but he'd seen the canceled check, the "hush money" of five thousand dollars that his father had paid George Powell in order that his daughter didn't cry "rape."

But that was crazy. They'd never made love…not that he hadn't wanted to. They'd come close a couple of times, and Nadine had seemed more than willing, but they'd never consummated their lust because Hayden had held back, thinking that he was protecting her honor, never wanting her to go through what Trish London had endured.

He shoved the throttle all out and the boys whooped in

glee. Their faces were red with the wind and spray from the water and their hair was damp against their heads. "I don't suppose either of you would like to drive," he said, and was met with loud shouts from each boy proclaiming that he should be the first to helm the boat.

"Hold on. You first," he said to Bobby. Slowing the craft, he balanced behind Bobby, ready to take over the wheel at a second's notice. The boy laughed as they cut across the choppy water, gaining speed near the center of the lake.

Impatiently, John demanded his turn at the wheel. By the time they'd circled the lake five or six times, the sky had turned a dark pewter hue. Lights glowed from Nadine's cabin, and smoke, barely visible in the fading light, curled from the chimney.

"Better drop anchor," Hayden said over loud protests from both boys.

"Just one more turn," John pleaded.

"And have your mother on my neck? No way." Hayden guided the speedboat inland and shut off the engine after mooring the rocking craft. He walked behind the boys as they scurried up the path to the front door and met their mother on the front porch.

"Look at you," Nadine said, eyeing their wet clothes and ruddy faces and clucking her tongue. "You're chilled to the bone."

Standing in the doorway, the light from the fire casting her hair in its fiery glow, she touched each boy fondly on the head. Hayden felt his diaphragm slam hard against his lungs. Her skin was creamy white, dusted with a few freckles across the bridge of her nose and her cheeks were two spots of apricot that contrasted with the deep, searing green of her eyes.

"Go on. Into the shower. Both of you," she ordered.

"But we're not dirty," John argued.

"You're wet and cold."

John looked about to argue further, but thought better of it as he tried to brush past her.

"And leave your shoes out here—"

"Yeah, yeah."

Dutifully both boys kicked off their sneakers and yanked off soggy socks before tromping inside. John turned just inside the doorway. "Oh, Mr. Monroe. Thanks."

"You're welcome."

"You can stay for dinner!" Bobby said, and Nadine's complexion paled.

Hayden, glancing at Nadine, shook his head. "I don't think so."

"Please," Bobby insisted.

"Another time." Hayden's gut twisted, and for the life of him he wondered why it was that dinner in this cramped, cozy cabin seemed so appealing. Maybe it was the house. Maybe it was the kids. Or maybe it was the woman. Another man's wife. His mouth filled with a bitter taste that wouldn't go away.

"Mom, make him stay," John pleaded.

"I don't think anyone can *make* Mr. Monroe do anything he doesn't want to."

"But he wants to. He's just bein' polite!" Bobby said, exasperated at his mother for being so blind.

"You could stay," she said, though there was more than a trace of reluctance in her voice.

"Wouldn't your husband object?"

She hesitated for a second, as if wrestling with her conscience, then shook her head. She looked about to say something, then held her tongue.

Hayden's jaw tightened. Was she the kind of woman who kept secrets behind her husband's back? Hayden had never liked Sam Warne, thought the guy was a whining, self-indulgent slob, but if Nadine had married him, she should honor her vows. Irritated, he stared at her. God, she was sensual—not in a model or Hollywood manifestation of beauty, but in a purely earthy, feminine way that bored right to his soul. Gritting his teeth, he swore to himself that he'd have nothing more to do with her. She was married and that was that. If she wanted to cheat on Sam or entertain men behind his back, so be it. But not with Hayden.

"I've got to get back anyway," he lied, trying to tell himself that the pine-paneled cabin with its river-rock fireplace and glowing coals held no appeal for him. No more appeal than the woman standing in the doorway. Before he changed his mind and decided that adultery wasn't such a sin, before he did something they'd both regret for the rest of their lives, he turned on his heel and walked rapidly back to the dock. Plunging fists deep into the pockets of his leather jacket, he bent his head against the wind. He'd go back to that morgue of a summer home, pour himself a stiff drink and try to make some sense of the corporate records of Monroe Sawmill Company. Somehow, some way, he'd shove all thoughts of Nadine from his mind.

THE LAST PERSON he expected to find waiting for him was his uncle. But there he was, big as life—Thomas Fitzpatrick himself, unfolding his tall body from the interior of a roomy new Cadillac that was parked near the garage. The Caddy's white finish gleamed in the light from a security lamp over the garage. Leo, barking furiously, neck hairs standing upright, ran toward Thomas.

"Stop!" Hayden commanded, and the dog, snarling lowly, did as he was bid.

"He looks like he could take your leg off," Thomas observed.

"Only when provoked." Hayden hadn't seen his uncle for a few years and he was struck again by Thomas's ageless quality. His hair was thick and white and there wasn't an ounce of extra padding on his trim body. His trademark mustache was neatly clipped and his eyes were shrewd. Somewhere around sixty, Thomas was as sharp as he'd ever been.

"Thought you'd probably show up sometime," Thomas said as he smoothed the flat of his hand over his hair. "That's why I waited. Bradworth said you called and I thought I could clear up a few company matters."

"I can handle it," Hayden replied, slightly rankled that his uncle thought he needed help deciphering the company books.

"Well, that's good to hear." Thomas rewarded Hayden with a wide smile. "The way Bradworth talked, I thought you might be turning the whole damned operation over to charity."

"Bradworth talks too much," Hayden said, retrieving a key from his pocket and unlocking the door. He shoved it open, and Leo, nails clicking, ran through the foyer.

"He only talks to the right people." Thomas accepted Hayden's silent invitation to walk into the house. As he did, his practiced smile fell. Hayden guessed that a host of memories crept through his mind. Absently Thomas touched the rail of the stairs and his lips rolled inward. Hayden could only guess what Thomas was thinking. This had been where Jackson Moore had hidden out overnight all those years ago when the whole town of Gold Creek thought he'd murdered Thomas's son, Roy. Just this past summer, the truth had finally come out and not only had Thomas's younger son's wife, Laura, confessed to the crime, but the entire town had learned that Jackson was Thomas's bastard son.

Hayden, never close to his uncle, was at a loss for

words. "Mom told me about Laura," he said, as much to break the ice as anything. "I'm sorry."

"Not half as sorry as I am," Thomas admitted as they walked into the den. "Brian's never gotten over it, I'm afraid.... He still works for the company, but..." Thomas shrugged, and his shoulders seemed a little more sloped. His life hadn't turned out as he had planned, Hayden knew. His son Roy had been killed; Brian had embezzled from the company and his wife had been found to be Roy's murderess. Toni...well, stubborn, strong-willed Toni was off to college back East and Thomas's political ambitions had all but died in the scandals involving his children. The rift between Thomas and Jackson, his bastard son, would probably never be repaired and he was estranged from his wife.

Hayden almost felt sorry for his uncle. Almost. He still didn't trust the guy. Thomas was as slippery as a seal in a tank of oil. Opening the old liquor cabinet, Hayden found a bottle of Irish whiskey with an unbroken seal. "Can I buy you a drink?"

Thomas nodded. "Guess you can afford it now."

Hayden pulled two crystal glasses from the cupboard, wiped them out with the tail of his shirt and splashed amber-colored liquor into each one. "To Roy," he said, handing his uncle a glass.

Thomas frowned, then touched his glass to Hayden's and downed his shot. "I wish that boy would've lived," he said.

"Me, too." Roy had been Hayden's friend. True, they'd oftentimes quarreled, and just before his death, Roy had proved himself to be a royal pain in the backside, but there had been years...many years while Hayden was growing up a lonely rich kid when Roy and Brian had been his only friends.

Hayden gulped the fiery liquid, feeling the heat slide

down his throat. Thomas tossed back his drink, as well, and accepted another shot of whiskey in his glass.

"To your father," Thomas said, and Hayden gritted his teeth. "May he rest in peace."

"And get what he deserves." Again the glasses clinked, but Hayden sipped his drink slowly this time.

"You're still blaming him."

Hayden's muscles tightened. "I just don't like anyone trying to run my life."

The silence between them stretched to the breaking point before Thomas, in an effort to change the conversation, asked, "Where were you tonight?" He threw off a dustcover and settled into a worn leather chair. Placing the heel of his shoe on the matching ottoman, he eyed his nephew as Hayden opened the damper of the fireplace and lit the dust-dry logs that had sat for years in the grate. "I heard the boat."

Hayden tensed a little. For an unnamed reason he didn't want to discuss Nadine. "Bradworth hired a woman to clean the place. She left a ring here and I took it back to her."

"By boat?"

"She lives across the lake."

Thomas scowled and glanced through the windows to the darkness beyond. The lake wasn't visible through the glass, but lights on the distant shore winked in the night. "Who is she?"

"Someone Bradworth got from an agency in town. HELP!, I think it was."

A shadow flickered in Thomas's gaze and the corners of his mouth tightened almost imperceptibly. "Nadine Warne?"

"That's right."

Thomas's eyes darkened, but he didn't comment and Hayden was left with the feeling that their conversation was unfinished, that Thomas knew something about Nadine that he didn't. Not that he cared, he reminded himself. What she did with her life, other than cleaning this damned house, didn't affect him.

Finishing their drinks, they discussed his mother and how she was coping since Hayden's father's death. Then the conversation turned to the string of mills he'd inherited. Though the largest sawmill was located in Gold Creek, there were other smaller operations in northern California as well as in southern Oregon.

"Those mills have been in the family for decades," Thomas said, leaning back in his chair. "Especially the one here, in Gold Creek. It was the first. Monroe Sawmill is a way of life—practically a tradition—to the people of Gold Creek. When times were tough during the depression, the company store or the sawmill and the logging company kept this town afloat. Even employees whose hours had been cut back were given credit to buy food and clothing for their families.

"Gold Creek depended upon the mill and the logging operation to keep it alive."

"That was a long time ago."

Thomas waved dismissively. "I know. But in the intervening years, through two world wars as well as the troubles in Korea and Vietnam, timber provided for the people of Gold Creek. Generations have depended upon the logging company and the sawmill for their livelihoods. That all may come to a grinding halt soon enough if the government tightens up on clear-cutting and logging old growth—but in the meantime we owe this town."

"Sounds like a bunch of political bull to me," Hayden observed. "I thought you had decided against running for public office a few years back."

Thomas placed his hands on his knees and stood.

His joints creaked audibly. The fire cast shadows on his patrician face and his expression was stern. "I can't tell you how to run your life, Hayden. Hell, even your father wasn't able to do that. But, one way or another, until you find a way to get rid of it, you own a majority interest in some valuable mills. Now, you can look at the corporation one of two ways—either you want it because it makes money for you, or you want it because it's the lifeblood of this community."

"I don't want it at all." Hayden studied his uncle a minute. "I thought you'd come here to try to buy me out."

Thomas's lips curved beneath his mustache and his eyes glimmered. "You remind me of Roy. He always cut right to the chase."

Hayden rolled his glass in his palms. "So what's it going to be?"

"I need a little time. Most of my cash is tied up in oil wells, at least temporarily. I'm still trying to buy some land north of here. I was interested in Badlands Ranch, but the owner is being stubborn." Thomas's eyes shadowed. He didn't like to be bested. "I'm interested in diversifying," he explained. "I've got enough invested in logging and sawmilling and I don't believe in putting all my eggs in one basket."

"Seems to me you've diversified a lot. Timber, sawmilling, real estate and oil."

"It's just a start." He clapped Hayden on the back. "I'm not going to pressure you, though. This company is in your blood whether you like it or not."

He walked out to his Cadillac before pausing at the car door. "The woman who Bradworth hired…?" Thomas asked, and Hayden felt his spine stiffen slightly.

"What about her?"

"Maybe you should tell me what's going on with that little piece," Thomas said, and Hayden's fists balled as the older man laughed. "Seems as if there's something more than the company in your blood."

"I GOT TWO days' detention," John announced at breakfast the next morning.

"For what?" Nadine asked, though she didn't really want to know. She wasn't in the best of moods. Ever since seeing Hayden again, she'd been on edge, her nerves jangled. She had to face him in less than an hour and wasn't looking forward to the day.

"Lack of respect," John answered. "Mrs. Zalinski hates me."

"She doesn't hate anyone," Nadine replied as she bit into a piece of dry toast she really didn't want.

"Oh, she hates me all right. Me and Mike Katcher. She hates us both."

Nadine chewed thoughtfully. Mike Katcher was trouble. No doubt about it. That kid reminded her a lot of Jackson Moore, a boy she'd gone to school with years before. Jackson, too, had been a troublemaker, a kid who had gotten into more than his share of fights, a boy who was constantly walking a thin line with the law. Years later, he'd risen above his past, returning to Gold Creek as a prominent attorney, a man who had cleared his murky reputation.

Nadine didn't think Mike Katcher would ever shape up. Mike's mother, too, was a single parent and she spent more time looking for another husband than she did with her son. "Look, John, why don't you give Mrs. Zalinski a break?"

"You'd better," Bobby advised. "Her husband's a cop and he might arrest you."

"You don't get arrested for locking girls in the bathroom," John said, and then turned a deep shade of red.

"Is that what you did?" Nadine asked. "John—"

"It was Mike's idea."

"Well, maybe you should come up with your own ideas." She glanced at the clock and gritted her teeth. "Look, we're going to talk this out this afternoon. And I'm going to call your teacher and Principal Strand and Mike's mother to straighten out this mess."

"Aw, Mom, *don't!*" John cried, horrified.

"We'll talk tonight."

"Promise me you won't call."

"Tonight," she replied, as the boys clambered down from the table and hurried out the back door. Despite the first drops of rain falling from the sky, they climbed on their bikes and headed toward the sitter's home to wait for the bus.

Nadine cleared the dishes and stacked them in the sink. John was becoming more and more defiant. Until this point, she'd been lenient with him, convinced that she couldn't come down on him too hard or he'd want to live with Sam. He couldn't, of course—she had custody. But Sam had been making noise about wanting more time with the boys and if he went to court again and John pleaded to live with his father... "What a mess!"

She'd have it out with John tonight and lay down the law. If he brought up living with his father again, then she'd deal with it. Hopefully it wouldn't come to that.

She placed a call to the school asking for a conference with John's teacher, then started collecting her cleaning supplies. Before she could concentrate on her son, she had to spend the day dealing with Hayden.

She passed by the small room that had been the pantry and she frowned. Inside, the shelves were filled with scraps of leather, buttons, paint and beads. In her spare time she created earrings and pins, hair clips, studded jackets and even tie-dyed shirts, whimsical designs of her own making; she'd begun to sell some of her work and had orders stacking up for more of her "wearable art." But lately it seemed that she didn't have an extra five minutes in each day, and she needed to devote hours to her craft if she ever wanted to make enough money from it to support herself and the boys.

"Someday," she told herself as she shut the pantry door and picked up her bucket of soaps and waxes.

She climbed into her old Nova, sent up a prayer that it wouldn't die and smiled wretchedly as the engine turned over on the first try. Wheeling out of the drive, she turned toward the north shore of the lake.

And Hayden.

CHAPTER SEVEN

HAYDEN'S JEEP, THE one Nadine had seen when she'd left yesterday, wasn't parked in the drive. Though the electronic gates were open, there was neither hide nor hair of him on the grounds. She knocked on the door, and when she didn't get a response, let herself in with the key she'd received from Bradworth.

"Hayden?" she called, and his name echoed back to her through the empty rooms. Strangely, she felt more alone in the house today than she had yesterday. She observed evidence that he'd been in the house. Drink glasses had been left in the den beside an opened bottle of Irish whiskey, a sleeping bag had been tossed across the top of the huge bed in the master suite and the shower stall was still wet with drips of water. She swiped at the shower sides with a towel and wondered how long he planned to camp out here. A couple of days? A week? A month? As long as it took to sell the place? Not that it mattered, she reminded herself.

Chasing wayward thoughts of Hayden from her mind, she spent three hours on the second floor, sweeping away cobwebs, cleaning two fireplaces and polishing the floors while she washed all the bedding she'd found in the closets. She plumped and aired out pillows and kept notes of repairs that were needed, from the leaky faucet in one of the bathrooms to the gutters that were overflowing with pine needles and downspouts that were clogged and rusted.

She also created a list of supplies and was oiling the banister leading to the first floor when the front door opened and a rush of winter-cold air swept up the stairs. Startled, Nadine nearly jumped out of her skin.

Hayden, carrying two sacks of groceries, strode into the foyer and stared up to the landing where she was working. His gaze was cold as a glacier in January. "You lied," he said, his lips white with rage.

"I...what?"

"You lied to me!"

"I didn't—"

He dropped the bags and took the stairs two at a time to loom over her. She felt as if she were stripped bare. "I don't know what you're raving about, but you scared the devil out of me just now," she said, feeling color stain her cheeks. "I didn't hear your car—"

Grabbing her wrist, he said, "I think the devil's still in you, woman."

"You're talking in circles."

"You're not married," he said flatly, and she stiffened. His gaze raked down her body to glance at her left hand, which was covered with a latex glove.

So that was it. She braced herself. "Not anymore. But I never said I was married," she replied hotly. "You jumped to conclusions."

"Then what was all that talk about your husband not minding if I stayed for dinner?" His nostrils flared in suppressed rage and his lips tightened in silent fury.

"He wouldn't."

"Of course he wouldn't!" Hayden whispered hoarsely, his face pushed so close to hers that she could see the movement of his nostrils as he breathed. "He walked out on you two years ago."

"I don't see that it's any business of yours—oh!" He

jerked her roughly to him. He was so close that a wave of his breath, hot and angry, fanned against her skin.

"I don't give a good goddamn whether you're single, married or a bigamist," he snarled, his nose nearly touching hers. "But, as long as you're working for me, I expect you to be honest."

Her temper grew hot. "You're a fine one to talk of honesty, Hayden!"

"I never lied to you."

"You left—"

She heard his back teeth grind together. "Did I promise you differently? Did I say I'd stick around?" His fingers dug into her upper arms. "Damn it, woman, I ended up in the hospital and by the time I was back on my feet you were gone—vanished into thin air!" A cold smile touched his lips. "But you had what you wanted, didn't you?"

"I—wha—"

"The money, Nadine. I know about the money."

"What money?"

Dropping her hand as if it were acid, he hurried down the stairs and kicked the door shut. The door banged against the casing. "Don't you ever, *ever* make me look like a fool again!"

"I don't think I have to help you. You seem to do a fine job of that yourself."

"Son of a—" He grabbed his sacks of groceries and stormed into the kitchen.

"You arrogant, self-serving bastard!" Nadine hissed after him. "How *dare* you come storming in here full of half-baked accusations and lies!"

A crash sounded from the kitchen and a string of swear words followed.

Furious, Nadine told herself to remain calm. Usually, she could keep a level head. Even when she imagined herself in love with Turner, she'd managed to stay composed. But every time she was near Hayden, her emotions were wound tight as a clock spring, her temper ready to explode. She clamped down on her teeth and picked up her dust rag. The smart thing to do, the reasonable thing to do, was to hold her tongue and cool off. Think before she acted.

But despite her arguments to the contrary, she half ran down the stairs and dashed into the kitchen where he was picking up a coffee cup that he'd knocked over. The ceramic mug had shattered and coffee and chips of pottery had sprayed upon the floor.

"Watch out!" he warned.

"I can handle this. I'm used to dealing with spills and broken—"

"Just leave it the hell alone," he cut in. "And while you're at it, leave me the hell alone, too!" He glowered up at her, swept the pieces together with a wet towel and, under his breath, muttered something about pigheaded women.

"You know, Hayden, if you're trying to impress me with this macho routine, it's not working."

"I'm not trying to impress anyone."

"Good. Now, maybe you can explain about the money you accused me of wanting."

He threw her a dark, scornful look.

"What money?" she repeated, ready to strangle him with her gloved hands.

"The blackmail money!" He slammed a cupboard door shut. "The damned hush money."

"Are you crazy? Blackmail? What're you talking about?"

He shoved two sets of fingers through his hair. "You know, Nadine, I told myself that you were different, convinced myself that your *family* was different, but in the end you proved that you and Trish and Wynona are the same kind of women—cut from the same greedy cloth. Maybe there isn't any other kind!"

"I don't know what you're talking about—"

"Like hell!" He strode over to her and ripped his wallet from his back pocket. His face was a dangerous shade of red and his lips flattened against stark white teeth. Eyes crackling with fury he yanked out a thick stack of bills. "Here you go, Nadine. Take it and leave. Consider your job here finished!" He slapped the bills into her hands, and she just stood there, too dumbfounded to speak. "If it isn't enough, if your deal with Bradworth is for more—just call him. He'll send you the rest."

"I haven't finished—"

"Oh, yes, you have, Nadine. You were finished a long time ago."

"You miserable—"

"You know where the door is."

"I mean the job. It's not finished."

He smiled coldly, cruelly. "Think of this as getting your walking papers."

"You'd like that, wouldn't you? Well, forget it. I intend to do what I was hired to do." With strength born of fury, she flung the bills back at him. "I signed a contract to clean this house and clean it I will, whether you like it or not! If I bother you, Mr. Monroe, you can make yourself and your ridiculous accusations scarce!"

"If you bother me? You quit bothering me a long time ago."

"Good! Then we don't have a problem, do we?"

His eyes narrowed a fraction. "I think we'll always have a problem." The air seemed to simmer between them. Nadine's pulse quickened and she gritted her teeth so as not to strike him. "I've got a job to do," she said, turning on her heel and heading back to the stairs. "And I'll get it done. All you have to do is stay out of my way!"

Easier said than done, Hayden thought as he strode to the den. Why did he let her get to him? He'd known a lot of women since he'd last dealt with Nadine. He'd worked with women, befriended few, slept with fewer still, but he'd never really trusted them. The women in his life, his mother, Trish, Wynona and Nadine had taught him from an early age about their priorities: money, money and more money.

There had been a few females that he'd met that hadn't seemed all that interested in his wealth. The women he'd dealt with in Oregon had had no idea that he was heir to a fortune, but he had been the boss—the owner of the logging company—and, for a small mill town, even the money he'd managed to make there had seemed a fortune to many of them. He'd never trusted their motives. Whenever a woman, a friend or lover, had gotten too close to him, he'd managed to cut ties with her.

Not that he cared. He whistled harshly to Leo and walked outside. A pale November sun was trying to warm the ground, but fog, in long, disappearing fingers, climbed up the trees and settled in a thick blanket over the lake.

Hayden kicked at a stone and sent it rolling toward the water. What was it about Nadine that made him see red? She wasn't always disagreeable, though he'd never met a more stubborn woman in all his life, but she had a way of rankling him to the point that he wanted to shake some sense into her or throw her on the ground and take her in a very primal way. He fantasized about her submission and realized it was his fantasy because she wasn't the kind of woman who would submit—those kinds of women turned him off. No, Nadine was a woman who knew her own mind, with a short fuse and a powder keg of emotions that was just waiting to be set off. It was the challenge in her eyes, the defiant lift of her chin and her sharp words that tied him in knots.

But she was dishonest. She'd already proved that much by lying about her marital status and trying to deceive him about the bloody money his father had paid her. Damn, what a mess!

Despite her deception, she fascinated him, intrigued him in a way that was as dangerous as it was impossible to ignore.

What was wrong with him? Just one look at her pouty lips, and he was ready to kiss her so hard, she'd have trouble breathing for days. Fool! Idiot!

Bradworth had contracted with her to work two weeks. Thirteen days were left. Surely he could rein in his emotions, manage to keep his hands off her and find a way to be civil to her for thirteen lousy days.

Shaking his head, he reached down and scratched Leo behind the ears. "I've never been a saint," he admitted. An understatement. "Dealing with that woman is probably going to kill me, but I can't let her win. If she can stand it, so can I."

Leo whined and thumped his tail.

His temper cooled, Hayden walked back to the house and locked himself in the den, trying to concentrate on the corporate records, but he heard her footsteps as she made her way to the kitchen. He called Bradworth, and asked a few questions, but was distracted by the sound of her humming an old Roy Orbison tune as she worked.

He drummed his fingers on the desk, tried to block her out of his mind and was half-crazy by noon. Angrily he slammed the books shut and convinced himself it was time for a break. Striding into the kitchen, he caught her, on her hands and knees, facing away from him, cleaning out a cupboard under the stove. His gut tightened as he noticed the way her jeans stretched across her rump and his mouth went dry when she looked at him over her shoulder, her red hair falling around her face and neck in untamed curls. "Is there something you want?" she asked him, and his vocal cords seemed to freeze.

He tried and failed to shift his gaze away from her. "I'm going out. Lock up when you leave."

"Yes, boss," she drawled, her eyes defiant. "Anything else?"

He shoved his hands into the pockets of his jeans and ignored the sensual curve of her lips. "Can't think of a thing."

She arched a fine mahogany brow, then turned back to her work.

"If you need me, you can get hold of me at the mill."

"I'll manage," she replied, never even glancing back at him and scouring the bottom of the cupboard as if her life depended upon it. She heard his keys jangle and his footsteps fade away. Once the back door slammed shut, she rocked back on her heels and blew her bangs from her eyes. She'd been able to sound cool and indifferent to him, but knowing he was in the house set her nerves on edge. She had listened for him, had expected to run into him at every corner, had found herself wondering what he was thinking. *He's thinking that he's the boss and you're the maid. That's all. And you're not even a maid he wanted. So get over it already. He's not worth it!*

If only she could.

THREE HOURS LATER, she'd locked the house and driven to Gold Creek Elementary. She hadn't seen Hayden again and had shoved any thoughts of him aside as she sat in a small chair at a round table in Wanda Zalinski's classroom. Nearing forty, Wanda was slightly plump and her long black hair, pulled back with two colorful barrettes, was streaked with gray.

Wanda's smile was genuine. "John's not a bad kid," she said, moving her hands as she talked. "He's just got a lot of energy and sometimes that energy isn't expressed in a positive manner. On the playground he's a ringleader and always in the middle of trouble if there is any. He doesn't always cause the trouble, mind you, but if there's a fight brewing, John's there.

"He's also back talked the music teacher and been disruptive in the library."

Nadine's shoulders slumped a fraction.

"On the other hand, John's extremely bright. In fact, a lot of times I suspect he's bored. I've given him a couple of special assignments and he's done very well with them. Right now, he's helping another student who's struggling."

Nadine cringed inside. John, who always taunted his younger brother, didn't seem a model teacher's assistant.

"Oh, don't worry," Wanda said, as if reading her worried mind. "He's doing well. The boy, Tim, is improving." She smiled encouragingly. "Academically, John's at the top of the class, and we're working on his social skills. If you reinforce at home, what we're trying to do here at school, I think we'll see a vast improvement by the end of the school year."

Nadine only hoped so.

"I...I, uh, was hoping John's father would come to this meeting."

"He had to work," Nadine said quickly.

"Well, please let him know. John needs strong role models, and you can't do it alone."

"Sam will help out."

Wanda managed a pleasant smile that didn't quite reach her eyes. She knew Sam, of course. Most of the people in town did. There had been gossip at the time of their divorce; no doubt Wanda Zalinski had heard it. Wanda's husband, Paul, a deputy for the sheriff's department, had even hauled Sam into jail one night when he'd been partying too late, been pulled over and failed a breath test for alcohol.

Gold Creek was a small town. Everyone knew everyone else's business. However, if Nadine, or Sam for that matter, ever needed anyone's help, they had a web of friends and relatives that seemed to go on forever. Nadine could suffer the gossip for the security. It was more than an even trade.

HIS FATHER'S OFFICE felt uncomfortable. Though Garreth had only spent one or two mornings a week at Monroe Sawmill in Gold Creek, he had the most spacious office in the building. At that, the room wasn't fancy—not like his office in San Francisco—but, by the standards of this mill, the room was impressive. Carpeted in commercial grade sable brown, the office boasted built-in metal shelves and a large wooden desk. Two chairs, worn orange vinyl, were situated near the window and a battered olive green couch had been pushed against the far wall. There were three filing cabinets and the walls were covered with pictures of Little League teams who had been sponsored by the sawmill company. Hayden wasn't in any of the pictures of the smiling boys dressed in uniforms of varying colors, but he recognized some of the boys he'd known as a kid. Roy Fitzpatrick was in several, along with his brother, Brian. Scott McDonald, Erik Patton, and Nadine's older brothers, Kevin and Ben, were on some of the teams from over ten years ago. Their pictures had faded with time, but there were more recent colorful pictures of kids who were probably still in school today. Without realizing what he was doing, he checked over most of the photos, his eyes scanning the grinning faces of boys dressed in uniforms that looked as if they were made by major league manufacturers. Nadine's boys weren't among the eager group in any of the shots.

Why had she lied about being married? he wondered for about the hundredth time.

His father's secretary, a small birdlike woman of about sixty named Marie Inman, was more than eager to bring him old files and reports and keep his coffee cup filled. She refused to call him Hayden, though he'd told her several times he preferred it to "Mr. Monroe."

Most of the company's accounts, payroll records and general information were on the computer, but Hayden was calling up old information—information from thirteen years before, so he sifted through dusty, yellowed printouts and general bookkeeping records, hoping that he would discover that his old man had lied, and that the check he'd waved at him under his nose was phony.

His gut grew tight when he found what he was looking for: a check made payable to George Powell for five thousand dollars. The notation was "return on investment." Some investment. Hayden's stomach soured as he remembered lying in the hospital in San Francisco, his leg in a cast, his body racked with agony between mercifully numbing shots of painkillers.

His father had visited him. Garreth's face had been florid, his blue eyes as cold as the bottom of Whitefire Lake. "This is what that little tramp wanted, Hayden." He waved a check in front of his son's nose. "Money. That's all. When women look at you, that's what they see—dollar signs."

Hayden had tried to protest, but Garreth raged on.

"I hope to God she's not pregnant! That would kill your mother, you know. And Wynona, Lord only knows what that sweet girl thinks."

"I don't care 'bout Wynona," Hayden had managed

to say. Strapped down to the bed, he felt cornered, like a bear in a trap.

"Well, you'd better care, son. Because she's planning on marrying you. That is *if* she survives. She's still in ICU, you know. Thanks to you! I don't know what you could've been thinking telling her you weren't going to marry her."

Hayden bit back the sharp retort forming on his tongue. The truth would only enrage his father further.

"Thank God for Dr. Galveston and all his connections. Wynona's getting the best care possible."

"I'm not going to marry Wynona," Hayden said firmly as a tiny dark-haired nurse swept into the room and added something to his IV.

"Just rest," his father insisted. "We'll discuss this later."

"I'm not—"

But Garreth had already huffed out of the room and soon the medication had dulled Hayden's pain as well as his mind. He had slipped away to blissful, painless unconsciousness.

In the intervening years, Hayden had hoped that his memory had been clouded, that the check that had been shoved under his nose either had never existed and was a figment of his foggy mind or had never been cashed.

From Nadine's reaction when he'd brought up the check, he'd hoped that his faith in her could be restored. But the notation in the general accounting books was right where it should have been, written two days after the accident.

Marie bustled into the room. "Can I get you anything else, Mr. Monroe? More coffee?"

"Not now. Thanks. And it's Hayden," he said. As she left the room as quickly as she'd entered, he looked around the office, smelled the remnants of stale tobacco in his father's humidor and wondered what the hell he was doing here.

THE NEXT FEW days at the Monroe house were tense. Hayden and Nadine tried to avoid each other, but even in a three-storied house the size of a manor, two people did bump into each other and Nadine dreaded each meeting.

He spent some of his time at the mill, some of his time on the phone, and a little of his time outside, doing a few of the repairs that she'd brought to his attention. Nonetheless, there was still a lot of hours when they were alone in the house, and Nadine, as if she had a sixth sense, knew where he was at just about any given second.

Which irritated her. She wanted to ignore him, to pretend that he wasn't around. But she heard the scrape of his boots, or the softer step of his running shoes, and sensed when he was in the room next to hers. Several times she'd caught him gazing at her, staring at her with those intense blue eyes that seemed to scrape down her body and penetrate her soul.

There was a new anger in him, a deep rage that he tried to hide, but was evident in the harsh set of his jaw and the tense cords in his neck that bulged whenever she spoke to him.

On Friday, she couldn't stand the strain a moment longer. She had just finished cleaning the fireplace in the living room. The ashes had been hauled outside, the andirons gleamed, the mantel had been polished and the brass candlesticks actually sparkled for the first time in years.

Wiping her hands on her jeans, she glanced into the oval mirror over the mantel and caught Hayden openly staring at her. Propped by one shoulder, he leaned against the heavy woodwork of the arch separating the dining room from the living room. His frown was deep, his eyebrows drawn together and if looks could kill, she would have already been laid in a coffin by now.

"Don't tell me—this doesn't pass the white-glove test," she said, watching a tic near his scarred eyebrow.

"I don't give a damn how clean it is."

"Then you shouldn't have hired me."

"I didn't."

"I'll be done by the end of next week," she said, and hid her disappointment that he didn't seem to appreciate any of her labors. She'd spent hours polishing the piano, washing the windows and dusting the chandelier while standing on a ladder and hand-rubbing each crystal teardrop of glass. The oak floors were waxed to a deep patina, and once the crew came out to shampoo the carpets, the living room would look as grand as it had years ago when Hayden's parents had thrown parties here. However, she wasn't going to let Hayden's pessimism infect her. She'd done a good job and she was proud of it.

"You know, Hayden," she said, unable to hold her tongue a minute longer, as she ran her fingers down the keys of the piano and the room seemed to shiver with the sound, "I don't understand why you're so hostile."

"I'm not."

She held his gaze steadily. "You act as if I did something horrible to you. Something unthinkable. Or else, you're substituting your guilt for rage."

"My guilt," he repeated, unfolding his arms. "*My* guilt?"

She walked a few steps closer to him. "The other day you mentioned money—blackmail money or hush money. I thought you'd really gone off the deep end at the time, and I tried to forget about it, but I can't. Just what is it you think I did?"

"I know about the five thousand dollars."

"*What* five thousand?"

Hayden's eyes darkened in anger. "The money my father paid yours so that you wouldn't come chasing after me, or spread rumors about us or claim that we'd slept together."

"Wh-what—?" Nadine's mouth dropped open, and she felt the blood drain from her face.

"That's right, Nadine, I found out. The old man brought me the check, shoved it under my nose in the hospital." His lips twisted into a cruel grin. "I thought you were different."

"There...there was no money. Your father lied."

"I thought so, too," he admitted. "Hell, I wanted him to have told me the biggest lie of all time. But he didn't, Nadine. The check was cashed. I saw the records when I went into the company office. The check was written two days after the boating accident and it was cashed three days later. Your hush money."

"No!" Her knees felt weak, and she placed the flat of her palm on the piano, making a horrid noise, to support herself.

"There's no reason to try to cover it up—"

"I never saw a dime of your damned money, Hayden," she said, stiffening her spine. "And your information is all wrong. We lost everything—our house, our savings, even our family—because of some investment scam your father dreamed up." Shaking inside as she thought about how they'd suffered, she grabbed her pails of polish and headed for the front door. "I never thought I'd say this, Hayden, but you're just like your father!"

She tried to barrel past him, but he caught her arm and swung her around. The pail flew out of her hand, clattering to the floor. One bottle of polish crashed, the plastic containers rolled crazily upon the hardwood and Hayden placed her between himself and the wall.

"Don't you ever compare me to him," Hayden warned.

"Then stop acting like him. Stop believing lies that

are all bound up in money! For God's sake, Hayden, be your own man!"

She saw his eyes blaze and the muscles in his face tense. He was breathing unevenly and his body was shoved hard against hers. Swearing, he suddenly covered her mouth with his and kissed her brutally. His lips ground over hers and he shoved his tongue between her teeth, tasting, touching, exploring.

Nadine's emotions were ragged, her patience worn thin. The assault caused her bones to turn to liquid and yet she didn't want to kiss him; she *didn't!* She tried to fight him off, but her hands, balled into tight fists ready to strike, slowly uncoiled and he captured her wrists, holding each by her side.

Her breasts were crushed, her abdomen flattened, her hips pinned intimately to his. Her mind closed to her arguments and she kissed him back, accepting his hungry tongue, her body thrilling at the feel of his hands as they released her arms and wound around her, dragging her closer still, until her clothes were suddenly too tight and she imagined herself making love to him, just as she'd imagined it years before.

He released her as suddenly as he'd taken her into his arms, and though she felt suddenly bereft, she wouldn't let him know that she tingled for his touch. "Was that supposed to convince me of something? Was I supposed to be tamed into believing all your lies? Did you think I would turn submissive because of one stupid kiss?" she threw back at him.

His eyes seared straight into hers.

"Don't ever touch me again," she warned. "As for your father's check. It never existed. You can balm your conscience any way you please, but I know the truth!"

"So do I, Nadine."

She glanced at her spilled bucket, thought the hell

with it, and marched out the front door. Her hands were trembling as she started her little Nova and tears stung the back of her eyes, but she wouldn't back down and believe his horrible lies.

She thought of her father living in a retirement center; she thought of her mother, remarried and raising her teenaged children in Iowa; she thought of her oldest brother, Kevin, now dead; and she thought of Ben, wounded in the Gulf War and finally being discharged from the army. He would return to Gold Creek to nothing. Her fingers tightened over the wheel and she nearly sobbed. She could lay the blame for her fragmented family directly at the feet of Garreth Monroe.

Tears drizzled down her cheeks but she sniffed them back. She had the weekend in front of her. A long, lonely weekend. The boys would be with Sam and she would try to forget about Hayden and the emotional havoc he wreaked upon her and her family.

COULD HE HAVE made a mistake?

Hayden kicked the empty pail and sent it rolling noisily toward the den. His muscles were tight, his mind cluttered and he wanted a woman. But not any woman. He wanted Nadine Powell Warne. He'd kissed her to punish her, to put her in her place by the most primal of means. Thinking about it now, he was embarrassed that he'd been so dominantly male, so savagely physical. And yet he'd enjoyed it. Kissing Nadine had turned him inside out and he'd wanted more. So damned much more.

Muttering a stream of oaths, he walked through the kitchen and out the back door. The wind was cold as it knifed through his shirt, but he didn't bother with a jacket. Inside he was hot, boiling. He headed to his Jeep. One drink at the Silver Horseshoe and then he'd decide what to do—whether to chase her down or not. Kissing her had been his first mistake.

He was about to make his second. Following her showed an incredible error in judgment, so he'd have to fight his natural instinct to take off after her.

However, as he climbed into the Jeep, he felt as if destiny had already tossed the dice. Deep in his heart he accepted the fact that later he'd wind up at Nadine's house.

"JUST FORGET HIM," she told herself as she pinned up her hair, peeled off her robe and stepped into the warm tub of water. But keeping Hayden out of her thoughts would be near impossible. Even two glasses of Chablis hadn't helped. She drank the first in anger and brought the second to the bathroom, hoping that a little alcohol and a warm bath would ease her aching muscles and dull the pain in her heart.

Why she cared about Hayden, she didn't know. He was often brooding, sometimes downright surly. Oh, sure, he could be charming, even funny, but those moments were rare.

During the past week she'd caught him watching her and each time her heart had taken flight. She'd seen the passion simmering in his eyes, known he'd felt the same damned electricity charging the air between them.

But why? Why was she drawn to men who only caused her pain? She took a long swallow of wine and wished she'd forget him, that his face and body wouldn't invade her dreams and that during the day she could ignore him.

She sank down to her chin and let the water soothe her sore muscles and balm her wounded ego. She still felt the warm imprint of Hayden's kiss, though it had been hours since she'd seen him. She took a cloth, dipped it in the water and rubbed it over her lips, as if to erase any impression or memory of the feel of his mouth against hers, but the rough terry-cloth fabric only served to remind her of the taste and feel of him. She'd turned to putty in his hands and now she felt ashamed that she had. He'd treated her roughly, pulled a male-domination act that should have soured her stomach. Instead she'd nearly collapsed onto the floor and begged him to make love to her.

"Stupid woman!" she whispered, tossing the cloth into a hamper in the corner of the bathroom and finishing off her wine in one long swallow. She detested women who were involved with men who didn't respect them and she'd vowed long ago never to join that pathetic club. And yet Hayden, with one forceful kiss, seemed to have easily stolen all of her brains along with her self-respect. "Idiot," she murmured, lathering her body and letting the warmth from the water invade her tired muscles. Only one more week, then she could kiss Mr. Big Bucks goodbye—or at least walk out the door. Kissing him would only prove dangerous.

Hershel started barking on the front porch, and Nadine scowled. Maybe the boys had left behind something they needed. With a last longing look at the bath, she drained the tub and stepped onto the mat just as the pounding began.

"I'm coming, I'm coming! Hold on to your pants!" she yelled as she cinched her robe around her waist and hurried through the living room.

She yanked hard on the door and a blast of cold air rushed into the house, billowing her robe around her bare legs and causing the fire to glow. Nadine's heart lodged in her throat as her gaze collided with Hayden's.

He was windblown, his face ruddy, his hair falling over blue eyes that were dark and dangerous. Without a jacket, he stood, hands braced on his hips, his features hard and set.

Since she was paralyzed, he pushed on the door and walked into the room. "I think we need to talk."

"Didn't we do enough of that already?" she taunted, and he caught her elbow, spinning her to face him as she tried to breeze past.

"We yelled at each other."

"That's how we communicate best."

"Oh, no, lady, you're wrong," he said, his eyes catching the light of the fire. He kicked the door shut, and she visibly jumped. "We communicate best another way." To prove his point he drew her into his arms and his lips settled over hers. He tasted of whiskey. The scents of tobacco and fresh air clung to him and he kept walking until her back was pressed against the wall.

She wanted to push away, but his supple mouth moved easily over hers, not hard and demanding as it had been earlier in the day, but hot and hungry, with a desperation that caused her blood to heat and her heart to pound. Her hands were placed flat against his shoulders, but she couldn't shove him away; her strength seemed to seep from her.

"Nadine," he whispered roughly as he lifted his head and gazed into her eyes. His hands moved upward to cradle her face and he kissed her again, so tenderly she thought she might cry. His fingers found the pins in her hair, and he gently tugged until her flame-colored curls, still damp, fell around her face.

His features were suddenly tortured, as if all his well-built barriers had tumbled to the ground.

"I told myself I shouldn't come here."

"I told you not to touch me again."

"I can't stop myself."

"Willpower, Hayden," she advised, though her own

was flagging. She tried to concentrate on the hateful things he'd said this afternoon, to focus her anger at him.

He traced her lips with his thumb and she shivered. "I never forgot you. I tried. But I never forgot you."

That was the alcohol talking. "You didn't recognize me that first day."

"You…" He touched her hair. "You've changed."

"So have you. We shouldn't—"

He pressed tender lips to hers, then lifted his head. "Where're the kids?"

"Don't worry, we're alone, but…" Her heart twisted. "Hayden, this is wrong," she forced out, her lungs tight, her skin beginning to tingle with his touch.

"It can't be. It feels right."

That was the truth, but Nadine was afraid the wine and Hayden's sheer maleness had gone to her head. She couldn't think straight, couldn't make him understand. "You said awful things."

"So did you."

The past reared its ugly head. "You didn't call. Years ago, after the accident, I waited, believing in you, but—"

"You didn't visit."

"I couldn't…my folks…oh!" His lips trailed down the slope of her neck and his hands found the knot of her belt. Her abdomen constricted.

Stop him! Stop him now while you still can!

He slipped one hand between the folds of velour and cupped her breast. Her skin tingled. It had been so long… so painfully long. A soft moan escaped her throat as his thumb brushed over the tip and her nipple responded, puckering and causing an ache to spread deep within her.

"Hayden," she murmured as he dropped to his knees, pulling her forward and off balance enough that she had to rest her weight against him in order not to fall. "Hayden, no…" But she didn't stop him when the robe parted and his lips captured that waiting bud. Deep in the hazy recesses of her mind, she realized that she was naked, that the robe covered only half her body, that his strong hands were kneading the small of her back as he took more of her breast in his mouth and suckled. Heat swirled at the apex of her legs, and when he lifted his head, leaving her nipple moist to the cool air, she groaned.

He pressed his face into her abdomen and she felt liquid fire between her loins. Her legs seemed to spread of their own accord as he kissed the downy triangle below her navel. "Let me love you," he whispered, his breath fanning that most sensitive part of her.

A small strangled cry escaped her as he kissed her intimately. Braced against the wall, she arched closer to him, to the sweet torture of his tongue, to the ministrations of lips and teeth that sought and found, teased and conquered. She wasn't aware that her robe had fallen away and in the firelight her naked body was visible to him. She didn't realize that his shirt had been cast aside and that her fingers were digging into the sinewy cords of his shoulder muscles. She began to shudder and quake, and he slowly pulled her down on the floor, to lie with him. His hands molded over her, and he kissed her lips before tasting of the sweetness of her nipples again.

"I've dreamed of this," he admitted. "Oh, I've dreamed of this so many times…." His lips found hers again, and he guided her hand to the waistband of his jeans. Her fingers worked of their own accord, and soon he was free of clothes, his body supple and sleek. She noticed several scars on his legs before her gaze landed on the length of him, hard and proud.

"Beautiful, beautiful, Nadine," he said, poised above her.

She writhed beneath him, feeling the soft scratch of his

chest hair against her breasts, smelling him and tasting the saltiness of his skin.

"I've waited a lifetime for this," he admitted.

Tears touched the backs of her eyes as his knees gently prodded her legs apart. "Me, too, Hayden. Me, too."

Their mouths met, tongues mated and Nadine lost all perception of time and space. He plunged downward and she arched up to meet him, eager for the feel of him. His movements were firm and hard, nearly angry, and she met each of his virile strokes with her own savage hunger.

The lights dimmed, the world seemed to spin, and in a breathtaking final surge, he thrust into her, falling against her and flattening her breasts as she shuddered with her own release. Thoughts reeling, her breath released in short pants, she clung to him and wished that she was thirteen years younger.

Then, they had had a chance. A future. But now they could have nothing. The course of their destinies was already set on vastly different paths. The best she could hope for was a short, passionate affair, the worst, a one-night stand.

CHAPTER EIGHT

NADINE STRETCHED AND sighed contentedly. Her dreams had been so wickedly sensual. She'd been with Hayden.... Her eyes flew open and she felt the weight of his arm around her waist, realized that the comforting warmth against her back was his chest and that the slight tickle at the back of her neck was Hayden's breath. His downy legs were angled beneath hers and she was as naked as a baby jaybird.

Oh, Lord!

She tried to scramble to a sitting position, but the hand splayed beneath her breasts pinned her close to him. "Awake?" he mumbled against her hair, and Nadine blushed.

"I can't believe that I...that you...that we—"

"Believe it," he whispered huskily, and the timbre of his voice caused a tingling to spread through her skin.

"Hayden, this is insane!"

"Maybe." He lifted her hair off her neck and placed a soft kiss against her nape.

Her silly body responded by trembling and she silently cursed herself. Sleeping with Hayden! Making love with him! Becoming one more of the women in his life who could be bought with a fancy trinket, a piece of jewelry or a few kind words. Just as her mother had predicted. A blush rose up the back of her neck as she remembered how easily, how eagerly, how desperately she'd wanted him. "This can't happen!"

"It already did." He kissed her ear, and she shuddered.

"Stop it! I'm serious—"

"So am I." He gently rotated her, forcing her to stare into slumbrous blue eyes. The hint of a smile played in the darkening shadow of his beard and for the first time since seeing him again she caught a glimmer of the boy who had captured her heart so many years before.

"We've behaved horribly," she said, but couldn't help the grin that tugged at the corners of her mouth.

"Wantonly," he agreed, his face a sudden mask of mock-seriousness. But his eyes twinkled.

"Without any responsibility whatsoever."

Nodding, he said, "We should be punished."

"Punished?"

"Mmm." He threw back the covers and his gaze raked down her body. "Let's start with you."

"Me?" she said nervously.

"You've been very, very bad." He brushed his lips across hers softly, deepened the kiss, then when she responded, drew back his head. "Uh-uh." Rolling her onto her back, he took both her wrists in one hand and held them over her head.

"Hey, wait a minute—"

"You wait," he said, his eyes darkening. "In fact, be as patient as you can." He kissed her again, longer this time, his tongue flicking into her mouth and scraping over her teeth. Nadine tried to return the kiss, to mold her mouth to his, but he lifted his head. "Patience," he growled.

"I'm not a patient person—ooh!"

Still holding her hands over her head, he ran his tongue down the length of her neck, leaving a slick impression. Her body arched upward and her nipples stood erect, anticipating his touch. So slowly she thought she might go mad, he kissed the cleft between her breasts and rimmed each nipple with his tongue. Heat exploded within her and the center of her womanhood felt empty and moist. Thoughts of their lovemaking long into the night filled her head.

His teeth found the tip of one nipple and nibbled. Nadine moaned. Her hips lifted anxiously. "Hayden."

"I'm here." To prove his point, he kissed her other breast, while his free hand lowered along her side, tickling the curve of her waist before settling against her hips. His fingers dug into the soft flesh of her rump.

An explosion deep inside rocked her and she bucked. Gazing up at him, she saw his pupils dilate and the sweat upon his forehead. So this was hard on him. Good. His muscles were tense, gleaming with perspiration.

"Patience," she whispered up at him, and with a groan, his mouth closed over hers again. His hand moved to part her legs and touch the soft wetness buried within. Her eyes closed and she lost track of time. Hayden's mouth and fingers seemed to be everywhere.

Small shudders rippled through her and she cried his name. Growling under his breath, he withdrew his hand and released her wrists. She arched upward, clinging to him, and he delved into her waiting moistness.

"Patience," she whispered throatily again.

"Like hell!" His thrusts were long and fierce and desperate as he joined with her. With a savage passion he cried out her name before collapsing against her, his sweat mingling with her own dewy sheen. "My sweet Nadine," he rasped against her hair as he breathed in thick gulps of air. "What're we going to do?"

Still wrapped in the gentle cloak of afterglow, she didn't worry. Not now. She kissed his sweat-soaked cheek, and her palms rubbed against his flat nipples. His chest hair was springy and soft.

As he rolled off her, she whispered, "Not so fast."

"What? Nadine? Again?" he said in wonder as she ran her tongue over his nipples and he shuddered. "So soon?"

His abdomen flexed as she kissed his navel, and when she lowered herself he groaned her name and gave in to the rising passion that was always simmering just under the surface whenever he was with her. Her lips and tongue played a special magic on him, and he knew in a moment of truth and ecstasy that he'd never get enough of her.

"TELL ME ABOUT your marriage." Hayden was seated at the small table in the kitchen, one bare foot propped on a nearby chair as he watched her pour coffee into two mugs. He noticed her robe move with her as she worked, the hem skimming the floor, offering him a peek at long slim legs, wrapping around her breasts and nipping in at her waist. Her hair was tied at her nape and her cheeks were still pink from a night of making love.

"There's nothing much to tell. It failed," she admitted, her lips pinching a little.

"Why?"

She set both mugs on the table and, gently pushing off his foot, sat in the chair he'd used as a stool. "We grew in different directions."

"Bull."

"It's true."

"Did you love him?"

She was in the process of blowing the steam across her cup, but looked up quickly at the question. Hesitating, she set down her mug and cradled her chin in one palm. "I don't know. I...well, I believed that it didn't matter if you loved someone or not. The important thing was to like and respect the person you married. Sam was... steady, or I thought he was. And he loved me. He told me I would learn to love him the same way, that all we needed was time." She sucked in her lower lip and shook her head. "Now," she said, "I realize that I was looking for a way to escape."

"From?"

"The problems at my house. When I was finished with boarding school, my mother had already left my dad and I felt that if…if I stuck around, I'd never get free." Guilt seeped into her green eyes. "I didn't have the money for college so I decided to get married." She avoided his gaze. "People had always called me a 'romantic,' but I guess I proved them wrong." Frowning, she climbed to her feet, snapped a couple of slices of bread into the toaster and turned her back on him.

He sipped the coffee and listened to the clock tick from the living room. Each second that passed reminded him of the years he'd spent away from her. Empty years. Wasted years.

Rubbing his jaw, he decided to gamble. Until they cleared up the past, there was no way they could even think about a future. Not that he was. He had no intention of falling in love with Nadine Warne or becoming a husband to her and a father to her kids. Yet here he was, comfortable as you please, drinking coffee and waiting for toast and eggs that she cooked for him. It bothered him a little as he watched her crack eggs into a skillet. She didn't want a quick affair any more than he did. But what else was there? Maybe, if they made love enough, the excitement would wear thin, the fantasy of their youth would be replaced by harsh adult reality. Because they were just playing out their teenage frustrations, weren't they? He took a long swallow of coffee and watched her rump sway beneath the robe. In his mind he saw her white, lightly veined flesh, felt her muscles rubbing anxiously up against him like a mare in heat. Clearing his throat, he forced his gaze to the window, away from the exciting movement of her body. She was only cooking eggs, for crying out loud!

Yet, dressed from shoulder to ankle in that damned robe, Nadine Warne was sexier than most women wearing string bikinis. "Damn," he muttered, and she visibly started, spattering grease on her wrist.

Swearing softly, she turned to the faucet and ran cold water over her arm.

Hayden was on his feet in an instant and when he reached for her arm, she drew it back. "I can handle this," she said, when he tried to touch her again.

"I just want to see—"

"If you want to help, watch the damned eggs." Spinning quickly out of his grasp, she headed for the bathroom and slammed the door behind her.

Hayden felt like a fool as he slid the eggs in the pan. What the devil was he doing here anyway? If he had any sense whatsoever, he'd climb into his Jeep and head back around the lake before he got himself caught in the mystery and mystique of a woman he barely knew yet felt as if he'd known for a lifetime.

"Eggs are done," he yelled, and when she didn't reply, he set the pan off the burner and turned off the stove. He buttered the toast and slid the eggs onto small plates and had settled down to wait when she emerged from the bathroom dressed in a long denim skirt and blue sweater. Her hair was braided away from her face and a dusting of powder colored her cheeks.

"You okay?"

"Right as rain."

"And your wrist?" He glanced at the red burn mark on the inside of her arm.

"I'll survive," she replied.

"I could kiss it and make it better."

She grinned a little. "I'll bet." Then, as if the subject

were already too intimate, she glanced at the table. "So you do know how to cook."

"Just the basics."

"I'm surprised," she admitted as she sat down.

"Why?" He reached for the blueberry jam and slathered a spoonful onto a piece of toast.

"I thought you had cooks and nannies and governesses to do all that."

"I did." He munched the toast and grinned, dabbing at a spot of jelly near his mouth. "But I walked out on my family after the accident and I learned by trial and error."

"Walked out?" She had been pronging a piece of egg, but her fork paused in midair. "Why?"

"The old man and I had a falling-out."

She waited, watching his facial muscles alter. Gone was his good mood, and in its stead was the same darkness that she'd begun to recognize. "You fought."

"More like a war."

"Over what?"

His eyes glittered with pent-up fury. "Over the worst possible thing—a woman."

"Wynona," she said aloud.

"Bingo."

"He thought you should marry her."

He hesitated for a beat, then nodded quickly. "That was the gist of it. I didn't think he should tell me who I should marry or when or even why. We started shouting at first, then, before you knew it, I threw a punch at him. That was it. By the time my mother found us, we were both panting and swearing and had done significant damage to the other. Mother tried to send me to my room. I was nearly nineteen, and instead I walked out the front door."

"But you returned?"

"Not until I'd proved myself, my own way."

"What about your parents—?"

"I hurt them," he said quietly. "Especially my mother. The old man, he had it coming, but I should've thought of my mom. She wasn't the best mother in the world, but, in her own way, she tried, and for the first six months after I left, I let her wonder if I was alive or dead. They sent out private investigators, of course. Eventually one of them caught up with me, a slimy bastard named Timms, but there was nothing they could do. I was legally an adult. So I told the P.I. to take a hike and then called my mother." He tossed a scrap of his toast into his partially congealed eggs. "I agreed to keep in contact with her if she'd call off her dogs. So we came to an understanding. I lived my life my way—they lived theirs differently. My dad was predictable. He cut me out of his will."

"But then how—?"

Hayden's mouth twisted into a cruel grin. "I guess he had a change of heart. Either that, or he knew that by giving me most of what he'd worked for all his life, he was taunting me from the grave."

"Oh, Hayden, you can't really believe he would do anything so cruel."

"You didn't know my old man, though, did you?" he spat out, his lips flattening over his teeth. "What was it you said the other night, something about him scamming your father?"

She swallowed hard.

"What was that all about?"

Nadine saw no reason to lie. She'd spent the night making love to him, the least she could do was explain to him why he was the last man on earth she should have taken to her bed. "As I said, my father handed every dime he'd ever earned to your dad, invested in some oil wells that were nearly guaranteed to make him rich. He had plans that wouldn't quit. College for all three of us kids. A new house and car for Mom. Retiring with money in the bank. But he came home one day and told us that it wasn't going to happen. That the well was dry, so to speak."

His eyes narrowed. "Go on."

She shuddered at the memories, and the cold spot in her heart seemed to grow. "It was as if all the life went out of my folks' marriage. Mom kind of clammed up. Not too long after that my oldest brother, Kevin, decided he couldn't handle life anymore and ended it."

Hayden's face was grim. "Because of the money?"

She shook her head quickly. "Because of a girl he was in love with. She didn't love him back.

"Kevin's death was more than my mother could handle. She divorced Dad and left us. Ben was through with high school and had joined up with the military and I was still away at school. Mom offered to take me to Iowa with her, but I decided I'd rather come home to be with Dad."

"And Sam?" he asked.

"And Sam."

He rubbed his temples with his fingers as if suddenly tired, but he didn't say a word and she felt compelled to continue. If he really didn't know the truth, it seemed imperative for him to understand her.

"I don't know what happened to your five thousand dollars, Hayden. If my dad got it, he never let me know about it. I assume that the money went to pay some bills or maybe for my schooling. We were always behind. However, there's always the chance your father lied."

"I saw the notation in the company books."

"Books can be fudged," she pointed out. "Did you see the check—the endorsed check—that proved my father got the money? And what does it matter if he did? It wasn't hush money, Hayden. It was repayment of a very small part of a debt. That's all."

Tipping his chair back, he stared at her. "I wonder what would have happened to us if there had been no check."

She wasn't a fool and knew he wasn't, either. She shook her head and swallowed a gulp of coffee. "Nothing would have changed. You were from one world, I was from another. I'd like to believe that circumstances kept us apart, but I know better. If we had really wanted to be together, our families wouldn't have mattered.

"As for right now, we both know that what happened between us last night was probably a mistake." She felt her throat catch on the words, but had to go on. There was no reason to delude themselves, much as she wanted to. "We both felt…pent-up sexual energy. That's all."

He scraped back his chair and carried his plate to the sink.

"We're wrong for each other. We both know it."

"Or so we've been told," he pointed out.

Her silly heart fluttered a bit and her palms began to sweat. She should leave well enough alone. She knew it. But she couldn't. "Are you trying to say that you want something more permanent? A woman with two preadolescent boys?"

He whipped around, his eyes dark. "I'm not the marrying kind," he said gruffly.

"Just the quick roll in the hay, let-me-show-you-how-we-communicate kind, right?" She felt her temper beginning to rise.

"I didn't make any promises."

"Good. Then you don't have any to break, do you?"

He strode over to her and physically lifted her from her chair.

"Without a doubt, you're the most beautiful and frustrating woman I've ever—"

"Put me down!" she commanded, her eyes snapping

fire, her heart breaking a thousand times over, though she wouldn't let him know it, not while she had an ounce of pride left. As he removed his hands, she furiously wagged a finger in his face. "I may be a lot of things, Hayden, but I'm not a woman who likes to be manhandled or shoved around or treated like a member of a lesser sex. I've spent the past two years standing on my own, making my way in the world, taking care of my boys—and no man, not you or anyone else for that matter, has the right to physically restrain me or tell me what to do in my own house." So angry she was visibly shaking, she added, "I don't remember inviting you over, Hayden, so rather than insult me any further, why don't you just walk out the door?"

His jaw tightened and the muscles in his neck bulged.

"I mean it. You obviously are looking for a way out of this.... Well, you've got one. I didn't seduce you and I didn't make any promises, either. So there's no reason for you to think that just because we spent the night together I expect some claim of undying love. I'm not seventeen anymore, Hayden. I'm a full-grown divorced woman with two boys. Believe it or not, I don't want a husband any more than you want a wife!" She flung her arm wide, taking in the expanse of her small cabin. "This may not look like much to you, but it's mine. Mine and my boys', and we've done just fine without you all these years. So just because you showed up on my doorstep, took the kids for a boat ride and somehow ended up in my bed, don't think I expect or *want* anything more."

"You're satisfied with an affair?" he asked, his features granite-hard.

"It's hardly an affair. An affair indicates that we cared for each other and the truth of the matter is we hardly know each other. I believe in telling it like it is, and it's history. It was nice, don't get me wrong. I enjoyed it, but it was only a one-night stand and it's over." Her insides were crumbling as she said the words, but she held her head high, intent upon making him believe her. She didn't want him to think that she did care for him, that she always had. She believed in clean breaks, even if the result was a cracked heart and shattered dreams.

"A one-night stand," he repeated, his lips barely moving. "A 'nice' one-night stand. You 'enjoyed it.' Do you hear yourself? What we did didn't even brush 'nice.' It was hot and wild and probably the best sex of my life. But it wasn't 'nice.'"

She cringed inwardly, but tilted her chin up. "And we both agree it's over."

"No way." He grabbed her again, and this time he kissed her, his lips clamping over hers, his hands manacling her wrists so that she couldn't push him away. Her knees threatened to turn to water, her heart pumped, her blood pounded in her temples at the assault of his tongue and mouth, and tears threatened her eyes. She stood stiff as a board, refusing to respond, denying that he had any power over her whatsoever. When he finally lifted his head and released her hands, she reacted swiftly, slapping him so hard that the smack resounded through the room and Hershel, from his position under the table, growled.

"It takes two for a relationship, Hayden, and I'm not going to be a part of something just for the sex. One-night stands and affairs aren't my style. You're the first man I've slept with in years...the only man I've slept with besides my ex-husband. I really don't believe in hopping into bed without some emotional commitment."

"There's that word again."

"I'm not talking marriage, Hayden," she said, managing to keep the sound of misery from her voice, though she felt wretched. "I just think two people should know each other, like each other, respect each other, before they take their relationship a step further."

"But you told me we don't have a relationship."

"That's right, we don't. What we have is a mistake. I work for you. You're my boss. But you're not my lover. At least not any longer." Her heart was thudding so loudly, she thought he could hear it; her fingers were clenched into fists that ached.

Slowly Hayden turned and walked to the back door. "It doesn't have to end this way."

Her heart was shredding into tiny little pieces. "Of course it does."

"Nadine—"

Knees threatening to crumple, she said, "Look, Hayden, let's be honest. You're not staying in Gold Creek forever and I'm not leaving. The most we could have together is a few weeks." Tears threatened her eyes but she held them at bay. "That's just not good enough. Not for me."

His eyes narrowed. "You do want marriage."

"Maybe," she had to agree. "Someday. But more than that, I don't want to be the talk of the town. I have a reputation and children to consider. Goodbye, Hayden." Her voice nearly caught as she watched him walk out the door. A few seconds later, she sagged against the wall and wondered if she'd made the worst mistake of her life. Last night she hadn't considered the fact that she could get pregnant, or that he could unwittingly pass a disease to her. She'd been foolish…beyond foolish, but she wouldn't be again. She was a mother, for crying out loud. She had responsibilities. She couldn't act so rashly. She couldn't let passion or lust sweep away all her common sense.

"Never again," she vowed, and wondered why that horrid thought scraped the bottom of her soul.

THE HUGE SUMMER house looked like a tomb. Inside, it was cold and dark. Flooding the house with electric light didn't add an ounce of warmth. Compared to Nadine's small cabin, filled with the scents of banked fires, meals once cooked, fresh coffee and Nadine's perfume, this rambling old summer home came up short. Big and beautiful, it was like every other object in his father's life: ostentatious and frigid.

Her cabin had been cluttered with shoes left on the back porch, jackets hung on pegs near the door, bicycles propped against the garage and afghans tossed carelessly over the arms of the couch and backs of chairs in the small living room. Cozy. Warm. Lived-in. *Loved.*

There had been life in that small cabin and, of course, there had been Nadine. He remembered her as she'd answered the door, still damp from the bath, her wet hair curling around her face, her robe allowing him a provocative glimpse of her skin.

"Hell," he ground out. The walls of the house seemed to close in on him. He considered a drink, but it was still hours before noon. Besides, the last time he'd had a drink he'd ended up at Nadine's house making love to her.

Spoiling for a fight, he whistled to Leo and walked back to his Jeep. He'd forget her by throwing himself into the problem at hand: what to do with the damned mills.

He didn't want to think what he was going to do with her.

He drove like a demon, hoping that speed would dull his need of her, hoping to shove all thoughts of her from his mind. He would spend a few hours with the books in his father's old office, then he'd walk through the sheds and talk to some of the employees, get a real feel for this cog in the operation of the chain of sawmills that were spattered around the state as well as in southern Oregon. He planned on visiting each individual operation, and this was as good a time as any. If he timed it right, the trip would take about two weeks, hardly long enough to get Nadine Warne out of his system, but a damned good start.

She'd made it clear how she felt about him, and he wasn't going to try and change her mind. He'd never forced himself upon a woman and didn't intend to start now, no matter how much his body wanted her. Shifting down, he took a corner too fast, eased up on the throttle and managed to round the hairpin curve and keep the Jeep in once piece. "You've got it bad, Monroe," he told his reflection in the rearview mirror. He'd never had to chase a woman down and charm her into his bed. More often than not, he was the one who'd been seduced. No woman had seemed worth the trouble and challenge.

No woman except Nadine.

But she was out of his life.

Forever.

CHAPTER NINE

HAYDEN WAS GONE. His Jeep wasn't parked in the drive, the old dog had disappeared, an answering machine, its red light already blinking, was hooked up to the telephone in the den and the sleeping bag he'd flung over the bed in the master bedroom was missing. He'd left. Without a word.

Nadine frowned to herself. This was what she'd wanted, wasn't it? A life without Hayden. She'd told him as much. So why should she feel any sense of depression? She usually wasn't a person to dwell on her mistakes, but she'd spent the remainder of her weekend thinking about Hayden and all the ramifications of making love to him. She'd kicked herself for not considering all of the problems that might arise *before* she'd tumbled into bed with him, but what was done was done, and now she had to live with the consequences.

Still, she felt a deep disappointment that he'd left. True, that without him her work would be easier; she could finish cleaning the old house more quickly and she wouldn't have to deal with the embarrassment of facing him again. Yet she was frustrated. No doubt about it. She'd put a little extra care into choosing her work clothes, fixing her hair and applying her makeup, silent testimony to the fact that she did care about him, if only just a little.

She spent the day finishing her intense cupboard-by-cupboard cleaning of the kitchen, then stripped all the floors. The stain in the foyer where Hayden had kicked over her bucket and some polish had spilled took hours of elbow grease. The telephone had rung several times while she was working, but she'd ignored it, and the answering machine had always clicked on. She hadn't heard the messages as she'd always been in another part of the house, but as she flung her jacket over her arm and picked up her supplies to leave, the telephone jangled again. This time she was near the den and couldn't help but overhear the one-sided conversation.

"Hayden?" A female voice asked, and then paused. "You there? It's me again. Wynona."

Nadine's heart seemed to slam through the floor.

"Hayden? If you're there, pick up," Wynona commanded. A few tense seconds of silence. "Great." Another pause followed by a lengthy sigh. "There's no reason to avoid me. You can't. You *owe* me." Nadine sagged against the wall, and Wynona's voice turned wheedling. "We've been through a lot together, baby. Let's not fight now. Give me a call. I'll be home all night, waiting to hear from you." After a few seconds, she clicked off, and Nadine, unaware that she'd been holding her breath, expelled the air in her lungs in a rush.

So Hayden was still involved with Wynona Galveston. Nadine's stomach soured at the thought, but she told herself not to jump to conclusions. The call was ambiguous and could mean anything. Besides, it didn't matter; Nadine had no claim to Hayden's affections or his attention. Just because they spent one night of lovemaking together... She let out a little strangled sound and then mentally kicked herself. She wasn't a simpering, love-besotted female, and she had lived long enough to accept that humans were sexual creatures. Her night with Hayden was either an act of rebellion or sexual fantasy, but it had nothing to do with love, so whatever his relationship was with Wynona, it didn't matter.

She argued with herself during the drive home and tried not to think of the last man she'd cared for. Hadn't Turner Brooks ignored her affections and fallen in love with his long-ago lover? Hayden would probably do the same and turn back to Wynona.

Yes, but you didn't sleep with Turner. You didn't make love with Turner. You didn't fantasize about living the rest of your life with Tur— "Stop it!" she ground out, switching on the radio and listening to a Garth Brooks recording of love lost.

Furious with herself, she snapped off the radio and pulled into the drive. She was too busy to dwell on Hayden or Wynona or anything but her sons, who, already home, tore out of the house at the sound of her car. They both flung themselves into her arms, and for the first time since hearing Wynona's voice, she felt better. As long as she had John and Bobby, who needed Hayden Monroe?

"I got an A on my math test!" John crowed. "And Tim, the kid I'm helping, he got a C, his best grade ever."

"Good for you." Nadine gave her eldest a squeeze.

"I didn't have a test," Bobby chimed in, not to be outdone. "But I made a new friend. His name is Alex and he just moved here from...from..."

"From Florida, you dweeb. His sister's in my class."

"I'm not a—"

"Of course you're not," she intervened, throwing her older son a warning glare. "And you, John, quit insulting your brother." Nadine kissed Bobby's forehead and rumpled John's blond hair. "Come on, you guys can help me fix dinner."

"What're we having?" John asked suspiciously.

"Hot dogs with whatever you want on them."

"All *right!*" Bobby shouted, seeming to have forgotten his older brother's insults.

After dinner, she helped the boys with their homework, then forced them into showering before they fell into bed. She spent the next three hours sewing and gluing studs and beads on a faded denim jacket that was an integral part of her collection. By the time she'd cleaned the kitchen and read her mail, it was one o'clock in the morning. Her head sank into the pillow and she hoped for exhaustion to claim her. It didn't. Though she was so tired she ached, she couldn't sleep. Wynona's message played and replayed in her mind, and Nadine was left to wonder why she should care so much about Wynona Galveston.

EACH DAY SHE expected Hayden to return, and each day she was disappointed. On Wednesday she received a letter from her brother, Ben, telling her that he was returning to Gold Creek before Christmas.

Thursday, she met her father downtown for lunch. He lived in a retirement center that was within walking distance to the heart of Gold Creek, but she always drove him to the restaurant. George Powell, at sixty, was no longer strapping. He walked with a cane, courtesy of a slight stroke several years earlier, and his hair was thin and gray. His apartment was small but adequate and he seemed comfortable if not happy.

As he eased his bulk into a worn red vinyl booth of his favorite restaurant, the Buckeye, he looked at his daughter. "Heard you been working for Monroe's attorney."

Nadine was flabbergasted. "How'd you hear that?"

"This is a small town, missy. Bad news travels fast."

"Aunt Velma!"

"So it is true. Keerist A'mighty!" He swiped a big

hand over his forehead. "What the hell do ya think you're doin', Nadine?"

"Dad, relax."

The waitress brought them plastic-encased menus, but they ordered without even glancing at the special of the day. "I heard Hayden's already taken over the house on the lake," her father said, once they were alone again. "Probably couldn't wait to get his hands on his old man's money."

"You hear a lot," she said, the muscles in her back tightening defensively.

"It's true, isn't it?"

She lifted a shoulder. "It's true—about him being there. Or at least he was. But I don't think he's interested in the money."

"Everyone's interested in money. You, me, your ma. Everyone. Hayden ain't any different, so don't you be puttin' him up for sainthood."

"Wouldn't dream of it," she said dryly.

"So he's at the house where you're working?"

"He was."

"Keerist!"

"It's a job, Dad," she said, though the lie tripped on her tongue. "Nothing more."

His green eyes, so like hers, sparked with disbelief. He looked about to say something more, thought better of it and played with the cellophane wrapper on a pack of crackers. The waitress brought their lunches—a bowl of soup and a chili burger for her father and a patty-melt with coleslaw for her. She was halfway through her sandwich when he asked, "Heard from your ma lately?"

Nadine's heart squeezed when she noticed the carefully disguised pain on his face. "Not recently."

His gray brows lifted a fraction, but he didn't say a word. They talked about everything and nothing, starting with the weather and ending with a rather heated discussion on how she should raise her boys.

By the time her father had paid the check, a ritual he insisted upon though Nadine paid half the cost of his rent each month, she slipped him the letter from Ben. A smile played upon his features as he read the contents of the letter. "He'll be back soon."

"In time for Christmas."

"Well, that's something to celebrate." He tried to hand the letter back to Nadine, but she slid it into the breast pocket of his wool jacket.

"You keep it, Dad," she insisted.

Outside the restaurant, the weather was cool. A pale sun pierced through the clouds, but the November wind was harsh as it tugged at Nadine's hair and brought color to her father's cheeks. Stiffly, her father slid into the front seat of her Chevy. She drove the few blocks to his apartment and stopped. Before he stepped out of the car, he turned to Nadine. "God gave you more than your share of brains, missy. If you use them you'll know that Hayden Monroe is trouble. Just like his old man."

"Dad." She touched him lightly on the arm to restrain him, and her heart was suddenly in her throat. She hated to ask the question preying upon her mind, but had to know the truth. "Hayden told me that his father paid you money. Five thousand dollars. To make sure that I would drop out of his life." A denial seemed about to form on her father's lips, so she added, "Hayden saw the check years ago and looked into the company books a few days ago."

"That son of a bitch!" Her father swore angrily and stared through the windshield to the rambling retirement complex he'd called home for two years.

"Dad?"

George let out an angry sigh. "Garreth paid me back some of the money I invested with him—a small part. I gave him nearly fifty thousand dollars, all our savings and the equity we had in the house at the time, and all I got back was five grand." He looked down at his feet, suddenly embarrassed. "Your mother called me a fool and she was right. When I finally got the check from Garreth, I handed over the money to her. I figured it was hers. Some of that money went to your education in that boarding school." He blinked suddenly, and his face seemed to age twenty years. "It broke Donna's heart, y'know, and broke us up. That investment with the Monroes was the beginning of the end." He shoved open the car door and eased himself out. "I can't really blame her, I suppose. Stan Farley has a huge farm in Iowa and he could give her everything she wanted." He glanced at his daughter as they walked up the cement path to the front door of his studio apartment. "Is she happy?"

Nadine nodded because she couldn't trust her voice. A searing pain still burned deep in her heart. Donna Powell Farley had found contentment with another man, over three hundred acres and two children who were not much older than her grandchildren. Stan Farley was a stable man, a decent man, a man whose finances were secure.

"Good, good," George muttered. "She deserves happiness." Resting a knotty hand on his daughter's shoulder, he added, "That's why you should keep your distance from Hayden Monroe. He's nothing but trouble and he'll only bring you heartache."

That much was true, she hated to admit. "So how about you, Dad? Are you happy?"

"Can't complain," he said, holding open the glass door for his daughter. "Got everything I need, right here at Rosewood Terrace."

EVERY MUSCLE IN Hayden's body ached from spending five days on the road. He'd logged in fifteen hundred miles and visited seven mills, talking with the employees, watching them at work, noting the condition of the equipment, stores of logs, contracts with logging companies and inventories of raw lumber. His had been a cursory scan at best, each individual sawmill would have to be reevaluated in depth. What he learned by talking to the men was their concerns of losing their jobs as there was less old-growth timber being cut due to dwindling resources, environmental concerns and government restrictions.

Most of the workers had been timber men for generations; their fathers and grandfathers had been part of a working tradition of men who had harvested trees and turned the forests into planed boards. The men knew only one craft.

Hayden climbed out of his Jeep and felt the weight of the world on his shoulders. Bradworth and Thomas Fitzpatrick had been right. People's lives and livelihoods depended upon him and his decision. How many employees, men and women alike, had shaken his hand and smiled at him and mentioned that they were glad the mills were still in Monroe hands? He'd noticed their worries—the knit brows, the eyes that didn't smile, the lips that pinched at the corners and he sensed the unasked questions of the workers: *Will I be laid off? Will you shut the mills down? Will you sell the machinery off, bit by bit? What will I do if there's no work? How will I feed my family, pay my bills, send my kids to college?*

Leo bounded into the bushes, scaring up a winter bird as Hayden trudged to the back porch and wiggled off one shoe with the toe of his other.

He opened the back door and stopped dead in his tracks. The house smelled of oil and wax, and every surface gleamed. The chairs were pushed carefully around the kitchen table where a crystal vase was filled with several kinds of fragrant flowers. Brass fixtures sparkled and the old wood floor shone with a fresh coat of polish.

Nadine. He felt a hard knot tighten his gut as he walked through the place and saw traces of her work—special touches such as the rearranging of pictures on the mantle, a grouping of candles on a table, another vase filled with flowers.

What was she trying to do? She'd been hired to clean, for crying out loud, and now it seemed that she had put her special stamp on the house. Blankets had been folded and tossed over the arm of the old couch in the den. Dry logs and split kindling had been set in each fireplace.

He climbed the steps to the second floor and noticed that each bed was made with clean bedding. In the master bedroom, the king-size bed was freshly made, one window cracked open to let in clear mountain air, dry kindling stacked on polished andirons in the fireplace and a large glass bowl half filled with water and floating blossoms rested on the bureau.

He smiled despite himself. Maybe she'd forgiven him. Then he caught his image in the mirror—his dirty jeans, faded work shirt, sawdust-sprinkled hair and a stupid grin pinned to his face. Because of her. What a damned fool he was! Glowering at his reflection, he turned and walked briskly into the bathroom, intent on cleaning up and forgetting Nadine. Obviously she was through working here. The flowers had to be the last touch; so he didn't have to worry about her again.

That particular thought was disturbing, though he didn't stop to analyze why. Eyeing the tub where he'd found her ring, he noted a bowl of colored soap and matching towels placed carefully on the racks. He twisted on the shower spray, stripped and tried to wash the grime and dirt and aches from the last few days from his body. He'd kept himself so busy that he hadn't had time to think about Nadine and whenever thoughts of her had crept into his mind, he'd stubbornly shoved them into a dark corner.

But now that he was back in Gold Creek, with only the choppy waters of Whitefire Lake separating them, he couldn't easily drive his images of her away. He leaned against the tiles and let the water cascade over his body. The steamy jets felt good; the only thing that would've felt better was Nadine's supple body lying underneath his. He remembered kissing her, touching her face, delving deep into the warmest part of her…

To his consternation, his thoughts had turned a certain part of his anatomy rock hard. Gritting his teeth, he twisted off the hot water spigot and sucked in his breath as the icy spray sent sharp little needles of frigid water against his skin. "Damn you," he muttered, and he didn't know if he was talking to himself or to Nadine.

NADINE CHECKED THE kitchen clock again and frowned to herself. Sam had promised to pick up the boys from basketball practice and drop them off. She dusted her hands on her apron, let her sauce simmer and told herself not to worry. They were less than an hour late; maybe Sam had decided the boys needed a little extra time to work on their shots. And yet…a niggle of doubt crawled through her mind. Sam knew that she was cooking dinner for her sons, that they'd both need a shower and they each had to tackle their homework assignments.

She glanced out the window and her eyes strayed to the lake and beyond to the thicket of trees she knew guarded Hayden's house. Her heart nearly stopped when she saw the lights glowing softly through the winter-bare branches.

So he was back. Or if not Hayden, someone close to him. Though she had told herself that she didn't care, that her job with him was nearly finished, that she had scrubbed her last cobweb out of the Monroe house and had composed a list of repairs that needed to be made, she felt her heart turn over. If only she could see him again. Maybe go over to the house for a final touch-up.... But she couldn't. She wouldn't. Instead, she'd spend the time writing down the names of a few local handymen and send the list to Bradworth in San Francisco. The lawyer, or Hayden himself, could oversee the mending of the porch rail and replacement of the gutters and so on. As for Nadine, she was out of there.

She felt a deep loneliness when she thought of Hayden, but she told herself firmly that she was over him. She glanced at the clock again, and lines of worry furrowed her forehead. She turned down the burner where the hot water was boiling, just as she heard the sound of a car in the drive.

"What's for dinner?" John demanded as he burst through the back door. Wrinkling his nose as he eyed the sauce, he sighed theatrically and rolled his eyes. "Stroganoff. Again!"

"I thought you liked Stroganoff."

"Bobby likes it. I hate it. I like goulash."

She could never seem to get this straight. "That's right. Well," she said, touching him fondly on the nose, "next time we'll have goulash. Now go shower. When you get out, dinner will be done. And help your brother—" Glancing worriedly to the back door, she asked, "Where is he?"

Avoiding her gaze, John licked his lips nervously and shifted from one foot to the other. "Bobby fell asleep in the car."

"But the school's only ten minutes away."

"Yeah, but...he was real tired." Without any further explanation, he dashed through the living room. Nadine heard the bathroom door shut as Sam, hauling a dead-to-the-world Bobby, walked into the kitchen.

"What happened to him?" she asked, worried that Bobby was coming down with some virus. Usually after a practice he was so wound up that she had to calm him down. Tonight he was fast asleep.

"I guess practice just did him in."

Nadine touched Bobby's forehead. Her fingers came away cool.

"Yeah, we really worked the boys," Sam said as he carried Bobby into the living room and laid him gently on the couch. Bobby sighed but didn't open his eyes. The smell of smoke mixed with stale beer, a scent Nadine recognized from her years of marriage to Sam, clung to her ex-husband, and she was instantly angry.

"He's not even sweating," she said.

"He was—"

"Somewhere where he shouldn't be." Sick inside, Nadine plucked a kernel of popcorn from Bobby's jacket. "Snacks after the game?" she asked, already knowing and dreading the answer. Anger surged through her blood.

"Well, you know how it is. Phil and Rick wanted to have a beer after the practice, so we stopped at the Buckeye for a quick one."

Nadine's back teeth ground together and silent rage swept through her. "While you were having your 'quick one,' what were the boys doing?"

Sam's face flushed scarlet and a defiant glint shone in his eyes. "I left them in the car. But I could see them through the window and I took them each a cup of popcorn—"

"Sam, how could you!"

"It was only for twenty minutes, Nadine!"

"But they could've been…oh, God, who knows what kind of scum lurks in the parking lot of the Buckeye at night. They're just children!"

"And they're fine, aren't they!"

"They could've been kidnapped or hurt or—"

"But they weren't, were they? They're both right as rain."

"I don't care."

"Listen, Nadine, I needed to talk to the guys," Sam nearly shouted. Then, as if hearing himself, he lowered his voice and plowed his fingers through his thinning blond hair. "With all the changes coming down at the mill, who knows what'll happen to our jobs."

"You could've brought them home first," she hissed, her temper still soaring.

Sam was unrepentant. "The Buckeye is only a few blocks from the school. It didn't make sense to come clear up here—"

"Clear up here? What is it—four, maybe five miles? Damn it, Sam, you could've called me. I would have picked them up."

Sam grimaced painfully. "I was busy. Me and the guys, we had things to discuss. Things you probably already know about."

"Things?" she repeated, not following this new twist in the conversation.

"Monroe. The Fourth. I heard he was already here, giving the boys a ride in the boat, making himself at home. With my kids!" Disgust curled his lip. "Jeez, Nadine, don't you ever learn?"

"I don't see what Hayden has to do with this!"

"Don't you? You can't be as blind to him now as you were in high school!"

She started to protest, but Sam was just warming to his subject. "What with 'Junior' owning the mill now, big changes are in the works. It's no secret that he plans to shut us down along with all his mills. Maybe one at a time, maybe all at once, but he'll close mills and consolidate or sell the entire chain of 'em, but believe me, whatever he decides, it won't be good for any of us. Including you. If I'm not working, I won't be able to come up with the support payments, so you'd better hope that 'your friend' keeps the mill open or he sells it to the employees."

"He's not my 'friend.'"

Sam lifted a skeptical thin blond brow and his nostrils flared a little. "Yeah, well, it might be interesting to know exactly what he is to you."

"My employer…or he was."

"Convenient. He pays you to clean his damned mansion."

Nadine squared her shoulders. Sam had never approved of her working, much less cleaning other people's homes, and yet she had to make a living while she took courses to better herself or tried to get her costume jewelry and clothes on the market. "It's a job, Sam, and from the sounds of things I don't think now would be the time to quit, do you?"

His eyes narrowed a fraction, and the smell of flat beer seemed to fill the space between them. "I think I'd better leave."

"Not until you hear me out, Sam Warne." Nadine blocked his path to the back door. "Don't you ever, *ever,* leave my sons alone in a parking lot again. And don't even think about driving them anywhere after you've had a few, okay?"

Sam winced. They both remembered the night while they were married when he'd rolled his pickup. If not for his safety belt, he would have been thrown from the crumpled vehicle and possibly killed. At that time he'd sworn off liquor. His abstinence had lasted all of three months.

"You can't tell me how to handle my sons," he said.

"Oh, yes, I can, Sam. And I will," she proclaimed. "They're my boys, too, and when it comes to their safety—"

"I don't have to listen to this." He hiked his jeans up beneath the sag that was his belly and stormed out. The back door slammed behind him and his truck, as he backed out of the drive, sent a spray of gravel beneath screaming tires.

"Mom?"

Nadine froze. Dread tore at her heart as she turned and found John wrapped in a yellow bath sheet, his skin blue, his hair wet and his eyes round. "You'd better get dressed or you'll catch your death."

"Don't yell at Dad."

"Oh, John." She folded him into her arms and felt his teeth chattering against her shoulder. "I don't mean to argue with him."

"It was okay. Me and Bobby, we were fine in the car."

"He shouldn't have left you."

"I wasn't scared."

"How about Bobby? Wasn't he afraid?" she prodded, knowing about her younger son's vivid imagination.

John shrugged a slim shoulder.

"Tell me."

"Well, just a little, maybe, but then he fell asleep and everything was all right."

She held her oldest son at arm's length and saw the pride in his reddened eyes, felt him square his shoulders. He was just too young to try to be the man of the house. Her heart squeezed painfully and she kissed his damp forehead. "Go on and get your pajamas on and I'll have dinner on the table." She gave him a playful swat on the bottom and he hurried upstairs to the loft.

By the time he came down again, she had a fire roaring in the grate and was trying to awaken a groggy Bobby.

John's appetite was enormous, and Bobby, though he usually liked Stroganoff, was glum and too tired to show much interest in food. After dinner, she bathed him, hauled him off to bed and turned out the light after John climbed into the top bunk. They were asleep before she finished the dishes.

Still inwardly seething at Sam, she made herself a cup of coffee, grabbed her sewing kit and glue gun and dragged the nearly finished jacket out of the closet. A few more beads and rhinestones dripping down one sleeve and it would be finished. She felt a small sense of pride. At least this jacket would be sold before Christmas. It was a special order from a bareback rider whom Turner Brooks had known during his days on the rodeo circuit. The woman, buying a horse from Turner, had seen a jacket Nadine had made for Heather and commissioned one for herself on the spot.

"Just make it a little more flashy," she'd said around a long, slim cigarette. "You know, a few more sparkles." Well, the jacket was definitely flashy.

The doorbell rang before she finished. Expecting Sam again, Nadine braced herself for another confrontation, flung open the front door and found Hayden, his hair windblown, his face flushed with the cold. Her stomach slammed hard against her abdomen.

"This is a surprise."

"For both of us," he admitted. "I didn't expect to come back here."

"Did I forget something this time?" she asked, her voice brittle, though her heart was pounding against her ribs.

He shook his head. "I'm the one who forgot."

Her brows drew together. "Forgot? Forgot wha—" Before she'd finished asking the question, he'd grabbed her and clamped his arms around her. His mouth found hers and with anxious, hungry lips, he kissed her.

She couldn't let this happen again! She wouldn't! With

all the strength she could muster, she tried to push him away. "Hayden, please…don't…"

Every muscle in his body grew rigid. Slowly he drew his head away from hers and stared into her eyes. What he saw in her gaze, she could only guess, but slowly he released her. "I…" He shoved the hair from his eyes and swore beneath his breath. "Hell, Nadine, I didn't mean to come on like a Neanderthal. But it seems I can't do anything else when I'm around you." He shook his head, disgusted with himself.

"What—what did you mean?" Good Lord, she could barely breathe and her voice sounded so weak and feminine she actually cringed.

A self-deprecating smile touched the corner of his mouth. "Just that I've missed you."

Sweet Lord, now what?

"I left here angry, said things I didn't mean and here I am trying to apologize." Swearing under his breath, he rolled his eyes. "I'm not very good at it."

"Not much practice, I suspect."

"You make me crazy, you know."

She couldn't help but smile. "I've missed you, too," she admitted, though she wanted to lie and tell him that she hadn't lost a moment's sleep over him, that she hadn't tossed and turned every night replaying their lovemaking over and over in her mind, that she didn't sometimes fantasize about loving him and becoming his wife and… Oh, God! Drawing herself up short, she shook her head. "This could never work, Hayden."

"You don't know that."

"We've already had this conversation, remember?" she said, though she wanted nothing more than to drag him into the house with her and throw herself into his arms. She trembled inside but held her ground.

"I just think we should start over. Take one step at a time."

Oh, God, why was he torturing her? "Why?"

"Why?" he repeated, glancing up at the dark sky, as if searching for the reasons. "Because I've gone slowly and steadily out of my mind without you. Because the house seems like a damned morgue without you there. Because…because I've missed you." His gaze settled on hers again, and there was honesty and desperation in his blue eyes.

Inside, she was melting. "I still don't want an affair."

"I'm not asking for one."

"Then what do you want?"

The question hung in the cool air between them, and she waited with her heart in her throat. "What I want is to get to know you, Nadine."

"You may not like me."

One side of his mouth lifted slightly. "I don't think there's much chance of that. Anyway, I'm willing to gamble."

"Damn it all, Hayden, why don't you just go away?" she said, her voice catching. "Leave me alone. Let my life go on as it was."

"I can't," he admitted, and he kissed her again. This time his lips were tender, his tongue undemanding. She sagged against him and realized with a sense of mounting dread that for the rest of her life she'd never be able to say no to Hayden Monroe.

CHAPTER TEN

HAYDEN HAD TROUBLE living up to his promise. Nadine had always exuded an earthiness that he found irresistibly sexy. Her jeans were snug, but not obscene, and yet he couldn't take his eyes off the sway of her rump as she walked. Her mahogany-red hair glinted with gold in the firelight, and her green eyes appeared large and dark above sculpted cheekbones. She served him coffee, then set about finishing work on some glittery jacket she was making for a woman he didn't know.

He settled in on the lumpy antique couch, propping one heel on the arm and watching her work as he sipped the coffee. "Decaf," she'd told him as she'd handed him a wide glazed mug. As if he cared. He wasn't here for the coffee.

She explained about trying to launch her career as a designer of exotic art and clothes or some damned thing— that she'd taken courses at the local junior college in color and art and fabric design, along with more traditional subjects of math and accounting and business law. She wasn't going to clean houses forever. When she finished the jacket, she held it up for his inspection.

"I'm not much of an authority on rodeo wear," he said dryly, and her eyes sparkled with merriment as she sashayed closer, the jacket swinging in front of her.

"Oh, sure. I just bet you want one for yourself."

"Right." A sarcastic smile touched his lips.

"Maybe for Christmas, hmm?" she teased. Her cheeks

were rosy, her lips pulled into a thoughtful grin. "Black denim with gold rhinestones. Kind of an Elvis look with—"

He grabbed her quickly, and the jacket slid to the floor as he pulled her down on top of him on the couch.

"Hayden, don't—" she said, but giggled as his arms surrounded her.

"Don't what?" he asked into her open mouth.

"I thought we weren't going to do this—"

"We're not." He kissed her, nibbling on her lower lip and causing shivers to race up her spine. Sighing, she opened her mouth to him and his tongue sought quick entrance. With sure strokes it touched the roof of her mouth and explored the insides of her cheeks before finding its mate.

Closing her eyes, Nadine kissed him back. She didn't protest when his hand cupped her buttocks, drawing her tighter to his hardness.

"You make me do things I've never done in my life," he admitted when he finally broke the kiss and stared up at her. He smoothed the cascade of red curls from her face and let his fingertips press gently against her neck, while his eyes strayed lower, to her breasts as they rose and fell against him. "However, wearing flashy clothes isn't one of them."

"No?" she teased, baiting him on purpose.

"I can think of better things." His gaze locked with hers, and he let his hand slide downward until he felt the weight of one breast in his palm. Nadine moaned softly, and his fingers squeezed. Desire swept through her in a hot torrent as his fingers fondled her through her clothes.

She closed her eyes, arching back, thrusting out her breasts.

"God, you're beautiful," he whispered, drawing her down and burying his face against her sternum. "I want you." He closed his eyes as if to clear his head and didn't open them again as he said, "I've wanted you from the first time I saw you in your dad's old pickup. I thought years and time would change that, but I was wrong. The reverse is true. I want you more now than I did as a kid."

Her throat closed in on itself so she couldn't swallow; she hardly dared believe him.

Pulling her down to him again, he held her tight and buried his face in the crook of her neck. "This is killing me, but we'll play it your way, Nadine. I don't know how, but we'll give it a damned good try."

He slapped her playfully on the butt, then forced them both into an upright position. Strain showed in the brackets near his mouth. "Do you really believe we can have a relationship without sex?"

"I don't know," she admitted.

"Well, I guess we'll find out. But let me tell you, it's gonna be hell!"

HAYDEN WAS TRUE to his word. He started showing up at her house on a regular basis and convinced her to keep working for him. He wanted her to hire the carpenters and handymen to oversee the repairs to the summer home while he spent his days at the mill. He never discussed his plans for the future of the company, and Nadine had never asked, though the few times she'd seen Sam, he was convinced that Hayden was going to do his level best to see that every employee of the company got his walking papers.

Fortunately, the boys hadn't told Sam about the fact that Hayden visited nearly every night, that sometimes he ate dinner with them or that he had taken them for speedboat rides across the lake. He'd promised to take them skiing as soon as the first storm dumped enough snow onto the mountains.

And they'd never made love again, though they'd come close a time or two when the boys were asleep upstairs and they were alone in front of the fire, but Hayden had always broken off their embrace and Nadine had been left feeling frustrated and doubting that she would much longer be able to abide by her own moral code.

As Christmas approached, there was more demand for her funky jewelry. She stopped by the Rexall Drugstore in the middle of town to check her inventory. The store, located on the corner of Pine and Main had a turn-of-the-century charm. It seemed more like an old-fashioned mercantile than a modern pharmacy. Paddle fans rotated to the strains of Christmas carols filling the store with soft music. Red and green tinsel was strung over the aisles, which were more crowded than ever with excess merchandise—cards, wrapping paper, gift ideas, decorations, even fruitcakes.

The rack that displayed her jewelry was near the front of the store, and as she approached the counter she realized that more than half of the original inventory had already been sold. There was a "lot of interest" in her pieces, the woman behind the counter confided to her.

Before she left, Nadine decided to buy a cup of cocoa at the back counter. She slid onto a vacant stool and dropped her purse at her feet before she recognized the girl sitting next to her as Carlie Surrett. Their gazes met in the mirror over the soda machine, and Nadine's insides went cold.

"Hello, Nadine," Carlie ventured, and Nadine forced a smile she didn't feel. Carlie was a beautiful girl with long, straight black hair and deep blue eyes. She'd been a model for some years, then turned photographer before she'd returned to Gold Creek only a few months before.

And she'd been the cause of Kevin's death.

This girl—this woman—had broken Nadine's oldest

brother's heart, and when he'd discovered his love was unreturned, he'd pulled his car into the garage of his apartment, closed the door and let the engine run until he'd died of carbon monoxide poisoning.

Nadine forced a greeting over her tongue. She told herself she couldn't blame Carlie, but couldn't fight the rage that burned in her heart. If only Carlie had treated Kevin more kindly, he might still be alive today.

Carlie's mother, Thelma, the waitress behind the counter, glanced at Nadine, snapped open her order pad and, without a smile, took her order. The pain between the two families had existed for years, and no one was able, or cared, to bridge the gap.

In a thunder of footsteps, five-year-old Adam Brooks, dressed in full cowboy regalia, scurried to the counter. His mother, Heather, and her sister, Rachelle Moore, were laughing, dragging shopping bags and obviously breathless as they walked down the aisle toward the back of the store. While Heather was petite and blond, and just beginning to show her pregnancy, Rachelle was tall and willowy, with long red-brown hair that fell to her waist.

"Rachelle!" Carlie gasped, then sent Heather a friendly glare. "You *knew* she'd be in town."

"I wasn't sure—" Heather hedged.

"Liar." Rachelle slid onto a stool next to Carlie. "I called her yesterday." She slid her packages under the counter and eyed the fluorescent menu displayed over the back mirror.

Adam scrambled onto a stool next to his aunt and began ordering a banana split, but Heather spied Nadine. "Just the woman I was looking for," she said as Rachelle and Carlie caught up on old times. "I need your help."

"Mine?"

"The studio. It needs all sorts of work and the doctor told me that I had to slow down." She patted her rounding belly. "So, after Christmas sometime I was hoping that you'd help me clean it up, maybe give it a fresh coat of paint—that sort of thing. If you have the time, of course."

"It shouldn't be a problem."

"Good. And I have a list of people for you—oh, where is it?" Heather dug through a voluminous purse, yanked out her wallet and dug through a compartment. "Here you go. All of these people showed an interest in some of your jewelry. That woman there—" she pointed a fingernail at the third name on the list "—owns a chain of boutiques around the bay area. She has a store near Fisherman's Wharf, one in Sausalito and a few sprinkled around Santa Rosa and Sonoma, I think. She displays some of my paintings and was *very* interested in your work. Give her…for that matter, give them all a call."

Nadine could hardly believe her good luck. She folded the scrap of paper into her purse and said, "Thanks."

"No trouble," Heather replied with a smile.

"Let me buy you a cup of coffee, at least."

"You don't have to—" Heather glanced along the length of the counter where Rachelle, Carlie and Adam were discussing the merits of marshmallow sauce versus pineapple on a sundae.

"I want to."

"All right." Heather eased onto one of the stools, and Nadine wondered how she'd ever been jealous of this woman who seemed to glow in her pregnancy. Her blond hair shimmered in the lights and her eyes sparkled with good humor. Obviously marriage was good for her and Turner Brooks was a good man, a strong man, a passionate man. A man Nadine had come to realize that she'd never really loved.

And what about Hayden? Do you love him?

The thought struck her cold, and she nearly dropped her cup of cocoa, sloshing some of the chocolate onto the counter. *Love?* Why, the notion was ridiculous! She couldn't, wouldn't fall for Hayden.

"Your father says there's talk at the logging company of trouble with the mill. Rumor has it that Garreth's son might sell it or scrap it out," Thelma said to Carlie as she slid a glass boat filled with bananas, ice cream and syrup toward Adam. With glee, he plucked the cherry from a bed of whipped cream and plopped it into his mouth.

"I thought you were going to share," his aunt Rachelle chided him, and Adam, a smile stretched long on his freckled face, shook his head.

"The mill's closing?" Carlie asked.

"It's not for certain yet."

"But this town will roll up and die," Heather observed.

Nadine looked at Carlie's mother. "Maybe it won't be shut down."

Thelma regarded Nadine with frosty eyes. "You just watch. Hayden Monroe's always been a pampered rich boy. Never done anyone any good, including that girl he was gonna marry. First he nearly killed her in a boat wreck, then he broke off the engagement." She clucked her tongue. "A real charmer, that one." She plucked a pad from the pocket of her apron and tallied the bill for a couple of men who were sitting at the far end of the counter.

Nadine said goodbye to everyone and thanked Heather again for the list of potential clients. She barely heard the strains of "Silver Bells" as she shoved open the door and walked outside. The cocoa in her stomach seemed to curdle when she thought of Hayden and the power he now had over this town. She'd grown up with the people who worked for him; their children were her own boys' friends. If Hayden did close down the mill, they might as well close down the town. Even Fitzpatrick Logging would be affected.

If Hayden sold the sawmill to a rival firm, there would be changes and the people of Gold Creek, God bless them, weren't all that interested in change. A new owner might bring in his own foremen, his own workers, his own office people and computer system. Jobs could be lost to other men and machinery.

It wasn't hard to see why the citizens of Gold Creek liked things to stay the same. They'd been raised in a timber town as their folks had been. Throughout the generations, logging in northern California had dwindled, but in Gold Creek it was a way of life.

And Hayden Monroe had the power to change it.

"JUST TAKE YOUR father's viewpoint into perspective," Thomas Fitzpatrick said, glancing through the window of Hayden's house to the lake. He'd spent the afternoon with his wayward nephew, trying to convince the boy to maintain a status quo. Hayden didn't seem to care what his father wanted nor did he seem all that interested in the fate of Fitzpatrick Logging. In fact, there seemed to be a new bitterness to him, a hardening of his features that Thomas hadn't seen in his previous meeting. As if Hayden knew something he shouldn't.

Thomas was sweating. He and Garreth had worked so well together. They'd built a monopoly here in Gold Creek and enjoyed ruling the town's economy, being Gold Creek's premier citizens. Well, at least Thomas had. Garreth had been more of a legend—what with living in the city and showing up only a few times a week at best.

Thomas cracked his knuckles as Hayden leaned back in the recliner. "What is it you really want?" Hayden asked, eyeing his uncle so intensely that Thomas, always cool, felt the need to squirm in his chair.

"For the time being, until I can come up with more cash, I want you to stay at the helm of Monroe Sawmill."

"And keep buying timber from Fitzpatrick Logging?"

"Of course. We have contracts—"

"You have a lot of things, Thomas. You and Dad." Hayden reached into a drawer and yanked out a stack of yellowed documents that had been forwarded to him, upon request, by Bradworth in San Francisco. He tossed them on the coffee table. "An interest in a soccer team that never got off the ground, a racehorse that couldn't win and oil leases for dry wells, to name just a few. Diversification—isn't that what you called it?"

Thomas tented his hands and nodded slightly, managing to hide his annoyance. "We've had our share of bad investments."

"More than your share, I'd say. In fact, it's my bet that the sawmill and the logging company are the only legitimate, profitable businesses that you're involved with."

"I'm just suggesting that you don't look a gift horse in the mouth."

Hayden's smile was cold. "Gift horse? I think the mills are more of an albatross than anything else."

Thomas's eyes snapped. "You always were too stubborn for your own good. Your father only wanted what was best for you."

"My father didn't give a damn for me, and you know it!" Hayden exploded. "I was just another one of his 'things.'"

Thomas pushed back his chair. "Just don't do anything foolish."

"You'll be one of the first to know it if I do," Hayden replied. "At the board meeting."

"What if I come up with an offer before then?"

Hayden's nostril's flared slightly. "Bring it to me. Then we'll talk."

Thomas left, and Hayden searched the den for a bottle

of Scotch or bourbon. He needed a drink. Grabbing a dusty bottle, he poured himself a stiff shot, then, with a growl, dumped the liquor down the bar sink and stared through the window into the coming night. His uncle worried him. The man was slick, oily. For the first time, Hayden wondered about selling out to him and giving him a complete monopoly in town—the owner of the only two industries.

Thomas would have more power than ever over people like Nadine.

He felt a pull on his gut and wondered what Nadine was doing.

Hell, why was it he couldn't stop thinking of her? Whatever his mood—happy, sad, frustrated, elated, worried—he wanted to share it with her. Ever since landing back in this two-bit town and seeing her bending over his bathtub, scrubbing as if her life depended upon it, he'd been fascinated with her.

Leo whined to go outside, and absently Hayden patted the old dog's head. "I know," he said, as he snagged his jacket off the hall tree near the front door. Within minutes he and the dog were driving around the curving road that followed the shoreline of the lake. The night was brisk, stars winked high above the canopy of spruce and redwood branches, but Hayden didn't notice. His concentration was focused on the twin beams of light thrown by his headlights and the single thought that soon he'd be with Nadine again.

"OKAY, OKAY, WE'LL put up the tree—but just the lights tonight. It's already late," Nadine told her boys. Upset over what she'd learned at the counter of the drugstore, she'd started home, passed the Boy Scout sales lot for Christmas trees and, on impulse, stopped and bought a small tree that she'd lashed to the roof of her car.

She was now holding it up for inspection on the back porch. Hershel growled at the tree, but the boys were delighted. "It's great, Mom," John told her, "but you could've gotten a bigger one. It's a little on the puny side."

"Yeah, like Charlie Brown's," Bobby chimed in, remembering a rerun of a Christmas special they'd seen.

"It's not that bad. With a little trimming, a few lights, and tons of ornaments, it'll be the best tree we've ever had," she insisted. "You'll see. Come on, Bobby, you help me get it inside, and John, look on the top shelf in the garage for the stand."

They wrestled the tree into the dusty stand, though the poor little pine listed to one side.

"It looks like it might fall down," Bobby said.

Nadine, still bent over the stand, shook her head. Pine needles fell into her hair and she had to speak around a protruding branch. "It'll be fine, once it's decorated."

"I don't know," John said, holding up his hand parallel to the wall and closing one eye to measure just how badly the tree leaned. "It could tip over."

"Hogwash. We'll just turn it so that it slants toward the corner. No one will ever know!" Nadine dusted her hands, eyed her handiwork, and had to admit to herself that the tree bordered on pathetic. "Just think Charlie Brown," she told herself as she poured water into the tray.

John was testing the lights, seeing which colorful bulbs still glowed after a year in the garage, by plugging the string into a wall socket, when there was a knock on the door. Hershel, searching the kitchen floor for scraps of food, bolted across the room, growling and snarling and nearly knocking over the tree as he raced by.

Bobby jumped onto the couch and peered out the window. "It's the guy from across the lake!"

"Mr. Monroe?" John asked, and his eyes were suddenly as bright as the string of lights at his feet. "Maybe he wants to take us on a ride in his boat at night! Wouldn't that be great!"

"Hershel, shush!" Nadine commanded. "And I doubt that he wants to take you two boys out on the lake tonight," Nadine added, but her heart seemed to take flight as she opened the door and found Hayden on the front porch. He loomed before her, and his musky male scent wafted on the breeze that crept into the room, billowing the curtains and causing the fire to glow brighter for an instant.

"Hey, did you bring your boat?" Bobby asked, jumping up and down on the couch in his excitement.

Hershel barked loudly.

Nadine snapped her fingers in her youngest son's direction. "Stop that jumping, Bobby, and you—" she whirled on the dog "—Hush! Right now!" She managed a smile for Hayden as she caught Hershel by the collar. "Welcome to my zoo." She swung the door open a little farther with her free hand, and Hayden stepped inside, only to kick the door closed behind him.

Nadine released the dog, and Hayden whispered to her, "This is the nicest damned zoo I've been to in a long time." His gaze found hers again and held. Her breath seemed to stop and time stretched endlessly. In those few seconds Nadine felt as if her future was wrapped up in this man, as if there were some unspoken bond between them.

"Come on, you can help us with the Christmas tree," John said, shattering the moment. "I didn't want to tell Mom that it was crooked, but it really needs some help."

Hayden shook his head. "I didn't mean to interrupt—"

"You didn't. John's right. You can help," Nadine said quickly.

Hayden's forehead creased. "I don't think I'm the right one to ask about this sort of thing."

"Hey, you're the only candidate who walked through the door," she joked, but no trace of humor entered his eyes.

"I've never put up a tree before."

"Oh, sure you have. When you were a kid…" Her voice trailed off when she saw the shadows crossing his eyes.

"When I was a kid, my mother hired a decorator to design a tree—actually a look for the house—around a theme, mind you, and I was never allowed to touch the creation." He eyed the tiny tree standing in the corner. "One year it was a Victorian theme, with huge bows and fake candles and lace, another something very sophisticated and contemporary—that year the tree was flocked pink. One other time it was sprayed gold and hung with red bells. There were strings of red bells all over the house—up the stairs, over the mantel, around the front door, in the foyer. Whatever some artist came up with, that was our look—but it was only skin deep."

"Oh, come on!" John said, sure that Hayden was pulling his leg. "A pink tree? And you didn't get to put it up?"

"Well, there's no time like the present to learn," Nadine said, despite the tears threatening her eyes. All her life she'd envied Hayden for his easy existence; she'd never really bought the "poor little rich boy" scenario, but now she wished she could ease his pain, tell him that she cared.

For all her family's lack of money, Christmastime had been a time of celebration. From the tinsel and candles on the mantel, to Sunday services at the church, where her mother would sing a solo in the choir, to cups of cocoa and bowls of popcorn as they decorated the tree with the meager decorations her mother had collected over the years—the same decorations that were probably trimming a tree on an Iowa farm.

Nadine wondered if her mother still made dozens of Christmas cookies and played her piano after dinner on Christmas Eve. She'd probably never know. The packages and cards she received never seemed to tell her much about Donna's life as a farmer's wife in the Midwest. A huge lump filled her throat, and she touched Hayden's fingers with her own.

"It's never too late to learn how to trim a tree," she said, driving away her own case of melancholy. "John will help you try to straighten it and Bobby and I will make some popcorn."

Bobby bounded from the couch and scurried to the kitchen, and John was all business as he explained what was wrong with the tree and how he proposed to keep it from leaning. "...the problem is," John confided to Hayden, "...Mom's a woman."

"I noticed," Hayden replied dryly.

"Well, women don't know nothin' about man things like hatchets and axes and—"

"I heard that, John," Nadine called from the kitchen. Smiling, she added, "Better be careful what you say or you'll be chopping all the firewood yourself...." Winking at Bobby, she plugged in the air popper and couldn't hear the rest of Hayden and John's discussion about the "weaker sex." Usually a conversation in that tone sent her temper skyrocketing, but tonight, with Hayden in the house, she decided not to take offense.

Bobby put a Christmas tape in his boom box, and by the time the popcorn, cranberry juice and cocoa were ready, Hayden and John had revived the little tree. Not only did it stand upright, but the first string of lights was winking between the branches. "How does it look?" John asked proudly.

"Like it was done by professionals."

Hayden shook his head. "Like it was done by amateurs,

the way it's supposed to be." They ate the popcorn by the fire, discussed the fact that the boys would be on vacation in less than two weeks and laughed as Hershel tried to steal kernels of popcorn out of Bobby's fingers. "He knows you're a soft touch," Hayden told Bobby. "Be careful of that."

"I'm not!" Bobby said, and to Nadine's surprise, Hayden grabbed the boy and wrestled him onto the floor. Bobby giggled and ended up on top, "pinning" Hayden until John joined in the fun. They rolled across the carpet, three bodies clinging together as one, laughing and muttering and working up a sweat.

Nadine watched in horror and awe. She'd seen the boys wrestle before, just as she'd watched her two brothers lunge and fight with each other when she'd grown up. Once in a while she'd even caught her father rolling around with Kevin and Ben. But Sam had never shown an interest in playing so physically with the boys. At the time she'd thought it a blessing, but now, seeing Bobby's red face and glowing eyes, watching as John leapt onto Hayden's back and unable to pull him down, started to laugh, she wondered if her sons had been missing out on some natural, primeval male bonding.

They crashed into a leg of the coffee table, and Hayden flopped onto his back. "You got me," he told the boys breathlessly, though Nadine suspected he wasn't near as winded as he put on.

"More, more!" Bobby cried.

"Not now, sport. I'm all in."

"No way," John said.

"That's enough, boys. Hayden's right. It's about time for bed," Nadine said.

After the usual protests and the fight over brushing their teeth and scrubbing their faces, both boys climbed into their bunks. Bobby was nearly asleep when Nadine bent over his pillow and kissed him, and John, too, was soon breathing deeply and evenly.

"You're lucky," Hayden told her, as he watched her pick up clothes that had been dropped everywhere on the floor. She tossed the small heap into a hamper.

They walked down the steps together. "Lucky? Because of the boys?" she asked, then smiled. "I know. I'll never regret marrying Sam if only because he gave me my sons."

"It doesn't take much of a man to conceive a kid. The hard part's the next twenty years." He helped her carry the popcorn bowl and glasses into the kitchen.

"So now you want kids?"

"No," he said quickly, and he might as well have stuck a knife in her heart.

"You might make a wonderful father."

His head jerked up quickly and his gaze sharpened. "You think so?"

"From what I've seen."

"I was just playing with the kids. That's all. It wasn't a big deal!"

"It was just an observation, Hayden." She placed the glasses into the dishwasher before she understood his reaction. As the light dawned, her blood began to boil. "It wasn't a hint, if that's what you're thinking."

"What am I supposed to think?"

"You're the one who showed up on my doorstep." She slammed the dishwasher shut and turned on him. "Was there a reason you came to see me? I mean something more than just to stop by and insult me? If you haven't noticed, I've done all right by myself these past couple of years. I take care of myself and my sons, and I don't need help from you or any other man for that matter, so if you think I'm in the market for a husband, you've got another think coming!" she said with more vehemence than she expected. She started to stride past him, but he hooked the crook of her arm with a hand.

"I'm sorry."

The words hung in the air between them, like icicles that wouldn't melt. She yanked her arm free. "I also don't need your pity, Prince."

"Believe me, you don't have it. I feel a lot of things for you, Nadine—some things I don't even understand myself. I respect you, I care for you, I admire you and sometimes I even envy you—"

She snorted. "You envy me. *That's* a good one."

"It's true. But in all the years I've known you, I've never, ever pitied you," he said firmly. "You know your own mind, take care of yourself, aren't afraid to stand up for what you think's right and I'll bet, if your back's to a corner or someone threatens your kids, you come out fighting like a she-bear. On top of that, you're the sexiest woman I've ever met in my life."

She supposed she should be flattered. She supposed she should take pride in his compliments. But all she felt was an empty void. Wrapping her arms around herself, she rubbed away the goose bumps that had risen on her flesh.

"Why did you come here?" she finally asked.

His jaw worked for a second, and the air between them became thick with emotions. "I came because I couldn't stay away."

"You act as if that's a curse."

He smiled crookedly. "Isn't it?" His eyes searched hers, and for a second she couldn't tear her gaze from his. Rather than answer, she quickly gathered up the empty boxes, which had held the tree ornaments, and carried them to the garage. Hayden followed her and helped her put the containers back on their shelves.

She started for the stairs to the back porch when he

reached for her, gently turning her in his arms and tilting her chin up with one of his fingers. The wind touched her hair and moonlight cast the darkness in silver.

"I was wrong," he said.

"About?"

"About not wanting you in my life. I don't understand it and I won't pretend to, but there's something about you that keeps me awake at night, something that I can't resist." Lowering his head, he brushed her lips with his own.

She trembled and let out a soft little cry as he folded his arms around her and his lips became more demanding. Somewhere in the distance a train rattled as it rode the rails of the old trestle bridge near town, and an owl let out a muted string of hoots from the high branches of one of the pine trees. The lake gleamed pearlescent, rippling as it lapped the shore. Nadine closed her eyes, drinking in the scent of Hayden—leather and soap and musk. Her arms circled his neck, and she didn't object when his weight dragged them down onto a gentle cushion of grass.

His tongue pressed against her teeth and she willingly parted her lips to him. She quivered when one of his hands reached below her sweater and long fingers splayed against the bare skin of her back.

Lifting his head for a second, he stared into her eyes and swallowed hard. "This is probably a mistake."

"Not our first," she said, managing a smile.

"Or our last?"

"I hope not."

He kissed her again, more fiercely this time, and his body, hard and wanting, pressed urgently against hers. His hands found her breasts and she arched upward, forcing each rounded swell into the gently kneading fingers that caused her blood to heat and pound in her ears. Deep inside, she began to melt. Like slow-burning oil, a liquid inside her began to simmer with want.

His mouth fastened over hers and she clung to him, holding him closer as he quickly discarded her sweater and bra, and found the anxious hard points that were her nipples. A current of electricity jolted through her as his tongue touched the tip of one breast. She cried out and her back bowed. One of his hands captured her buttock and forced her closer to the rock hardness that was his manhood. He rubbed against her and groaned as he began to suckle. Nadine's thoughts swirled crazily in a whirlpool of starlight and rainbows. She didn't think, only felt, and when the zipper of her skirt opened with a quiet hiss, she was eager for the touch of his bare hands against her skin.

He was quick. He skimmed her of her clothes and guided her hands to help him remove his own shirt and jeans. Without releasing her, he kicked off his running shoes and writhed out of his jeans until at last, beneath the pale disc of the moon, they were naked, their bodies gleaming white, their muscles straining together.

From the bathroom window, still cracked open, the strains of a soft Christmas ballad filtered over the noises of the woods, and the cool air caused a chill that only stoked the fires of their passion hotter still.

Hayden kissed her eyes, her cheeks and lips before lowering himself along the slim arch of her neck and the circle of fragile bones at the base of her throat. She whispered his name and he moved downward, touching the point of each breast with his tongue and licking a hot path down her sternum and over the soft flesh to her navel, where he pressed a hot, insistent kiss.

Moaning, Nadine arched upward and he captured her hips with his hands, kissing her, nibbling at her, caressing her with his tongue as he explored each crease and curve of her body. She clutched fistfuls of his hair as he smoothed his tongue over her so intimately that she thought she might break. The heat within her became lava from a volcano buried deep in her soul. She cried out as the first quake rocked her.

"Hayden!" she screamed, though her voice was only a throaty whisper. "Hayden, please..."

He came to her then. As her body was still in the throes of pleasure, his lips claimed hers and he parted her legs with his knees. "Make love to me, Nadine," he growled into her open, waiting mouth. "Make love to me and never stop."

"Yes, oh, yes—"

He thrust into her then and she welcomed him, sheathing his manhood, becoming one with him, feeling the sweet white-hot heat within her build yet again. Her arms surrounded him and she met each of his thrusts with her own needful movements.

This was so right, so right, she thought as once again she gave herself up to the passion that only he could inspire. Her fingers dug into his shoulders as his rhythm increased and a cry passed her lips. Then his muscles coiled, and he shuddered and fell against her with his own answering call.

"I love you," he said in a rush of breath. "Damn it all, Nadine, I think I love you."

CHAPTER ELEVEN

LOVE? HE LOVED her?

Four days later, while driving home from Coleville, Nadine was still trying to absorb this bit of information, but told herself not to believe words whispered in the throes of passion. He'd never said those three magical words again, and she wasn't kidding herself into believing that he'd meant them.

True, she'd been battling her own conflicting emotions for Hayden, but she'd tried to keep herself from fantasizing that love was involved. Attraction, yes. Lust, definitely. But love? She wasn't sure that romantic ideal existed. Her own parents hadn't found happiness, nor had she. Many of her friends had married and divorced; only a handful had stayed together, and they were often unhappy. There were a few exceptions, of course. Turner and Heather seemed blissfully, ecstatically in love and Heather's sister, Rachelle, was madly in love with her husband, Jackson.

But their marriages hadn't stood the test of time—though certainly their love had.

Her fingers tightened over the wheel as she rounded a hairpin curve on the west end of the lake and thought about the long hours after making love to Hayden near the lake. They'd returned to the house, drank wine and had cuddled together on the couch until the fire had died.

He'd come back the next night, eaten dinner with them and helped finish decorating the tree. Hayden had even helped John with his science report on the depletion of the ozone layer. Once the boys had fallen asleep, she and Hayden had walked outside and again given into their passion.

She'd seen Hayden each night and looked forward to greeting him at the front door. Sometimes he smelled of sawdust and oil, and she'd known he'd been at one of the mills. Other times he carried the scent of leather or soap with him, as if he'd just come from the shower.

He'd brought wine for her, soda for the boys and had taken it upon himself to fix the chain on Bobby's bicycle, getting himself greasy in the process and delighting her youngest son. Hayden Monroe certainly knew how to carve his way into her heart.

She couldn't be falling in love with him, she told herself, and wouldn't let it happen. Her runaway emotions were on the loose and it was time to rein them in.

"What a mess," she told herself, and clicked on the radio. She hadn't wanted an affair with any man and certainly not Hayden, yet she was involved with him up to her neck. She thought about him constantly and, as she had throughout her trip from Coleville, she tried to concentrate on her work.

Elizabeth Wheeler, the owner of Beth's Boutique, had been encouraging. She'd ordered three more jackets and two dozen pairs of earrings.

"They're going like hotcakes. Kids as well as adults," Beth had confided in Nadine two hours earlier. "If you can't get them here by Christmas, I'll want them for spring!"

Nadine smiled to herself. It seemed as if her life was turning around, despite everyone's dour predictions about Hayden Monroe and his grim effect upon the town. Even Nadine's father seemed a little happier, and though he wouldn't confide the reason for the spring in his step when they'd gone to lunch this afternoon, Nadine suspected that he was interested in another woman for the first time in years. He'd hardly dated since her mother had walked out on him, but there was definitely something different about him in the past couple of days and she didn't believe his change in mood was just because the spirit of Christmas was in the air or because Ben was on his way home. No, the twinkle in her father's eyes could only be attributed to the attentions of a woman. But whose attentions?

Time would tell, she decided, turning into the drive and spying Hayden's Jeep.

He was waiting for her, legs outstretched, ankles crossed, hips resting on the fender. Her heart skipped a beat and she wondered fleetingly if there was a chance for them. In a millisecond she pictured herself as Hayden's wife, living in the manor across the lake, spending hours with Hayden, making love with him, having more children.... Reality broke the spell. Hayden wasn't going to stay in Gold Creek. He would probably sell his string of sawmills, perhaps even close some of them, and he didn't want a wife and especially not any children; she'd learned that much. Being the product of an unhappy marriage, with unrealistic goals placed upon his young shoulders, Hayden had decided from an early age to depend upon no one but himself. He didn't want a wife and kids.

As her silly bubble of happiness burst, she parked near the garage. With Hayden, she had to live for the moment and forget about a future.

Forcing a smile, she slid out of the car and was rewarded with a crushing embrace and a kiss that sucked the breath from her lungs and made her bones as weak as jelly.

His body fit intimately against hers, and the realization that she loved him hit her like the proverbial ton of bricks.

For weeks she'd been denying it, burying her feelings, telling herself her emotions were on the rampage because she'd been without a man for so long. But now, with his arms around her, his lips devouring hers, his hands possessive, she knew she'd lost her heart to him and she doubted she'd ever retrieve it.

He lifted his head to stare into her eyes. "God, I missed you," he said hoarsely as he captured a handful of her hair and twined his fingers through the thick, red curls. Her heart seemed to crack.

"I saw you this morning," she pointed out, thinking of their goodbye kiss on the front porch at one-thirty.

"That was a long time ago."

"Mmm. Too long," she admitted. "I missed you, too," she admitted.

"I could tell." He slapped her on the rump playfully, but let his hand settle over the curve of her hip.

"Could you?" She wound her arms around his neck and licked her lips provocatively. "How?"

He groaned. "You're wicked, woman."

"And you love it."

He laughed and kissed her again. "I have half a mind to carry you into the house, throw you on the bed and ravage you until you beg for mercy."

"The half a mind part, I believe."

His eyes flashed. "Well, I guess I'll just have to prove it to you." Quickly he scooped her up and threw her over his shoulder in a fireman's carry.

"Hayden, no!" she cried, laughing as the blood rushed to her head and her hair nearly swept the ground. Hershel yipped and bounded in excitement, trying to lick Nadine's face. "Please, put me down!"

"You asked for it."

"No, I— Hayden, oh, come on—"

He started packing her up the back steps to the door. "How much time do we have before the boys get home?"

"They'll be here any minute."

"Liar."

"It's…it's the truth!"

He set her on her feet, but his arms still surrounded her and he kissed her again. Already breathless, her heart pumping, she kissed him back and playfully darted her tongue between his lips.

"You're asking for trouble."

"Am I gonna get it?" she asked.

He chuckled. "You *are* bad."

"Only with you."

"It better be only with me." His eyes sizzled electric blue just as the sound of shouts and bicycle tires crushing gravel reached her ears.

"See," she taunted.

Hershel gave an expectant bark and streaked down the lane toward the coming noises. With a sigh, she touched a finger to his lips. "I don't think we're alone anymore."

His mouth curved sardonically. "I'm a patient man, Nadine. I'll wait."

John's old bike rounded the corner, and Bobby's smaller two-wheeler was right behind him. Before the bike had stopped, John had leapt off his seat, letting the bicycle fall into the yard.

"What's for dinner?" John demanded as Hershel jumped and barked.

"A surprise."

"Uh-oh." John pulled a face, and Bobby, leaning his bike against the garage, wrinkled his nose.

"Let's go to McDonald's," Bobby suggested.

Nadine shook her head. "No way. I'm not driving back to Coleville tonight. Besides, you like pasta salad—"

"Yuk!" John said. "I *hate* salad."

"This is different. It has chicken and cheese and—"

"And it's still salad," John said.

"We can have Kentucky Fried Chicken," Bobby, ever the fast-food junkie, suggested.

Nadine was starting to fume. "I said we're not going to—"

"I'll take you out."

Nadine turned on Hayden, as if she'd heard him wrong. "But the boys have homework and—"

"You need a night off. Besides, I've bummed more than my share of meals around here."

"Come on, Mom!" Bobby cried.

"Yeah, let's go."

Nadine glared at Hayden. "Why do I have the feeling that I've been conned?" she asked, glancing back to the boys. "I wasn't kidding about the homework."

"We'll do it. Okay? When we get back!" John said.

"Before the TV goes on."

John rolled his eyes before racing after Bobby into the house.

"Lighten up about the homework," Hayden suggested.

"So now you're telling me how to be a parent?" she asked, though she wasn't angry. "What makes you such an expert?"

"I was a kid. A kid who was expected to get straight A's, a kid who was supposed to be the best football player, baseball player, chess player and leader of the debate team. My folks wanted—no, make that *expected*—me to be the smartest kid in my class."

"Were you?" she asked.

His grin turned devilish. "Until about seventh grade. Then I became the biggest hellion."

"I bet your parents were proud," she teased, before she saw the storm clouds gathering in his eyes.

"I doubt that was the word my father would have used to describe anything I did."

Before she could say anything else, the boys had thundered out of the house. They all piled into Hayden's Jeep and he drove into town.

Hayden took them to a small restaurant in the mall near the tricinemas. For the first time in their lives the boys, seated on one side of the booth, were encouraged to order anything off the menu as Hayden insisted this night was his treat. Nadine tried to protest, but he wouldn't hear of it, and in the end, John and Hayden each ordered a steak, Bobby stuck with a hamburger and Nadine chose grilled salmon. The boys were in heaven.

"Why can't we do this all the time?" John asked as he struggled to cut his steak.

"Because it's not practical," Nadine replied.

On the seat of the booth between them, Hayden folded his hand over hers. "Sometimes it's better not to be practical." His fingers fit into the grooves between her own and she tingled a little.

"Everyone should keep his head," she said. "And think of the consequences of what they're doing."

"We're just eating," John pointed out. "That's no crime."

"But we can't do it all the time because we can't afford it."

"He can!" Bobby said, pointing a fork at Hayden.

"That's right," John chimed in, focusing on Hayden. "Katie Osgood says you're the richest man in Gold Creek. But Mike Katcher thinks it's Mr. Fitzgerald."

Nadine was horrified. "John, it's not polite to—"

Hayden held up a hand. "I don't know about my local status and I really don't care. My father was a very wealthy man. I inherited a lot from him, but it doesn't mean a whole lot to me."

"Well, it should," John said. "Money talks. That's what my dad says."

Nadine wanted to drop through the floorboards of the restaurant.

"He does. Dad is always talking about money," Bobby added as the waitress approached. Luckily the subject was dropped.

Hayden let the boys order dessert and the conversation stayed light as John plowed into apple pie with ice cream and Bobby picked at a huge piece of six-layer chocolate cake.

Upon instruction, both boys thanked Hayden and he made a point of telling them to call him by his first name.

This is going much too fast, Nadine thought, and realized that it wasn't just her heart that would be broken when Hayden left. The boys, too, would miss him. For their own sakes, she had to make sure they didn't get too emotionally attached to a man who would soon return to his life in the city.

Later that night, as she was tucking Bobby into bed, she smoothed his hair from his forehead and gave him a kiss. "See ya in the morning," she said before turning out the light.

"Mom?"

"Hmm?" She looked over her shoulder at the top of the stairs.

"Are you going to marry Mr. Mon—Hayden?"

She froze, hoping that Hayden, in the living room below, hadn't heard her youngest son's question. John leaned over from the top bunk and stared at his mom, waiting for her answer. Her throat felt like sandpaper, but she shook her head.

"Why not?" Bobby wanted to know.

"He hasn't asked her yet, you dope."

"It's more than that. I…Hayden…we…well, we live in different worlds."

"But you like each other," Bobby pointed out. "He's here a lot."

"Liking each other is not enough."

John propped his head up with his hand. "If he asked you, would you say 'yes'?"

That was a tough one. "I don't think so."

"Aw, Mom!" Bobby said with a sigh. "If you married him we could have everything we wanted. New twenty-one-speed bikes, a big house, a boat that goes real fast like his—"

"And an airplane. Like Mr. Fitzpatrick. Katie Osgood says—"

"I don't care what Katie Osgood says," Nadine snapped at John. "Now, you just close your eyes and go to sleep, and that goes double for you," she added with a smile for Bobby.

Quickly she descended the stairs. "Trouble?" Hayden asked as she reached the first floor.

"Nothing serious," she replied, as he took her into his arms and placed a kiss upon her forehead. She melted willingly against him and wished she could think of a way to protect herself and her children from the great void that would appear in their lives when he locked the doors of the manor across the lake forever.

SELL OUT TO Thomas Fitzpatrick. The offer was tempting. Uncle Thomas hadn't pulled any punches, which surprised Hayden as he studied the buyout offer. Thomas wanted all the mills and was offering a decent price, if not top dollar. The deal was neat. All Hayden had to do was sign on the dotted line and make an announcement at the next board meeting. Since he owned controlling interest, no one could raise a stink. So why was he hesitating?

Because of Nadine. If he sold the mills and put the summerhouse on the market, he would be closing the door to Gold Creek forever and turning his back on Nadine and her children. He smiled as he thought of the boys. The older kid, John, was a handful. Bright and cocky, he was sure to give his mother more than her share of gray hairs, and the younger boy…he was difficult in his own way—a kid who struggled in school and was always at the mercy of his older, stronger brother.

They didn't know how lucky they were, he decided. If only he'd had a brother or a sister with whom he could have shared his problems, confided his darkest secrets and beat the living tar out of when he'd been angry.

The phone rang, and he picked up on the second ring. He nearly slammed the receiver back into its cradle when he recognized Wynona's wheedling voice. "Hayden? Thank God I caught you."

The irony of her words settled like lead on his shoulders. "What do you want, Wynona?" he asked without much interest.

"I want to see you again. We need to talk."

"Talk to Bradworth."

He could almost feel her seething through the wires. "There are things we need to discuss. Important things. Things that I don't want to confide in a lawyer."

"Guilty conscience?" he mocked, and he heard her swift intake of breath. He didn't feel the slightest bit of remorse.

"I'm coming to see you."

"Won't do any good, Wynona. I'm leaving town."

"But—"

"Goodbye," he said, and slammed down the receiver. The phone started ringing again, but he didn't bother answering, just took the stairs two at a time and started planning a weekend away from Gold Creek and the mills and Thomas Fitzpatrick and contracts. Away from the guilt.

But not away from everything. He planned to take Nadine and her boys with him.

SAM CLAPPED HIS hands and yelled up the stairs to the loft. "Come on, guys. Chop! Chop!"

"Give them a break," Nadine reprimanded. "It was the last day of school today. They're wound up."

"Good. We got lots to do." To the rafters, he called, "Hurry up."

"Coming!" John hollered down.

"So what's the rush?" Nadine asked. She didn't want to sound suspicious, but Sam wasn't usually so anxious to be bothered with the boys. Not that he was a bad father, nor neglectful. He just wasn't usually so attentive.

In a clatter of footsteps the boys hurried down the stairs. After quick kisses to Nadine's cheeks, John and Bobby, their overnight bags slung over their shoulders, were herded out the back door toward Sam's waiting pickup. The passenger door opened with a loud creak just as Hayden's Jeep pulled into the drive.

"What the hell?" Sam said under his breath. "I wonder what *he* wants."

"He's coming to see Mom," Bobby offered and started waving enthusiastically. "He comes all the time."

Sam sent Nadine a sharp glance over his shoulder. "Is that right?"

"Well—"

"And he takes us fishing, and riding in his boat, and to fancy restaurants," Bobby added.

John, sensing the change of atmosphere in the air, didn't add anything to the conversation.

"He said he'd take us skiing, too."

"Bobby, I don't think Dad wants to hear everything that Mr. Monroe has talked about."

"He said we were supposed to call him Hayden," Bobby corrected, and Nadine had to grit her teeth.

Hayden parked next to Sam's pickup and stretched out. Taller than Sam by nearly three inches, with broader shoulders and harsher features, he looked hard-bodied and tough. "Hayden, you've met Sam, I think."

"At the mill," Sam supplied, his eyes narrowing a fraction. "And a long time ago. Company picnic, or something."

Hayden extended his hand, but Sam ignored it.

"Is there something you want?"

Hayden offered a practiced smile. "I just came to see Nadine and the kids."

Sam bristled a little, and Nadine wondered again where his sudden sense of fatherhood had come from. "Well, you'd better say 'hello' now because the boys are leaving with me. For the weekend."

Hayden's lips stretched into a wide grin, as if he harbored a secret he wouldn't share. "Have a great time."

"We always do," Sam said stiffly as he climbed into the cab of his truck and roared off.

"What was that all about?" Hayden asked.

"You know perfectly well, Hayden Monroe. I think it's called marking his territory. The boys were going on and on about you and all the things you've done for them and Sam got his fatherly hackles up." She glanced at the disappearing truck. "About time."

"So," Hayden asked, placing his hands on her waist, "does that mean you're free for the weekend?"

"It means I'm alone."

His grin turned positively evil. "Not anymore. I'm taking you out—"

"Where?"

"It's a surprise."

"I don't like surprises."

"You'll like this one," he guaranteed.

"Hayden, I don't think—"

"Humor me. Believe me, you won't be disappointed."

HE WAS RIGHT. Three hours later, as the Jeep rounded a final curve through the pine trees in the mountains, Nadine held her breath. Lights glowed through the windows of a rambling, three-storied lodge. Built of cedar and pine, with a wide porch, the building was settled in a thicket of pine trees and nearly twenty miles from the nearest small town.

Inside, the walls were raw wood, aged dark without a hint of varnish and covered with paraphernalia of the Wild West—saws, wagon yokes, axes and picks, even a full-size canoe. Wagon-wheel chandeliers offered flickering light. "I was afraid you were going to take me somewhere stuffy."

"Me?" he laughed. "Never."

They were seated near a bay window decorated with a cedar garland and sprigs of pine and mistletoe. Soon a waiter poured the wine Hayden had chosen, then took their orders. A hurricane lantern flickered on the cloth-covered table and reflected in the glass. Nadine sipped her wine and talked with Hayden before noticing, through the window, snow beginning to fall in thick, heavy flakes.

"If this keeps up, we could be trapped here all night," Hayden teased.

"I don't think so."

"Would it be so horrible?" he asked, the light from the lantern reflecting in his warm blue eyes.

"I'm a mother. I have responsibilities."

"The kids are with their dad. And your answering machine's on. If there's a problem, you'll know about it."

"Why Mr. Monroe, I think you're trying to seduce me," she teased, and her pulse jumped.

"Count on it." Her throat went dry as he touched his glass to hers with a soft clink, then finished his wine in one swallow.

They talked through courses of Caesar salad, French onion soup, stuffed trout and raspberry mousse. Hayden told her he'd found a buyer for the sawmills and that he was considering the offer. Her heart felt as if it had been pierced by a sharp needle as she considered the fact that he might soon be gone, perhaps before the first of the year. A coldness settled in her stomach and seeped through her limbs. All along she'd known that he would leave, of course, but she'd never let herself think about the date; it had seemed a long way into the future, some indefinable time that she would worry about come spring…or maybe summer. But now? She managed to pretend that his talk of selling the sawmill didn't bother her, that she was sophisticated enough to deal with the inevitable fact that they would soon be separated by time and distance, but the small puncture wound in her heart seemed to rip a little more with each of her breaths.

She didn't notice the time passing, nor did she observe the snow that had accumulated on the ground around the lodge. She concentrated totally on Hayden, the inflexible line of his jaw, the angles of his cheekbones, the way his lips barely moved as he spoke.

By the time they'd finished coffee, two inches of snow had fallen. "Looks like we're here for the night," Hayden observed as he paid the bill and glanced outside.

"Doesn't your Jeep have four-wheel drive?"

His grin crept from one side of his mouth to the other. "Yes, but it would be a waste not to take advantage of the room I've already paid for, don't you think?"

"What I think," she said, standing as they left the table, "is that you should have asked me first."

He pulled her into a shadowy corner near the lobby. "All right. I'm asking." His eyes held hers. "Will you spend the night with me?"

She swallowed hard and considered all the reasons she should tell him to take her home. Staying would only prolong the heartache and keep the pain alive, and yet she couldn't resist. "Of course I'll stay with you," she whispered, knowing that he didn't realize she meant for the rest of her life.

THE ROOM SPRAWLED across most of the top floor. Lustrous hardwood peeked out from beneath thick Oriental carpets and the furnishings of the suite were crafted to look antique. A hurricane lamp sat on the corner of the mantel in the bedroom occupied by a queen-size canopy bed.

A bottle of champagne stood chilling in a stand, and through the French doors leading to a private deck, Nadine noticed steam rising from an outdoor hot tub in a thick cloud, reminding her of the morning fog on Whitefire Lake.

"This is quite a place," she observed, running her hand over the curve of the bed frame.

"It's nice." He struck a match to the fire and lit the lantern before turning down the lights.

"You've been here before?" Why it mattered, she didn't know, but she didn't want to be just one in a long line of the women he'd brought here.

He nodded, watching her reaction in the beveled glass mirror over the bureau. She felt a jab of pain, but hoped he didn't notice. In the firelight, his features seemed harsher, more male, and the thought of him with another woman... Oh, God, she loved him too much. "With whom?" she asked, her voice sounding oddly strangled.

While icicles formed in her heart, he had the audacity to smile. "A woman."

Oh, God.

She fought the urge to walk straight out the door, and when he stood behind her and placed his hands on her shoulders, she wished she could find the strength to shake them off. But her willpower seemed to vanish at his touch and her skin heated beneath his fingertips. "Do I know her?"

"You've met, I think. A long time ago."

Wynona. She felt like such a fool and her shoulders drooped a little. He pulled her closer and whispered into her ear. "I was here with my mother. I was ten or eleven at the time, I think."

Relief flooded through her, and when she met his gaze in the mirror again, she saw the hint of laughter in his crystal-blue eyes. "You are a rotten, mean, miserable—"

"Prince," he supplied, and she couldn't help but grin as he twirled her in his arms.

"You're the king now, you know."

He shook his head. "Not me. Just a regular Joe."

"Regular Joes don't do this—" She motioned to the room and deck.

"They should," he said, as he lowered his lips over hers and dragged her onto the bed with him. She quit arguing and gave herself body and soul to him. The doubts and fears in her mind were stripped away as surely as were her clothes. The old bed creaked as he removed her jacket, sweater and slacks and, while she was dressed only in her bra and panties, he tore off his own clothes. His shoes clunked as they hit the floor and were followed quickly by his slacks and shirt. In the firelight, his chest seemed bronze, the swirling black hairs darker than ever. His body was taut and strong, and she was reminded of a Native American warrior, so sinewy were his thighs and shoulders. But his eyes were blue, a tribute to his Anglo ancestors.

"This is the way it should be," he whispered, as his arms folded around her and he nibbled at the skin of her neck. Her pulse jumped and her blood flowed like liquid fire through her veins. His chest hair was stiff and curly against her skin and he seemed all hard and angular where she was soft and supple. His mouth found hers, and he kissed her long and hard, his tongue exploring, his hands moving sensually along her rib cage.

He shoved her bra away from her breast, kissing the nipple with featherlight strokes that caused her to writhe and arch against him.

"Slow down," he said, his lips brushing her breasts, his breath caressing her nipple. "We've got all night."

It sounded so good. She cradled his head against her breast as he removed the rest of her clothes. She reveled in his touch and her heart pounded as his fingers grazed her nipple before he lowered his mouth and teased her with his lips and tongue. His hands sculpted her back, holding her firmly to him, making her feel the length of his hardness pressed deep against her abdomen.

His hands worked magic as they explored her, touching her in intimate places, causing her heart to beat as rapidly as the wings of a hummingbird. Lovingly he caressed her, moving with a slow steady hand that only increased when her body requested a faster tempo.

The room seemed to spin, the heat within her coiled, whirling so quickly that she closed her eyes. But still the candlelight was there, in bright vibrant colors that exploded behind her eyelids and caused her body to quake in violent convulsions that ripped a primeval sound from her throat. "Hayden," she cried in that foreign voice.

"I'm right here," he assured her as she clung to him. He let her body slow, and only when her breathing was even and her eyelids fluttered open, did he kiss her again. "Okay, love, now it's my turn," he said.

She reached for him, but he picked her up and carried her outside where the cold air brought goose bumps to her flesh. "Are you crazy? What're you doing?" she cried as he set her into the hot tub and followed after her. "It's freezing out here."

"Not in the water."

"But—"

He kissed her and cut off further protests, and there in the steamy water, with snowflakes sticking to their hair, he gently prodded her knees apart and claimed her for his own.

LATER, WRAPPED ONLY in a bath sheet, she dialed her home, accessed her answering machine code and discovered no messages, so she hung up feeling less irresponsible. Hayden came up behind her, stripped away the bath towel and forced her back to the bed.

The night passed quickly in a haze of lovemaking and glasses of champagne. They fell asleep sometime before dawn and when she finally awoke, the sun was high in the sky, glistening off six inches of fresh snow. Hayden stood by the window, dressed only in his shorts, staring at the trees. When he heard her stir, he turned and spying her sprawled upon the bed, grinned mischievously.

"This is the way I'd like to wake up every morning."

Her traitorous heart skipped a beat, but she ignored it and stretched lazily.

Hayden's gaze moved to her breasts, covered only by the sheets, and he stifled a groan. "We'll never get out of here if you don't quit that."

"Quit what?" she taunted, and he swore under his breath.

"You little tease."

"Me?" she asked innocently, and he crossed the few feet and threw himself over the bed.

"Yes, you."

She laughed as he pinned her beneath the covers and kissed her.

"You are the most exciting, impulsive and impossible woman ever to set foot on this earth."

"May I take that as a compliment?"

"Take it any way you like." He kissed her gently, then propped his head up with one hand. "If you don't get up, you're in for serious trouble, lady."

She knew that. But she didn't want this bliss to end. She stroked his beard-roughened cheek with her hand and touched the tiny scar that sliced through one of his brows. "What's this from?" she asked, and watched as his smile faded.

"Compliments of my old man."

"But how?"

"We had a disagreement. He couldn't get through to me with words, so he used his fist. Not here…but he hit me so hard I fell and cut myself on the stair rail. I think I was fifteen."

Her stomach squeezed in pain. "What was the fight about?"

He snorted. "I can't even remember." He was stretched out on the top of the sheet and she saw the other scars on his body, neatly stitched gashes on his legs.

"And these?"

He glanced down when her finger touched one of the bluish marks. "From the accident," he said coldly.

"The what?"

"In the boat. With Wynona."

"Oh." She drew back her hand, but he threaded his fingers through hers and sighed.

"It's okay. That all happened a long time ago. Now,

you'd better get up. I'd love to spend the rest of the weekend here, but unfortunately duty calls."

"The mill?"

"The mill," he replied grimly, as he reached for his slacks. "But before we go back, we should eat breakfast. Steak, eggs, pancakes—the works."

She shook her head. "How about coffee and a piece of toast?"

"Whatever your heart desires," he said, kissing her lightly on the forehead before throwing back the covers and exposing her naked form. With a sardonic smile, he kicked off his slacks again. "On second thought…"

BY THE TIME they returned to Gold Creek, the sun was low in the sky. Nadine thought about the work stretched out before her; she had promised Elizabeth new merchandise. Two of the jackets were complete, the third was almost done, but she only had about a dozen pairs of earrings finished. Then there was some Christmas shopping and planning the traditional meal for her father, the boys and Ben. *And Hayden?* Was that possible?

Hayden folded his hand over hers. "You could come spend the rest of the weekend at my house."

The offer was tempting. "I don't think so. I've got a lot of work to do—"

He placed his hand on her knee, and his gaze slid in her direction. "Won't it keep overnight? I'll build a fire and we'll have eggnog and you can help me with my tree. Remember, I'm still an amateur at this."

"You're twisting my arm."

"I'll bring you back early in the morning, I promise."

"I've heard that one before," she said with a chuckle. "This time I'm going to hold you to it."

They stopped by Nadine's place, where she gave Hershel fresh food and water, checked the mail and the phone messages, grabbed a small suitcase with a change of clothes and her makeup, and then they were on their way. In Gold Creek they purchased a Christmas tree, a stand and some decorations along with a few supplies and groceries.

Darkness had settled on the lake as they pulled into the drive of Hayden's house. Through the tall trees, the lights of the house winked brightly.

"That's odd," Hayden said, his hands tightening over the wheel as they rounded the final bend and the headlights of his rig washed over the shiny finish of a white Jaguar. "Damn it all to hell," he ground out as he stood on the brakes and the Jeep slid to a stop.

"Who's here?" Nadine asked, uneasiness tightening into a hard ball in the pit of her stomach.

"Wynona," he ground out, stepping down from the Jeep.

Nadine froze. *Wynona Galveston was here? Through the locked gates and inside the locked house? As if she had her own key?*

Hayden was striding furiously up the front walk when the door burst open, and Wynona, her supple body framed by interior lights, appeared.

"Thank God you're here," she said, smiling brightly. Her blond hair caught in the moonlight as she ran from the front door and threw herself into Hayden's arms.

Nadine held back a small cry. Her insides shriveled and she felt the urge to run, to get as far away from Hayden as possible. But she kept her wits about her and took a deep breath. His relationship with Wynona might not be what it seemed.

Gathering her courage, Nadine found the door handle of the Jeep and slowly let herself out. The air was cold, blowing off the lake in wintry gusts. A thin layer of clouds partially obscured the moon, but she could see clearly as Hayden slowly peeled Wynona's arms from around his neck.

"…but you have to help me," Wynona was saying, tears frozen in her eyes.

"I don't have to do a damned thing."

"You *owe* me."

"I told you before I owe you nothing." His voice was harsh and callous. Nadine felt bitter and betrayed.

"How can you be so cruel?" Wynona demanded, sobbing openly. "If it weren't for you—"

"Don't start this."

"You nearly killed me," she cried, tears running freely from her eyes.

Nadine's stomach turned sour. She shouldn't listen to this. Yet she couldn't turn away.

"I didn't—"

Wynona's fury unleashed. "The accident was your fault, Hayden. It was your fault I nearly died, and damn it all to hell, it was your fault I lost the baby!"

CHAPTER TWELVE

A BABY?

Nadine's knees nearly gave out. Hayden and Wynona had created an unborn baby who had died in the boating accident? Oh, God, what was she doing here? Pain seared her soul. She'd believed him, she'd loved him, she'd given herself to him; and Hayden hadn't even thought enough of her to tell her the truth. "How can you be so cruel?" Wynona broke into hysterical sobs, and Nadine felt as if she'd been hit in the stomach by an iron fist. She leaned against a tall pine for support and wished she'd never become involved with him again, never heard Wynona's pathetic pleas. Her stomach roiled to think she'd imagined she'd loved him—a man who had— Oh, God, little by little she was dying inside.

Hayden swore loudly. "Damn it, Wynona, don't you think you've got your facts twisted a bit?"

"You were there, Hayden. And you abandoned me. For some cheap little small-town whore—ouch!"

Stricken, Nadine glanced up and saw Hayden grab Wynona by the shoulders and give her an angry shake. "Don't you ever talk about her—"

"Oh, Christ, don't tell me you're still in love with her!" Wynona's eyes narrowed, and the tears seemed to melt away. As Nadine drew closer, Wynona's gaze collided with hers and she sucked in her breath. "Well, I'll be," she whispered, shaking her head. "You still have your little redheaded piece of—"

"Stop it!" He shook her again.

Wynona's eyes were frigid and her lip curled. "Just like your old man, aren't you, Hayden? One woman was never enough for him and it looks like you're just the same."

He dropped her as if touching her skin had scorched his fingers. "Get out, Wynona."

Rubbing her arms, she said, "You haven't seen the last of me. You and your father *owe* me. Big-time. Promises were made. Nothing's changed just because he died."

"Like hell. I'm in charge now."

"And you're trying to cut me off!"

"Take it up with Bradworth. Maybe you can strike a private deal with him."

She tried to slap him, but he was too quick. He caught her wrist in his hand and shoved her back. "Don't be stupid, Wynona."

"You bastard! You sick, filthy bastard!"

"Flattery will get you nowhere," he said, and she yanked her hand away. Throwing a scathing glance at Nadine, she strode into the house, grabbed her purse and fur coat, and with the mink waving behind her like a sleek banner, she stormed to her car.

She threw the Jaguar into reverse, backed into a tree and smashed her taillight. Metal crunched and glass splintered. Wynona shoved the car into Drive and roared away, tires spitting gravel, one red taillight winking brightly through the trees.

Nadine was shaking so badly, she could barely move. She thought she might throw up as the pieces of Hayden's past fit together into an ugly, painful puzzle.

"What do they say about a woman scorned?" Hayden asked.

Nadine couldn't answer. Her mouth was dry as cotton, her guts twisted and the pain in her bruised heart wouldn't go away. "I think I should leave," she said, tears threatening her eyes.

"Because of what Wynona said?"

She nodded, and the first drops of rain started to fall from the sky, touching her cheeks and splashing on the ground. "There was a baby?" she whispered, her fists clenched so tightly, her fingernails dug into her palms. She prayed that she misunderstood, but the hardening of Hayden's jaw, the tightening of his mouth at its corners only confirmed the worst of her fears. The bottom of Nadine's world seemed to fall out from under her.

"Yes, there was a baby, but it wasn't mine."

"Hayden, don't lie—"

"I'm not, damn it!" He grabbed her and dragged her wooden body close to his. "You have to believe me."

"But you never said a word," she cried, her trust in him unraveling as quickly as old seam in an antique dress. How could she have trusted him, made love to him, given her heart to him when she knew so little about him?

"There are reasons."

"Reasons? What reasons? You didn't want me to know because then I wouldn't be so easily seduced, is that it? Or were you trying to make yourself look better in my eyes?" Icy rain was falling heavily now, trickling in the gutters and pooling on the walks. Frigid drops drizzled down Nadine's face and throat.

"Of course not!"

"Then why?"

His jaw worked and he closed his eyes. "The baby was my father's."

Nadine gasped, and her insides churned as wildly as the storm-tossed lake. "Your father's?" She couldn't believe it. Wouldn't. "But you were engaged to her. Come on, Hayden, you don't really expect me to believe that—"

"That my father would seduce a woman half his age?

That she would be flattered by his attention since she couldn't have mine? That Wynona Galveston was more interested in Monroe money than she was in me or my dad?" he asked, shoving his wet hair from his face. "Which part is so unbelievable?"

"It never came out that she was pregnant. In all the press about the accident. Never once—"

"Her father is a doctor. He hushed it up. It was part of the deal he made with my dad... Oh, hell, it's complicated. Come inside before we're both soaked. You may as well know the whole sordid story."

"I don't think I should—"

He held her hand in his and looked into her eyes with such pain and torment, she couldn't say no. "I must be crazy. I should just walk away from all this."

"No, you shouldn't." His thumb rubbed gently across the back of her hand. "Just hear me out."

Telling herself she was a fool of the highest order, Nadine helped him unpack the car. Her insides were knotted, and she told herself she was only prolonging the agony by watching him start a fire. "We'll eat first," he said, and she didn't argue. She wasn't sure that she wanted to hear all of the details of his affair—or his father's—with another woman, but knew that if there was any chance of a future for them, she had to.

She heated clam chowder and warmed the bread. They ate in the den, in front of the crackling flames, sipping wine and trying to ignore the tension that seemed to mount with each slow tick of the grandfather clock.

"I never loved her," Hayden admitted, setting his empty bowl on the coffee table.

"You don't have to—"

"She was handpicked by my mother. From the right family. Her father was a doctor and her mother had inherited 'old money.' She was pretty and smart and my mother thought she'd make the perfect match. Her parents, too, were thrilled at the prospect. Even Wynona bought into the plan. But I wasn't about to be bullied into marrying someone I didn't really care about. Oh, I liked her. A lot. What was there not to like?

"What I didn't know, and my parents didn't realize, was that most of Wynona's inheritance didn't exist. Her father had sizable debts that he'd incurred while going to school and he had a little problem at the racetrack. He liked to bet on the ponies. The family still had money, of course, but not the kind of wealth my mother expected. Most of what was left of the Galveston fortune would be passed on to their son, Wynona's brother, Gerard. So, I was the perfect catch.

"Remember the Mercedes I left in the sawmill lot the day I met you?" She nodded and he said, "Well, it was an engagement present from my father. To Wynona and me. Only, there was no engagement. So I didn't accept the gift and my old man was furious."

Nadine remembered the day as vividly as if it had occurred just last week. Meeting Hayden had changed her life forever. She stared at him now, his features solemn in the firelight, his eyes lifeless. "When I wasn't interested in her, Wynona was desperate and then…my father stepped in. I don't really know when they started their affair. I've told myself that it had to have happened *after* I'd told her I wouldn't marry her, but I'm not so sure. She was pregnant. Oh, hell!" He stood and walked to the fireplace, adding a small log and watching the flames devour the mossy oak.

"I didn't know about their affair at first, nor did my mom. Dad had always had a thing for women, younger beautiful women, and Mom had always turned her head. She would rather suffer his infidelity than divorce him and admit that she couldn't hold her man. How she put up with him, I'll never know. Remember I told you that my mom and I stayed at the lodge in the mountains? Well, she took me there once when she walked out on dad after learning that he was involved with his secretary. But, as always, she went back to him."

Nadine felt as if she'd been led down a private stairway and into a dark room where she didn't belong. "I don't think I want to know the rest—"

"I want you to. While my mom was trying to patch things up with Wynona and me, my dad was already taking her to his bed."

"And she got pregnant."

"Right. Then all hell broke loose." He stared at Nadine, saw the doubts in her eyes and took her hand between his two larger palms. "Believe me, Nadine, I never slept with her. The baby couldn't have been mine."

"There was no mention of a baby in the paper."

"Lots of things were left out," he said flatly. "As I said, her old man was a doctor and made sure that no one learned that she was pregnant. Oh, a few medical people knew, but they kept their mouths shut."

"Oh, God, Hayden. This is too much," she said, shaking her head. "Even if the baby wasn't yours—"

"It wasn't," he said firmly, his nostrils flaring.

"It died. *Died* in the accident. Your half brother or sister."

He took her into his arms and held her close. She felt near tears, for a baby who had never had the chance to live, for Hayden who had endured the hardship of being fathered by a man who had never known the meaning of the word *love* and for herself. She loved him. With all her stupid heart, she loved him and yet there was so much she didn't know about him. He'd been raised in a different world from hers and there was so much pain between their families.

"You may as well know it all," Hayden said, holding her close.

"There's more?"

"I wasn't driving the boat."

"But the accident report—"

"Shh." His breath ruffled her hair. "Wynona blamed me because we had a fight. Because of the baby, she begged me to marry her and I wouldn't. She was out of her mind and told me she was going to kill herself. I didn't really believe her but she ran out of the house and down the dock. I chased after her, and managed to get into the boat before she took off, but she was already at the helm. She tore away from the dock as fast as she could and I let her drive. I figured it would do her good to let off steam. So I didn't try to wrestle the helm from her. She tried to scare me, driving recklessly, but I didn't stop her. I saw the other boat before she did and yelled at her, but it was too late. The other guy bailed out and we struck the fishing boat broadside."

"But everyone thinks…the police reports…"

"They said I was the driver. For insurance purposes. No one was supposed to drive the boat but members of the family. There was some restriction because the boat was so powerful. Lots of other people did, but when the accident occurred, everyone thought I was behind the wheel. I was unconscious for a couple of days and by the time I came around and the police talked to me, my dad had told me what to say. I didn't want to, of course, but he convinced me it would look best for everyone. Especially Wynona. She was already blaming me for the accident because I was the reason she took the boat in the first place. And I felt guilty about the baby. For once I believed my old man and rather than cause more of a scandal, I went along with the story." He sighed. "For keeping my mouth shut so long, my dad finally paid me off." He motioned to the room around him. "With this."

She wanted to believe him, to trust him, but needed time to sort through his story, decide for herself what was fact and what was fiction. Slowly she pulled herself out of his embrace and asked a question that had been on her mind for years. "There were rumors, Hayden. Lots of them. You had a reputation." She eyed him thoughtfully. "A girl named Trish London."

"Hell."

Again a sick feeling. "You were involved with her?"

"Yes."

"And she was sent to stay in Portland with her sister to have your baby?"

"What?" His head snapped up and his eyes focused hard on Nadine. "There wasn't a baby. Dad gave her family money, true, but she left because her mother was unfit to care for her. Her older sister offered to give her a place to live and help her with college. Trish really didn't have a choice. She'd already been branded in this town, so she took off. Wrote me one letter. Trish and I had an affair, I won't deny it, but we were careful." He looked at her long and hard. "In fact, the only woman I haven't been careful with has been you. Until the past couple of weeks I never wanted children and I was damned careful to make sure that I didn't sire any."

His world was so different from hers. Money was and always would be the answer. He grew up learning that money could solve any problem. She heard his change of heart toward a family, but she wasn't sure she believed him. There was just so much to learn.... "What does Wynona want from you now?"

His lips curled in disgust. "What do you think?"

"Money."

"Right. The old man didn't leave her much and she

wants more, plans on suing his estate for what she considers her share."

So it all came down to money. And it always would. As long as Hayden was the rich boy, money would always rule his life.

She stood quickly. He reached for her but she drew away. Why was she prolonging this agony? Why didn't she just leave him now, break it off, save herself and her children any further heartache?

He drew her into his arms, but she resisted. "I think I should leave," she said again, her heart breaking into a thousand pieces.

"You don't believe me."

Fighting tears, she placed her hand along his jaw, felt the beard stubble in her palms and nearly broke down. "That's the problem. I do believe you. I believe that you're right. For the rest of your life you'll live in a world I can't begin to understand, a world run by money. You said you didn't want a wife and children and I said I didn't want a husband. However, there's no future for us. There's no reason to prolong this any further."

He touched her and she fell back a step. "Don't."

"Nadine, listen, I—"

"Shh." Placing a finger against his lips, she shook her head. "It's over, Hayden. It really never did exist. We can be happy now, knowing we fulfilled our childhood fantasies, but we can't expect this to go on indefinitely. You're planning to sell the mill, and what then?"

He didn't say a word, and she suddenly felt as cold as the bottom of the ocean. "Believe me, this is for the best." Turning quickly, she headed for the door, hoping to feel his hand on the crook of her elbow, silently praying that he'd grab her and tell her he couldn't live without her, dying with each step as she approached the door.

Finally she heard him move, heard his footsteps behind

her. Her heart leapt unexpectedly when she thought he would crush her to him and tell her that he wouldn't let her go.

Instead he said, "I think you'll need a ride."

HAYDEN KICKED HIMSELF for being such a damned fool. She'd only been gone eighteen hours and he was going out of his mind. Like an idiot, he'd decorated the house by himself and now he sneered at his attempts at Christmas spirit. The house with lights and tinsel and a tree near the fire was as cold as the feeling in the middle of his heart. All the decorations and lights and gifts in the world wouldn't make up for the emptiness he felt without her and the boys. He'd even bought gifts, wrapped them and placed them under the tree. For Nadine and her kids. Not that she'd want them.

He'd learned long ago that everything came with a price, and her price was his loss of freedom and a life in Gold Creek. The freedom part he could handle. The family part he surprisingly decided he would embrace. But Gold Creek and his father's sawmills? He could still sell them, of course, but that thought was beginning to sour his stomach and he didn't want to be a part of the "idle rich." No way. Selling out to Thomas Fitzpatrick or some other rich timber baron was the coward's way out.

He climbed into the Jeep and drove into town. Snow had been predicted, and the first flakes were starting to collect on the ground. Good. It didn't matter if the whole damned lake froze over. Hayden couldn't get any colder.

The Silver Horseshoe wasn't very crowded on the twenty-third of December. A few of the regulars hung out at the bar, several younger guys played pool and Hayden recognized a few faces. Erik Patton, who worked at the mill, was huddled over a mug of beer, a cigarette burning in the ashtray beside him. Ed Foster, who had recently retired from the coaching staff at Tyler High, was nursing a tall one, and Patty Osgood Smythe gave him the once-over as he approached the bar. There were other people there, as well, men who seemed to bristle when he slid onto his stool. In the mirror behind the bar, he caught a few hard glances cast his way and knew that some of these men and women were dependent upon him for their livelihoods.

He ordered an ale, nibbled at peanuts and wondered what life would be like if he settled down in Gold Creek for good. What if he buried the past, made peace with his father and took over the helm of the sawmills? He could go through the company books, make restitution where it was necessary. If other people had been swindled by his father, maybe there was something that could be done. Better late than never.

He could run the mills. He had the education and the experience. What he didn't have was the employees behind him. That would take time. No one really trusted him.

A gust of cold wind followed a newcomer into the bar. Hayden glanced over his shoulder and spied Ben Powell, Nadine's older brother, as he sauntered in. His dark hair cut military-short, Ben surveyed the room in one glance, caught sight of Hayden and froze. "I figured you were back," he said, his features hard, his hazel eyes cold. "I heard that your father had died."

"That's right."

"Running things, are you, now?"

Hayden nodded. "Let me buy you a beer."

Ben's mouth twisted into a mirthless grin. He reached into his pocket and threw a couple of bucks onto the polished counter. "I don't want any of your money, Monroe." To the bartender, "Give me a draft—anything you've got on tap." Leaning closer to Hayden, Ben said, "Well, I'm back, too. For good. So just stay out of my way."

"Might be hard."

Ben's eyes narrowed.

"Why's that?"

"Because I'm going to ask your sister to marry me."

"You're what?" Ben asked, paling a little.

"You heard me."

Ben's reactions were quick. With skill learned in the army, he hauled back and landed a right cross to Hayden's face. Hayden's head snapped back, but he heard the rip of cartilage and felt blood gush from his nostrils as he stumbled against the bar.

A woman screamed as all eyes in the bar turned toward the two men squaring off.

Quickly he was on the balls of his feet, spoiling for the fight. It would do him good to hit something, and Ben's angular face seemed a ready target. "Come on," he taunted, "brother."

"You bloody son of a bitch!" Ben came at him again, and Hayden sidestepped the blow.

The bartender vaulted over the bar. "Enough. You're outta here, mister," he said to Ben, but Hayden waved and found a cocktail napkin to staunch the flow of his blood. "Don't you two know anything about the Christmas spirit?"

"Outside!" Ben demanded, but Hayden only laughed.

"It's over," he said to the bartender. "Let me buy this man a drink. Hell, I'll buy a round for everyone."

The bartender hesitated, but the small crowd in the bar cheered, and Hayden felt that for the first time since he'd returned to Gold Creek, he was beginning to belong. Still eyeing Ben, the bartender started pouring drinks.

Ben's expression was thunderous; his eyes narrowed in fury. He grabbed his glass of beer and poured it slowly onto the floor. Without bothering to pick up his change, he turned on his heel and left.

"Who was that guy?" the bartender asked.

"Someone with a grudge," Hayden said. "And it's only going to get worse." Just wait until Ben found out that he and Nadine had been sleeping together. All hell was bound to break loose. Hayden grinned. Ben wouldn't make such a bad brother-in-law.

"You did what?" Ben roared, his face florid, his hands balled into tight fists of rage.

Standing at the dining room table, Nadine smoothed the foil wrap around a game that she'd bought for John. Christmas cookies were baking in the oven, and the exterior lights glowed in the falling snow. If not for Ben's bad mood and her heartache over Hayden, this Christmas could be the best one in a long, long while. "I said I went out with Hayden last night," she repeated, unnerved by the fire in Ben's eye. She'd been happy to find him in the house, waiting for her, his duffel bag stuffed in a corner of the living room. But he'd come at her like a tiger.

"You've been seeing him again? Damn, what do you think you're doing?" Ben strode in front of the fireplace, his back stiff, his eyes flashing with anger. "Does Dad know?"

"Yes," she replied sweetly. "And he's given me his blessing, just like you."

"But Monroe—"

"Stop it, Ben! You can't walk back into my life and start big-brothering me all over again. I'm a grown woman, for God's sake. I take care of myself and my children, and you have no right, no right whatsoever, to tell me what to do or start second-guessing my judgment. Besides—" she taped the package and worked on the bow, avoiding his eyes "—I think it's over. I left his place and it was pretty much understood that we wouldn't see each other again."

He opened his mouth to say something, thought better of it and leaned a shoulder against the mantel. "Good—just remember what that bastard and his father did to this family."

Her head snapped up and she pinned him with a glare meant to cut steel. "I haven't forgotten, Ben, but it's time to bury the past, don't you think?"

"Never."

"It's Christmas."

"So I've heard," he said cryptically.

"Well, I've at least come to terms with what happened. You'd better, too."

"Why? So you can marry the bum?"

Her spine stiffened. "No. It's over with Hayden."

"You wouldn't do anything as stupid as marry him, right?"

"Marry him?" she repeated, her heart tugging. "I don't think you've got to worry about that."

He rubbed the back of his neck uneasily. "He hasn't asked you?"

Her heart thudded painfully. "It won't happen, Ben. Don't worry about it." The bell on the stove rang softly, indicating that the cookies she was baking were done. She left the package to take out one sheet of apple squares and shove in another of pumpkin bars.

The house smelled of warm cinnamon and nutmeg, fragrant pine and bayberry candles. A fire blazed in the hearth; the Christmas tree glowed warmly in the corner, its lights reflecting in the windows. Everything was perfect, except the house seemed empty. Even with Ben here. The boys were still with Sam, and Hayden... God only knew where he was and what he was doing. She glanced out the window, past the snow falling upon the dark waters of the lake to the pinpoints of light she knew were burning from the Monroe home.

She didn't hear Ben approach. His voice startled her. "More snow's been predicted. Looks like we might have a white Christmas."

A lonely white Christmas, she thought, burning herself on the hot cookie sheet as she brushed up against it. "Hmm."

Ben found a knife and cut himself a gooey apple square.

"Help yourself," she said, teasing, as she handed him a napkin. "Milk's in the fridge. Or I can make coffee—"

He waved away her offer. "Don't bother." When she glanced through the window again, he said, "You're really hung up on that bastard, aren't you?"

"I told you I'm not seeing him again. I told him so tonight." Glancing back at him, she saw the ghost of a smile touch his thin lips. "But if I change my mind, I expect you to keep your mouth shut about it."

Ben smiled coldly. "You always did have a way with words."

"So did you. Now, come on, make yourself useful. I bought new bikes for the boys, and you can put them together. I'll even make you something to eat. Something more than cookies."

"I'm not all that hungry. I'll just have another one of these—" he said, and winced as he grabbed the knife. For the first time she noticed that the knuckles on his right hand were swollen. "What happened to you?" she asked, and he cut another bar from the pan.

"I, um, had a little altercation down at the Silver Horseshoe."

"A fight? You've been in town less that twenty-four hours and you've already been in a fistfight? Didn't you learn anything while you were in the army?"

"The guy had it coming."

"Oh. Okay, sure," she said sarcastically as she peered into the oven. "Who was the guy and what did he do?"

Ben didn't say a word, just looked at her and she knew. Her heart sank. Her brother had rolled into town, run into Hayden and promptly tried to punch out his lights.

"You already saw Hayden? That's how you found out about us?" she said, sick at heart. "What happened?"

"He tried to buy me a drink."

"And you hit him. Nice, Ben. Real nice."

"He had it coming," he said, rubbing his wounded hand with his fingers. "Has had for years."

Nadine shook her head. One part of her wanted to run to Hayden, to see that he was all right. The other wanted to slap her older brother across his self-righteous chin. "So you took it upon yourself to defend my honor."

Ben rubbed his jaw and for the first time seemed slightly contrite. "I couldn't help it, Nadine. The bastard said something about marrying you."

BEN'S WORDS HAD stuck with her. *Marriage? Hayden was talking about marriage?*

She couldn't still the beat of her heart, and expected him to show up on her doorstep. But he didn't. Nor did he call. Nadine was beginning to think that Ben hadn't heard Hayden correctly or that Hayden had been teasing Ben, just to get a rise out of him.

She considered calling Hayden, but didn't. Nothing had really changed. Though Hayden had mellowed a little on his stance about children, he still didn't want to be tied down. Never had, never would. He'd said as much.

Nadine slept restlessly, thinking of Hayden, and Ben left early the next morning to spend the day looking for an apartment he could rent, as well as visit their father.

Nadine kept herself busy cooking and cleaning,

wrapping a few presents and putting the finishing touches on the house. By the time the boys arrived home, she wanted everything to be perfect. She glanced across the lake more times than she could count and found herself listening for the whine of Hayden's Jeep's engine.

The phone rang and she nearly jumped out of her skin. She answered with a breathless hello and was disappointed when Sam told her he was running a little late; he and the kids were at a Christmas party and he'd bring the boys home a little later.

"When?" Nadine asked.

"Does it matter? There's no school tomorrow."

"I know, but—"

"Don't worry, Nadine. They'll be home in a little while."

A few hours later, Sam was true to his word. He brought the boys into the house and dropped their overnight bags in the middle of the living room. His face was red and his eyes a little glazed from too much partying. Snow melted off his boots and clung to his collar.

"Hey, Mom, there's already presents under the tree!" Bobby said, his eyes as round as saucers.

"A few from me."

"Any from Monroe?" Sam asked, his eyes as cold as the December storm.

Bobby was already checking the brightly colored packages. "Santa's still gonna come, isn't he?"

"You bet. I baked some cookies today and you and I will make a special batch tomorrow."

"Aw, Mom, there's no such thing as—" John started to protest, but Nadine cast him a sharp look that shut him up.

Sam lingered, taking in the cozy room and frowning. "The boys say you're pretty thick with Monroe."

"We've seen a little of each other."

He lifted his hat and rubbed his head. "You might as well know that I don't approve."

"I figured that," she said, bristling.

"And don't tell me it's none of my business."

"What I do with my life—"

"I'm talkin' about the kids, damn it. They're seeing entirely too much of the guy." Sam was getting angry, and the drinks he'd obviously consumed had begun to affect his speech. He waved one arm wildly to make his point. "That son of a bitch is gonna close the mills—"

"He wouldn't do that, Dad," John said.

"What would you know about it?"

"I like him. He's a good guy."

"What he is," Sam said, weaving a little, "is a no-good, pampered rich bastard, and I don't like him buying fancy things for my boys."

"It's not like that, Dad," John argued.

"You back-talkin' me?" Sam asked, lunging a little as he caught John by the collar.

"Let go of him!" Nadine stepped in front of her son as if to use her body as a barrier. "Don't you dare lay a hand on him," she warned.

But Sam was suddenly mad at the world. "You're too easy on the kids. Git out of my way." He tried to push Nadine aside, but she held her ground.

"You'd better leave."

"Why?" He rolled back on his heels and smiled sickly. "So you can entertain your rich boyfriend?"

"That's enough!"

Sam's glazed eyes narrowed in hatred. "So have you given it to him yet? You always wanted to. Don't think I didn't know it. Every time we were in bed, you were thinking about him, imagining that I—"

"Stop it!" she cried, marching to the door and opening

it. Cold wind crept in and the fire stoked higher. "Go on, Sam. Go sleep it off."

"I think I'll stay here. Too dangerous for me to drive."

"I'll call someone."

"Come on, Nadine. Let me stay. For old times." His grin turned into a leer and he started for her, but tripped on the edge of the rug. "Goddamn it," he said, reaching for anything to keep his balance. He stumbled over the coffee table, caught hold of the branch of the tree and grabbed on, but the little Christmas tree was no match for his weight. It toppled to the floor and one branch fell into the fireplace. With a rush of air, the dry needles ignited and flames consumed them.

"Oh, God! Sam, watch out! Boys, get out quick!" Nadine cried, and when her sons stood immobile, she screamed. "Now! Outside, run over to the Thornton's, have them call the fire department!"

Trying to get free of the tree, Sam was screaming. Both boys took off through the front door and Hershel gave chase. Nadine ran to the kitchen, grabbed the fire extinguisher and started spraying, but it was too late, the fire had caught on the rug and curtains. Flames leapt high in the tree and though Sam was free, his clothes were on fire. He was screaming horribly.

She didn't hear him arrive, but suddenly Hayden was there, shouting orders, yelling at her to go outside to the lake, kicking at the tree with his boots and dragging a writhing Sam from the conflagration.

Adrenaline pumped through Nadine's bloodstream, she grabbed a photo album and her purse from a table, and then she, in horror, helped Hayden drag Sam outside, down the rise in the ground, toward the lake. They yanked off his clothes, leaving him in his underwear. His screams filled the night and snow melted on his skin.

Nadine glanced frantically around for her boys in

the darkness, but they and the dog had disappeared and her little cottage, her pride and joy, the only possession she held dear had become an inferno and reflected in bloodred shadows on the snow.

"You're gonna be all right," Hayden said to Sam.

"Help me. God Almighty, help me."

"Help's coming." Hayden took Nadine's hand. "Stay with him but give me your keys."

"My what—?" But she was already digging through her purse. In the distance, she heard the first wail of a siren.

Hayden stripped the keys from her shaking hands and ran toward the house. She screamed at him until she saw him climb into her little Nova, back the car as far from the conflagration as possible and park.

"Oh, God," she whispered, still searching the night for her children. "John? Bobby? Please, please—" They wouldn't have run back into the house, would they? Searching for her, the boys wouldn't have gone into the kitchen through the back door?

Terror squeezed her heart and she heard Sam moan. Dropping to her knees she tried to hold his hand and comfort him, keeping snow against his skin as she searched the darkness.

Hayden jogged back to her as the first window exploded.

"Oh, God—the boys?" she cried.

"They'll be fine," he said, wrapping her in his arms and kissing her forehead. "Thank God. Just hang in here. Be strong." In a second he released her and was bending over Sam. "Help will be here soon." And for the first time Nadine realized how close Sam had come to death. She heard her children running along the shoreline with the neighbors, and thankfully Jane Thornton, a nurse who worked at the county hospital and lived on the south shore of the lake was with them. She immediately tended to Sam as Nadine gathered her boys close.

Flames shot through the dry roof of the house, flickering red fingers reaching hellishly toward the black night sky, and tears began to fall from Nadine's eyes. Everything was gone. Everything she'd worked for, every possession she'd held dear.

"You're safe now," Hayden whispered into her ear.

"But the cabin—"

"It can be rebuilt."

"No, I—everything's in there—"

"Not everything," he said, his voice rough, tears glistening in his eyes. "You've got me. And the boys. Forever."

She glanced up at him, hardly daring to believe him.

Sirens wailed closer. Firelight shone in his eyes. The stench of smoke filled the air. Trucks with firemen rolled into the yard. An ambulance slid to a stop and paramedics quickly took over, helping Sam. Within minutes they'd taken him to County Hospital after assuring Nadine that he would survive.

She watched for over an hour as the firemen doused the flames and her cabin was reduced to a dripping, blackened skeleton.

When the firemen finally left, tears drizzled from her eyes. "It's gone," she whispered. "It's all gone."

Hayden held her tighter. "I came here to ask you to be my wife, Nadine, and when I saw you in the fire, that there was a chance I could lose you, I...I knew I'd never live without you. Marry me." He kissed her on the lips. "Please. Tell me you'll be my wife."

"I—"

"I love you," he said, and his face was serious with emotions that burned deep in his soul. "Make this Christmas our first as a family."

She laughed and cried at the same time. Relief mingled with happiness as snow settled on the remains of a cottage where she'd brought her children into the world, suffered through her divorce and made love to Hayden.

Her gaze drifted over his shoulder, past the dark depths of Whitefire Lake to the lights glowing in the distance. Her new home. With Hayden.

Her throat so thick she could barely speak, she gathered her boys close. "I guess we get to start over," she said, her eyes shining as she stared into Hayden's eyes. "Of course I'll marry you."

EPILOGUE

FROM THE LANDING on the stairs of her new home, Nadine tossed her bridal bouquet to the crowd gathered in her foyer. A scream of delight went up when Carlie Surrett caught the flowers.

Half the town had been invited to the hastily planned wedding, including the Surretts, in an attempt to mend all the old rifts. A pianist was playing love songs on the baby grand in the living room and guests mingled and danced, talked and laughed and sipped champagne.

As she descended toward the crowd, Nadine spied Hayden, dressed in a black tuxedo, his eyes as blue as a summer morning. "It seems to be some pagan tradition that we dance," he whispered into her ear.

Nadine smiled up at him. In the living room, they started the dance, with a crowd of onlookers watching. Tiny white lights were strewn in the potted plants and twelve-foot Christmas tree in the corner. Eventually, one by one, other couples followed their lead. Heather Brooks, draped in shimmery pale blue, danced with Turner, who, dressed in a Western-cut black suit, his blond-streaked hair unruly as ever, winked broadly at Nadine. "I get the next dance," he said, and Hayden grinned. "Not on your life."

Rachelle and her husband, Jackson Moore, took a turn about the floor and Rachelle's hazel eyes were full of a secret only a few people knew. In the spring, she and Jackson would become parents. She laughed up at her husband and he held her with a possession that bordered upon fierce.

"Everyone's happy," Hayden said.

"Mmm." Even her father, sitting in the corner chair, was talking and laughing with Ellen Little, Heather and Rachelle's mother, and Nadine's heart warmed.

Only Ben seemed out of place. Grudgingly, he'd accepted Hayden as his brother-in-law. Since Hayden had decided to stay in Gold Creek and run the sawmills he'd inherited, not as his father had from a distance, but here, as a citizen of the town, Ben had decided he might turn out all right.

The fact that Hayden approved of his new wife's career and was willing to help her get started with her wearable art had convinced Ben that Hayden wasn't all bad.

Even John and Bobby were having a good time, though John spent entirely too much time at the punch bowl with Katie Osgood.

The music changed, and Hayden drew his wife through the French doors to the back deck. "Hey... What?" she asked, as he led her, running through the snow and dark night, down a lighted path to the shores of the lake. "Are you crazy?" she cried, as he pulled her to the ground and her dress was suddenly wet from the snow.

With a devilish grin, he scooped up a handful of the icy water and held it to his bride's lips. "Drink," he ordered, "and let the God of the Sun or whatever bless us."

"I think he already has." She sipped the water from his hands and looked deep into his eyes. "You're going to be a father."

"I'm what—?"

"John and Bobby won't be the only children," she said, and watched as he blinked rapidly.

"Oh, God."

"Happy?"

In answer, he drew her into his arms and kissed her long and hard, but she pulled away, and giggling, offered him a scoop of lake water.

"Don't be greedy," she said, as he touched his lips to her palm and the water dripped through her fingers.

"Me?" His blue eyes sparked with an inner fire and his fingers twined in her hair, dragging her face to bare inches from his own. "There's only one thing on this earth I can never get enough of, lady," he vowed, his voice growing gruff with conviction, "and you may as well know that one thing is you."

His lips found hers, and as an owl hooted softly in the trees, Nadine was certain she heard the ghosts of the lake whisper their blessing on the rich boy of Gold Creek.

* * * * *

HE'S MY SOLDIER BOY

PROLOGUE

Whitefire Lake, California
The Present

PROLOGUE

CARLIE SURRETT!

That woman had been the bane of Ben Powell's existence for over eleven years and he'd thought…no, he'd *vowed* he would never lay eyes on her again.

"Yeah, and you're a damned fool," he said to himself as he brushed off the snow that had collected around his collar. Still cursing his luck, he yanked open the door of his secondhand pickup and reached inside. A six-pack of beer was on the worn seat, and he slipped one of the longnecks from the carton. With a frown, he opened the bottle by placing the edge of the cap on a rusted fender and snapping down hard—a trick he'd learned ages ago when he'd first enlisted. The cap spun off into a snowbank and foam spewed over the lip of the bottle to run down his fingers as he lifted the beer to his mouth and took a satisfying pull.

Why couldn't he get Carlie out of his mind?

Muttering oaths under his breath, he kicked the door shut and stared at the rubble that had been his sister Nadine's lakeside cabin. Once charming, the cottage was now only twisted black metal, charred beams and a sagging soot-covered chimney. Ash and debris. Nothing worth saving.

Nadine had asked him to rebuild it. His eyes narrowed on the snow drifting on the cold pile of ash. Did she really want to give him a job or was her offer merely a handout to her only surviving brother, a man who had to start over in this shabby little town? After her wedding today, Nadine would be able to build a damned palace on this side of the lake. She could hire a bevy of architects, builders, and yes-men who would bow and fawn over the new Mrs. Hayden Garreth Monroe IV.

Damn! He should be pleased, he told himself. Nadine had struggled for years. But was marrying Monroe, that class-A bastard born with a silver spoon wedged firmly between his teeth, the break she deserved? Why not just sell her soul to the devil?

And why invite Carlie to the ceremony?

"Son of a bitch." Angry at himself and the world in general, Ben picked his way over the frozen path to the dock. His knee hurt like hell, compliments of embedded shrapnel from that skirmish in the Middle East, and his pride had been bruised and battered over the course of the past decade, starting over a decade ago in this very town. With Carlie Surrett. Beautiful, seductive, treacherous Carlie. She'd managed to destroy Ben's brother as well as rip Ben's world apart in the bargain.

And now he'd have to face her again. All because of his sister and her insistence that it was time to let bygones be bygones. "Thanks a lot, Nadine."

Through the snow swirling to the ground, he shot a glance across the angry gray waters of Whitefire Lake where lights glowed warmly from the windows of Monroe Manor—Hayden's mansion on the lake. Smoke curled lazily from the chimney and twinkling Christmas lights, still glowing though the holiday season was long over, glimmered in the gloomy day. *I hope you know what you're doing, Nadine,* he thought anxiously. She was the only person left in the world that he really cared about. He'd never forgiven their mother for turning her back on the family when the going got tough, and his father... well, the old man had never gotten over Kevin's death...

which brought Ben's thoughts back to Carlie again. Always Carlie. He scowled darkly, then took another long swallow from his bottle.

A north wind, raw as January, blew across the choppy surface of the water and sliced through his dress uniform.

Today was the big day—the day of reckoning, or rejoicing, of ignoring decade-old feuds and, in Ben's opinion, of doom. He should be on his way to the wedding, but he couldn't stomach all the small talk, gossip and curious stares his presence was bound to inspire. No, he'd wait until the last minute, then stand in the back and watch his sister make one of the biggest mistakes of her life.

He glanced at his watch. The ceremony was scheduled to start in less than an hour. His guts twisted just thinking about the fact that he'd probably see Carlie there. He'd been furious when Nadine had told him that Carlie was on the guest list.

"Are you out of your mind?" Ben had demanded of his sister. "It's bad enough you're going to marry Monroe—" He'd caught the mutinous set of his sister's jaw and held up a hand in surrender. "Sorry, Nadine, but I never did like the guy and you know it as well as I do. I'm not gonna stand here and tell you that all of a sudden I think he's a wonderful choice—"

"Enough, Ben," she'd warned.

He'd plowed on. "But if that isn't bad enough, you invite *Carlie Surrett?*"

"It's time to bury hatchets, Ben. All of them."

"You've really lost it, Nadine. First marrying Monroe, that's… Well, it's damned unbelievable. But inviting Carlie…"

"Just behave yourself," Nadine had said, her green eyes glittering with an impish light that meant she was scheming again.

"You don't have to worry about me. I'm the model of civility."

"Yeah, right. And I'm the pope. Save that one for someone who'll believe it."

She'd turned the conversation back to rebuilding the cabin. The topic of her wedding had been effectively closed and she was going to have her way come hell or high water. Ben, like it or not, would have to abide by her whimsical, *I'm-the-bride-and-I'll-do-as-I-damned-well-please* wishes.

So he was stuck. "Hell," he ground out. He didn't want to think about Carlie. Not now. Not ever. He'd planned on avoiding her the rest of his life. That woman was trouble. No two ways about it. Beautiful, headstrong, kick-you-in-the-gut trouble.

Telling himself that she probably had more sense than to show up at Nadine's wedding, he finished his beer. Certainly she wouldn't want to cause all the old speculation again. Or would she? Carlie Surrett had been a woman drawn to the spotlight, a woman the camera loved, a woman whose brush with celebrity, though fleeting, had been real.

Frowning, he slipped a small pair of binoculars from his pocket and held them to his eyes. Monroe Manor loomed larger than before. With snow clinging to the eaves, the three-storied Cape Cod looked like something from Currier and Ives.

Charming, he thought with a sardonic sneer. Well, he hoped his mule-headed sister knew what she was getting into by saying "I do" to the likes of Monroe.

Give it up, Powell! He's marrying her and she's happy. As for seeing Carlie again, you can handle it. Couldn't be much worse than what you went through in the action you saw in the Middle East. Or could it?

Ben allowed himself a grim smile. He'd willingly

return to combat rather than stare into Carlie's erotic blue eyes ever again.

Through the magnification of the binoculars, his gaze skimmed the banks of the lake, past frozen, empty docks, ancient sequoia trees, stumps and rocks to land on the shoreline by the old church camp. He saw a movement, a flash of deep blue and he adjusted the glasses.

His heart nearly stopped. His muscles tightened as she came into focus: a long-legged, beautiful woman staring across the water. Her black hair was braided loosely and coiled around the back of her head, but a few strands whipped across a face that was branded in his memory forever. She looked as if she could grace the cover of a fashion magazine in her long black coat, thrown open to reveal a gauzy blue dress that skimmed her ankles and offered a view of her elegant throat.

His fingers tightened over the binoculars as she turned, staring straight at him, her cornflower blue eyes as warm as a June day, her cheeks pink from the cold, her full lips glossy and turned pensively down at the corners. Drawing in a frozen breath, Ben waited for a wave of disgust to sweep through his blood, but instead of revulsion he felt a pang of regret for all the could-have-beens that would never be.

"Fool," he ground out, though he kept the field glasses to his eyes.

Model slender, she stood in heels, her long coat billowing in the breeze. She shivered and tightened the belt as snow melted against her cheeks and turned to jewellike drops in her ebony hair.

"Great." He forced the binoculars from his eyes. No doubt about it. From her getup it was obvious that she was going to the wedding. So much for hoping she had the brains or common decency to decline.

So, whether he liked it or not, he'd have to face her

within the hour in front of a hundred guests. His stomach knotted at the thought of his father and how the old man would react to seeing Carlie Surrett, the woman who, in George Powell's rather prejudiced estimation, had brought nothing but agony and disgrace to the family, the woman he blamed for the death of his first-born son.

There would be a scene and Nadine's wedding would be ruined. "Damn," Ben swore at the world in general. He knew what had to be done. It meant facing her alone. Dealing with the infamous Ms. Surrett would be best accomplished without a crowd of wedding guests peering over his shoulder and whispering behind his back.

It wasn't that he wanted to see her alone, he half convinced himself; he had no choice.

Jaw set, he stalked back to his battle-scarred pickup and climbed inside. Throwing the rig into reverse, he told himself that he was just going to talk to her and set her straight on a few things before they squared off at the wedding.

He owed it to his father. He owed it to Kevin. And most importantly, he owed it to himself.

CRAZY. THAT'S WHAT SHE WAS. *Certifiably nuts!* Showing up at Nadine Powell Warne's wedding to Hayden Monroe would be more than asking for trouble; she'd be begging for it!

Carlie shivered, rubbing her arms as she followed the snow-encrusted path that rimmed the rocky banks of the lake. Snowflakes caught in her lashes and her braid was loosening. She should just go to the wedding and get it over with or turn tail and run. Instead, she was out here, in the middle of nowhere, second-guessing herself.

This was all Rachelle's fault. Her best friend had insisted that Carlie put the past to rest and accept Nadine's olive branch to bridge the gap between the two families.

But it wasn't Nadine who worried Carlie. Nadine was happy, content with her life, ready to forgive and forget; that much was evident by the fact that she was marrying Hayden Monroe, a sworn enemy of the Powell family.

But Ben was a different matter. A different matter entirely. Carlie's heart squeezed a little when she thought of him, but she closed her mind to such traitorous thoughts. She'd see him today, try and be pleasant and that would be the end of it.

An icy blast of wind ripped through the thick wool of her coat and she shivered. The sounds of muffled traffic on the road winding around the perimeter of the lake reached her ears, and for a second she thought she heard the sound of a truck's engine much closer than it should have been, as if someone else had seen the open gates to the old church camp and pulled into the long-abandoned property. Silly. She was alone.

Her satin heels slid on the icy ground and she decided she should turn around, climb into her worn-out Jeep Cherokee and drive to Nadine's wedding where she belonged.

Ha! What a joke! *Where she belonged!* That was the problem. She didn't *know* where she belonged. It certainly wasn't in the town of Gold Creek, California, where she'd been born and raised, and it didn't take a genius to realize that she didn't really belong at Nadine's wedding where she'd have to see Ben again.

Her heart tripped a little and she bit down on her lip as she shoved aside a frozen cobweb dangling from a low-hanging pine branch. In her mind, she'd played the scene of meeting him again over and over again, silly fantasies of a love long dead. If it had ever existed at all.

A thorn caught on the sleeve of her coat as she walked along a curtain of cedar and spruce trees rimming the shore. She paused, extracting the barb.

On the day of Rachelle's wedding the lake had been blue and serene, the mirrorlike surface reflecting the mountains that spired above the timberline. But this afternoon, with the winter wind ripping through the ridge of peaks to the north, the gray water was whipped to an angry froth, whitecaps rising and falling above murky depths. Tiny particles of ice had begun to form in the water that lapped along the rocky banks and the low-lying clouds were a thick mist, the same mist that was a part of the old Native American legend.

The sight of the chilly water brought back memories. Some happy, others painful, all tracing back to her youth. It had been on these very shores where Carlie had first been kissed, where she'd tasted her first sip of wine, where she'd given away her virginity... She'd been young, naive, believing that she could someday change the world, trusting in true love and never once thinking that tragedy, shame and scandal could touch her.

Fool! Drawing in a cold breath, she remembered running away from the small town of Gold Creek with its narrow minds and wagging tongues. The comfort and security of her home had crumbled, turned to hostility and pain, and all the joy she'd felt growing up in this small community had disappeared. So she'd left and put time and distance between herself and the pain, tried to forget that she'd ever heard of the Powell brothers.

She'd run as fast and far as possible, to the bright lights and dazzle of Manhattan—to the noise, the bustle, the glitter—always hoping that she would leave the heartache and humiliation of this small Californian town behind her. Unfortunately the past had always been nipping at her heels. Dogging her. In New York. In Paris. In Alaska. The dark shadow of Kevin's death clung to her tenaciously, never far away, never to be lost, always clutching at her subconscious.

An icy blast of wind cut like a knife, and she shivered. If she'd learned anything in the past ten years it was that she could depend upon no one but herself and that she'd damned well better hold her head high.

A twig snapped. Carlie spun, quickly searching the undergrowth. Probably just an animal, but she couldn't stop the goose bumps from rising on her arms. She stared into the thickets of brush and trees, but saw no one. Skeletal berry vines clawed along the ground; oak trees, naked in winter, reached gnarled branches up to the steely sky; and overhead, a hawk circled in the falling snow, but no one appeared from the shadows of the trees.

Just your imagination, she told herself. *Just because you're back at Whitefire Lake and caught up in memories you should have buried a long time ago.* She turned, intent on hurrying back to the open area of the campground where she'd parked the Jeep. Her gaze landed squarely on the one man she had hoped to avoid.

Ben Powell.

A very real ghost of the past appeared on the shores of the lake. It was fitting, she supposed, and ironic. She tried not to gasp and managed what she hoped would appear a confident smile.

Dressed in his crisp military uniform, Ben Powell wasn't a man to fear, just as certainly as he wasn't a man to love. But he was definitely as hard and cruelly handsome as the pictures she'd tried not to conjure up in her mind for a long, long time.

His sensual lips were compressed into a firm, uncompromising line, and his face, honed by years in the army, was angular and stern; not a single trace of his boyish features—the features she'd held dear in her heart—remained. Eyes, beneath flat dark brows, snapped with unrestrained hostility, and Carlie wondered how in the world she'd ever thought she'd been in love with him.

Where was the kindness, the humor that had been such an integral part of the boy she'd once secretly hoped to marry?

He stood ramrod straight, his dress uniform starched, his cap square on his head, and he glared at her with undisguised hatred.

"All dressed up and no place to go?" he asked, his voice as sharp as the bite of the wind.

So much for pleasantries.

"I could say the same about you." Her gaze drifted from his shoulders to his spit-and-polished shoes.

His chest was still broad, his waist trim, his hips as lean as ever. He hadn't even had the decency to start to bald. His hair was as thick and coffee brown as it had been all those years ago and his eyes, hazel, shot with silver, could cut right to her soul.

"I don't suppose you came here to escort me to the wedding?" she asked, deciding to give as much as she got.

He snorted.

"I didn't think so." She rolled back the cuff of her coat and glanced at her watch. "We probably should get going. We're already late."

"I can't believe you were invited."

Echoes from the past rippled through her mind as an old memory surfaced and she thought of the first night she'd been with him. She swallowed hard and kept her mind on the present. She didn't think for a minute that Nadine wouldn't have told him her name was on the guest list. No doubt Ben's sister had warned him. So what was his game? "Believe it, Ben. I don't show up where I'm not wanted."

"That's not the way I remember it."

She felt the color drain from her face, but she inched her chin up a notch, refusing to give him an inkling that she remembered with crystal clarity the party she'd crashed, just to be with him. "Look, you don't have to pretend to like me—"

"I won't."

"Good. Then we're even," she lied, her pride ruling her tongue.

His lips tightened at the corners.

"Now all we have to do is endure your sister's wedding. We don't have to speak, touch or so much as look at each other. Then, after the reception, you can go your way and I'll go mine."

He rubbed the back of his neck and seemed to wrestle with something on his mind. "I just didn't happen to show up here," he said. "I was at Nadine's dock and I saw you through field glasses." The stubborn set of his jaw didn't alter. "You're right, I knew you were invited to the wedding, but I thought I should warn you."

"About what?"

He stared at her long enough that she was certain he'd studied every pore on her face.

"My dad won't appreciate your being there."

"Your dad didn't invite me."

"You're not wanted, Carlie."

That stung, but she wasn't a virgin in the pain department. "Not by you maybe, but—"

"Not by me ever."

The old wounds opened, but she wouldn't give Ben the satisfaction of knowing he still had the ability to hurt her. She shook her head and sighed. "I was hoping that it wouldn't be like this between us."

"It couldn't be any different."

"Why?"

"Because Kevin's dead, damn it. Don't you remember?"

"Every day of my life." She swallowed back that old, painful lump that filled her throat when she thought of Ben's older brother. "But—" she forced the words over her suddenly thick tongue "—nothing I can say or do will bring him back. We have to let it rest. Both of us."

He looked as if he planned to disagree. Shadows darkened his clear eyes and he quickly glanced away, past her, to the mountains rising in the distance. Seconds drummed by, punctuated by the silence that stretched between them. A tic throbbed near his temple and his jaw was clenched so hard, she wondered if his teeth were being ground into his gums. "I don't think we should talk about this," he said at length, but his voice was less harsh; the accusations in his eyes had faded.

"The way I remember it, you don't think we should talk about anything!"

"Fair enough."

"Good. Because we—or at least *I*—have a wedding to attend." The brisk air crackled between them and he didn't reply. Again, the silence was deafening and it was all she could do to stand her ground under his hard, uncompromising gaze. "Are you always this rude," she asked impulsively, "or did the army teach you how to be a jerk?"

"You just seem to bring out the best in me."

"I don't remember handing you an invitation to bulldoze your way over here and insult me. This time, Ben, you're doing the crashing." She turned, intent on leaving him, but he moved quickly, reaching out, his hand clamping firmly over her elbow. He spun her back to face him with such force that his cap fell into the snow. For a breathless second she remembered him as he had been: impetuous, young, bold, sought after by most of the girls who had attended Tyler High. And she, Carlie Surrett, had been flattered that she'd caught his attention—even if she'd had to chase him a little to get it.

His gaze settled on her mouth. The breeze seemed to die and they were alone. Two people, man and woman, lost in a swirl of snowflakes and icy air. In the span of a heartbeat she thought he might kiss her, and her lips felt suddenly dry. How could she even let one single memory of the love they once shared into her heart? It had all been so long ago.

"I'm surprised you're back," he said roughly, his eyes narrowing, his warm breath fogging in the cool air. "I heard you were married."

Her spine stiffened slightly. "For a while."

"Didn't last?" He raised a dubious black eyebrow. "I can't imagine why."

"Irreconcilable differences," she said, ignoring the little bit of pain that still remained when she thought about her short-lived marriage. "I believed in monogamy. He thought it was a drag."

Ben's skepticism was etched on his face, but she told herself she didn't care. What Ben Powell thought of her didn't matter. Squaring her shoulders, she was determined to change the subject. "What about you, Ben? What're you doing back in Gold Creek? Unless things have changed, there's no army base for hundreds of miles."

"I'm through with the military."

She eyed the buttons of his uniform, the medals decorating his chest. "Doesn't look that way."

"The wedding was news to me when I got back to town. Didn't have anything to wear. The trunk with my tux hasn't arrived yet."

So he still had a sense of humor—cynical though it was. And his eyes, angry and smoldering, were staring at her with an intensity that caused the chilly air to be trapped in her lungs.

She had to remind herself that she wasn't going to fall for his sex appeal again. Not now. Not ever. Quickly she yanked her arm from his. "We'll be late."

"You shouldn't go, Carlie. Not after what happened."

She felt like dying. All the old pain and shame ripped fresh holes in her heart.

"My old man, if he sees you…" Ben's brows drew together.

"He'll get over it," she said, though she didn't know if she was up to facing the censure and accusations in George Powell's eyes. "This is Nadine's day. If we're smart, none of us will do anything to spoil it."

Backing up, she nearly stumbled, then turned and strode briskly back to her vehicle. She could feel him watching her as she climbed into the Cherokee, twisted on the ignition and pumped the gas. The engine turned over and in a plume of blue exhaust, she drove away from the little campground by the lake, away from the ghosts of the old legend and away from Ben Powell, a man she'd loved with all of her naive heart and a man who had all but destroyed her.

Had it really been eleven years? A decade of carrying around a load of guilt she should have unstrapped long ago? She switched on the defroster, clearing the suddenly misty windshield.

"Forget him," she told herself angrily. He was wrong for her then, even more wrong for her now. Not that she wanted him—or any man for that matter. It had taken a while, but she'd grown up to be her own independent woman.

She wiped at the fog the old defroster couldn't make disappear. Her fingers came away from the windshield wet and cold. Forgetting Ben Powell was easier said than done. She'd already spent so many years trying and had obviously failed. Why else would she care what he thought of her?

Gritting her teeth, she took a corner a little too fast, the Jeep's tires skidded and spun and she slid into the oncoming lane. From years of practice negotiating the icy roads in Alaska, she turned into the slide and guided the Cherokee back to the right-hand lane. Her heart was pounding, her hands tight around the steering wheel and she couldn't help remembering Ben and how much she'd once loved him.

It had been summer when she'd crashed that party, a warm July night filled with the sound of crickets and thick with the scent of honeysuckle. She'd been young and reckless and anxious to experience all that life had to offer.

Because of Ben Powell. Ben with his irreverent smile, his intense hazel eyes and his promises.... Dear God, why couldn't she forget him? Why did just the sight of him inspire memories that she'd kept locked away in a dark corner of her heart and promised herself that she'd never open?

As an old Fleetwood Mac song about the chains of love filled the interior of her vehicle she hummed along.

Despite all Carlie's vows to herself, her mind circled backward in time to the hot summer nights that had changed the course of her life forever....

BOOK ONE

Whitefire Lake, California
Eleven Years Earlier

CHAPTER ONE

"MAYBE WE SHOULD turn back." Carlie gnawed nervously on the inside of her lip, but continued to paddle forward. She didn't usually second-guess herself, and she'd always been adventurous, but this time she questioned her own wisdom as she dipped her oar into the water and glanced over her shoulder to her friend, Brenda, paddling steadily at the stern of the small rowboat.

Dusk gathered lazily over the lake. Water skippers and dragonflies skimmed the clear surface and mosquitoes droned in the early-evening air.

"Turn back now? Are you crazy?" Brenda asked, clucking her tongue in disappointment. With springy red curls, freckles and eyes the color of chocolate, Brenda was new to Gold Creek, but she and Carlie were fast becoming friends. "This was your idea, remember?"

"Can't I change my mind?"

"Not now." Brenda shoved her oar into the water and threw her shoulders into her stroke. The small boat skimmed closer to their destination, an abandoned log cabin on the south side of the lake.

The Bait and Fish, lights glowing warmly from the windows, slid by. Flickering neon signs announcing favorite brands of beer stood in stark relief against the weathered old boards. In the distance, near the north shore, speedboats dragged water-skiers. Carlie recognized Brian Fitzpatrick at the helm of a racing silver craft that rimmed the shoreline and left a thick rippling wake over which an experienced skier, probably Brian's younger sister, Toni, was balanced on one ski.

"What a life," Brenda said dreamily as she glanced at the sleek speedboat.

"You'd want to be a Fitzpatrick?" Carlie shook her head. "With all their troubles?"

"They've got *soooo* much money."

"And *soooo* many troubles. Haven't you heard about the root of all evil?"

"So, let me sin a little."

Carlie laughed, enjoying the breath of a breeze that fanned her face and lifted her hair off her shoulders. Though the sun had set in a blaze of gold and pink behind the mountains, the July air was hot and sticky.

Their destination loomed ahead, a thicket of pines surrounding an ancient cabin with rotting, weather-beaten shingles for a roof and rough log walls. No one knew who owned the property, but the single acre was referred to as the "old Daniels's place" by most of the people in town. Jed Daniels built the cabin for his bride just before the turn of the century, and successive generations of Daniels' kin had used the place as a summer cottage. Eventually the Daniels family was spread too far and thin to keep up the house, but if the place had ever been sold, no one in town talked of it.

Carlie eased the rowboat to the old dock of weathered pilings and broken boards. Though the house was dark, music and laughter drifted through the broken, boarded-up windows, and she recognized an old song by the Rolling Stones.

She bit her lower lip and worried it over her teeth. What was it about her that was always seeking out adventure or "looking for trouble," as her father had so often said?

"She's just curious, nothing wrong with that." Her

mother, Thelma, had quickly defended her only child on more than one occasion. "She's got a quick mind and she gets bored easily."

"Dreamin', that's what she's doin'. Thinkin' she can become some hot-damn New York model. Where I come from that's called being too big fer yer britches," Weldon Surrett had stated as he'd sat at the kitchen table smoking a cigarette.

"Where you come from, a six-pack of beer and a deck of cards were considered big-time," her mother teased gently, then adjusted the skirt of her uniform and kissed her husband on the cheek. "See you after my shift." Thelma had always been defensive of Carlie. Sometimes she went too far and was overprotective. Carlie blamed it on the fact that her mother couldn't have any more children. A hysterectomy one year after Carlie's birth had denied Thelma the large family she'd always wanted. Consequently, Thelma had poured all her motherly affection, concern and love onto her only child. If it weren't for the fact that Thelma's job at the Rexall Drugstore in town kept her busy, she would surely have suffocated Carlie with all her good intentions long ago.

"This is the place?" Brenda asked skeptically as she eyed the dilapidated cabin.

"Uh-huh."

"You sure you heard right?"

"Positive."

"And Ben Powell will be here?" Brenda lifted a doubtful eyebrow.

"I heard him talking to his brother," Carlie said as the boat rocked softly against the dock. She'd run into Ben and Kevin at the new video store that had opened up near the supermarket. The boys had been arguing about which movie to rent when Kevin had looked up and caught her staring at them. Carlie felt a little jab of guilt when she remembered the spark of interest in Kevin's eyes when he'd caught her gaze.

Kevin was older than Ben and had spent a year away at college before Kevin's grades had slipped and the money had run out for his education. Now he was working at Monroe Sawmill and was unhappy with his life. He and Carlie had dated several times, but then she'd stopped seeing him. Kevin was seven years older than she, and was much too serious and possessive. By the third date, Carlie had known that their relationship was doomed. He began calling twice a day, demanding to know where she'd been, jealous of her friends and the time she'd spent away from him. After three lousy dates!

She'd never really broken up with him because they'd never really gone together; she'd just stopped going out with him. He spent a lot of his time at the Buckeye Restaurant and Lounge, drinking beer and watching sports on television through a smoky haze as he relived his own days of glory as one of the best basketball players to ever graduate from Tyler High School.

Carlie shuddered, thinking of Kevin. Too many times he'd wanted to touch her, kiss her, get her alone. They hadn't had one thing in common and she probably didn't have much more with Kevin's younger brother, Ben.

So what was she doing here? Crashing a party because of Ben Powell, Kevin's younger brother? *Boy, Carlie, you are looking for trouble!*

She tied the boat to one of the sturdier pilings, walked carefully across the bleached boards and hiked along a weed-choked path to the broad front porch, where an old rocking chair swayed slightly with the breeze. The sound of voices grew louder, some from inside the house, others from around back, but a heavy chain and padlock on the front door suggested they find another entrance.

"I'm starting to have second thoughts about this,"

Brenda admitted. "It's kind of creepy, you know. Aren't there laws about criminal trespass and breaking and entering?"

"I thought you didn't want to turn back!" Carlie, too, was torn. She remembered another party, less than a year before, when a group of kids were gathered at the Fitzpatrick house on the other side of the lake. Things got out of hand and Roy Fitzpatrick, the golden boy of Gold Creek, heir to the Fitzpatrick fortune, had been killed.

Jackson Moore was suspected and arrested for the crime, but Carlie's best friend, Rachelle Tremont, had given Jackson the alibi he needed to avoid being indicted. Jackson had walked away from jail a free man, but he'd left town, leaving Rachelle with a soiled reputation and a broken heart.

The aftermath of the party had been devastating, but now, even remembering the hell the Fitzpatricks and Tremonts had gone through, Carlie still couldn't turn around. The lure of seeing Ben was greater than her fear of being caught breaking some kind of minor law. She walked off the porch and took an overgrown trail of flagstones toward the back.

Why she was so attracted to Ben, she didn't know. He should be the one boy in town to avoid, considering the fact that he was Kevin's younger brother. But everything about Ben appealed to her—his rugged good looks, his easy, slightly cynical smile, his open irreverence for all things monetary.

Shorter and more compact than Kevin, Ben wasn't quite six feet, but he was more muscular and his hazel gaze seemed to burn right into her soul. So here she was, acting like a sneak thief, sticking her nose where it didn't belong and stepping around the corner to…*nearly run right into him.*

She gasped and Brenda, walking behind her bumped against her backside.

Ben didn't seem the least surprised. Stripped to the waist, wearing faded Levi's with split knees, he stopped dead in his tracks. A bottle of beer dangled from his fingers and a slow, lazy smile spread across his beard-darkened jaw. "Carlie, right? Carlie Surrett?"

She nodded, her throat dry, her heart hammering.

"And I'm Brenda." Her friend stepped out of Carlie's shadow to introduce herself.

Ben seemed amused. His lips twisted upward a little and an intense spark of interest lighted his hazel eyes. Never, not for one second, did his gaze waver from hers.

Carlie swallowed hard and shoved a handful of hair over her shoulder. She suddenly felt awkward and wondered why she'd been so stupid as to come party crashing.

"Kevin isn't here," Ben said, taking a long pull from the beer. Carlie watched in fascination as he swallowed. Sweat trickled down his neck and his Adam's apple moved slowly.

"I didn't come looking for Kevin."

One dark brow shot up. "Who then?"

"Nobody," she lied and heard Brenda's sharp intake of breath. "I just, um, heard there was a party."

He leaned a palm against the rough sides of the building and moved his fingertips restlessly along one hand-hewn log. She noticed his tanned arms, the muscles of his shoulders, the veins bulging beneath his skin. "So this is what you do...crash parties?"

"I didn't know it was engraved invitation only."

He smiled at that. "We were just trying to keep it small. Avoid a fiasco like what happened at the Fitzpatrick place."

"No one knows we're here."

"No one?"

Brenda shook her head.

"You can trust us," Carlie said, wondering why she felt like baiting him.

"Can I?" His eyes narrowed a fraction. "Kevin seems to think you're his girl."

She felt the hackles on the back of her neck rise. "Kevin's wrong."

He took another swig from his beer. "So why he'd get the wrong information?"

"Look, I don't think it's a good idea to discuss—"

"Kevin got too serious," Brenda cut in. "Besides, he's too old for her." With a shrug she walked past Ben and Carlie. "I'll let you two work this out."

"There's nothing to work out," Carlie protested. Heat climbed up her neck and she was suddenly aware that coming here was a big mistake. "Look, maybe Brenda and I should take off."

"You just got here."

"I know, but—" She waved in the air.

"You weren't invited."

"Right."

"It doesn't matter." His gaze held hers and her mouth turned to cotton. The sounds of the night, deep croaks from hidden bullfrogs and the soft chirp of a thousand crickets, were suddenly muted. The fragrance of wild roses soon to go to seed, filtered over the acrid odor of burning wood and exhaust.

"Let's go check out the action. That's why you're here, aren't you?"

"Brenda and I were just taking a turn in the boat. We heard the music…." It was a little bit of a lie, but she couldn't admit the reason she'd shown up here was because of him.

"You want a beer?" His gaze was neutral, and yet she felt as if he were challenging her.

"I guess."

With a shrug, he turned and walked barefooted along the dusty path. Nervously, Carlie followed him to what had once been a backyard. Gravel had been strewn near a dilapidated garage, and several cars, pickups and motorcycles had been parked in the rutted lane. A stack of bleached cordwood partially covered with blackberry vines, seemed to prop up a sagging wall of the garage. Kids sat on bumpers of cars, on the drooping back porch or wandered into the house through an open door. A rusted lock was sprung and lay with an equally neglected chain that had slid to the floorboards.

"Who owns this place?" she asked.

"One of the guys here—" Ben took the time to point to a pimply-faced boy of about nineteen who was trying to build a fire in an old barbecue pit "—lives in Coleville and claims his uncle is the Daniels's heir who ended up with the cabin. He says the uncle is trying to sell it."

"And he doesn't care if your friend has a party?"

Ben slanted her a sly grin. "What do you think?"

"That the uncle doesn't have a clue."

"Smart girl."

Ben introduced her to some of the guests, most of whom were a little older than she was—kids who worked in the mill or the logging company or the Dari-Maid, some with full-time jobs, others who were spending their summer back in Gold Creek until they returned to college in the fall. She knew some of them of course, but there were a lot that she'd never seen before.

Brenda had already grabbed a beer and was trying to make conversation with Patty Osgood, the reverend's daughter. Patty was a couple of years older than Carlie, but already had enough of a reputation to turn her father's hair white, should the good reverend stumble upon the truth.

Patty sat on the edge of a stump, her long, tanned legs stretched out from shorts that barely covered her rear end and a white blouse knotted beneath her breasts. Her flat abdomen and a flirty glimpse of the hollow between her breasts left little to the imagination.

Patty wasn't a really bad girl, but she liked to flaunt the gorgeous body the good Lord had seen fit to bestow upon her—and hang the consequences. She'd dated a lot of boys in town, but now her eyes were on Ben.

"Well, well, well…" Erik Patton said when Carlie and Ben moved in his direction. Erik dragged on his cigarette and shot smoke out of the side of his mouth. "I didn't think you'd ever show your face at a beer bash again." Leisurely, he plucked a flake of tobacco from his tongue and eyed his friend, Scott McDonald. Both boys had been friends of Roy Fitzpatrick and believed Jackson Moore had killed Roy last fall. Most of the citizens of Gold Creek agreed, though Jackson had never been indicted. Only a few people in town believed in Jackson's innocence. Carlie belonged to that small minority and it obviously bothered Erik, who had given her a ride to the Fitzpatrick summer home on that fateful night.

Goose bumps rose on her arms. "I was just—"

"Save it, Surrett," Erik said through a cloud of smoke. "We were all there. We know what happened."

"Jackson didn't—"

"Oh, sure he managed to get Rachelle to claim they'd been together all night, but we all know that's a pile of crap. She just made up the story to give him an alibi."

"She wouldn't!"

"Sure she would." Erik let out a sigh of disgust. "She made it with him and she didn't even know him, did she? Face it, she's a slut."

"Shut up!" Ben ordered, but not before Carlie could lunge at Erik.

"Don't you ever—"

Ben grabbed her arm. "That's enough," he said with quiet authority aimed in Erik's direction. "Maybe you want to apologize."

"I just call 'em as I see 'em."

"Then you're blind!" Carlie said.

Eyes slitting as if he were sizing up the enemy, Erik glared at Ben but had the good sense to back down a little. "Forget it. Forget I said anything."

"That's more like it." Ben's gaze could have cut through lead and the smell of a fight filled the air.

Carlie could hardly breathe and she noticed that all conversation had died and a dozen pairs of eyes were trained on the two boys who were squaring off. She wanted to die a thousand deaths. "Leave Carlie alone, Patton," Ben said loudly enough so that everyone got the message. "She's with me."

Erik flicked his cigarette into the gravel and ground the smoldering butt with the toe of his boot. "Your loss, man."

Ben's smile was crooked but self-assured. "I don't think so."

Carlie felt Ben's fingers tighten over her arm and her heart pumped a little faster.

Scott spit into the scrub oaks, his eyes dark with disgust. "You can have her," he muttered.

Embarrassment rushed up Carlie's neck as she remembered the pickup ride to the Fitzpatricks' lakeside cabin. She and Rachelle had ridden in the cab of Erik's truck and Carlie, because of lack of space, had been forced to sit on Scott's lap. She'd giggled and flirted with him, unaware that what was to happen that night would put her at odds with almost everyone in town—including Erik Patton and Scott McDonald.

She'd been naive then, younger and foolish and the thought that she'd actually been that close to Scott made her skin crawl.

She should have learned her lesson.

So what was she doing here hoping to catch Ben Powell's attention? Didn't she have enough trouble with Kevin?

The fingers clamped around her forearm didn't move and her skin tingled slightly. "You certainly know how to create a scene," he said quietly.

"Maybe I should leave."

With a lift of his shoulder, he let go of her arm. The warmth of his fingertips left soft impressions on her arm. "Up to you." His silver-tinged gaze touched hers and her throat caught for a second.

"We'll stay…for a while," she said, as the night closed around them and the fire cast golden shadows over the angles of his face. Someone had a portable radio, fiddled with the dial and the strong notes of "Night Moves" by Bob Seger wafted through the air.

"Good." Ben stuck close to her the rest of the evening, but he never touched her again and any little flame of interest in his eyes was quickly doused when he talked to her.

She listened to music, nursed a beer, talked to some of the kids and always knew exactly where Ben was, whom he was talking to and what he was doing. It was silly really, but she couldn't help the attraction she felt for him.

"He's interested," Brenda told her when it was near midnight and the party was breaking up.

"I don't think so."

"Definitely interested," her friend maintained. "He watched you when he didn't think you were looking."

"Really?" Carlie whispered just as Ben left a small group of his friends and approached the girls.

"Need a ride?" Ben slipped his arms through a faded denim shirt. He didn't bother with the buttons.

"We've got the rowboat," Carlie said, managing to hide her disappointment.

"It'll fit in the back of my truck." His gaze touched hers for just a heartbeat. "It's no trouble."

"I don't think—"

"We'd love a ride," Brenda cut in as she glanced at her watch. "There's no way we can row back to my house by curfew."

"But—"

Ben wasn't listening to any arguments. He followed them to the back of the house, waded into the thigh-deep water, dragged the rowboat to shore, then swung the small craft over his head. Lake water drizzled down his neck and the back of his shirt, but he didn't seem to notice.

"I don't think this is a good idea," Carlie whispered to her friend.

"You wanted to be with him, didn't you?" When Carlie didn't answer, Brenda gave her a nudge. "Go for it."

BEN SHOVED THE rowboat into the back of his father's truck and told himself he was an idiot. Why borrow trouble? Why take Carlie home?

Because you can't help yourself!

He now understood his brother's fascination with Carlie Surrett. Reed-slender, with thick black hair that fell to the middle of her back, high cheekbones, lips that always looked moist and eyes that sparked with a misty blue-green intelligence turned his insides to jelly. No wonder Kevin had been so hot for her. But it was over. Kevin had said so himself.

Ben might have felt guilty taking Carlie home a couple of weeks ago, but Kevin had sworn just the other night that he was over Carlie Surrett. They'd been down at the Silver Horseshoe, the local watering hole, tossing back a few beers after Kevin's shift at the mill.

"She's too much trouble, that one," Kevin had said, signaling the waitress for another round. "So I broke up with her and I found someone else."

"I thought you were in love with her. She's all you could talk about for…what…two or three weeks."

Kevin snorted. "We only went out a few times." He fished into his front pocket of his jeans for change and avoided his brother's intense stare. "'Sides, you and I know there's no such thing as love. All a big lie. Made up by women with their stupid ideas that they get from books and movies."

"You believe that?" Ben had known that Kevin had turned cynical over the years after losing his chance to play basketball in college, but he hadn't believed his older brother could be so hard-nosed and jaded. A few weeks ago, Kevin had been on cloud nine, talking about Carlie Surrett as if he intended to marry her. And now he thought love was just an illusion.

"Look at Mom and Dad," Kevin said, as if their parents' ill-fated union was proof of his opinion.

Ben scowled and picked at the label of his bottle. His parents, Donna and George Powell, after fighting for years had separated and were now divorced. The battles had started long ago and had always been about money—the kind of money the Monroes and Fitzpatricks had and the rest of the town didn't. For as long as Ben could remember, his family had been one of the many "have-nots" and this point only became crushingly clear when his father had lost all the family's savings on some lamebrained investment scheme concocted by H. G.

Monroe, owner of the sawmill for which George and Kevin worked, and one rich, mean son of a bitch.

"So who's the girl?" he asked his brother rather than think about the past. "The one who's replaced Carlie Surrett?"

Kevin's lips turned down. "No one replaced Carlie," he said defensively as a buxom waitress, wearing a skirt that barely covered her rear, left two more bottles on the glossy mahogany bar. In one swift motion, she emptied the ashtray and quickly picked up the crumpled bills Kevin cast in her direction. "Keep the change," he said with a smile that invited trouble.

"Thanks, sugar."

"No problem."

The waitress moved through the smoke to a table in the corner. Kevin took a long swallow from his bottle. As if they'd never been interrupted, he said, "I'm seein' a girl named Tracy. Tracy Niday from Coleville. Ever hear of her?"

Ben shook his head and Kevin seemed relieved.

"Is she nice?"

"Nice? Humph. I'm not lookin' for nice." Kevin's eyes darkened a shade. "But she's…simple. Doesn't have big dreams of goin' to New York, becoming a model or some such bull. She's just happy that I take her out and show her a good time."

"And Carlie wasn't?"

"No way. No how." Kevin scowled and reached into the pocket of his flannel shirt for his pack of cigarettes. "Carlie has big plans—thinks she's gonna be some hot-damn model or somethin'. Didn't want to be tied down to Gold Creek and…oh, hell, she was a load of trouble. I'm better off without her." He lit up and shot a plume of smoke out of the corner of his mouth. "If you ask me, she was all screwed up over that Roy Fitzpatrick murder.

Her and that friend of hers—Rachelle Tremont—are both more trouble than they're worth."

And that had been the end of the conversation about Kevin's love life. Ben hadn't believed that his brother was truly over Carlie and so he'd questioned her when he'd first found her climbing out of the boat at the dock. But her story had been close enough to Kevin's to convince Ben that they weren't seeing each other anymore.

He watched as she wiped her hands on the front of her shorts. "Hop in," he said, opening the driver's side of the pickup and wondering why he felt a twinge of relief knowing that Kevin wasn't interested in Carlie any longer. He and Kevin had never dated the same girls— there seemed to be an unwritten law between them when it came to going out and heretofore maintaining their silent code hadn't been a problem. Kevin was a few years older than Ben, and no conflicts had arisen. Until Carlie. Until now.

Carlie was the youngest girl Kevin had ever taken out, and, without a doubt, the most gorgeous. He noticed the shape of her buttocks and the nip of her waist as she slid onto the old seat of the truck. He didn't question that she could become a successful model and he didn't blame her for wanting to taste more of the world than Gold Creek, California, had to offer.

He wanted to get out of town himself.

He rammed the truck into gear. "Where to?" he asked the girls.

"My place," Brenda said quickly. "It's a little ways from the old church camp."

"Just point me in the right direction." Ben shoved the Ford into first and the truck bounced along the rutted lane. Near a dilapidated mailbox, he turned south on the county road that rimmed the lake. Carlie reached for the radio, but Ben shook his head. "Hasn't worked for a few months now," he said, his fingers brushing her bare leg as he shifted into third. His fingers skimmed her thigh and he felt a tightening in his gut.

Carlie felt the touch of his fingers, and her skin tingled. She pretended to stare out the dusty windshield, but she watched him from the corner of her eye. He squinted slightly as he drove and the planes of his face seemed more rugged in the dark cab. He was dark and sexy and dangerous.

The porch light was burning at Brenda's old farmhouse. Ben unloaded the rowboat, and, following Brenda's instructions, propped the boat against the side of a concrete-block shed. "Thanks for the ride," Brenda sang out as she ran up the cement walk. "I'll talk to you tomorrow, Carlie!" She dashed up the steps and disappeared into the house as Ben climbed behind the wheel.

"Now where?" he asked, glancing in her direction and noting that she'd moved to the far side of the cab, as if she didn't want to chance touching him.

"I live in town. The Lakeview Apartments on Cedar Street—one block off Pine."

"I've been there." He slashed her a smile that was white in the darkness and caused her heart to flip.

"Then you know there's no lake and no view." She relaxed against the worn cushions and rolled down the window. Fresh air blew into the cab, ruffling her hair and caressing her cheeks.

A train was passing on the old railroad trestle that spanned the highway into town as the lights of Gold Creek came into view. They passed the Dari-Maid and turned at the corner of Pine and Main by the Rexall Drugstore, the store where her mother had worked for as long as Carlie could remember.

Though she was nervous just being alone with him, she hoped he didn't notice. Her palms were sweaty, her throat dry and her heart knocked loudly as the night seemed to close around them.

He took the corner a little too fast and the truck's tires squealed as he pulled into the parking lot near her parents' apartment complex. Built in the thirties, the Lakeview was comprised of three six-plex town houses. On the exterior, the bottom floors were faced in brick while the upper story was white clapboard. Black shutters adorned paned windows and though the apartments weren't very big, they still held a certain charm that her mother loved. "Just like home," Thelma, who had been raised in Brooklyn, New York, had told her daughter on more than one occasion. "You can't find quality building like this anymore."

As the pickup idled, Carlie reached for the door handle.

"You don't have to go in," he said, drumming his fingers on the steering wheel.

Her fingers froze in midair. "It's late."

"Not that late." He turned off the ignition and the ensuing silence was suddenly deafening. She could hear her own heartbeat and the hum of the security lamps that shed a blue light over the pockmarked asphalt of the parking lot.

"I've got to work in the morning."

"So do I."

She turned to face him and barely dared breathe. Lounging against the driver's side door, Ben was openly staring at her and his eyebrows were drawn together as if he were trying to piece together some complicated, mystical puzzle. He fingered his keys. Silence was thick in the truck. She swallowed hard.

He reached across the cab, lifted a lock of her long black hair and let it drop again. "Why did you show up at the cabin tonight?"

"I told you—"

"I know what you said, but I was wondering if there was another reason."

"No."

"You're sure that it's over between you and my brother?"

Her heart was beating so loudly, she was embarrassed. "It never really got started, Ben. It just didn't work," she said honestly.

"Why?"

"I liked Kevin…I still do, but he wanted to get more serious than I did…." Before she realized what he was doing, his fingers slid beneath her hair, found the back of her neck and drew her face to his.

"So what are you? Just a party girl?" he asked, his breath fanning her lips.

Oh, God, she could hardly breathe.

"No, but—"

His lips found hers in a kiss that was hot and wet and promised so much more. His mouth moved easily and Carlie couldn't help the little groan of pleasure that escaped her. Somewhere in the back of her mind she knew that kissing him was asking for more trouble than she could ever hope to handle, but she couldn't stop herself and she didn't protest as his arms surrounded her, pulling her close against him. His chest was rock hard and bare where his shirt didn't quite close and his mouth moved easily over hers.

She felt as if she were melting inside when he finally let go of her.

Her heart was thundering as he slid back to his side of the truck and ran an unsteady hand through his hair. "Damn!" His breathing was loud and he cast her a glance that could cut through metal. "You—"

"I what?" she asked, bristling a little. After all, he'd kissed her. Not the other way around.

"You're…well, you're just not what I expected. Son of a—"

"Gun?" She tried to break the tension building in the cab.

"Close enough." His fingers still shook a little as he placed them over the steering wheel. So he had been as affected as she. That little bit of knowledge helped because she was surprised at her own reaction. She'd kissed her share of boys during high school and some of the kisses had been pleasant, but she'd never felt so downright shaken to her toes.

"I'd better get going." He reached for the keys still dangling in the ignition.

"You want to come in…for a soda, or some coffee or something?" Lord, that sounded so immature. They'd just been at a beer bash and shared a kiss that was as deep as the night and she was offering him coffee like a middle-aged woman in a commercial on television.

Hesitating, he glanced in her direction, appeared to wrestle with a silent decision, then pocketed his keys. "I don't think this is a good idea."

"Probably not." Relieved, she laughed and climbed out of the truck.

Now what? she wondered as she waited for him to round the fender and walk to the front door. Her fingers fumbled a little as she pushed the key into the lock and turned softly. The door opened silently and her cat, in a streak of gray, bolted inside.

"Get locked out, did you, Shadow?" Carlie said, thankful for the distraction. "That's what happens when you don't come in when you're called." With the cat at her heels, Carlie walked quickly and quietly down the hall to the kitchen where she snapped on the light. Shadow sprang to the counter and perched on the windowsill.

"You've got a friend," Ben observed.

"Most of the time, but she's a little fickle."

"Like you?" he asked and she felt heat flood up her neck. Of course he'd think she was as flighty as the stupid cat. There was no telling what Kevin had told his brother.

"I'm a lot of things," she said, opening the refrigerator door and pulling out a carton of milk. She sniffed the edge to be sure the contents weren't sour, then poured some into a saucer and placed the dish in the corner by the back door. "But definitely not fickle." The cat hopped off the sill, trotted over to the saucer, wrinkled her nose, then began to lap greedily.

"No?" Ben twisted a kitchen chair around and straddled the back.

"We've got cola, or lemonade or I can make coffee."

"The soda's fine."

She poured two glasses, rattled ice out of a tray and plopped a couple of cubes into each glass. "I just want to know that we're not together because of Kevin," Ben suddenly tossed out.

"What? That's crazy!" She nearly dropped the glasses. Was he serious?

"Some girls would date a guy's brother to get back at him."

"I don't want to get back at anyone!"

"And some would try and make him jealous."

"Do you really believe that?" she asked, dumbfounded. His eyes turned sober. "I don't want to."

"Good, because I'm tired of talking about your brother, okay? I told you that I was never really serious about him. Either you believe me or you don't."

"I just want things straight."

"Me, too."

He stared at her a long minute, then took the glass from her outstretched hand and lifted it a bit. "Cheers."

"Here's mud in your eye."

"Better than a foot in the mouth, I guess." He smiled then, a long slow smile that touched a corner of her heart, before he placed the glass to his lips.

Carlie's heart did a stupid little somersault and she knew that she'd misjudged her reaction to him. She'd hoped that after meeting him, her fascination for him would fade, but instead, the more she was with him, the more intrigued she was and try as she might, she couldn't forget that single, long kiss.

"I heard you plan to leave town," he said. She guessed his information had come from Kevin. "That you've got big plans to model. L.A. or New York. Right?"

She felt heat flood her face. "It's a dream," she admitted. "I worked on the school paper, taking pictures. And so after I graduated, I took a job in Coleville at a studio, just doing grunt work—filing, typing, developing negatives—that sort of thing. And then the owner of the studio—his name is Rory—asked me to pose for him. So I did."

Clouds gathered in his eyes. "So the rest is history?"

She lifted a shoulder. "Hardly."

"No contract with the Ford Agency?"

"Not yet." She relaxed a little. He was teasing her and the twinkle in his hazel eyes wasn't malicious—just interested.

"I don't blame you for wanting to get out," he admitted, then drained his drink.

"You don't?" She didn't believe him. Kevin had acted as if Gold Creek was the end-all and be-all. She'd suspected that he hadn't always believed it, but that once he'd lost his basketball scholarship and his dreams in the process, he'd forced himself to settle for a job in the mill and now was rationalizing...or pouring himself into a bottle. Though she'd never voiced her opinion, she thought Kevin spent too many nights on the third stool of the Silver Horseshoe Saloon holding up the bar and watching sports on television. He'd even given up on city-league basketball with friends. She expected his brother to feel the same.

"Sure. I don't plan to hang out here any longer than necessary."

"What're you going to do?"

"See as much of the world as I can. Maybe join the army. My dad thinks I should enlist first and let the military pay for my schooling when I get out."

"You want to go into the army?" she repeated.

"Why not?" He slanted her an uneven grin. "You know, join the army, see the world."

"I don't know. It sounds so…rigid and well, kind of like prison."

"It'll be a challenge."

"You have a thing for guns, or something?"

"I have a thing for adventure." His eyes glimmered a fraction as his teeth crunched down on the ice cube. All at once she could imagine him creeping through some foreign jungle, rifle slung over his back, searching out the enemy. There was a part of Ben Powell that seemed dangerous and forbidden—a part of him that longed to walk on the edge.

"It's peacetime, remember?" she said, feeling more than a little nervous. She hated guns. Hated war. Hated the military.

"There's always action somewhere."

"And you want to be there."

"Beats sitting around this Podunk town and ending up hoping that the mills don't shut down and praying that some jerk like H. G. Monroe III keeps on handing out paychecks that barely cover your bills." He frowned darkly and his jaw grew hard. "I don't plan on working at the Bait and Fish for the rest of my life and I'm sure as hell not going to sign up with the Monroes or the Fitzpatricks."

"But you would with the army." Carlie didn't bother hiding her sarcasm. Her father had worked at Fitzpatrick Logging for nearly thirty years. He was a foreman and made decent money. Time after time Weldon Surrett had told his only daughter that Thomas Fitzpatrick had given him a job when there was no work, he'd kept the logging company running in bad times and good, he'd spotted Weldon as a dedicated worker and promoted him. Carlie was convinced her father would lay down his life for Thomas Fitzpatrick, even though she didn't completely trust the man.

When Roy, Thomas's eldest son, had been killed last fall, her father had cried and forced his small family to attend the funeral. It had been painful that rainy day and the fact that Carlie had sided with Rachelle in defending Jackson Moore had caused friction in the family as well as friction at Weldon's job.

Almost everyone in town believed that Jackson Moore had killed his rival. Everyone but Rachelle and her friend, Carlie. It had been an argument that simmered around the apartment for weeks after Jackson Moore left town.

She took a sip of her drink. "I, um, think Thomas Fitzpatrick isn't all bad," she said, though, truthfully, the few times she'd met him, she'd been uncomfortable. Thomas, tall and patrician, had looked at her intently each time and his smile had seemed to have a hidden meaning that chilled her blood.

"I'd hate to see what you consider 'all bad.'"

She wiped a drop of dew from the side of her glass. "Look, years ago, Fitzpatrick gave my father a chance and he's kept him on, even when Dad was out with back surgery. Dad never missed a paycheck."

Ben's jaw tightened into a harsh line. "Yep. Fitzpatrick. Helluva guy. He and Monroe. Peas in the same dirty pod." He scooted back his chair, handed her his glass and shoved his hands into the front pockets of his jeans. "I guess I'd better shove off. Big day at the Bait and Fish tomorrow."

"You don't have to leave," she said, hating the fact that they'd come very near an argument.

"It's late." With a bitter smile he strode to the front door and she followed. "Thanks for the drink."

She thought he might kiss her again and he stared at her for a heartbeat that caused her throat to catch. His gaze lingered on hers a second longer than necessary. "Good night, Carlie," he whispered, his voice rough.

She leaned forward, expecting to be taken into his arms, but he opened the door and disappeared, leaving her feeling empty inside.

Disappointment curled in her stomach as she watched him through the narrow window. The pickup bounced out of the parking lot and disappeared into the night. Touching the tip of her finger to her lips, she closed her eyes and wondered if she'd ever see him again.

"I HEARD YOU were with Carlie." Kevin lifted his head from beneath the hood of his Corvette long enough to stare his brother hard in the eye. "At the lake the other night. Some of the guys said you met her at the Daniels's place and wound up taking her home."

"Does it bother you?" Ben asked, wishing he hadn't stopped by Kevin's rented house unannounced. His brother was checking out his one prized possession—a six-year-old Corvette with engine problems. Keeping the car running cost Kevin nearly every dime he earned at the sawmill. Glossy black and sleek, the car seemed to hug the asphalt of the driveway.

"Bother me?" Kevin slammed down the hood and leaned a hip against a low-slung fender. "'Course it bothers me. She's trouble, man. I told you that before."

"You also said that you were through with her, that you were going with someone else…a girl from Coleville."

"Tracy," Kevin agreed, wiping his hands on a greasy rag. "I am."

"So it doesn't matter—"

"Like hell!" Kevin said, bending a little so that the tip of his nose nearly touched Ben's. "That little bitch gave me nothing but grief. Nothing! If you're smart, you'll stay away from her!" He opened the car door, slid inside and started the Corvette with a roar from the powerful engine. Blue smoke jetted from the exhaust as the sports car idled for a second, backfired and died. "Great," Kevin ground out. "Now what?"

Ben ignored his brother's question. "You've still got a thing for her."

Kevin stiffened, but his mouth twisted into an ugly little smile as he glared up at Ben through the open window. "No way. I'm through with her. Used goods."

Ben's fists clenched and he gnashed his back teeth together to keep from uttering a hot retort. He hadn't come over to Kevin's to pick a fight with him. No, he'd just stopped by to clear his conscience and make certain that Kevin didn't still hold a torch for Carlie because, for the past three days, ever since taking her home from the lake, Ben had thought of little else than her easy smile, glossy black hair and blue eyes. During the day, when he was supposed to be stocking the shelves or selling fishing tackle, thoughts of her had invaded his mind. And the nights were worse—he'd already lost three nights' sleep,

tossing and turning, remembering the feel of her body
against his when he'd kissed her.

Muttering under his breath, Kevin climbed out of
the car, checked under the hood one more time and, in
exasperation, tossed the dirty rag into a box of tools. He
reached into the pocket of his shirt for his cigarettes and
his face creased into a frown. "Probably needs a whole
new engine." Then, as if he remembered why his brother
had stopped by, he added, "Look, if you want Carlie
Surrett, I'm not standin' in your way. She's all yours.
She doesn't mean a thing to me."

"You're sure?"

Kevin flicked a lighter to the end of his cigarette, then
let out a long stream of smoke. "It's your funeral."

Ben wasn't convinced that Kevin didn't still harbor
a few unsettled feelings, but it didn't really matter. Ben
had laid all his cards on the table. "So how'd you find
out that I was with her at the lake?"

Kevin snorted. Smoke curled from his nostrils. "This
is Gold Creek, remember? Bad news travels fast."

CHAPTER TWO

BEN DIDN'T CALL. Not the next day, nor the day after. Carlie began to believe that she'd imagined the passion in his kiss.

"Face it," she told her reflection as she stared into the oval mirror mounted over her bureau. "It wasn't a big deal to him." She brushed her long hair until it crackled, then braided the blue-black strands into a single plait that fell down the middle of her back. Shadow was curled on the window seat in her room, washing her face and obviously unconcerned about Carlie's love life.

"I shouldn't care, you know," she said with a glance at the gray tabby. Shadow did her best to ignore Carlie and continued preening. In disgust, Carlie tossed her brush onto the bureau. "You make a lousy sister, you know," she said, wishing she had someone in whom to confide. She considered Brenda, but shoved that idea quickly aside. Brenda was too gregarious; she didn't know how to keep a secret. But she could always confide in Rachelle.

Or she could just forget Ben. He obviously wasn't interested in her and she wasn't the type to go chasing after boys. Or she hadn't been until she'd become interested in the younger Powell brother.

Grabbing her purse, she headed for work. Upon her mother's urging, she snatched an apple from the fruit basket on the table, and walked outside. The morning air was already hot, the dew melted away. She left the windows of her car rolled down and turned the radio up as she drove the few miles to Coleville and her summer job. What she'd do come September, she hadn't really considered.

She didn't have enough money to go away to school, and she'd applied at a local junior college, but she wasn't convinced that academics was in her future.

Neither is Ben Powell, she told herself firmly as her mind strayed to him. Why had she met him this summer, when she was already confused about the rest of her life? She didn't need to be so distracted by a boy who hardly knew she existed.

Disgusted that she couldn't put him out of her mind, she spent the next five hours in the photography studio concentrating on her work. She developed negatives, helped frame some of Rory's, her boss's, most recent shots and generally tidied up the studio. Rory didn't seem to believe in the connection between cleanliness and God.

"I have to be creative," he'd told her when she mentioned the general mess. "I can't be bothered with trivial things." He was joking, of course, but Carlie had taken it upon herself to pick up the clutter around the studio, clean the kitchen and bathroom, and vacuum the carpets. She couldn't bear to work in a pigsty.

Rory didn't seem to notice. However, he was adamant that she model for him when he was doing an advertising shoot for local merchants or creating his own portfolio.

Rory had told her time and time again that she was wasting her time on the wrong end of a camera.

"Thousands of girls would die for what you've got," he said as he set up the studio for a shoot. Mrs. Murdock was coming in with her two-year-old son and her border collie. "The camera loves you. Look at these——" He waved pictures he'd taken of Carlie, showing off her high cheekbones and blue-green eyes. "The face of an angel with just the hint of the devil in those eyes of yours. I'm telling you, Madison Avenue would eat these up."

"I like to take pictures, not pose," she'd replied, though the idea of modeling held more than a little appeal.

"So spend a few years in front of the lens. Make some bucks, give it your best shot before you grow old and fat, or God forbid, fall in love." Rory was a tall man, thirty-five or so, with a dishwater-blond ponytail that was starting to thin and streak with gray. His face was perpetually unshaven and he never wore a tie. "Now, do we have any Christmas props? These pictures are a Christmas gift for Mrs. Murdock's husband, even though Christmas is what—seven months away?"

"Five," Carlie said. "I'll check the upstairs." She climbed the rickety staircase and opened a door. The attic was sweltering and dusty. She dug through some boxes and came up with several sprigs of fake holly, some red candles that had already melted a little and a stuffed animal that looked like a reindeer. She even uncovered a rolled backdrop of a snow-encrusted forest.

Carrying the box downstairs, she blew her bangs from her eyes. "There's not much," she admitted as the front bell chimed and Mrs. Murdock strolled into the reception area. She held a perfectly behaved border collie on a leash and her dynamo of a two-year-old son was wearing a white shirt, red-and-green plaid vest and black velvet shorts. Red knee socks and black shoes completed the outfit.

She offered Carlie a tired smile. "I know this won't be easy," she admitted as she licked her fingers and tried to smooth a wrinkle in her son's hair. He jerked his head away with a loud protest. "Jason's in the middle of the 'terrible twos,' but my husband would love a picture of him with Waldo." At the moment Jason was tugging hard on Waldo's leash and the dog was sitting patiently.

Carlie led the entourage back to the studio where Rory was adjusting the light.

Mrs. Murdock's prediction was an understatement.

Jason pulled at his bow tie, cried, pitched a fit and generally mauled the dog, but both the collie and Rory were incredibly calm. By the end of the shoot nearly two hours later, Carlie's patience was frayed, Mrs. Murdock had lost her smile and Rory wasn't convinced any of the shots he'd taken would be satisfactory. "Keep your fingers crossed," Rory suggested as they locked up for the night. "I'd hate to go through that all over again."

The thought was depressing. "I'm sure at least one of the shots will turn out," she said, hoping to sound encouraging.

"If today was December twentieth, I would worry. As it is, we still have a lot of time for retakes."

Carlie groaned inwardly at the thought. She drove home in her hot little car and felt positively wilted. Sweat collected at the base of her neck and dotted her forehead, and her clothes, a black skirt and white blouse, were wrinkled and grimy.

Wheeling into the parking lot, she nearly stood on the brakes. Ben's truck was parked in the shade of a larch tree and he was leaning against the fender, arms crossed over his chest, as if he had nothing better to do.

He glanced up when he saw her and shifted a match from one side of his mouth to the other. His lips twitched in what one might consider a smile.

She cut the engine and climbed out.

"Thought I might find you here," he said, taking the match from his mouth and breaking it between two fingers.

"Have you been waiting long?"

Shaking his head he glanced at his watch. "A few minutes."

She couldn't stop the wild beating of her heart. He looked much the same as the last time. Again he wore faded blue Levi's, but this time a white T-shirt stretched across his chest. His gaze was lazy when it touched hers. "I wondered if you wanted to go for a drive. Up to the lake or something."

"I thought you'd forgotten all about me."

Again the sexy smile. "Forget you?" He let out a silent laugh. "Is that possible?"

"It's been a while since I heard from you."

"I've been busy." He leaned one hip against the truck's fender and waited. "So what do you say?"

"Just let me grab my suit."

The apartment was empty and Ben waited downstairs while Carlie dashed into her room, stripped out of her work clothes and threw on a one-piece sea-green swimsuit. She couldn't believe that he was actually waiting for her. Her heart pounded as she stepped into a pair of shorts and a sleeveless blouse with long tails that she tied under her breasts. She ran a brush over her hair, touched up her lipstick and was back downstairs in less than ten minutes. She felt breathless and flushed as she wrote her parents a quick note and let Shadow inside.

Once they were in the parking lot, he unlocked the truck and held open the passenger door for her. She climbed into the sun-baked interior and wondered why, after hearing nothing from him for the past few days, he'd decided to pick up where they'd left off. Or had he?

With a roar the old truck started and Ben eased the Ford into traffic.

"Did something happen?" she finally asked.

His brows fastened together as he squinted through the windshield. Frowning, he reached across her, into the glove compartment and extracted a pair of sunglasses.

"Happen?" he asked, sliding the shades onto the bridge of his nose.

"Well, I just figured that you didn't want to see me again."

"You figured wrong," he said with a trace of agitation. He stopped for a red light, rolled down the window and rested his elbow on the ledge. "Besides, I thought I should make sure that I wasn't stepping on Kevin's toes."

She nearly dropped through the seat. "What's he got to do with this?"

"Nothing. But I wanted to double-check."

"Double-check? This is my life—" she began, but held her tongue. It didn't matter anyway. Obviously Kevin understood how she felt and Ben was here with her now. Still, the thought galled her.

As they drove through the outskirts of town, Ben fiddled with the dial for the radio and found a station that mixed old songs with newer recordings.

"I thought that didn't work."

"Fixed it." He sent her a quick glance as they approached the sawmill. Ben's expression changed and his jaw grew hard as the truck sped along the chain-link fence surrounding the yard. Thousands of board-feet of lumber were sorted according to grade in huge stacks and a mountain of logs waited to be milled. Trucks, many bearing the logo of Fitzpatrick Logging, roared in and out of the yard and men in hard hats waved to the drivers.

Cranes hovered over huge piles of logs and forklifts carried planed lumber from sheds. The shift was changing and men sauntered in and out of the gate. They laughed and smoked, shouted to friends and brushed the sawdust from their shirts and jeans.

Kevin's sleek Corvette was parked in the lot between the dusty pickups and station wagons.

"So why don't you work at the mill?" she asked,

sensing him tense as they sped past the activity at the sawmill.

"Don't you think two Powells bowing down and paying homage to H.G. III is enough?"

"It's a good job."

"I prefer the hours at the Bait and Fish."

She slid a glance in his direction and noticed the way his hands gripped the steering wheel—as if he were going to rip it from its column.

"You don't like the Monroes much, do you?"

"I try not to think about them."

She lifted a brow and he caught the movement.

"Okay. It's like this. I just don't appreciate the way Monroe does business. He lives in a mansion in some ritzy neighborhood in San Francisco, sent his son to private schools, flies into Gold Creek in a company helicopter once, maybe twice a week, does some rah-rahing and claps a few men on the back, then speeds back to his country club for eighteen holes of golf before he plants himself in the clubhouse. Like some damned visiting royalty."

"He's rich."

"So that gives him the right to use the sweat of people's backs to pay for his yacht harbored in the marina?"

"That's the way it works."

"At least Fitzpatrick has the guts to stick around Gold Creek," Ben said as he shifted down and turned onto an abandoned logging road that curved away from the lake and switchbacked through the forested hills.

"I thought we were going swimming at the lake."

"We are."

"Unless my sense of direction is way off, we should be driving toward the setting sun instead of away from it."

He laughed then and the anger that had been radiating from him since they passed the sawmill faded. He touched her lightly on the back of her hand with strong, callused fingers. "Trust me."

Her heart flipped over and she knew she'd trust him with her very life.

They drove slowly, past fir and maple trees that allowed only a little of the fading sunlight through a thick canopy of branches overhead. Dry weeds brushed the belly of the truck as it labored up the steep grade. The radio began to fade and Ben snapped it off as the forest gave way to bare hills that had been stripped of old-growth timber. The scarred land looked as if it had been shaved by a godlike barber who took huge cuts at the remaining stands of old growth. Where the land had been logged, nature was taking over. A fine layer of grass and brush, dotted with a few scrub trees, began to reclaim the rocks and soil between the rotting stumps. Farther on there was evidence of reforestation, small fir and pine trees planted by man and machines to replenish the forest and provide the next crop of timber for another generation of loggers and sawmill men.

"The lifeblood of Gold Creek," Ben observed wryly.

It was the truth, whether he meant to be sarcastic or not. For generations, Gold Creek had depended upon its rich stands of timber. Though the town had been optimistically named during the gold rush when a few miners had discovered glittering bits of the precious metal in the streambed of the brook that flowed into Whitefire Lake, timber was the real gold in the area. The fortunes of men like the Monroes and the Fitzpatricks had been founded and grown on the wealth of the forest.

Ben drove until the road gave out and he parked in a rutted, overgrown lot that had once been used as a base for the machinery that winched the trees up the hillside and a parking lot for logging trucks that had hauled the precious timber back to Monroe's mill.

He grabbed a backpack and slung it over his shoulder. "Come on," he said and she climbed out of his pickup. They left the truck and followed a path that was flanked by berry vines and brush. Eventually the forest resumed and Carlie struggled against the sharp incline. She was breathing hard as they passed through shaded stands of trees that had never been touched by a chain saw. Birds flitted through the trees, while squirrels scolded from hidden branches. The earth smelled cool, and far in the distance she heard the sound of water tumbling over rocks.

"Where's the river?" she asked.

"No river. Gold Creek."

"Clear up here?"

"Has to start somewhere." They continued to climb and Carlie's legs began to ache. "You know, I'm not really dressed for mountain climbing," she said as the back of her heels began to rub in her tennis shoes.

"It's just a little farther." He grabbed her hand and helped her through the woods. She tried not to concentrate on the feel of his fingers twining with hers.

"What is?"

"A place I heard about at the store."

"You're not taking me fishing, are you?" she teased, but he didn't answer, and the warmth of his hand over hers was as secure as a promise. They hiked for another twenty minutes before the forest began to thin. The trees eventually gave way to an alpine meadow, complete with a profusion of wildflowers blooming between thin blades of sun-bleached grass. Butterflies fluttered in the dying sunlight and bees droned lazily.

Still holding her hand, Ben led her through the knee-high grass to the head of a spring where clear water spilled into a small ravine and washed along the rocks as it tumbled downhill.

"Gold Creek," he said.

"I thought the creek started at Whitefire Lake."

"Technically it does," he agreed, "and if you look on a map there's probably another name for this particular brook, but since all this water rushes down to the lake and runs out to feed Gold Creek, I'd say this is where it all starts." Leaning down, he ran his fingers through the water.

"Why'd you bring me up here?"

His hand stopped beneath the clear, shimmering surface. Straightening, he let the water drip from his hands and touched the line of her jaw. His fingers were cool and wet, his eyes dark with the coming dusk. "I wanted to be alone with you," he admitted with the hint of a smile. "No Brenda. No Kevin. No parents. Just you and me."

"Why?" She hardly dared breathe. Her chest was so tight, she thought it might burst.

"I thought we got started on the wrong foot the other night."

She swallowed against a knot in her throat. "I was starting to believe that we didn't really get started."

"Silly girl," he whispered. He shifted and the fingers that had traced her jaw moved around her neck, pulling her gently to him as his lips found hers in a kiss that was filled with wonder and youth and the promise of tomorrow.

Carlie's knees felt weak and she didn't protest when the weight of his body pushed them both to the soft bed of dry grass near the water.

She wound her arms around his neck and opened her mouth to the gentle pressure of his tongue. A curling warmth started somewhere deep in her abdomen and spread outward, racing through her bloodstream, causing her skin to tingle. He flicked the tip of his tongue against the ridges along the roof of her mouth, touching her teeth and delving farther.

Was this wrong? she wondered, but didn't care. Nothing that felt this right should be forbidden.

Groaning, he flung one leg between hers and kissed her harder, pressing hot lips against hers anxiously.

"Carlie," he whispered when he lifted his head and stared down into her eyes. "Is this what you want?"

"I just want to be with you," she said, not thinking about the words, just anxious to assure him that she cared. She touched his cheek with her fingers, then ran them along the back of his neck and drew his head down to hers.

Her lips were wet and eager as they kissed again and she didn't stop him when his fingers found the knot at her blouse and untied the cotton fabric.

Somewhere in the back of her mind she knew that she should tell him no—that she should cool things off before she lost control, but she couldn't. Her blouse parted and his hand surrounded her breast. Through the shiny fabric of her suit, he touched her, kneading the soft mound, causing her nipple to tighten.

Stop him. Stop him now a voice in the back of her mind cried, but she ignored the alarm and kissed him with more fever than before. She felt the cool air touch her shoulder, knew that he was lowering the strap of her swimsuit and before she could say a word, his hot lips had pressed a kiss to the top of her breast.

A low moan escaped her throat as he tugged and the suit fell away, baring the breast to the last rays of sunlight. "So beautiful," he whispered gently, his breath hot as he took the nipple between his lips and tugged.

"Ben," she whispered, her voice rising on the breeze. "Don't tell me to stop."

"I can't," she murmured, closing her eyes to the feel

of his callused hands kneading her flesh, the warmth of his mouth drawing hard on her nipple. Her hips raised anxiously from the nest of dried grass and desire ran hot and thick through her veins when one of his hands moved lower to cup one of her buttocks.

Somewhere, far away, a train whistle blasted, echoing up the mountainside.

Ben tensed, abruptly pulled away, looked down into her eyes, and with a stream of oaths rolled away from her to lie spread-eagled on the grass. He flung an arm over his eyes and said, "Get dressed."

His harsh words were like a slap. Feeling like a fool, Carlie adjusted the strap of her suit and rebuttoned her blouse. "Is...is something wrong?"

Sighing loudly, he shoved his hair out of his eyes and stared up at the dusky sky. "I didn't plan to bring you up here and seduce you." His brows drew together in a serious line of vexation. "Oh, hell, maybe I did."

Her back stiffened a bit. "You wouldn't have forced me to do anything I wasn't ready for."

He glanced at her, his eyes dark and unreadable. "You don't know me, Carlie."

"I know you well enough."

"Damn it all anyway!" He rolled over, grabbed the bag he'd let drop to the meadow floor and took her hand again. "We'd better get back. It's getting dark and I don't trust myself alone with you."

"I thought that's what you wanted."

"Don't you get it? I don't know what I want and I was about to do something that might take away all of our options! Hell, what a mess!"

Cheeks inflamed, she adjusted her clothing and walked away from him to the cliff. Staring over the tops of trees, she saw the glimmer of water.

She heard him approaching and tensed when he

wrapped his arms around her waist to link his hands beneath her breasts. "Hey, look, I'm sorry. Things were just moving too fast for me."

"I wasn't the one—"

"Shh. I know. Believe me, I take all the blame."

With a sigh, she leaned back against him and wrapped her arms over his. "No blame," she said. "It just happened."

"And it will keep happening unless we use our heads." For a second he was silent and she felt his breath ruffle the hair at her crown.

"You see the lake?" he said, as if trying to change the subject.

"Mmm."

"Now look to the south. Over here." He moved, rotating her body. "The town."

The first lights were beginning to twinkle from the valley, shimmering up against the darkening sky.

"If you look hard enough, or with binoculars, you can see the railroad trestle bridge, city hall and the sawmill."

She followed his gaze and noticed the railroad tracks cutting through the valley. The trestle bridge spanned Gold Creek just on the outskirts of town.

"I didn't think you'd been up here before," she said, once her heart had stopped drumming and she could trust her voice again.

"I'm just telling you what I heard from some of the guys who come into the store. Come on. We'd better get back." He rummaged in his backpack, drew out a flashlight and started leading her down the trail.

Night settled over the forest and by the time they returned to Ben's truck, they were following the steady beam of his flashlight. Carlie heard bats stir in the trees, felt the breeze as they flew low, but she wasn't afraid. Probably because she was with Ben.

Silly, she told herself, but she trusted Ben. It came as a shock to realize that if she didn't stop her runaway emotions, she might just end up falling in love with him.

CHAPTER THREE

"Come on. It's not every day I get the afternoon off!" Carlie said, insisting that Rachelle drop the magazine she was reading as she sat on an old patio chair on the back porch of her mother's house. "I'll buy you French fries and a Coke."

"What if I want lemonade?"

"Whatever!" Carlie blew her bangs out of her eyes and waited as Rachelle told her mother what the girls had planned. Rachelle found a way to avoid dragging her little sister, Heather, with them and they drove into town with the windows down. Carlie's T-shirt clung to her back as she parked her car near the Rexall Drugstore.

Kids on skateboards zoomed along the sidewalk, while mothers pushed strollers and adjusted sunbonnets. Heat waved up from the sidewalk and street.

Inside the store, ceiling fans whirred, but did little to lower the temperature. Carlie fanned herself with her hand as they looked into a glass case filled with costume jewelry.

"You're seeing *Ben* Powell?" Rachelle repeated, lifting her eyebrows as if she hadn't heard her friend correctly. "But I thought—"

"I know. You thought I was dating Kevin. I did for a few weeks. We went out a couple of times and it didn't work out. I thought I told you."

"You didn't say anything about Ben."

"I didn't know Ben." Carlie paused at a rack of sunglasses and tried on a pair with yellow lenses.

"Not you," Rachelle advised.

"I know." She replaced the glasses and turned her attention back to the jewelry case. She fingered a set of turquoise-and-silver earrings, held one of the big hoops up to her ear and frowned at her reflection. "I just met him the other night, at a party. Then…well, we took a drive into the mountains."

"Are you going out with him?"

In the mirror, Carlie saw her own eyes cloud. "He hasn't called. It's been nearly a week."

Rachelle tossed a shank of auburn hair over her shoulder as she eyed the pieces of bargain jewelry on the sale rack. "So you haven't actually dated him."

"Not really," Carlie said. Her time with Ben in the mountains hadn't been much of a date, and yet she'd remembered each second so vividly that even now she tingled a little. She was determined to see Ben again. She'd always been a little boy crazy, or so her mother had claimed, but she'd never been quite so bold. Usually boys had sought her out, as in the case of Ben's older brother, but this time, it looked as if she would have to take the bull by the horns and do a little pursuing. The thought settled like lead in her stomach and she wasn't particularly comfortable with the role. But it was long past the days when girls sat by the phone praying it would ring. Women's lib wasn't a new concept. So it was time to push aside the traditional roles and go for it. Right?

They walked through a section of paperback books and magazines and ended up sitting on the stools at the back counter. The menu was a big marquee positioned over the soda machines with interchangeable letters and numbers that were backlit by flickering fluorescent bulbs.

Carlie waved to her mom, glanced at the menu, but

ordered her usual, a chocolate Coke and large order of fries.

"I'll have the same," Rachelle said, "except I'd like a cherry Coke."

"You're making a mistake," Carlie teased and she noticed Rachelle shudder as if the thought of mixing chocolate and cola in a drink concoction was disgusting.

"I thought you had to work today," Thelma said to her daughter as she scribbled their orders onto a pad, ripped off the page and clipped it to a spinning wheel for the fry cook.

"There wasn't much happening at the studio, so Rory gave me a few hours off."

"Are you going home? You could start dinner...."

"I, uh, already have plans. I'm meeting some kids at the lake." She noticed the lines of strain around her mother's eyes and lifted a shoulder. "But I could swing by the house first."

"Would you?"

"Sure."

Thelma busied herself making milk shakes for a crowd of preteen boys. The shake machine whined loudly.

"What's so special about Ben?" Rachelle asked.

"Everything."

"Come on. You can be more specific."

"I wish." Carlie couldn't even explain her fascination with him to herself. "I just saw him a couple of weeks ago and really noticed him. I'd seen him before, of course, but never really paid much attention." She blushed a little. "You know I've never been shy—"

"Amen."

"So...I came up with a way to meet him." She gave a quick version of crashing the party by the lake and Rachelle's good mood seemed to fade, as if she were reliving the night of the Fitzpatrick party.

"I thought you'd learned your lesson."

Carlie grinned. "I guess not."

"So your interest in Ben has nothing to do with the fact that he and Kevin are brothers?"

"Believe me, I wish they weren't."

Thelma placed dewy glasses of soda in front of them. "Fries will be up in a sec," she said with a wink. Carlie fingered her straw until her mother was out of earshot again. "I know that being interested in Ben is...well, kind of strange."

"*Crazy* is the word I'd choose."

"But I can't stop thinking about him."

"You?" Rachelle smiled and Carlie knew what she was thinking.

While Rachelle had barely gone out, and had spent most of her time with her nose in a book, Carlie had dated most of the guys on the basketball and swim teams. Not seriously, of course. She'd never "gone" with any boy for over two months. That had been the problem with Kevin. He'd started talking about the future, their future, here in Gold Creek. When she'd mentioned her dreams of seeing some of the world, he'd pouted, told her that she was setting herself up for a fall, that she should get real and realize that the best she could expect was a small house in Gold Creek, a good husband who worked in the mill and a couple of kids.

No, thank you. She wasn't ready to settle down yet. There were places to see, people to meet and then, someday, maybe, she'd come back. She had the rest of her life to get married and raise a family....

Carlie swirled her straw in her drink. Thelma dropped two plastic baskets of French fries onto the counter. "I'm not supposed to say this around here," she said, "but these are a nutritional disaster."

Grinning, Carlie plucked a hot fry from the basket

and dipped it in a tiny cup of catsup. "That's why they're so delicious."

Her mother winked at her. "Don't forget dinner."

"I won't."

She chatted with Rachelle and Carlie until the next wave of patrons came in. "Uh-oh, looks like duty calls." With a friendly smile, she whipped out her order pad and offered coffee to a couple of men who looked as if they'd just got off the early shift at the mill.

Carlie knew why her dreams of leaving Gold Creek were so important to her. Her mother had told Carlie time and time again not to make the same mistakes that she had. "Not that I regret anything, mind you," she'd told her daughter one night as she rubbed a crick from her lower back and reached in the medicine cabinet for the Bengay. Thelma Perkins had once had dreams of being a dancer, but she'd fallen in love with and married Weldon Surrett. She'd gotten pregnant with Carlie and put away her ballet shoes forever.

Rachelle munched on a fry. "Don't you think it's a big mistake getting involved with brothers?"

"First of all, I wasn't 'involved' with Kevin and secondly…" Carlie plucked the cherry out of her drink and dropped it into her friend's glass. "Well, it shouldn't matter."

"It matters when you go out with a guy's best friend. It has to be worse if they're related."

"So now you're the authority."

Rachelle smiled sadly. "I just know that I wouldn't want to share anyone I cared about with Heather."

"Heather's not the type to share."

"Neither am I," Rachelle said and Carlie wondered if Rachelle was thinking of Jackson Moore, the only boy she'd ever cared for. "The way I see it, if they've both dated you, it's got to cause some kind of friction between the two brothers."

She did have a point, Carlie silently conceded, and truth to tell, she'd been concerned about the same thing, but she didn't want to think about it. "I told Kevin it was over weeks ago."

"Did he believe you?"

"Well, it took him a while, but, yeah, he got the message. He's dating someone else now. Some girl from Coleville."

"Ben tell you that?" Rachelle wiped her fingers on a paper napkin.

"No, I heard it from Brenda."

"Ahh, the source of all truth," Rachelle teased.

"Of all gossip," Carlie corrected as they finished their drinks and French fries.

HOW SHE FELT for Ben didn't have anything to do with his brother, she told herself later as she gathered her hair into a ponytail and made a face at her reflection. After washing her hands, she started on dinner as she'd promised her mother, but she had trouble concentrating.

Ever since being with Ben in the mountains, she'd thought of little else. She had never let another boy touch her—not that way—and she remembered each graze of his finger against her skin, his breath in her hair, the way he cradled her breasts.... "Oh, stop it!" she snapped, causing Shadow to look up from her nap on one of the kitchen chairs.

Carlie threw herself into the task at hand. The chicken was cooked and she was supposed to piece together a potato salad. Not too difficult.

She sliced the already-boiled eggs and added them to the bowl of chopped onions and diced potatoes before starting on the dressing.

Maybe she should just forget about Ben. After all, he hadn't called. He probably wasn't interested in a girl he considered his brother's castoff. Besides, she really didn't have time to get involved with a boy from Gold Creek.... *But who was she kidding?* She was already involved. Up to her eyeballs!

Muttering to herself, she added salt, pepper and paprika to her concoction of mayonnaise and cream. She tasted the dressing and wrinkled her nose. Not quite like Mom's, but it would have to do. Snapping off plastic wrap, she covered the salad and shoved her efforts into the refrigerator before racing upstairs to change.

For Ben.

Not that he even wanted to see her.

However, Carlie was impulsive and she believed in going after something she wanted. Right now, be it right or wrong, she wanted Ben Powell. Despite everyone's advice to the contrary, she knew she'd do whatever she could to make Ben notice her.

Knowing she was asking for trouble, she drove to the Bait and Fish, a small general store perched on the south side of the lake. Built in the 1920s, the store was flanked by a wooden porch and a covered extension that housed two old-fashioned gas pumps. Faded metal signs for Nehi soda and Camel cigarettes were tacked onto the exterior as was an outdoor thermometer.

So this was it. Do or die, she thought when she recognized Ben's pickup parked in the gravel lot. Her fingers were suddenly sweaty on the steering wheel. She parked her car, wiped her hands on her shorts and reminded herself that there wasn't a law against buying soda. She hadn't been in the Bait and Fish for half a year. Pocketing the keys to the car, she walked up the front steps and shoved open the screen door.

A bell tinkled as she stepped inside. Three large rooms

connected by archways wandered away from the central area near the cash register where Tina Sedgewick, a spry woman nearing sixty, was working.

Carlie saw Ben from the corner of her eyes. Balanced atop a ladder, he was fiddling with wires to an old paddle fan. He glanced her direction as the door opened and a half smile curved his lips. *As if he'd been expecting her!* She felt suddenly foolish, but there was no turning back.

"Well, hi, stranger," Tina said, catching sight of Carlie. She'd been seated on a stool behind the register and working on a piece of needlepoint. With blue-tinged hair and a weathered complexion, Tina had worked at the Bait and Fish longer than she'd been married to the owner, Eli Sedgewick, which, according to Carlie's mother, was close to forty years.

"How're you, Mrs. Sedgewick?"

"Can't complain, though, Lord knows, I'd like to." She set her needlepoint aside and prattled on, asking about Carlie's folks, her job in Coleville and her plans after the summer was over. Carlie tried to keep her concentration on the conversation but she could feel Ben's gaze hot against the back of her neck.

"Don't suppose your ma is with you." Tina glanced out the window to check the parking lot, as if she expected Thelma to appear.

"She's at work."

With a sigh, Tina clucked her tongue. "Work, work, work, that's all everybody does anymore. You tell her to come up and visit us once in a while. Eli—hey, look who's come visitin'."

Eli Sedgewick was leaning over a glass display case of fishing equipment, loudly discussing the merits of gray hackles, some kind of fishing fly, with an older man Carlie didn't recognize.

Two other men sat around a potbellied stove in the corner, swapping fishing tales.

Eli, fishing hat studded with different flies, straightened, squinted through thick glasses and smiled as he recognized her. "Well, Carlie girl, about time you showed your face around here," he said. "Your pa retired yet?"

"Not quite."

The customer asked Eli a question and he turned back to his serious discussion.

Carlie walked to the coolers at the rear of the store, eyed the variety of sodas and settled on ginger ale. As she walked back toward the cash register, she stopped at Ben's ladder. "So now you're an electrician?" Carlie asked, her stomach filled with a nest of suddenly very active butterflies.

"Jack-of-all-trades, that's me."

"Or a soldier of fortune?"

He hopped lithely to the ground and dusted off his hands. "Absolutely." Offering her a smile that caused her heart to turn over, he snapped the ladder shut and yelled toward the fishing lure section, "You can try it now, Mr. Sedgewick."

"What? Oh, well, yes…" Sedgewick disappeared behind an open door and flipped on the appropriate switch. The paddle fan started moving slowly.

"What'd I tell ya?" Ben asked, obviously pleased with himself.

"I'll never doubt you again."

His grin widened. "I'll remember that." He turned his intense hazel eyes in her direction. "You come here lookin' for me?"

"No, I…just stopped in for a soda." To prove her point, she flipped open her can of pop.

"Come on, Carlie. You haven't been in the store in months," he said and she couldn't argue, not after he'd obviously overheard her conversation with the Sedgewicks.

"Don't flatter yourself," she said, tossing her hair off her shoulder defensively.

"I'm just telling you what it looks like to me." He carried the ladder back to a storage closet and tucked it inside. Carlie, embarrassed, wondered if the conversation was over and if her relationship, what little there had been of it, with Ben was over, as well.

She paid for her soda and walked outside. She'd been a fool to come by here. She'd known it and yet still she'd come, irresistibly drawn, as if a powerful magnet had forced her to wheel into the Bait and Fish.

"Idiot," she muttered as she climbed into the hot interior of her car. She jammed the keys into the ignition and the motor turned over.

"Hey, wait!" Ben strode out of the store, the screen door slamming behind him.

"For what?" She eyed him through her open window and wondered why she didn't ram the little car into gear and roar out of the lot in a cloud of dust and righteous indignation.

"I didn't mean to embarrass you."

"Well, you did." She just wanted to get away from him. Enough was enough. She couldn't chase him forever and let herself look like an idiot.

"I'm sorry." He stopped by her car and leaned down so that he could stare into her eyes. "I'm glad you came by."

"I'm not."

"Carlie," he said and his voice was like a caress on the soft-blowing breeze. "Look, can we start over?"

She swallowed hard. She didn't want to see the kind side to him, not when she'd made a fool of herself. "Maybe we should just finish. It would be easier."

"But not as much fun," he said and the streaks of silver

in his eyes seemed more defined. "I've been meaning to call you—"

"But," she prompted, ready for a string of excuses.

"But I'm working two jobs and well…I didn't know if it was such a good idea." He didn't have to mention the passion that had flared between them whenever they were alone, but there it was, still thick in the air, hovering between them. He leaned both arms on the edge of the window and kicked out a hip so that he could stare at her. His fingers grazed her arm and her pulse jumped in anticipation. "I really am glad you stopped by."

She didn't want to hear any platitudes. Not now. "I'm on my way to the lake. I should really go."

Frowning, he checked his watch. "I don't get off until seven. How long are you staying at the lake?"

"Until six-forty-five."

He cocked an interested dark eyebrow. "Not another fifteen minutes?"

"I don't think it's such a good idea," she said, repeating his words and mocking him. With a sigh and a lift of her shoulders, she threw her little car into gear. "I've got to be home for dinner."

"Is that right?" He didn't believe her. The cocksure grin told her he knew she was lying, but he didn't call her on it. At least not yet. Straightening, he slapped the open window with his bare palm. "Well, I guess I'll have to catch you another time." With that he turned on his heel and dashed up the two steps to the porch, leaving Carlie to seethe in her car and wonder why she couldn't just forget him. He was trouble. No two ways about it. She should listen to Rachelle's advice and forget him.

She ripped out of the parking lot in a spray of gravel and imagined Ben laughing at her. So what was she doing chasing after him like a lovesick puppy? He was just playing with her and she certainly didn't need the aggravation. So he'd kissed her. Big deal. Lots of boys had kissed her and she hadn't fantasized about it, made it seem as if the sun and the moon and stars were involved in a simple touching of lips. But she hadn't been willing to let any of the other boys strip her of her blouse or loosen the straps of her swimsuit. No one else had put his lips to her breasts and— "Forget it!" she told herself as she stepped on the gas and pushed the speed limit of the winding road around the lake. At the public boat landing and park, she nosed her compact car into a sliver of a parking space. "Forget him."

She grabbed her towel and beach bag, locked the car and started down the trail through the trees to the swimming hole. She'd cool off, talk with some friends for a while, swim, then go home *before* seven o'clock! She had to forget him. Anything else was just begging for emotional suicide.

"SHE'S A PRETTY thing, ain't she?" Mrs. Sedgewick said to the world in general as Ben strode back into the store. He didn't comment but saw the old lady swallow a smile at his reaction. Why was everything so complicated when it came to dealing with Carlie? Yes, she was a pretty girl. Yes, he was interested in her. Yes, he'd like to date her. And yes, he couldn't pry her from his mind, try as he might. But all his instincts told him to turn the other way and run anytime he came in contact with her.

Kevin had warned him about her and yet, try as he would, Ben couldn't seem to get the girl out of his blood. Kissing her had been a mistake, a kick-you-in-the-gut kind of mistake that messed with his mind.

He had enough trouble without Carlie. His father had never been the same since his divorce, and his sister, Nadine, seemed about ready to bolt to the altar with Sam Warne, her boyfriend of the past few years. Kevin, well, he was already screwed up. Ever since he'd lost his basketball scholarship, he hadn't been the same.

Ben needed to keep his wits about him. He was the only Powell left with a lick of sense.

"Why don't you take the rest of the day off?" Tina suggested. "Not much business this afternoon."

"You sure?" Ben was surprised.

"Hell, yes!" Eli said as he straightened a few ten-pound sacks of dog food. "It's slow today."

Ben didn't need any more encouragement. Between his hours working in the woods during the week and his weekend job at the Bait and Fish, he didn't have much time for himself. Not to mention the matter of Carlie Surrett. He should avoid her like the plague, but as he waved to Tina, walked outside and noticed the sun lingering over the horizon, he knew he'd follow Carlie to the lake. "Just like the stupid lemmings," he thought as he ground the gears of his old truck and headed to the public easement where most of the kids hung out.

He saw her car in the parking lot and smiled inwardly. Pocketing his keys, he almost whistled. He had the rest of the day off and didn't have to be back at the tackle shop until noon tomorrow. He considered the ragged pair of cutoffs he kept in a bag on the floor of the cab and decided they'd have to suffice for a swimming suit. *Well, Miss Surrett,* he thought as he climbed out of the hot interior of his old truck, *you're in for one helluva surprise.*

LIKE A MIRROR, the lake reflected the forest and surrounding mountains. Speedboats pulling water-skiers, dinghies drifting with fishermen and motorboats trolling through the smooth waters caused the only ripples to appear on the lake's glassy surface.

Carlie ignored a group of kids huddled around a cooler

and a radio and walked to the end of the dock. She kicked off her sandals, sat on the edge and dragged one toe through the cold water. What was she doing getting herself tied in emotional knots over Ben Powell? As soon as she had enough money saved, she was leaving Gold Creek and she didn't need any complications—romantic or otherwise—holding her down. Closing her eyes, she pressed her palms to the sun-baked boards of the pier and lolled her head back.

Tranquillity had just settled over her when she felt footsteps reverberating on the tired boards of the dock. She was about to turn around when a pair of hands clamped possessively over her shoulders, thumbs to her back, fingertips resting on the slope of her breasts.

"I didn't think you'd come this early," she said, and a deep-throated chuckle was her response. Blinking open her eyes, she stared upward, where the sun silhouetted the handsome face of a man...but not Ben's. The smell of cigarette smoke and stale beer floated on the breeze. She froze as she recognized Kevin.

"Expecting someone?" he asked with a grin.

She scooted away from him. "What're you doing here?"

"I was with some friends, saw you and thought I'd say hello." He rubbed his chin. "We need to talk."

She tried not to be wary. He was, after all, Ben's brother, as well as a man she'd recently dated. She should give him the benefit of the doubt. Squinting up at him, she said, "What do you want to talk about?"

"Us."

Her throat closed. "There's nothing more to discuss."

"I miss you, Carlie," he said, his expression lifeless.

"I thought you were dating someone else."

"It didn't work out." He shoved a hand through his brown hair and scowled down at the water.

This was getting complicated and she felt a little guilty. "Look, Kevin, I'm seeing someone—"

"Ben. I know." His expression hardened and the look in his eyes was as cold as the depths of the lake. "Hell, don't I know?"

"I don't understand what you want from me, Kevin," she said, wrapping her towel around her shoulders as she stood and faced him. He was tall and intimidating, but he didn't scare her. Kevin wasn't a bad person, just confused.

"I don't know, either. I know it didn't work for us and I suppose I'm as much to blame as anyone, but I'm not sure I can deal with you being Ben's girl. I loved you, Carlie. More than anyone else ever could."

Her heart twisted a little. "You don't, Kevin, and I'm... I'm not anyone's girl."

He reached for her, but she stepped away. "Please, don't—"

His lips flattened suddenly. "No one's girl, eh? Oh, right. You're your own woman, going places, off to see the world." When she didn't answer, he cast her a disdainful look filled with pain and anger. "Who're you kidding, Carlie? You don't have any more chance of getting out of this hellhole of a town than the rest of us. You're trapped, baby, just like everyone else."

Trembling a little at the fierceness in his tone, she stepped backward and nearly fell off the dock. She had to scramble to maintain her balance.

"Kevin!" Ben's voice thundered from the parking lot and Carlie wanted to die.

Kevin's expression turned ugly as he watched his younger brother run to the dock. "Big mistake, Carlie," he said, turning back to her and stripping the towel from her fingers. His gaze raked down her body. "If you really want to get out, you'd better not tie yourself down. Especially not to Ben. He'll break your damned heart." With that piece of advice he dropped the towel and strode down the planks of the dock and met his brother who was running toward the pier.

"She's all yours," Kevin said with a dismissive motion of his head.

"I'm not anyone's!" she insisted again, though her face burned with shame.

"Carlie—"

Ben's voice followed her as she turned and dived into the clear, cold water of the lake. Damn the Powell boys. Both of them. Who did they think they were, snarling over her like two tigers coveting a prized piece of meat? Why couldn't she just forget them both? Kevin was bad news and everyone told her that getting involved with Ben would be courting disaster. The writing was already on the wall.

The water caressed her skin and she swam under the surface, determined to put as much distance between herself and anyone named Powell. Who needed them, she thought, and her heart tugged a little as her lungs began to burn. She kicked upward, through the cool depths and, as her head broke the surface, gasped for air. Treading water she looked back at the dock and saw Ben kicking off his shoes.

She felt a little shiver of anticipation as he looked her way and stripped off his shirt. Her throat tightened as he dived neatly into the water and started swimming her way. She had two choices: swim toward him or toward the opposite shore. Gauging the distance, and the rate he was plowing through the water, she knew she didn't have a prayer of reaching the distant bank. Still, she could give him a good run for his money.

Again she dived under the surface and swam toward the middle of the lake, but at an angle, toward the

Fitzpatrick place. Within a minute her lungs began to ache, but she kept going and only surfaced when she was starved for air and her lungs were on fire.

Her head emerged and she saw him, still coming, swimming unerringly in her direction. With a kick, she surged away from him, but within a matter of minutes, he was next to her, his hands sliding against her wet skin, his fingers surrounding her arms.

"Wh-what are you doing?" she asked between gasps.

"This." His lips found hers and he tasted of salt and clear water. She had to tread water to stay afloat.

Kicking away from him, she said, "I don't appreciate your getting your big brother's approval to—"

He pulled her roughly against him. "Kevin has nothing to do with us." He kissed her again, and wound his arms around her torso. His body was hot and wet against hers and her heart beat anxiously to a new and wild drum.

"We'll drown out here."

He lifted his head and smiled, a flash of white so devilish that her heart turned over. "I'll keep you safe, Carlie," he vowed. "Come on." He pulled gently on her hand before letting go and swimming back to the dock. With only a second's hesitation, she followed him, swimming in his wake, feeling the ripples splash her face and knowing that she was beginning to fall in love with him.

Not now! her mind screamed. She had plans for her life and those plans didn't include being tied to a hometown boy. But he was different and changed her way of thinking. He wanted to see the world—he'd said as much. Maybe they could see it together.

By the time she reached the dock she was exhausted. He helped her onto the weathered planks and they sat together, side by side, not touching, breathing hard and listening to the sound of crickets and frogs over the constant lapping of the lake.

"Listen, Ben," she said, when she could finally speak again, "I don't like you talking about me to anyone. Especially Kevin."

"I didn't."

"He seems to think we were going together or something." She didn't add that he said he had loved her.

"Are we?"

The question hung between them, unanswered and she dragged her toes through the water. "You tell me," she finally said.

He smiled then and chased away all the doubts in her heart as he kissed her. But he never answered her question.

"THOSE POWELL BOYS are trouble," Weldon Surrett said as he cleaned his hunting rifle and offered his daughter some unrequested advice. They were seated on the back deck, he drinking a beer, she sipping a tart lemonade. The sun had set, a few stars winked in the sky and the lights of Gold Creek cast a glow into the bank of heavy clouds that were rolling in from the west. "I think you'd best avoid both the boys."

"Who says they're trouble?"

"Ever'body. Now, the old man, George, he's okay. Worked every day of his life for the sawmill, but Kevin's always complaining and showing up late for work. Got the reputation of a troublemaker. I'll just bet his brother's the same." He paused to light a cigarette and let it dangle from his lips.

"You don't work at the mill and besides, just because two people are related doesn't meant they think the same. Look at you and Uncle Sid," she said, feeling a need to defend Ben. They'd started dating just this past week and tonight was the third night they were scheduled to go out to a new action movie at the twin cinemas in Coleville. Obviously her father thought she and Ben were becoming too close.

"But half the people in this town get their paychecks from Monroe Sawmill and our trucks take logs over to the mill all day long. The drivers see and hear things and word filters back. Kevin's a pain in the backside. Always has been. Got himself an attitude that nearly cost him his job a couple of times. The only reason he's still there is Monroe seems to like George. I was worried when you first dated him and I was relieved that it ended so quickly."

"There was nothing there, Dad. We only went out a couple of times."

He drew hard on his cigarette and let smoke drift from his nose. "But now you're with the other kid. Six of one, half a dozen of the other, if you ask me." He took a long swallow from his glass and called over his shoulder. "Thelma, how about another beer?"

"How about you gettin' it yourself and helping with these dishes?"

"I'll get it." Carlie was glad for an excuse to avoid another lecture. She walked through the sliding door into the kitchen and opened the refrigerator. "Leave the dishes, Mom. I'll do 'em."

Her mother smiled. "You vacuum tomorrow. I'll take care of the dishes."

"It's a deal." Carlie popped the cap of a can of beer and walked back outside.

"Thanks," her father said as he stubbed out his cigarette. He poured the brew into his glass, took a sip and set his drink on the table. "Now, about the Powell boy—"

"Dad, please."

"It's not a good idea to date brothers—" He picked up his rifle again and ran his fingers along the barrel.

"I already told you, Ben and Kevin are different."

Her father opened the Remington, snapped it shut and hoisted it to his shoulder, where he squinted through the sight. With a satisfied grunt, he set the rifle on the small table. "Just be careful, honey. Boys are territorial and dating two brothers is—"

"Asking for trouble, I know. Believe me, I've heard the lecture. About a million times," Carlie said as thunderclouds rumbled in the distance.

"Good. Then maybe you learned something. Looks like it might rain." He rubbed the back of his neck. "You know, I saw Thomas Fitzpatrick today and he asked about you."

Carlie squirmed a little. "He's still mad 'cause I stood up for Rachelle and Jackson."

"He didn't seem angry," Weldon said thoughtfully as he gazed over the railing. "He just asked what you planned to do after the summer's over."

She tried to ignore the little chill that scurried down her spine. "I think he might offer you a job," Weldon said hopefully. "You could work for him and go to the community college. Give up all those crazy notions of yours about New York City."

"He wouldn't give me a job."

"Oh, I think he might," Weldon argued. Then as if an unpleasant thought had come to mind, he frowned and snagged his beer. "Sometimes he takes a special interest in a kid from town, helps him out with jobs and loans for college. That sort of thing."

"Helps *him* out?"

"Or her," Weldon said.

"Has he ever helped out a girl before?" she asked, suddenly uneasy. She'd felt the weight of Mr. Fitzpatrick's stare at company picnics or in church and it made her feel uncomfortable.

"I don't know." He reached for his pack of cigarettes, found it empty and crumpled the cellophane wrapper in his big hand. He settled on his chewing tobacco instead and twisted open the can. "Come to think of it, I can't say I ever heard of him working with a girl."

"So why would he want to help me?"

"Maybe 'cause you're my daughter." Her father contemplated his tin of tobacco. "Who knows? I'm just sayin' we can't afford to look a gift horse in the mouth." Placing the tobacco next to his gum, he rubbed his lip pensively. "You didn't win yourself any points by sidin' with Jackson Moore, but then, Thomas has probably figured it's time to let bygones be bygones."

Carlie wasn't convinced. Thomas Fitzpatrick's memory was long and hard. Few people ever crossed him and though she respected him as her father's employer, there was something about Fitzpatrick that bothered her. She hadn't admitted as much to Ben, of course, when the subject had come up because Fitzpatrick had been good to her family. However, the truth was that she still felt uncomfortable around him. He looked at her a few seconds too long when he didn't think she noticed and his gaze had drifted from her face to her chest and lower more than once.

"Well, I think I'll check on the news," her father said, grabbing his rifle and walking inside, but Carlie watched as the night turned black and she shivered despite the day's heat that lingered.

CHAPTER FOUR

"YOU'RE DOING WHAT?" Ben couldn't believe his ears.

"I'm gonna marry Sam," Nadine replied, lifting her chin a notch, daring him to argue with her before she turned her attention back to the dishes in the sink.

"Why?"

She didn't answer, just kept wiping the plates and stacking them in the drainer. She and Ben still lived in the little house by the river with their dad. Kevin had a place of his own, and their mother… Ben didn't want to think of Donna Powell, how she'd left her family all because of Hayden Garreth Monroe III and his scheme to fleece the Powell family out of all their life savings.

Hate burned through his veins and he stared past her through the screen door. Outside, Bonanza, his father's yellow lab, lay in the shade of a maple tree and a bottlebrush bloomed along the porch. The garden, once a source of his mother's pride, was overgrown and dry. Clouds filled the sky and the air filtering through the patched screen door was sultry and hot.

The Powells had once been a happy family. Ben remembered his mother playing the piano and singing as she worked in the house they had in town. She spent her afternoons in the library, earning a little extra income, but her hours had increased when George had sold their house and moved out here, by the river, to this sorry two-storied home that they rented.

The money from their home in town, the savings

earmarked for retirement and children's educations, had been invested with the almighty himself: Hayden Garreth Monroe III. Even Monroe's rich brother-in-law, Thomas Fitzpatrick, was part of the scheme to invest in oil wells that turned out to spit only worthless sand. Everything the family had ever saved had been lost, Kevin's dreams had died an agonizing death and he'd lost his scholarship.

Kevin had felt he had no choice but to drop out of college and follow in his father's weary footsteps by working for Garreth Monroe. Everything that had ever gone wrong with the Powell family could be laid at the feet of the Monroes and yet Nadine had seen fit to fall in love with the heir to the Monroe wealth—Hayden Garreth Monroe IV. It hadn't worked out, of course, and Ben was glad, though it would have been sweet irony to see Nadine marry the guy and get a little of their money back.

But Garreth had been engaged to a woman of his social standing. Ben had hoped Nadine had gotten over the jerk, but to marry Sam Warne, a boy she didn't love? That wasn't an answer, it was desperation. "I don't get it," he told her as she wiped her hands on the dish towel.

"Nothing to get." She snapped the wet towel and folded it over the handle of the oven door.

"You set a date?"

"Not yet."

"Good!" Ben kicked out a chair and sat down, glaring at her stiff spine. "You can't marry the guy just because Monroe's not interested."

Her lips compressed and when she looked at him her green eyes sparked with self-righteous fury. "We all have our ways of getting out, don't we, Ben?"

He didn't answer.

"Didn't you go visit the army recruiter today?"

"How'd you know?" All of a sudden, he was on the

defensive. That was the trouble with arguing with Nadine; she had an uncanny way of turning the tables on you.

"You don't have to be Sherlock Holmes to figure it out. The recruiter called today, confirming an appointment on…" She ran her finger along the calendar stuck onto the wall next to the kitchen phone. "Let's see…Friday at—"

"I know when."

"Good. Now, do you know when to stick your nose back into your own business? You can sit there and be my judge and jury all day long, but at least I'm not running away to the army and messing around with a woman my older brother's in love with."

Ben's head jerked up. "Kevin's not interested in Carlie."

Nadine let out a snort of disbelief.

"He's been seeing some girl in Coleville—"

"Tracy Niday. Yeah, I know." She slid into the chair next to Ben and arranged the salt and pepper shakers around the napkin holder. "But they broke up and if you ask me, he fell pretty hard for Carlie. The way I see it, his interest in Tracy was all a rebound thing, because Carlie hurt him."

"That's not what he told me," Ben said stubbornly. He didn't want to believe that Kevin was emotionally entangled with Carlie. Not now. Now when he, himself, was becoming involved with her.

Nadine looked him straight in the eye and smiled sadly, as if she thought he were the most stupid beast to ever walk the earth. "You have to read between the lines, Ben. It's hard for you, I know. You like things in black and white, no gray areas. Cut-and-dried. But that's not how the world works."

"And that's why you're gonna marry Sam, because of some gray area?"

She flushed and stared at her hands. "It just seems like the thing to do."

"Isn't it a 'rebound thing' because of Hayden Monroe?"

"It's over between Hayden and me."

Ben clamped his hands under his arms and leaned back in his chair. "Tell me you love Sam."

She opened her mouth, closed it and sighed. "I'm not sure I believe in love anymore."

"Liar. You're still in love with that jerk Monroe, aren't you?"

"He's out of my life," she said, her voice a little husky.

"So Sam's second best."

"Sam has always cared about me," she said simply, lacing her fingers together and biting her lower lip.

"You're settling, Nadine."

Her restless green eyes lifted to meet his. "It's my choice, isn't it, Ben? Don't worry about me, I've learned from my mistakes. Besides, I think you've got your own battles to fight."

THE PARK WAS nearly empty because of the threat of a thunderstorm. Picnic tables were vacated, the barbecue pits cold, the playground equipment without children.

In a private copse of fir trees, Carlie lay on a blanket with Ben, nibbling at her sandwich of French bread, cream cheese, turkey and sprouts. They'd decided upon a picnic and a few little thunderclouds hadn't changed their plans.

Ben had seemed quiet all afternoon. He smiled rarely, and his eyes were troubled and dark.

"Something's bothering you," she said, tossing pieces of bread to the ducks that were hovering near the edge of the water. With loud squawks and fluttering of wings, two vied for the delicacy.

"I'm fine."

"What you are is a terrible liar." Throwing the final scrap of bread to a brown mallard who had waddled close to the blanket, she glanced up at Ben. His mouth was firm and set, his jaw tight, the skin over his cheekbones stretched thin. Lying across the blanket, leaning on one elbow, he'd brooded for nearly an hour. "What gives?"

"I'm thinking of joining up."

She didn't think she'd heard him right. "You're what?"

"I talked to an army recruiter today."

The bottom dropped out of her world. "But why?"

Avoiding her eyes, he reached into a small cooler and pulled out a Coke. "Things are happening."

"What things?"

"Nadine's going to marry Sam Warne."

"So?"

"So it's a big mistake."

"But really none of your business."

"She said the same thing," he admitted. He twisted off the bottle cap. "But I can't just ignore it. The fact is, he's ruining her life."

"You don't know that."

"She doesn't love him," he said flatly, then nearly drained the bottle.

Carlie shook her hair loose from its braid and considered Ben. So he did believe in love after all, but he didn't want to think that people got married for a lot of different reasons: family pressure, sexual fulfillment, pregnancy. It wasn't a law that two people had to be in love before they signed a certificate of marriage and, from the marriages Carlie had seen, she was certain more often than not, love wasn't a major factor in the decision.

Nadine, the little that Carlie knew of her, was a practical person who knew her own mind. If she wanted to marry Sam Warne, Carlie guessed, Nadine had her reasons. Nonetheless, she wanted to understand the source of Ben's concern, so she played devil's advocate. "Why do you think she's going to marry Sam?"

"Because she can't have the jerk she really loves." He rolled the empty bottle in his hands and stared across the water. A heron skimmed the surface only to fly gracefully away as thunder rumbled over the hills.

"The man she loves?"

"Don't you remember? I thought everyone in town knew the old scandal. Nadine and Hayden Monroe, the younger, were an item not too long ago. He got bored with his socialite girlfriend, Wynona Galveston, messed around with Nadine and then, when push came to shove, returned to Wynona's waiting arms and promptly took her on a boat ride that nearly killed her. Yep, that Hayden Monroe, what a prince of a guy he is." Ben's words were bitter as his eyes narrowed on the distant shore. "Good riddance."

"So what've you got against Sam?"

Ben snorted. "He's okay, just a little too...normal for Nadine. And, you've got to admit, Hayden Monroe with his speedboat and big bucks is a tough act to follow."

"Maybe it'll work out." She pushed herself upright and scooted close enough so that her shoulder touched his. Tucking her knees to her chest, she rested her chin on her arms. "You can't solve all the world's problems, you know."

He glanced at her and offered a self-deprecating grin. "I can try."

"Is that why you think you have to join the army?" she asked, trying to ignore the tiny hole in her heart that ripped a little more each time she thought of Ben tromping through some humid foreign jungle, or marching across acres of hot enemy sand, or rappelling down a sheer cliff to drop into hostile terrain. Her stomach squeezed painfully and she reminded herself that it was peacetime. If Ben joined the army now, chances were he'd be stationed stateside or maybe at a base in Europe.

"I'm joining because I can't stay here. Nothing ever happens in Gold Creek. There's just a lot of broken dreams and borrowed promises." The wind off the lake kicked up, ruffling his hair, smelling of water. "I don't think I can sit around and watch another generation of Fitzpatricks and Monroes rape the land and make a fortune off the sweat of other men's backs." He cocked his head to look at her. "Besides, who're you to talk? You don't plan to stick around."

She couldn't argue with that, and yet, because of Ben and the last few weeks she'd shared with him, she'd been second-guessing herself, telling herself that a small town in California wasn't such a bad place to live. She'd fantasized about staying here and marrying Ben. Would it be so bad? Who needed adventure? Who cared about faraway places—the bustle of Manhattan, the romance of Paris, the exotic allure of the Caribbean? What did the world have to offer that she couldn't find in Gold Creek?

Her train of thought was on a fast track and gathering steam when she put on the brakes. She was ready to change her life and her dreams. All because of Ben. Her throat felt suddenly thick and as she gazed into the hazel depths of his eyes she knew that she would willingly, even gladly, push aside all her dreams of the future just to walk down the aisle with him and become his bride.

As if he could read her thoughts, he brought his face closer to hers and his breath fanned her face. "You're the only doubt I have," he admitted, his voice deep and rough. "If I hadn't met you, I wouldn't think twice about signing on the dotted line and shipping out."

Her heart turned over as the first drops of rain began to fall. "You don't have to say—"

"Shh." He placed a finger against her lips. "I know I don't have to say or do anything. I'm just telling you how I feel, Carlie."

Her throat was suddenly dry as a summer wind.

"And I've never cared for anyone the way I care for you. When I'm with you, I don't want to ever leave and when I'm away from you, I can't stop thinking about you." His gaze searched the contours of her face and his fingers found hers. "I don't understand this and God knows I didn't want it to happen, but I think I'm falling for you, Carlie Surrett, and if there was anything I could do to prevent it, I would."

"Ben—"

The finger pressed harder against her mouth and she kissed the soft pad. Rain drizzled from a darkening sky as he outlined her lips, then pushed against her teeth until her mouth opened. Still staring into her eyes, he explored the recess of her mouth, touching the back of her teeth and lightly rubbing the tip of her tongue.

Carlie moaned softly, opening her mouth as his finger withdrew. He gathered her into his arms and his lips melded over hers with a possession that drew the breath from her lungs. Thoughts swam in her head, but all her doubts were chased away and she was only concerned with the here and now, with this lonely park by the lake and Ben...wonderful Ben. His hands were magic as they slid beneath the hem of her T-shirt and massaged the muscles of her back.

Fires ignited deep in her most secret self, a warmth invaded her blood and a deep, dusky need controlled her.

He kissed her eyes, her lips, her neck, and when he came to the circle of bones at her throat, he pressed his tongue against her skin. A tremor swept through her and she felt heat rise in her blood.

His fingers scaled her ribs to feel the weight of her breast and she arched against him, filling his palm, wanting more. He yanked the T-shirt over her head, then, lying on his back, he drew her down to him, so that

she was lying atop him as he took her into his mouth.
Through the lace of her bra, he suckled, drawing on her
nipple, pressing against the muscles of her back so that
he could take more of her into his mouth.

Arching her neck, wanting to fill him with the love
that was burning in her soul, she clung to his shoulders.
She felt him pause to remove the scrap of cloth that
restrained him and then his tongue and teeth and lips
were kissing her, on her shoulders, between her breasts,
on the flat wall of her abdomen and lower. He drew off
her shorts, rimming her navel with his tongue as the fine
mist of rain collected on her back.

"Love me, Carlie," he whispered gruffly against her
bare stomach and she writhed her answer against him.

She didn't consider the consequences of the step they
were about to take, didn't think about how easily she
would give him her virginity, nor did she doubt that the
union of their bodies was anything but destiny.

Kissing him and feeling the wonder of his sinewy
muscles, she stripped him of his shirt and soon they were
naked in the darkness, protected by the trees, silently
touching and kissing. Feverish, she pressed her tongue
into his mouth, felt him stiffen as her hands played with
his flat nipples.

There was no turning back. As thunder cracked and
lightning sizzled in jagged streaks across the sky, Ben
rolled her onto her back, gazed into her eyes and with the
determination of a man whose sole purpose is to claim
one very special woman, he entered her.

She let out a silent scream at the pain, but soon he was
rocking over her, giving of himself only to take away,
moving as surely as the sea flows to the sand and then
retreats. The pain disappeared and her body swayed in
a perfect rhythm with his and the blood in her veins ran
hot. With a moan she dug her fingers into his shoulders

and danced with him. Ribbons of light fluttered behind her eyes and as lightning streaked the sky she bucked upward, her body convulsing as the ribbons shredded with an explosive wave of heat that flashed behind her eyes and sent her soul soaring to the heavens. Ben fell against her, his body slick with rain and sweat. "Carlie... beautiful, loving Carlie," he cried, expelling ragged breaths against her neck.

Slowly she floated back to earth, still clinging to him as the wind and rain tore at their bodies. When he lifted his head, he smiled down at her and chuckled. Shoving an unruly lock of wet black hair from her cheek, he sighed loudly and shook his head. "You usually have all the answers. Now what're we going to do?"

She giggled and wiped a drip of rain from the tip of his nose. With a gruff voice that she didn't recognize as her own, she whispered, "Hey, soldier, what about an encore?"

THEY RAN TO the pickup. Their clothes were streaked with mud, their hair sopping wet, their spirits laughing upward to the dark clouds that had the nerve to block the moon.

Carlie cuddled close to Ben as he flipped on the radio and pulled out of the empty lot. Stephen Stills was singing "Love the One You're With" as the windshield wipers slapped raindrops from the glass. Ben's truck splashed through puddles on the road back to town and the sky was inky black. Only the occasional oncoming headlight flashed over the interior of the cab, giving Carlie a chance to stare at Ben's handsome features. Would he really sign his life away and join the army, leaving Gold Creek forever? Her heart squeezed though she knew she was being foolish; she, too, was planning to shake the dust of this small town from her heels.

But now, after making love, after realizing what it was

to give yourself to one person, she wondered if she would have the guts to leave. What if Ben didn't go? What if he stayed here and worked for Thomas Fitzpatrick or Hayden Monroe, putting in hour after hour, shift after shift, day after day and year after tedious year?

Her throat tightened. She could never ask him to give up his dreams, to stay here forever.

So what if you get pregnant? her wayward mind nagged. She hadn't planned on making love with him, nor had either of them taken precautions. Though she knew the chances of it happening were slim, there were people who conceived children the first time they made love.

Made love.

She bit her lip and wondered about a baby possibly growing inside her: Ben's child. Oh, Lord. She was torn between being in awe of the miracle of life and knowing that neither she nor Ben were emotionally equipped to raise a child.

The truck sped along the road, toward the glow of lights that shimmered up against the heavy clouds, the town of Gold Creek. Hadn't she sworn that she'd never live her life here, that she'd see the world before she settled down to raise a family, that she wouldn't make the same mistakes her parents had? And yet, a part of her would give up all her glamorous plans for a future of adventure and fantasy if she could know that Ben Powell would love her forever.

They drove down Main Street and stopped at a red light. He glanced in her direction and must've read the confusion in her eyes. "Regrets?" he asked, touching her hand.

"None," she assured him. "You?"

He laughed and kissed her cheek. "What do you think?"

The light changed and Ben crossed traffic just as the sound of sirens split the night.

Two police cars, lights flashing, sirens screaming gained on the old pickup.

"Great," Ben said, pulling over, but the cruisers sped past, sirens wailing shrilly. "Accident," Ben said and Carlie felt a cold drip of fear slide down her spine. She watched as the police cars rounded the corner of Main Street and Spruce. Ben stepped on the throttle. "That's Kevin's street," he said with a shrug though his brows drew into a worried line.

Of course nothing was wrong with Kevin. Just because he lived on Spruce Street was no reason to believe the police were after him.

But Ben didn't turn onto the side street leading to the Lakeview Apartments complex. Instead, as if drawn by some kind of morbid magnet, he turned onto Spruce and a ball of ice tightened in Carlie's stomach. "What're you— Oh, God!"

The cruisers were parked cockeyed in front of the house Kevin shared with a roommate. Colored lights strobed the sky. A fire truck and rescue van were already pulled into the driveway. Several firemen and police officers were scattered around the yard. Some talked into walkie-talkies, some huddled together, others were in the garage huddled around Kevin's shiny Corvette.

Neighbors filtered out of their houses and the whole scene played out in slow motion.

Ben yanked out the keys and jumped out of the pickup before the truck had come to a complete stop. Carlie scrambled out behind him. "What's going on here?" Ben demanded of the first policeman.

"Get back, boy!"

Ben ignored him. "My brother lives here!" he said when the officer tried to restrain him.

"Who's your brother?"

"Kevin Powell. He—" His voice broke when he stared into the officer's grim face and Carlie's lungs seemed to give out. She couldn't breathe. Her blood pounded in her ears.

"Your brother's dead, son," the officer said, sadness etched on his features. "Your sister found him. They took him over to County General, but it was too late."

"Oh, God," Carlie whispered, her knees threatening to buckle. This was all a horrid dream. That was it…a dream. She watched as if from a distance.

"No, you're wrong!" Ben threw off the policeman's arm. "Kevin—he's here. He lives here!"

"Son, I'm telling you—"

"You're a liar!" Ben screamed.

Carlie thought she might be sick. She tried to reach for Ben, but he twisted away from her.

"Kevin's okay, Carlie! He's okay!" Ben yelled. "He's okay!"

"I'm sorry, kid. Maybe I should get you a ride—"

"Like hell. Kevin's okay! He's okay!" Ben repeated. His features were etched in fury and disbelief, his body tense and spoiling for a fight as rain sheeted from the sky. "I don't know why you're lying to me!"

"Look, son, if you don't believe me—"

"What's going on here?" a senior officer intervened and Carlie, willing her knees not to give out, stood next to Ben.

"There's been some kind of mistake," she said, her voice nearly failing her. Kevin couldn't be dead. He just couldn't. "This is Ben Powell, Kevin's brother, and—"

"Then you've got your work cut out for you," the officer cut in, staring at Ben. "Your sister's not dealing with this very well and your father has been taken to the hospital with chest pains. I know this is difficult, but you've got to face it."

Carlie's legs turned to water. Deputy Zalinski caught her before she slid onto the muddy ground.

"You're wrong!" Ben said, backing away from the policemen. Rain flattened his hair and ran from the tip of his nose and his chin. "You're wrong! Kevin's okay! He has to be!"

"Get a grip, Powell," the officer said evenly. "We can take you to the hospital—"

"No way!"

"Ben," Carlie said, walking up to him and touching his arm. Her lips were trembling and tears filled her eyes. "Come on—"

"Let go of me," he snarled, yanking his arm away, his eyes filled with dark, unspoken accusations. Carlie's heart turned to stone when she saw the sudden hatred in the angry line of his mouth.

"We're investigating this as a possible suicide," the officer said. "But we're not certain of anything. Not yet. It looks like alcohol could've been involved and—"

"No! Man, this is crazy—" Ben cried, but the anger left his features, replaced by cold, certain fear. "No!" he screamed, his fists clenched as he turned his head to the sky. "No! No! No!"

Tears washed down Carlie's cheeks. She reached for Ben again, but he backed away, nearly stumbling on the curb before he turned around and ran through the night, abandoning her and racing under the streetlamps, faster and faster through the rain. She took a step forward to chase him, but Zalinski restrained her.

"Give him time to deal with this."

"But I—"

"He needs some space. He's had a helluva shock."

But I love him, she cried mutely, feeling the officer's

strong hands restraining her as Ben disappeared around a corner.

"He'll be okay," the officer assured her. "It'll just take a little time. He needs to be alone for a few minutes, but don't worry about him, I'll send a squad car after him."

Carlie, numb, couldn't say a word.

The officer motioned for one of the paramedics. "Hey, Joe, you got a blanket and a cup of coffee?"

"Comin' right up."

Carlie barely heard the exchange. She was still staring down Spruce Street where neighbors had clustered and stood whispering and shaking their heads, but her eyes were still searching for Ben.

A blanket was tossed over her shoulders and a disposable cup of warm coffee placed between her fingers, but she didn't move. She wanted to run after Ben, to hold him, to kiss him, to make love to him again and tell him everything would be all right. But he didn't want to hear her lies, nor did he want her comforting touch.

Shivering, Carlie began to sob. Deep, racking, pain-filled sobs. For Kevin. For the Powell family. But mostly for Ben.

BOOK TWO

Gold Creek, California
The Present

CHAPTER FIVE

CARLIE SLID HER Jeep between two cars and told herself she just had to get through the ceremony, then she could leave. Watch Nadine Powell Warne become Mrs. Hayden Monroe, say congratulations and be off.

Except that she'd have to see Ben again! Ben the Impossible. Ben the Cruel. Ben the Terrible. She could give him a thousand names but it wouldn't change the fact that she'd have to pretend that he meant nothing to her, that the past was dead and buried and that she was content to live her life without him. Which, of course, she reminded herself, she was.

How ironic that they were both back in Gold Creek after years away. She hoped that he was just passing through, staying only long enough to watch the wedding ceremony, then climbing back into his beat-up pickup and taking off for parts unknown.

She'd leave, too, if she could, but her father's health wasn't what it once was. The doctors thought he'd had a series of tiny strokes, and he'd been forced to stop working for a while, maybe forever. Carlie's mother was sick with worry. Carlie, as the only child, had offered to stick around until things were settled.

And she'd found a job. Not just a job. A "career opportunity" Rory Jaeger, her old boss, had told her when she'd approached him about working part-time. He'd scoffed at her proposal. Hadn't she been a New York model? Hadn't she seen Paris? What could she possibly want with his little business? She'd explained that though she didn't need work, not desperately, quite yet, she needed a studio to develop her pictures. *As well as a place to put down a few roots—shallow ones perhaps, but roots nonetheless.*

Rory had become more interested and they'd struck a deal. For a small investment, she could own half the shop. He was close to retiring anyway and they'd shook hands on their agreement, sealing her fate to stay in Gold Creek for at least a year, probably longer, at which time she could sell her interest back to Rory or to someone else, upon Rory's approval.

The documents were being drawn up by the lawyers and within the week she would become part owner of the shop. If she needed extra income, she could drive to San Francisco and talk to a modeling agency there and she'd called her old agency in New York, giving the owner, Constance, her telephone number and address. The modeling was a long shot; she hadn't been in front of a camera in years and she didn't have much interest in trying to revive a career that had barely gotten off the ground. Still, she couldn't afford not to keep all her options open.

So she was stuck in Gold Creek for a while and she'd just have to be able to face Ben if she ran into him again, which, in a town this size, was a foregone conclusion.

She locked her Jeep and started walking to one of the largest houses built upon the shores of Whitefire Lake. The house was cozy, despite its size. Now, in the coming twilight, Monroe Manor looked like something out of an old-fashioned Christmas card. Snow was piled on the third-floor dormers, golden light glowed warmly through frosted windows and smoke drifted lazily from a chimney. Icicles hung like crystal teardrops from the gutters that separated the house from the garage. Two dogs, one black-and-white, the other a yellow Lab, wandered through the tree-covered acres.

It's now or never, she thought, wondering what she would say to George Powell. Before she could second-guess herself, she rang the doorbell and prayed that she would be inside before Ben arrived.

She heard the rumble of a truck's engine as the door opened and a boy of about seven or eight, with red-blond hair, freckles and mischievous hazel eyes stood before her. Dressed in a black suit and white shirt, he shoved out his hand in a gesture that looked as if it had been practiced a hundred times over. "Hi, I'm Bobby."

Ah. Nadine's younger son. "Pleased to meet you. I'm Carlie." She shook his hand firmly.

His nose wrinkled thoughtfully. "You're the model, aren't you?"

Laughing a little, she said, "I was, but that was quite a while ago."

"Wow! Wait until I tell Katie Osgood. She said you wouldn't show up and that—"

"Robert!" A short, blonde woman whom Carlie recognized as Ben and Nadine's aunt Velma, came to the rescue. "We're glad you could come," she said with a smile, then shooting a warning look to Bobby.

"Thanks."

Bobby, suddenly remembering his manners said, "Oh...um, can I take your coat?"

"Sure." Carlie peeled out of the coat and watched as the boy tried diligently not to let the hem drag as he carried it upstairs. He looked over his shoulder at the landing. "You're s'posed to sign the book!"

"The guest register," Velma clarified, "when you have a minute. Now, come on in." She touched Carlie on the arm. "The ceremony's going to start in about ten minutes, so you might want to grab a seat pretty quick."

The doorbell chimed and Carlie's stomach tightened, thinking that the next guest might be Ben. Rather than wait for round two of their argument, she walked through the foyer to the living room where folding chairs had been set up to face the fireplace. Soft music drifted through hidden speakers to vie with the sounds of laughter and conversation flowing through the spacious rooms. Flowers and ribbons decorated the walls and stair railing and the scents of carnations, roses and lilacs mingled with an underlying smell of burning wood.

She recognized more than a few people. The Fitzpatricks, though separated, were together. Despite rumors of impending divorce, Thomas sat by his wife, June, and their daughter, Toni. As Carlie walked in, Thomas glanced in her direction. Beneath his mustache, his lips curved into a quick smile of recognition, but quickly faded and Carlie was reminded of all the times she'd met him as a girl—and how uncomfortable he'd made her feel.

Along with the Fitzpatricks, the Reverend Osgood and his family, as well as the Nelsons, Pattons, McDonalds and Sedgewicks, were already taking seats.

"About time," a voice called from the stairs. Carlie's best friend, Rachelle, was hurrying down the steps. Her mahogany-colored hair was curled and fell to the middle of her back. "I was afraid you were going to chicken out," Rachelle teased. "Looks like I lost that bet."

"You *bet* on whether I'd come or not?"

Rachelle winked. "Couldn't help myself. There was this pool, you see. Heather, Turner, Jackson and I—"

"I don't want to hear it!" Carlie said, though she relaxed a little at her friend's gentle teasing. "And I hope you lost big-time—thousands of dollars. You deserve it. Besides, I wouldn't have missed this for the world."

"Oh, sure. Remember, Carlie, I know you. I can just imagine how desperately you wanted to be here." Grinning, Rachelle grabbed Carlie's hand. "Jeez, you're freezing!"

"I stopped for a walk around the lake."

Rachelle's eyes narrowed a fraction, but the smile didn't leave her lips. "Getting your nerve together?"

"Something like that."

"Think you can handle seeing Ben again?"

Carlie lifted a shoulder in nonchalance. "Now that I'm here, I guess I don't have much choice, do I?"

"It won't kill you," Rachelle predicted with a knowing smile. "In fact, it could be fun."

"Fun? Yeah, about as fun as having all my teeth extracted."

"You might be surprised."

"Don't count on it." But Carlie felt more relaxed than she had since she'd decided to attend the wedding. She'd been friends with Rachelle for as long as she could remember. "Friends for life," they'd once pledged and so far, despite the miles and years that had separated them, they were still as close as sisters.

"Come on," Rachelle urged, "Heather and Turner have saved us seats up near the front."

Rachelle pulled on her hand and soon Carlie was standing in front of a folding chair facing the fireplace. She didn't see Ben come in, but she knew the moment he entered, sensed his presence, as surely as if she'd watched him stride across the threshold. The air against the back of her neck felt suddenly chilled, but her shoulders burned where his gaze bored into her. Cold and hot—like dry ice. Ignoring the temptation to glance over her shoulder, she sat in her chair and watched the ceremony unfold.

Reverend Osgood stood before the fire as Nadine's older son, John, gave the bride away. Then, while Carlie's throat grew tight, Nadine Powell Warne and Hayden Monroe IV stared into each other's eyes and pledged their lives and their love for all time.

To have and hold...from this day forward. Bits and pieces of the traditional words filtered through her mind, and she thought back to her own wedding day, so distant now. She and Paul had stood before a judge and the entire ceremony had lasted less than ten minutes. Cold, stark, without feeling.

Just like her short-lived marriage.

Blinking rapidly, she turned her attention back to the preacher. "You may kiss the bride."

Reverend Osgood didn't have to repeat himself. With a rakish grin, Hayden took Nadine into his arms and kissed her with a passion and love that nearly melted Carlie's bones.

Only one man had kissed her with the same blinding passion that Hayden so obviously felt for his wife, and that man was standing somewhere near the back of the room, regarding the ritual with jaded eyes.

Holding his bride at arm's length, Hayden winked at her, then, as the piano player began playing, they walked between the beribboned chairs and mingled with their guests.

"Don't you just love a wedding?" Heather said on a sigh. Her blond hair was curled away from her face and she wore a shimmery pale blue dress that didn't hide the fact that she was pregnant again. Dabbing at her eyes with a handkerchief, she sighed. "It's so romantic."

Her husband, Turner, looked at his wife and clucked his tongue. "Women. Emotional." He grinned irreverently and Heather rolled her eyes.

"Men. Stoic."

"That's me," Turner replied, but he linked her hand with his as their son, Adam, ran toward the tiered cake and punch bowl to take stock of the refreshments.

Jackson laughed as they walked past the den. "Bring back memories?" he whispered to his wife, though Carlie overheard and understood that he was talking about this very room where Jackson and Rachelle had taken refuge, where they'd first spent the night together, where Jackson had been hiding when he'd been hauled into the sheriff's office for questioning the next morning.

"Great memories," Rachelle said, blushing slightly. Her hazel eyes twinkled wickedly. "I just wonder why Deputy Zalinski wasn't invited."

"You're trouble, Mrs. Moore," Jackson said as he guided her away from the crowd.

"Absolutely," she replied while Carlie, wanting some time alone, wandered toward the stairs where Nadine and Hayden were posing for "spontaneous" snapshots. Velma clicked off a picture as Nadine's boys, John and Bobby, rushed into the foyer.

Bobby tugged on his mother's skirt. "Katie Osgood's trying to sneak some of the champagne," he said, his eyes wide.

"Is she?" Hayden said. "Well, we'll just have to see about that."

"That girl's a wagonload of trouble," Velma said, rewinding her film.

John yanked at his bow tie. "Troublemaker," he snarled at his younger brother.

"It's true!"

"Yeah, and it's true that you're a dweeb!"

"Later, boys," Nadine said, but Hayden glanced pointedly toward the fountain and a girl of about nine or ten dashed quickly out of the room.

The older boy, John, saw Carlie for the first time. "You're—"

"John, this is Carlie Surrett," Nadine said. "We're really glad you could come."

"Thank you," Carlie replied, then shook John's hand. "Nice to meet you."

"She's a model," Bobby supplied.

John's face wrinkled and he glanced up at his mom. "Is she the one who posed for the swimsuit issue of *Sports Illustrated?*"

"Don't I wish," Carlie said, and John grinned.

"Forgive them," Nadine said as her sons caught up with a group of other children about their age.

"Nothing to forgive."

"They're pretty impressed with your life."

"If they only knew," Carlie replied, thinking of the loneliness she'd felt in New York. "Believe me, it's not as glamorous as it seems."

Nadine and Hayden were called away and Carlie found herself alone. She wondered where Ben was, decided it didn't matter and wandered over to the fountain for a glass of champagne. *Just a little while longer,* she told herself as she sipped from a fluted glass and took a seat on a window ledge near the stairs. Then the ordeal would be over.

BEN TRIED TO keep his eyes off Carlie. After all, there was no reason to torture himself. If she felt she had to make a statement and show up, who gave a rip?

His father, for one. George had declined giving his daughter away, proclaiming that one time was enough. He'd blamed every member of the Monroe family for stripping him of his life savings. Though Hayden Garreth Monroe III and Thomas Fitzpatrick were solely responsible for the scheme, George still blamed everyone associated with the rich men. Including Nadine's new husband whom he considered "a spoiled playboy with too much money and too little sense."

George had watched the ceremony without any trace of emotion. His lips had tightened when he'd noticed Carlie, but he'd held his tongue and only stayed long enough to shake Hayden's hand and hug his daughter, then had asked his new friend, Ellen Tremont Little, the woman who had sat with him and been the only person to coax a smile from his lips, to take him back to town.

Nadine, for her part, had braved her father's disapproval

and had refused to let anyone spoil her day. She'd gone upstairs for a moment, returned to the landing and, to the surprise of everyone, thrown her bridal bouquet into the group of guests milling around the base of the stairs.

Girls squealed, hands raised, fingers extended, but the airborne nosegay had landed squarely in Carlie's lap. She'd been sitting on the window seat, staring out the window when the bouquet had soared over the anxious fingers to rest against the blue of her dress. So startled she nearly dropped the flowers, she'd blushed a dozen shades of red.

Fitting, Ben thought, his jaw tightening a little. Hadn't Carlie always been the center of attention? Even now, at Nadine's wedding, she'd somehow managed to steal the show. Hell, what a mess. He would have walked up to Carlie and made a comment, but he didn't want to ruin Nadine's happiness by causing a scene. So he held his tongue and glowered at the woman who had been on the edge of his thoughts for too many years.

Leaning a shoulder against the archway separating the living room from the foyer, he kept his distance— from Carlie and the dangerous emotions that always surfaced when he thought of her. He snatched a glass of champagne off a silver tray carried by a waiter, then drained the drink in one swallow. Restless, he had to keep moving. He walked into the living room and noticed that the folding chairs had been stacked, the carpet rolled back, and Hayden and Nadine were dancing together for the first time as man and wife. He couldn't stand it. He needed some air. Turning his back on the bride and groom, he shoved open the front door and strode outside.

Carlie watched him leave and let out her breath. Maybe now she could relax a little. She forced her fingers, wrapped tightly around the stem of the bridal bouquet, to loosen.

From a baby grand piano tucked in a corner of the living room, strains of the "Anniversary Waltz" drifted through the hallways. Nadine and Hayden glided across the soft patina of the old oak floors. The guests, citizens of Gold Creek, dressed in suits or tuxedos and dresses of vibrant silk or simple cotton, talked among themselves, watching the newlyweds, laughing and sipping champagne that flowed endlessly from the fountain.

Hayden and Nadine danced as one. He whispered something in his bride's ear and Nadine tossed her head and smiled up at him, her green eyes flashing impishly, her red hair reflecting the soft illumination of the tiny lights.

Carlie saw the exchange, noticed Hayden brush Nadine's forehead with his lips as he guided her around the floor. Other couples joined the newlyweds.

Heather and Turner swept by. They looked like a cowboy and a lady, he in a black Western-cut suit and polished boots, she in quivering pale silk. They swayed around plants decorated with a thousand tiny lights and behind them, even though it was long past the season, the Christmas tree loomed twelve feet to the ceiling.

As the dance floor became more crowded, Hayden and Nadine disappeared through the French doors. No one but Carlie seemed to notice.

At last she could go home. She'd done her duty. She found her coat in the closet of an upstairs bedroom and, after saying hasty goodbyes to Rachelle and Heather, she started for the door.

"Carlie?" Thomas Fitzpatrick was wending his way through a crowd of guests and making his way toward her. Her muscles tightened, though he posed no threat. A distinguished-looking man with patrician features, silver hair and a clipped mustache, he smiled evenly as he approached her and she told herself that she'd imagined his leers all those years ago.

Still, she didn't completely trust him. She'd seen what his hatred could do—even to his own kin. Hadn't he tried to blame Jackson Moore, his illegitimate son, for the death of Roy, his favorite child? He'd pitted one of his sons against the other, never recognizing Jackson, then allowing him to take the blame for a murder he didn't commit. No, Thomas Fitzpatrick was no saint, but only a few people had ever had the nerve to stand up to him and Carlie had been one of those very few.

"Can I have a few minutes of your time?" he asked, touching her arm with the familiarity of a favorite uncle.

"I was just leaving."

"Please…it will only take a few minutes. It's about your father."

Her heart nearly stopped. What was wrong with Dad? Surely Thomas wouldn't lay him off now, not while he was still recuperating. Dread inching its way into her heart, she followed the richest man in Gold Creek into the kitchen, where there were only a few caterers filling trays.

"I know things are difficult right now for Thelma and Weldon," Thomas said, his forehead furrowing in worry.

Carlie braced herself against the counter. "It's hard. Dad doesn't like being cooped up."

"Understandable." Thomas smiled, that cold snakelike smile that chilled Carlie to her bones. "He's been a valued employee at the company for years."

Here it comes! Carlie's fingers curled over the smooth marble edge of the counter.

"This is difficult for me, you understand, and I'm willing to do anything I can to help out, but I can't leave his job open indefinitely."

Oh, God.

"I don't think Weldon would expect that and the man who's taken over his position temporarily is willing to stay on indefinitely. In fact, he's insisting that he needs more job security and that's not an unreasonable request as he has a family to support."

"Don't you think you should be discussing this with my father?" she said, unable to hide her irritation. Her parents weren't rich; they, too, needed the job security Fitzpatrick Logging had always provided. There was no way her mother's small salary and tips from working at the soda counter at the drugstore would begin to pay their bills.

"I'll speak to Weldon tomorrow," Fitzpatrick agreed. He stroked the corner of his mustache with a long finger. "And you have to understand that it's hard for me to make a decision like this. Your father could retire, of course—"

"But not at full benefits."

Thomas sighed. He seemed genuinely unhappy. "Unfortunately, no."

"What's he supposed to do?" she asked, anger beginning to burn through her blood.

"As soon as he's well enough, I'll find him a job—a decent job, mind you—with the company. However, he won't have the same responsibilities as he did while he was foreman."

"Or the same salary."

Thomas lifted the shoulder of his expensive wool suit. "I do have a way to help out."

She didn't believe him and she didn't bother hiding it. "My folks aren't interested in your charity, Mr. Fitzpatrick."

"Of course not." He offered her a tentative smile. "The reason I'm bringing this all up to you is that the company annual report is due in a couple of months. We always had the photographs taken by Rory Jaeger."

Was it her imagination or was Thomas smirking behind his cool blue eyes? She nearly shivered, for she was certain that he already knew every intimate detail of her life.

"I worked for him a long time ago."

"And, as I understand it, you'll be working with him again."

So he did know! Carlie wondered if there was any word of gossip in Gold Creek that Thomas Fitzpatrick didn't hear. "It looks that way. If things work out."

"Good. Then I was hoping I could ask you to do the pictures for this year's report. We'd need shots of the logging camps, the trees that are growing through reforestation, and photographs of the other phases of our business—oil wells and the like."

"Have you talked to Rory about this?"

"He insisted on throwing the business your way and, in light of your father's situation, I thought it was a good idea."

As if he ever did anything noble. She itched to tell him to take his business and shove it, but she was more practical than that. She was in no position to turn away a job. Any job.

"What do you say?"

She hesitated, then looked him squarely in the eye. "I'll call you once I set up shop."

"Looking forward to it," Thomas said amiably as he handed her his business card. His gaze lingered on hers a second longer than was normal and Carlie swallowed hard. Was it her imagination? He placed his hand on her shoulder, as if feeling the texture of her dress. The touch was intimate and Carlie took a step away. "Give my best to your dad."

He walked back to the living room to join his wife and daughter. June stiffened at his touch on her elbow and Toni didn't even look his way.

Wealth didn't guarantee happiness, Carlie thought,

tapping the narrow edge of his card against the counter, grateful her interview with him was over. Thomas Fitzpatrick might be one of the richest men in Gold Creek, but he'd already buried one son, and his second was in the legal battle of his life and his third—his bastard— Jackson Moore, refused to even speak with him. That left Antoinette "Toni" Fitzpatrick, pretty and petite, with dark blond hair and blue eyes and an attitude that wouldn't quit.

It was rumored that Toni was more trouble than his other children combined.

Yes, Thomas was an unhappy man. Carlie stuffed his card into her purse and walked through the back door.

Outside, the night was still and snow continued to fall. Thousands of tiny lights illuminated the gazebo and boathouse, to reflect in the dark, shimmering waters of the lake. Somewhere overhead an owl hooted softly.

It was peaceful here. Serene. If she let herself she could forget all her problems with her family. With the Powells. With Thomas Fitzpatrick. With Ben. She frowned at the thought of him—handsome and rigid in his military best. A man who saw the world in terms of black and white, wrong or right, good or bad. No in-between for Ben Powell.

She turned, intending to slip through the breezeway when she saw him, standing near the far side of the gazebo, snow collecting on his shoulders and in his hair.

"Just can't tear yourself away, can you?" he said without bothering to hide his animosity.

"I was about to leave."

"*After* your little chat with Fitzpatrick."

She glanced to the house and the kitchen window where the lights cast squares of light onto the snow. Inside, the caterers were busy refilling trays. Carlie could watch their movements as clearly as if she were in the room. Obviously Ben had seen all of her exchange with Fitzpatrick. "We had business to discuss."

His lips tightened at the corners. "He's trouble, Carlie."

"So you've finished insulting me and now you're giving me warnings?"

He lifted his shoulder, as if he really didn't give a care, but the rigid set of his jaw said otherwise.

"You know, the same could be said about you," she pointed out.

He leaned one hand against a leafless oak sapling, then dusted off the snow that clung tenaciously to the bark. "I just thought you should know."

"'Forewarned is forearmed'—isn't that an old army saying?"

"Take it any way you like," he said hotly. He moved dangerously close to her. "Besides, what do you care, from the looks of it, you've got Thomas Fitzpatrick wrapped around your little finger."

"I don't even know him."

"It won't be long, Carlie," Ben predicted harshly. "I saw him with you. He's on the scent and a man like that usually gets what he wants."

"You're crazy." Thomas Fitzpatrick? Interested in her? The idea was outlandish. Or was it? Her skin crawled.

"Just watch out."

"You're serious."

"Absolutely, and you'd better open your eyes or quit playing that you don't know what's going on."

"He's a married man and old—"

"—enough to be your father. I know. Big deal. He wants you, Ms. Surrett. So the question is whether you're going to go for the bait. Fancy house, all those businesses, more money than you can count. What about it, Carlie?"

"You're unbelievable."

"Tell me that in a couple of weeks. The way I figure it, Fitzpatrick will make another move by then."

She lifted her hand as if to slap him, but he caught

her wrist and his eyes flashed fire. "Don't even think about it!"

"You bastard."

His mouth twitched into a sarcastic grin. "Now we're getting somewhere." He let go of her hand.

Shaken, Carlie decided to have it out with him. Obviously they couldn't both live in this tiny little town, trying to avoid each other, hoping to steer clear of the other person's path. Tilting her chin, she eyed him speculatively. "You know, you don't have to hate me, Ben." Her words seemed to echo across the lake. "It's not part of the rules."

Ben winced and looked at her sharply, his eyes narrowing on her face. "I don't—" He moved back, snapped his mouth closed and glowered angrily, as if he were suddenly mad at the world.

"You don't what? Hate me?" She almost laughed. But her heart soared at the thought that there was a chance they could, at the very least, be civil to each other. "You have a funny way of showing it." Shoving her hands in her pockets, she walked through the tiny drifts of snow to get closer to him. "It would be a lot easier if we could get along."

"I don't think so."

"You'd rather despise me."

He raked fingers through his hair and squared his cap on his head. "It just makes things easier."

"You don't believe that," she said, feeling suddenly bold. There was anger in his dark gaze but something else, as well. Doubts? Passion? Memories of the love they'd shared? She wondered what he'd think if he knew the truth—all of the painful truth.

"I don't think it matters."

"How long are you staying in Gold Creek?"

He wanted to lie, to tell her that he'd be on the next

bus out of town, but the deceit would catch up with him. "I don't know."

"A few days?" She stepped closer. Too close. The scent of her perfume wafted through the cold air. "A week?" Her face turned up to his, defying him, challenging him to lie to her. "A month?" She was so near that he saw the reflection of the Christmas lights in her eyes.

"Why does it matter?"

"I just wonder how often I'll run into you and how I'm supposed to act? Like a complete stranger? Or maybe just an acquaintance, someone you've heard of but don't really know? Or maybe a friend? No—that wouldn't be right, now would it? We'd be bending the rules." Her nostrils flared just a fraction. "I know," she said, tossing from her face the few strands of hair that had fallen out of her braid. "I'll act like a jilted ex-lover. You know, a girl who had all her hopes and dreams pinned on the boy she loved only to find out that he didn't care about her at all. Yeah, that's it. Like someone who was unjustly accused of something and who didn't even get the chance to defend herself." There was more she wanted to say, but thoughts along those particular lines were dangerous, made her vulnerable, which, right now, she could ill afford.

His back teeth ground together, and as she stared up at him with those damned blue eyes it was all he could do not to touch her, not to grab her by the arms and shake some sense into her, not to drag her body close to his and shut her up by kissing her so long and hard, she could barely breathe. Instead he just stared down at her, like a statue, the trained soldier he was, his face a mask of disinterest. "Act any way you like, Carlie," he said harshly and winced a little inside when he saw the color drain from her face. "You can do whatever you want, 'cause I really don't give a damn."

CHAPTER SIX

THOMAS FITZPATRICK SWIRLED a drink in his hand and stood near the window of his office. He tossed back a large swallow of Scotch, felt the alcohol hit the back of his throat and burn all the way down to his stomach. It was still morning. Ten-fifteen. Too early for a drink except on special occasions: birthdays, anniversaries, the signing of a particularly good deal. Or the day a man's served with divorce papers. From the corner of his eye he glimpsed the neatly typed documents from some high-powered lawyer in San Francisco. James T. Bennington. A tiger. The best. June was going for blood.

He swallowed the rest of his drink and poured another. Two would be his limit. Sitting at the desk, he stared down at the divorce papers. Signed, sealed and delivered. His wife had actually filed. She had more guts—and pride—than he'd ever given her credit for.

Being served had been humiliating, but not surprising. His reconciliation efforts with June had been feeble. They'd just gone through the motions of seeing a marriage counselor, engaging in a few "dates," trying to figure out what to do with the rest of their lives. All that time and money had been wasted. June wanted out. She was tired of Thomas's deals and his women. When Jackson Moore had come back to town and discovered that Thomas was really his father, all hell had broken loose. June had known the truth, of course, but it had been a well-kept secret. The boy had even been kept in the dark and Thomas had continued his on-again, off-again affair with Sandra Moore, Jackson's sexy, loose-moraled mother. He smiled as he thought of her. Sandra, of all his mistresses, had most touched his heart.

June had found the strength to move out and take their daughter, Toni, with her. Though Toni was old enough to be on her own, she'd still been living at home, here in Gold Creek. Thomas's baby. His little girl. His princess.

He sighed. He didn't really blame his wife. The love they'd once shared had died a long time ago. Sandra Moore wasn't his first mistress, nor had she been his last.

There had been lots of other women. Bosomy, beautiful females he'd met when he'd been out of town. Young women who had pretended an interest in him but were really impressed with his wealth.

He sipped this drink slowly and set the glass on the table as he settled deeper in his chair. The old leather creaked.

He thought of Carlie Surrett. Lord, she'd turned into a beauty. His fingers moved slowly up and down his sweaty glass. Years ago she'd caught his eye, but he'd drawn the line at girls still in their teens. If he remembered correctly, she'd left town because of that scandal with the older Powell boy, Ken or Conrad…no, Kevin. That was it. He'd committed suicide, or so everyone thought, because he'd loved Carlie and she'd broken up with him and become involved with his younger brother—that arrogant kid who ended up joining the army. There had even been some scandal about pregnancy, but no one knew for sure if that was true. Carlie certainly hadn't come back to town with a kid tagging behind her.

Pulling on his mustache, he thought long and hard, as he always did when he considered something he wanted. Without realizing what he was doing, he shoved back his chair, walked to the bar and plopped a couple of ice cubes into his glass. He caught his reflection in the mirror and scowled. Age was creeping up on him. Age and disappointment. He hadn't wanted to lose Roy years ago, and he didn't want to suffer the pain and financial strain of a divorce now. He'd hoped Jackson would forgive him and that somehow he'd end up with Turner Brooks's ranch. He'd even tried to wrangle the sawmills from his nephew, Hayden. Nothing had worked. He seemed to have lost the Midas touch he'd once possessed.

So now he wanted Carlie. She was old enough, and he was soon to be single. Nothing was standing in his way. Unless she was involved with someone; he'd have to check. It wouldn't be hard to find out all about her.

Carlie's father, Weldon, worked for him as a foreman at the logging company. Good man. Steady worker. Company man. Carlie was Weldon's only daughter and he'd disapproved when she'd taken off for the city. Weldon had grumbled about her getting too big for her britches though Thomas suspected that Weldon was covering up because he was hurt that his only daughter had run off to the city.

Rumor had it that she'd been married, briefly, but that wasn't confirmed. Thomas didn't really know much about her except that she and Rachelle Tremont had backed up Jackson Moore to prove that he hadn't killed Thomas's eldest son, Roy. Grief stole into his heart as it always did when he thought of Roy. God, he'd loved that boy. So had June. He'd been so bright, so athletic, and Thomas was sure there wasn't anything Roy couldn't do if he set his mind on it.

While Roy was alive, June had been a different person. Afterward, she was a shell of the woman she had been—a bitter shell. She had no longer turned a blind eye to Thomas's affairs.

The whole family had started to unravel when Roy

was killed. Brian… Hell, Brian was never half the boy Roy had been and then he'd married that tramp, Laura Chandler, who'd trapped him into marriage and who, it turned out years later, had actually killed Roy.

So Carlie Surrett had been right, and grudgingly Thomas admired her principles. Among other things. Her long legs, her blue eyes, her perfect face. No wonder she'd been a model. He felt a restless stirring between his legs, something he hadn't felt in a long, long time and in his mind's eye he saw himself seducing Carlie, lying with her on silk sheets.

It didn't matter that she was less than half his age. She was an adult, a gorgeous adult, and she was single. Rumor had it that she wasn't rich and after all, her father was still working at the mill, struggling to make ends meet.

He folded the neatly typed documents and shoved them into his desk drawer. He decided to find out everything there was to know about Carlie and her family. The strengths and, more importantly, the weaknesses. He pushed the button on his intercom and told Melanie, his secretary, to get Robert Sands, a slick private investigator, on the line. For the right amount of money, Sands would leave no stone unturned and would find out all the dirt there was on the Surretts—finances, illegitimate children, affairs and any other little skeleton they'd like to keep locked in their closets.

For the first time all morning, Thomas Fitzpatrick smiled.

"WE'LL SEND A crew over to clean up the debris at the lakeside site." Ralph Katcher, Ben's foreman, reached into the back pocket of his jeans for his tin of chewing tobacco and propped one leg on the small step stool in the trailer Ben used as the official offices of his new company. It had been nearly two weeks since Nadine's wedding—two weeks since he'd seen Carlie—and Ben had spent that time buried in his work, trying to start his own construction business. "The Hardesty brothers are looking for work and they'll be able to salvage whatever's left," Ralph added.

"It's not much." Ben stood and stretched. He'd been sitting behind his beat-up desk for hours and his neck ached. He reached for the coffeepot still warming on a hot plate. "Nothin' much but the chimney. I was over there the other day."

"Leave it to Lyle and Lee. Believe me, they can find something out of nothing. 'Sides, the Hardestys work cheap. Best scrappers in the county."

"Good enough. Coffee?"

Ralph shook his head, and chuckled. "I'll pass. I'm about to head out for a beer. Besides, that sludge looks deadly."

"It is," Ben agreed, pouring the coffee into a chipped cup and taking a sip. Scowling at the bitter taste, he set his cup on the clutter of paperwork strewn over his desk and picked up his pencil again. The best decision Ben had made since he'd returned to Gold Creek was to hire Ralph. A hard worker who was supporting an ex-wife and a son, Ralph was glad for the work and had pointed Ben in the direction of several potential jobs.

Ralph pinched out some tobacco and laid it against his gum.

Ben pointed to the tin with his pencil. "*That's* the stuff that'll kill you."

"Yeah, but if it's not this, somethin' else will," Ralph replied with a grin that showed off flecks of brown against incredibly white teeth.

"I guess you're right."

"What about the house on Bitner? Mrs. Hunter's place?"

"It's a go. I'll start looking things over today and let

you know what needs to be done. She seems to know what she wants."

"That's Dora for ya."

Ben rotated his neck and heard some disquieting pops. "I'll talk to Fitzpatrick tomorrow. There's got to be some repair work at the camp." Ben hated to ask for work from old Thomas. Ever since seeing him with Carlie at Nadine's wedding... The pencil he'd been holding snapped between his fingers.

"It would be nice to get a little money out of that old skinflint." Ralph had been out of work for nearly a year since a back injury had sidelined him from his last job with a major construction company, which was owned in part by Thomas Fitzpatrick. Since the accident, the company had laid off more people than it hired and Ralph hadn't been offered his old job because it had no longer existed: the company had gone out of business. Since then, Ralph had worked doing odd jobs—carpentry, chopping wood, even general yard work before he'd been introduced to Ben over a beer at the Silver Horseshoe. They'd struck a deal and he'd been working for Ben ever since. Ralph was grateful for the job and Ben was sure that he'd found the best foreman in the county. A burly man with muttonchop sideburns and slight paunch that hid his belt buckle, Ralph worked hard and was honest. Ben couldn't ask for more.

Ralph grabbed a dusty Mets cap off the rack near the door, then slung his denim jacket over his shoulder. "Well, it looks like we're gonna be busy."

"That's the plan."

"You won't hear me complainin'." Ralph stepped out of the old trailer and jogged to his pickup.

Ben took another swallow of bitter coffee, before dumping the rest of the foul stuff down the toilet. He'd start a fresh pot in the morning.

Stretching so that his back creaked, he thought about leaving, then sat down again in the worn swivel chair behind his metal desk. He shuffled a few papers, and wondered when he'd feel confident enough to hire a secretary. Not right away. He picked up a manila folder and let the check fall into the mess that was his desk. Fifty-thousand big ones. More money than he'd ever seen in his life and he hadn't even had to sign for it. All because he was now related to Hayden Monroe IV. Ben shouldn't take it—just stuff the damned piece of paper into an envelope and send it back, but he was too practical not to realize the value of this—a peace offering—from his sister's new husband.

"I just want to set things straight," Hayden had told him when he and Nadine had returned from their week-long honeymoon in the Bahamas. "For the past."

"That had nothing to do with me," Ben had replied.

Hayden's jaw had clamped tight. "This was my idea, not Nadine's. Hell, she doesn't even know about it."

"Deal with my dad."

Hayden had leveled him a gaze that could cut through solid steel. "I did, Powell. Now this is between us. Just you and me. Think of this money as an advance or a loan or a damned gift, I don't care, but rebuild Nadine's cabin the way she wants it. You can take your profit off the top, then pay me back when you can." Hayden's gaze had brooked no argument and the nostrils of his nose—a nose Ben had nearly broken just a few weeks ago—had flared with indignation.

It was a generous offer, one Ben could hardly refuse, so he'd agreed, but he'd had the proper legal papers drawn so that it was duly recorded that he was borrowing money from Monroe and the debt would be repaid within four years.

Ben had grown up believing that a person earned his

way in the world, that he couldn't expect something for nothing, and he wasn't going to accept Hayden Monroe's money just to ease his new brother-in-law's conscience. This was a business matter. And a chance to rebuild his sister's cabin, so family loyalty was involved. However, the sooner he paid back the debt, the better he'd feel.

Satisfied, he filled out the deposit slip for his new business and stuffed the paperwork into his briefcase. His father had called him a fool, referred to Hayden's investment as "blood money." Well, maybe George was right. It didn't matter. For once Ben wasn't going to kick the golden goose out of his path.

He'd been frugal, picking up this old trailer from Fitzpatrick Logging for a song, and putting it on an empty lot on the outskirts of town zoned for commercial use. He'd bought the weed-infested lot from a man who lived in Seattle and who had once planned to retire in the area. Later, because of the downturn in the California economy, the owner had changed his mind about his retirement plans and gladly sold the piece of ground to Ben. Once the lot was paid off, Ben planned to build himself an office complex, but that dream was a long way off. First he needed to line up more work than just the construction of a lakeside cabin for his sister and the renovation of the old Victorian house on Bitner Street.

Ben's bid for the Bitner job had been lower than any of his competitors' because he was hungrier and he wanted a real job, not a handout from his brother-in-law. Mrs. Hunter, the owner of the building, wanted it to be brought up to date: cleaned, repaired, remodeled, "whatever it takes" to get it ready to sell. She was a sly woman who had a vacancy that she hoped to fill and she'd decided Ben would make a perfect tenant for her downstairs studio. "We could do a trade. You get free rent and I get a little knocked off the bill?" She'd smiled

sweetly, bobbing her head of blue-gray curls, but Ben
had declined, preferring to keep a little distance between
himself and the people who hired him.

However, Dora Hunter wasn't to be outmaneuvered.
"You think about it," she'd told him during their last
conversation. "It could be mighty convenient and I could
come up with a deal you'd be a fool to pass up."

Ben had decided right then and there that there was
a shrewd businesswoman with a will of iron lurking
behind the grandmotherly persona of apple cheeks
and rimless spectacles. At seventy-eight, Mrs. Hunter
was tired of the problems associated with owning and
managing an apartment building and was ready to retire
to Palm Springs to be closer to her daughter and good-
for-nothing son-in-law. She'd confided in Ben as she'd
signed their contract. "He's a bum, but Sonja loves him,
so what does it matter what I think? Besides, there's the
grandchildren…" She'd clucked her tongue. "Hard to
believe that man could father such adorable boys. Ahh,
well…" She'd put down the pen, looked up at Ben with a
twinkle in her blue eyes and stuck out her hand. "Looks
like we have a bargain, Mr. Powell."

"Ben." Her grip was amazingly strong.

"Only if you call me Dora."

"It's a deal."

So Ben had a contract for his first "real job," and
it felt good, damned good, even if he wouldn't make a
ton of money. He had a chance to prove himself and, if
Mrs. Hunter—Dora—was satisfied with the quality of
his work, word would get out. In a town the size of Gold
Creek word of mouth was worth more than thousands of
dollars of paid advertising in the *Clarion*.

The Hunter apartments and Nadine's cabin were
just the beginning of his plan. He figured there were
ample opportunities in Gold Creek, Coleville and the

neighboring communities. He intended to specialize in remodeling rather than developing new projects. A lot of the buildings in Gold Creek were steeped in history and charm but nearly desolate in the way of modern conveniences. Most of the commercial property in the center of town had been built in the early part of the century and though attractive and quaint, needed new wiring, plumbing, insulation, heating and cooling systems or face-lifts.

Ben was determined to find work, even if he had to swallow his pride and offer his services to Fitzpatrick Logging, though that particular thought stuck in his gut. He locked the single-wide trailer behind him. In the army, he'd learned about construction and had taken enough college courses at different universities and through correspondence to graduate as a building engineer.

Now all he needed was a break or two. Hayden Monroe had given him his first. Dora Hunter had provided the second. It was just a matter of time, then maybe he'd settle down in this town, find himself a wife and... Thoughts of Carlie crashed through his cozy little dreams and he threw a dark look at the sky. Why couldn't he get her out of his mind? Ever since the day of Nadine's wedding, when he'd first spied her through the binoculars, he hadn't been able to quit thinking about her. She was on his mind morning, noon and night.

And, as before, nights were definitely the worst, he thought, grimacing as he strode across the gravel to his pickup. He'd spent the past week tossing and sweating in his bed or under the spray of an ice-cold shower. Whether he wanted to admit it or not, Carlie Surrett had gotten into his blood again.

But not for long. She definitely wasn't the kind of woman he intended to spend the rest of his life with. A hot-tempered New York model, a sophisticated photographer—an *artiste,* for God's sake. No, the woman he'd finally ask to marry him would be a simple girl, born and raised in this small town with no ambitions other than to have a couple of kids and enjoy life. He knew it was an antiquated picture of the American family, but it was exactly the kind of family he'd wanted ever since he'd left the army.

He had no room for Carlie in his life.

Besides, she was the last woman he should want. He had only to remember back to that horror-riddled night of Kevin's death....

"Don't!" he told himself as he noticed the first fat drops of rain fall from the sky.

Muttering under his breath, he threw his briefcase onto the seat of the old truck and had started the engine when he saw the dog—a dusty black German shepherd—lying near the side of the trailer. He hesitated, knowing he was taking on more than he'd bargained for, then let the truck idle.

Whistling softly, he climbed out of the cab. The shepherd's ears pricked forward for a second and he snarled.

Ben lowered himself to one knee and began talking softly.

The dog growled.

"This is not a way to make friends and influence people," he told the animal.

They didn't move for a while, each staring the other down, before Ben whistled again.

The dog didn't respond.

"Come on, boy." Ben inched closer and watched the shepherd. Balanced on the balls of his feet, Ben was ready to spring backward if the dog decided to lunge. "Okay, now what's going on here?" he asked as the animal issued a low warning. The shepherd tried to get up, stumbled and Ben saw the blood, a sticky purple pool, beneath the animal's belly. With surprising speed, the dog attacked, snapping, and Ben jumped back. Now what? He couldn't leave the animal there to die.

Knowing he was probably making a mistake, he climbed into the truck, found his leather gloves, a shank of rope and a thick rawhide jacket. After spreading a tattered blanket in the bed of the truck, he approached the dog calmly as he worked the rope into a slipknot.

"Okay, boy, let's see what you've got," he said.

The animal lunged again, but Ben was ready for him, avoiding the sharp teeth as he slipped the noose over the dog's head and barked out his own command. "No!"

The animal froze.

"Down!"

Still no movement.

"That's better." Ben fashioned a muzzle with some hemp and braved the snarling jaws to quiet the animal. For his efforts he was nipped on the sleeve. "You are a bastard," Ben ground out, enjoying the fight a little. "I'm gonna win, you know. Whether you like it or not, I'm taking you to the nearest vet and you're going to be stitched up so you can bite the next idiot who tries to take care of you."

Carefully Ben carried the writhing dog to the truck and laid him, snarling and frustrated, on the tattered blanket. "Stay!" Ben commanded, knowing the dog was too weak to stand or leap from the vehicle. He climbed in the front, snapped on the wipers, threw the rig into gear and headed into town, hoping that Dr. Vance and the veterinary clinic were still on the west end of town.

What was wrong with him? Ever since he'd landed in Gold Creek, he seemed destined on some sort of collision course with fate. First his battle with Hayden Monroe, then Carlie—hell, what a mess that was—and now the dog. The damned dog. One more problem that he didn't need.

CARLIE RUBBED THE kinks out of her neck. She'd spent a long day in the darkroom and couldn't wait to get home to a hot shower, a glass of wine and a good book.

Just before leaving the studio, she'd called Thomas Fitzpatrick, agreed to take the photographs for the logging company's annual report, and wondered why she felt as if she'd sold her soul to the devil. The man was just offering her work, after all; it wasn't as if he'd committed a major sin. He'd visited her father, as promised, and broken the news to Weldon that his job couldn't be held. Her father, always a prideful man, hadn't fallen apart. In fact he'd been grateful that Fitzpatrick had promised to find another position for him as soon as Weldon was fit enough to spend four or five hours at the logging company. "You can work as many hours as you want, kind of ease into the job again," Thomas had told Weldon as he'd clapped him on the back. "The logging company's just not the same without you."

Her father had eaten it up, but Carlie had been unsettled by Fitzpatrick's practiced smile and easy charm. She remembered that he'd once planned a career in politics and she didn't trust him any more than she would a king cobra. He was too smooth to be real. And then there was all that trouble and scandal concerning Jackson.

So why are you planning to do business with him? her tired mind demanded. *For the money.* Pure and simple. Just in case the bastard had lied to her father.

As for Ben's insinuations about the man, they were just plain false. She'd spoken to Fitzpatrick several times, her senses on guard, and each time he'd been a gentleman. Ben, damn him, had been wrong.

But he'd been wrong about a lot of things, she thought darkly, wondering if he had an inkling of the fact that he'd nearly been a father.... The pain in her heart ached and she shoved those agonizing thoughts far away, where no one could ever find them.

She drove to her parents' apartment and managed a smile as she opened the door. "Hi! Thought I'd stop by—" She stopped in midsentence as she felt in the air that something was wrong—dreadfully wrong.

"Carlie?" Her mother's voice shook a little and her footsteps were quick as they carried her down the stairs. White lines of strain bracketed her mouth and she looked as if she'd been crying.

"What's wrong?" Carlie asked, her heart knocking.

"Thank God you're here." Thelma's voice cracked and she had to blink against an onslaught of tears. "It's your father. He's…he's in the hospital."

"The hospital?" Carlie whispered, her heart pounding with dread.

"He…he got that numb feeling again—you know, I told you it happened a couple of times before—and he couldn't move very well and I called the emergency number and an ambulance took him to County General…. Oh, Lord, it was awful, Carlie. I stayed with him for a couple of hours, just to make sure he was resting, but then the doctor convinced me I should go home, that there wasn't anything more I could do. I didn't want to leave him—" Her voice cracked and Carlie hugged her mother tightly.

"Shh. He'll be fine," Carlie said, hoping for the best and knowing that her words held a hollow ring.

"They're sayin' it might be a stroke—a bigger one. Oh, Lord, I can't imagine your father all crippled up. It'll kill him, sure as I'm standin' here."

"Oh, come on, Mom, don't think that way," Carlie said, though she was smiling through her tears. *A stroke?*

Thelma sniffed, attempted a smile and failed miserably.

"I tried to call you, but by that time, you were already gone."

"So what did the doctor say? What exactly?"

"A lot of things I didn't understand," she admitted and wiped her eyes with the back of her hand. "The gist of it is that your father's out of immediate danger, whatever that means."

"Well, it sounds encouraging."

"I'm not so sure." Thelma wrung her hands and walked into the kitchen with Carlie, fearing the worst, following behind. "They've taken more tests and well, they practically wore poor Weldon out with all their poking and prodding...." Her voice faded and she stared out the window to the rainy winter night. "All we can do is pray."

Carlie's heart seemed to drop to her knees. Her father couldn't be seriously ill, could he? He'd always been so big and strapping—a man's man. Now he was frail?

"Come on, Mom," she heard herself saying as she walked on wooden legs. "Let's go see how he is and I'll talk to the doctors. Then, if we think we can leave him, I'll buy you dinner."

"You don't have to—"

"Don't be silly, Mom. I *want* to. Now get your coat."

Thelma didn't argue and Carlie ushered her out to the Jeep. The ride to the hospital took less than thirty minutes and Carlie spent the entire time willing her father to live, to be as strong as he once was.

She'd always depended upon her father. Whenever she had been in trouble, she'd turned to him, listening to his advice. He was kind and strong, not well educated, but wise to the world and she'd adored him. Even when they'd argued, which had happened more frequently in her teenaged years, they had never lost respect for each other because of the special bond they shared.

It had been he, not her mother, who had been hurt when Carlie had turned her back on Gold Creek. He, who had in those first few months when she'd been starving in Manhattan, sent her checks, "a little something extra to help out," though she knew he'd grumbled loudly and often about her decision to move to New York. He'd never liked the idea of her modeling, wearing scanty clothing and being photographed; he'd felt personally violated somehow. However, Weldon Surrett had offered a hefty shoulder when she'd needed to cry on one and then been baffled when she no longer reached for him.

He hadn't approved of her love for Ben. Years ago he'd warned her about both Powell boys. She'd ignored him and when, in the end, he'd been right, he'd never mentioned the fact. Of course, he hadn't known that she'd been pregnant when she'd left Gold Creek. That little secret was hers and hers alone.

Her father had been hurt badly enough when she'd gotten married on the spur of the moment but had tried his best to like his new son-in-law, though they'd met only once and Paul had been disagreeable. But Weldon hadn't so much as said "I told you so" when the marriage had failed.

Oh, Dad, don't die, she thought desperately. She wasn't done needing a father. For the past few months she'd convinced herself that she'd returned to Gold Creek to help him, when, she decided as she squinted through the drizzle on the windshield, it had been she who had needed help to figure out what to do with the rest of her life.

One thing was certain. It was time she stopped running. Time to face her past. Time to mend fences. Time to start a new life. Time to tell her father she loved him and time to deal with the one loose end in her life, the one dangling thread that still had the ability to coil around and squeeze her heart: her feelings for Ben.

But she couldn't think of Ben now, not when her father was battling for his life. She drove the Cherokee into a spot near the emergency entrance, slid out of the Jeep and hunched her shoulders against the rain as she and her mother dashed across the puddles forming on the asphalt of the parking lot.

On the third floor of the hospital, in a semiprivate room, Weldon Surrett lay in the bed, his face slightly ashen, the left side slack. He was sleeping and his breathing was labored.

"Dad?" Carlie whispered, and he blinked his eyes open. It took him a second to focus before he smiled a little. "How are you?"

"Still kickin'," he replied though he coughed a little and his tongue seemed thick.

"You gave us both a scare."

He chuckled and coughed again. "Keeps you on your toes."

"Sure does." She grabbed his hand and held it tightly between her own. His grip was weak, but he was still the man who, singing in a deep baritone as he arrived home from work each evening, would scoop her up in his arms and swing her in the air. He'd smell of smoke and the outdoors and he would force her to sing along with him while her mother clucked her tongue and told them they were both mindless.

"Don't suppose you brought me a beer?"

"Not this time."

"Smokes?" he asked hopefully.

"The doctor would kill me, and I thought you gave those up years ago."

"Smokeless ain't the same," he said. "But I'll take chew if ya got it."

"Like I always carry around a can of tobacco," she said with a smile.

"You should've today," he managed to get out.

"Don't talk," she said, still holding his hand. "You go back to sleep and we'll stay with you awhile."

"Sorry I'm such lousy company."

Her throat clogged. "You're good company, Dad. You always have been."

He squeezed her fingers before closing his eyes again and Carlie fought the hot sting of tears. "I love you, Daddy," she whispered and though he didn't open his eyes again, she felt him try to squeeze her hand a second time.

They waited until he'd drifted off, then Carlie decided it was time she spoke to the doctor. Her parents had led her to believe that her father had suffered a "mild stroke," which was stronger than the smaller ones he'd experienced. The doctors hoped that after a little recovery, some intensive physical therapy, new medication and a change in diet, he'd be able to resume most of his usual activities. But seeing her father looking so weak, as if he'd just walked a thousand miles, she knew better. And it scared the living daylights out of her.

BEN SAT AT the computer, the one luxury he'd afforded himself, and worked with the rough drawings Nadine had given him. At first she'd wanted to rebuild the cabin as it was, but Hayden and Ben, agreeing for the first time in years, had suggested that she'd need something a little more modern, with two bathrooms instead of one and a couple of bedrooms rather than a single. She could still keep the loft, but she'd have an expanded kitchen and a fireplace that served as a room divider so that it could be seen from both the kitchen/nook area as well as the living room.

"Looks like I'm outnumbered," she'd responded, with a slight trace of irritation in her voice.

"It's just more practical," Ben had explained.

"But I liked it the way it was."

"So did I." Hayden had wrapped his arms around his wife's waist and kissed her on the neck. "This will be essentially the same floor plan, but a little more modern."

"You can even have a laundry room," Ben had quipped.

"And a sewing room with enough space for your machine, a desk and—"

"Okay, okay, already! I'm convinced," she'd said with a smile. "Just as long as I get to design the room layout."

So here he was, struggling with her rough sketch, adjusting the size of rooms and placement of walls for duct work, support beams, plumbing, electrical wiring and taking into consideration the slope of the land, watershed and a million other things that would be required before the county would approve her plans.

By noon he was stiff from sitting, so he drove into town to the Buckeye Restaurant and Lounge. The establishment hadn't changed much in the years that he'd been away. The booths were still covered in a time-smoothed Naugahyde.

"Ben Powell!" Tracy Niday, dressed in a gingham dress and brown apron, slid a plastic menu onto the table in front of him. "I heard you were back in town."

"You heard right."

"Just passing through?" she asked.

"I think I'll be sticking around for a while."

"Coffee?"

"Please. Black."

He opened the menu as she hurried back to the kitchen. He'd known that Tracy was in town, of course; Nadine and his father had written him while he was in the service. She'd been nearly destroyed after Kevin had died. Three weeks later she'd dropped the bomb with a mind-numbing announcement that she was pregnant with Kevin's baby. Ben had already left Gold Creek when Tracy had told his father the news.

She'd given birth to a healthy baby boy eight months after Kevin had been buried. George had helped her out a little as her own family had nearly disowned her. Things were better now, or so Nadine had told him. Tracy worked at the bank during the week and put in a shift or two at the Buckeye on the weekends.

She returned, flipped over his coffee cup and poured the coffee from a fat glass pot. "You know," she said as she set the pot on the table and grabbed her pad, "Randy would love to meet you."

Randy was her son. His nephew. He felt a jab of guilt. "Sure. Anytime."

"You mean it?"

"Give me a call." He reached into his wallet and drew out a business card. "I'd like to see Kevin's boy."

For a second he thought she might cry. Her brown eyes glistened and she cleared her throat before taking his order and moving on to wait on the next booth.

Tracy had never married, though, according to Nadine she'd dated several men seriously. She'd spent the past ten years taking care of her boy and trying to better herself. She was pretty, one of those kind of women who seemed to get more good-looking as the years passed.

She returned to Ben's table, talked with him, laughing and joking, smiling a little more than she did with the other patrons as she served him a ham sandwich, potato salad and a crisp dill pickle.

"Don't make yourself scarce," she said when he'd taken the final swallow from a coffee cup she seemed determined to keep filled.

"I won't." He left her a decent tip and waved as he

walked out the door. A weak winter sun was trying to break through the clouds and the puddles of water, left over from the rain, shimmered in the pale light. He climbed into his pickup and drove to the veterinary clinic where he was told that the shepherd, though dehydrated and suffering from malnutrition, was on the mend. The hole in his belly was probably compliments of a fight with another dog or a wild animal and though the beast had lost a lot of blood, he would survive.

"I've called around," Dr. Vance said as he rubbed the lenses of his glasses with the tail of his lab coat. "None of the shelters or other vets have any anxious owners looking for their pets. I even checked with the police department. He's got a collar, but no license, so there's no way of knowin' where he comes from." He patted the groggy animal on the head. "But my guess is that the dog is a purebred and someone's taken care of him. He's been neutered and had his teeth cleaned within the last year, and look at this—" he showed him the dog's feet "—his toenails have been clipped, fairly recently, so I don't think there's a worry of rabies, though I'd inoculate him."

"If I decide to keep him."

The round vet smiled, showing off a gold tooth that winked in the fluorescent lights dangling from the ceiling. "You've got yourself a hefty bill here for a dog you're gonna turn loose on the streets." Again he patted the shepherd and the dog yawned. "Besides, every bachelor needs a dog. Someone to come home and talk to. Believe me, a dog's better than a wife. This here shepherd won't talk back."

"I heard that," Lorna, the doctor's wife and assistant, called from the back room.

"Listenin' in again?" he yelled back at her.

"Hard not to overhear you griping."

Dr. Vance rolled his eyes and mouthed, "Women!" as if that said it all.

Ben agreed to have the dog vaccinated, then paid his bill. It took most of his patience not to be offended when the shepherd growled at him. "Okay, Attila," he said, leading the animal outside and to his truck, "if you so much as snarl at me while I'm driving, I'm letting you off right then and there. You're history." The dog snorted as Ben helped him onto the sagging bench seat, but he didn't bare his teeth, nor did he try to bite, which Ben decided, was an improvement over the day Ben had first found him.

"Just for the record," he said, as if the beast could understand him, "I don't want a dog."

Settling behind the steering wheel, Ben thought of Dr. Vance's words of wisdom about marriage. Vance was probably kidding; he'd been married forever.

Ben had already decided he needed a wife—but not Carlie Surrett. Yet, just at the thought of her clear blue eyes, lustrous black hair and intelligent smile, his gut tightened.

He wanted her. It was that simple. And though he could deny it to himself a thousand times, he had to admit the truth. "Damn it all," he muttered, slapping on the radio. The dog let out a low growl of disapproval, which Ben ignored.

His house, a rental, was located on the outskirts of town. Once inside, he offered the dog food and water, then left him on a blanket in the laundry room. He had to meet some of the men who were going to clean the debris from Nadine's lot, then he had to do a little work over at the Hunter Victorian. He'd figure out what to do about the dog a little later.

As for Carlie—God only knew what he'd do about her. CARLIE WAS BONE weary. The past couple of nights she'd spent hours at the hospital with her father or talking with the doctors who attended him. Though Weldon Surrett had suffered a mild stroke, he would recover. His speech had already improved and he had partial use of his left hand and arm. He was frustrated and cranky, but if he changed his lifestyle, gave up high-cholesterol food, avoided cigarettes and kept active, the prognosis was encouraging.

However, he was stuck with months of physical therapy. He would eventually be released from the hospital, but he wouldn't be able to work at any kind of strenuous labor for a long, long while.

He was too old to retrain for a desk job, and even if he were a younger man, he would never be happy cooped up inside, shuffling papers, filing and working with figures.

It looked as if he would have to retire early, as Thomas Fitzpatrick had suggested, and hope that whatever savings he and his wife had accumulated over the years would be enough to get them through. Thelma would still work of course, and Carlie intended to help out, though her father had been adamantly against the suggestion. Eventually, he'd collect Social Security, but those checks were still a few years away.

"We'll manage," he'd said from his hospital bed.

"But I can help—"

"This is my problem, Carlie, and I'll handle it. Now don't you say a word to your mother or go getting her upset. We've made it through rough times before, we can do it again."

Reluctantly Carlie had dropped the argument when she'd seen the determined set of his jaw. Any further discussion would only have made him angrier and more upset and might have brought on another attack.

Now her stomach grumbled at her as she walked through the foyer to her apartment and noticed that the baseboards had been stripped from the walls. Mrs. Hunter, Carlie's landlady, had told her that she was going to renovate the old place in hopes of selling out. She'd even approached Carlie about buying the old Victorian house on the hill.

At the time, Carlie hadn't been sure she wanted to stay in Gold Creek; now, with her father ill, she'd decided to stay, at least for a while. She'd seen a lot of the world and was surprised at the feeling of coming home she'd experienced upon returning to this cozy little town, a town she'd once left without a backward glance.

"Well, hello there!" Mrs. Hunter opened the door to her apartment to walk into the vestibule. She was dressed in a raincoat and carried a floral umbrella of purple and pink. "I thought you were my ride down to the center," she said, peering out one of the tall leaded-glass windows that flanked the front door. "Smorgasbord tonight, you know."

"You'll have a good time."

"I hope so. Last time the food was overcooked, you know, tasted like shoe leather, but the company's usually good. Let's just hope Leo Phelps doesn't drag out his harmonica. Why they let him play after dinner, when everyone else wants to get on with cards or bingo, I'll never know." She pulled a plastic bonnet from her behemoth of a bag and spread it over her newly permed gray curls. "Oh, here they are now. By the way, the workmen are still here, probably just finishing up, so if you run across a handsome man in your room..." She let the sentence trail off and laughed.

"I'll know what to do," Carlie teased as Mrs. Hunter walked onto the porch and closed the door behind her.

Still smiling to herself, Carlie gathered her mail and started up the stairs. She lived on the third floor, the "crow's nest" Mrs. Hunter called it, and Carlie had come to love her apartment. The turret, where she kept her desk, had nearly a three-hundred-and-sixty-degree view, and the old wooden floors, and hand-carved window frames held a charm that she'd found lacking in more modern apartments. Running her fingers along the time-worn rail, she hiked her way up the steep stairs and told herself that the climb would keep her in shape. There were drawbacks to living here—the heating and cooling systems were ancient, the windows rattled and she'd seen more than one mouse sharing her living quarters, but she still loved her tiny rooms tucked high in the eaves of the old house.

On the landing, she stepped over an electrical cord strung across the hall before it snaked through her front door. "Hello?" she called, not wanting to scare the workman as she entered.

Ben stood near one of the windows, his hip thrown out, his arms crossed over his chest.

Her heart missed a beat and she stopped dead in her tracks.

A tool belt was slung low over his hips and the sleeves of his work shirt were rolled over his forearms displaying tanned skin dusted with dark hair.

"Well, Carlie," he said with a brazen smile that touched a dark corner of her heart. "I wondered when you'd show up."

CHAPTER SEVEN

CARLIE COULDN'T BELIEVE her eyes. Ben? Ben was the contractor—the workman who was going to be walking in and out of the house, with his own set of keys, his own set of rules and his own damned swagger? She felt suddenly violated and insecure. The fact that he was in her apartment, her private sanctuary, made her blood boil. After the way he'd treated her, he was the last person she wanted prowling about her home. Let the windows rattle. Let the faucet drip. Let the damned roof leak, but for God's sake, never let Ben Powell in here. "What're you doing here?" she demanded as he placed a screwdriver to her window frame and played with the pulleys in the old casing.

"What does it look like?"

She ground her teeth in frustration. "I *know* about the work that has to be done, I just don't understand why *you* had to do it!"

"I got the job." He grimaced a little as the rope slid between his fingers and the window dropped suddenly. With a grunt, he shoved the old pane up again and tightened the screw.

"But you're not living here, are you?" she asked, her world suddenly tilting as she remembered the empty studio apartment on the first floor that Mrs. Hunter had wanted to rent. Mrs. Hunter had mentioned that she might trade the rent for work around the house.... Oh, no! He couldn't live here—no way, no how! This small set of rooms was her private place, her shelter! She wasn't going to share it with the one man who had the ability to wound her.

"I'd be moving in tomorrow if your landlady had her way." He shoved his screwdriver back into his tool belt and his eyes glinted a bit. "However, so far I've resisted."

"She can be pretty persuasive." Carlie tossed her purse on the couch.

"Can she?" he asked, one corner of his mouth lifting skeptically.

"Very."

"I guess I'd better avoid her."

"Like you do with all women," she challenged, and his head jerked up, his smile fading quickly away.

"Only the ones that I think will be trouble." He reached into his open toolbox, withdrew a plane and turned back to the sill, as if he planned to fix the damned window this very night.

"And that doesn't take in the entire female population?" Carlie was spoiling for a fight and she couldn't control her tongue. It had been a long week, worrying about her parents, thinking about Ben, wishing she could just start over.

"Not quite." He glared pointedly at her and she blushed. He seemed so much more real today. The last time she'd seen him at Nadine's wedding, he'd worn his military uniform and he'd seemed untouchable and remote. Distant. A soldier on a three-day pass. But today, dressed in faded jeans with worn knees and thin fabric over his buttocks, a tool belt and work shirt with the sleeves rolled over his forearms, he was decidedly more human and, therefore, more dangerous.

"You obviously don't want me here," he said as he shaved off some of the casing. Sawdust and wood curls fell to the floor.

"You got that right."

"Look, it's just a job, okay?" He scowled, as if he felt uncomfortable.

"A job in my house."

"Live with it, lady." He uncinched his belt and it fell to the floor with a thud that echoed in her heart. She averted her eyes for a second; she couldn't even stand to watch him remove one article of clothing without thinking back to a time when she would have liked nothing more than to lie naked with him in a field of summer wildflowers.

But she couldn't afford to feel this way; the strain on her already stretched emotions would be too much. She couldn't be around him until they'd dealt with the past, cleared the air and started fresh. She wasn't in the mood to pick up the old pieces of her life and start fitting them together, but she didn't have much of a choice. Not if she was being forced to see Ben on a daily basis.

"This job going to take long?"

"Are you asking if I'm gonna be underfoot for the next couple of weeks?" He frowned, then ran his fingers over the newly smoothed wood. "That's a distinct possibility."

"I'm not crazy about the idea."

"Neither am I." He glanced up at her, and when their gazes touched, the breath seemed knocked from her throat. Damn the man, he had no right to look so sexy. "Couldn't one of your men—"

"So far I *am* my men." He set the plane back in the toolbox. "Does it bother you so much—that I'm here in your apartment?"

"It makes me uncomfortable."

"Why?"

"Why?" She rested one hip against the back of the couch. "I guess there're about a million reasons," she admitted.

"Name one."

"You're an arrogant bastard."

He grinned. "Name two."

"You've tried your best to do nothing but insult me from the minute you stepped into town." Crossing her arms over her chest, she added, "I can read all sorts of accusations in your eyes, Ben, but I don't understand them."

"I'm not accusing you of anything."

"Like hell! Every time we're together you insinuate that I'm some kind of...of criminal or something— that I did something terrible and wrong and God only knows what else." She took in a long breath and asked the question that had haunted her for so many years. "Just what was it I did to hurt you so badly?"

"You didn't hurt me."

"I damned well did something. You took off out of town like a dog with his tail tucked between his legs."

"My brother was dead, damn it!" He kicked the tool belt across the floor, sending it crashing into an ottoman. "Dead! And you...you..."

"I what?" she demanded, her lungs constricting, old memories burning through her mind.

"You didn't care."

"Oh, Ben—"

He held up a hand, to cut off further conversation. "Forget it, Carlie. Let's just start back at square one. You didn't do anything. Okay? Not a damned thing!" But a tic jumped near his left eye and the muscles in the back of his neck grew rigid.

"Wrong." She shook her head and thought hard, rolling back the years, allowing the blinding pain of the past to surface. For over a decade she'd kept it bottled up, tucked away in a dark corner of her mind, collecting cobwebs, but now she let all of her suspicions surface. "It was because of Kevin," she said quietly, finally saying the words that she'd denied so long. "Somehow you blame me for what happened to him."

Ben didn't say a word, just stared at her as if she were Eve in the Garden of Eden, offering him forbidden fruit, trying to open his eyes to things better left unseen, forcing him to face the truth.

Shoving away from the couch, she picked up his heavy belt and walked the short distance that separated them, her footsteps muffled on the worn Oriental carpet. He never stopped staring at her and she only quit moving when the toe of her shoe nudged the tip of his worn sneakers. She dropped the belt at his feet. "You've blamed me, though I don't know why. There was nothing I could do. Nothing either of us could do. We couldn't have stopped Kevin from driving into that garage and letting the engine run."

The air grew thick with cold. Rain pelted the windows and dripped down the sill into the house. Ben's eyes narrowed a fraction and a deep anguish shadowed his eyes.

"Whether it was an accident or suicide, we weren't to blame," she said, wishing she could touch him and erase the pain that still lingered in his gaze.

"You don't know that."

Her heart ached for all the years they'd let the past keep them apart, for all the misunderstandings, the hatred and mistrust. "What could either of us have done?"

"I could have been there for him. I knew he was having problems," Ben said gruffly. His throat worked and he stared at her with a venom so intense, she shuddered.

"Did you think he'd take his life?"

"No."

"Neither did I."

Ben snorted. "But I suspected he was in love with you and I didn't care. Nadine even warned me, but I still took you out, bragged about it, even told him I thought I might marry you," Ben said. His face was filled with self-loathing.

"Marry me?" she whispered, her heart aching.

"I'd thought about it. He'd tried to talk me out of it, claimed that you weren't the marrying type—too interested in seeing the world." He slammed the window shut and the room seemed suddenly still.

"Ben, I didn't know—"

"You knew a lot, Carlie," he said, his lips curling into a sneer of disgust, his gaze suddenly dark and menacing. He grabbed her by the shoulders, his eyes fierce, his expression haunted. "He loved you, Carlie. We both should have known it, but we didn't want to. We were too wrapped up in each other to care about someone else. I rationalized everything—he was dating Tracy so it was okay for me to start seeing the girl that he couldn't forget."

"You've got it all turned around," she said, but she remembered the day on the dock when Kevin had surprised her and professed his love. She'd conveniently forgotten how wounded he'd been.

"Do I?" Ben snarled, his face flushed in anger, his hands clenching and stretching in frustration. "Why didn't you tell me about the letters, Carlie?"

"The letters?" she repeated. "What letters?"

He offered her a smile that chilled her to the bones. "You know the letters. The ones that Kevin wrote to you."

"I didn't get any—"

"Liar!" His fingers dug into the soft flesh of her upper arms. "We found some of the letters he hadn't gotten around to sending to you and they were pretty explicit about your relationship."

"There was no relationship!" she said. "I'd broken up with him, if you can even call it that. There wasn't even a reason to break up. We only had a few dates and I just told him I couldn't go out with him anymore."

"But those dates…they were powerful, weren't they?" he said, his hold punishing.

"I don't know what you're getting at, Ben."

"I know about the baby."

Her heart stopped suddenly and she hardly dared breathe. "*What* baby?"

"The baby you wouldn't have. Kevin's baby."

"Kevin's baby? What are you talking about? I never had a baby.…" Her voice failed her as her heart tightened in painful knots.

"Because you wouldn't," he snarled in disgust. The look he sent her was pure hatred.

"Oh, Ben, if you only knew."

"I do know. You were too selfish—"

"Hey wait a minute!" She shoved hard on his chest. "You don't know me, Ben Powell! Not at all. You didn't stick around long enough to find out, did you?"

"I know you wanted to get rid of the baby."

"I didn't want to get rid of any baby," she said, her throat closing as she shook her head in misery. Anger rushed through her veins. "You've got everything all twisted around. You think I was pregnant with Kevin's child and…and that I had an abortion?"

Horrified at his accusations, she watched the play of emotions contort his face. He was serious! He really believed this insane bunch of lies. He didn't say a word, but condemnation sizzled in his gaze and she died a little inside. If only she could reach out, touch his hand, explain…but the censure on his face was devastating.

Her knees nearly gave way when she thought of all the wasted years. All the lies. All the pain. Leaning against the wall for support, she shook her head. "I didn't…I never…Kevin and I…we didn't ever get that far."

"Don't lie to me, Carlie. It's too late."

"You should know better, Ben," she said, fury taking hold of her tongue again. Eyes shimmering with unshed tears, she inched her chin up a notch and pinned him with her furious gaze. "You are the one man who should know the truth!" Her heart shredded a little. It wasn't Kevin's baby she'd wanted all those years ago, it was Ben's. She'd hoped for a miracle, that though they'd made love only one night, that she would become pregnant. At the time, she'd wanted desperately to bear his child, and she'd been ecstatic when she'd skipped her period. But her euphoria had been short-lived. Though she'd taken an in-home pregnancy test that had showed positive, within weeks, she'd miscarried. Alone. The doctor had kept her secret and she'd never felt more miserable in her life.

A tear drizzled down her cheek, but she sniffed hard before any other traces of her regret tracked from her eyes. "Don't you remember?" she demanded, pride stiffening her spine. "I couldn't have been pregnant, Ben, because when I was seeing Kevin, I was still a virgin."

He had been reaching for his toolbox, but he froze.

"That night on the lake. In the rain? That's the night I lost my virginity, Ben!" she said, wounded and furious all in one instant. "And I didn't give it to Kevin. I gave it to his brother." *And I got pregnant. With your baby. Our baby!*

He stared at her in disbelief and she shook her head. "I don't know why you want to believe this ridiculous story—"

His face drained of color. "You were a—"

"Too bad you weren't paying attention," she said bitterly. "You could have saved yourself a whole lot of time and trouble hating me for something that was so obviously a lie!"

"I don't believe—"

"I don't care what you believe," she said in righteous fury. "You can think what you want! But the truth of the matter is that I gave my virginity to you, Ben, and if I'd been lucky enough to get pregnant it would have been with your child!" *It had been with your child!*

"But—"

"Kevin never touched me!"

His jaw clamped tightly together.

"I can't believe that you let some lie and your own guilt twist things around so that you hated me for all these years. Why didn't you come to me, Ben? Why didn't you let me explain rather than set yourself up as judge and jury?" Trembling inside, she motioned to the door. "You've always been wrong about me. You were wrong then and you're wrong now. I think you'd better go," she said firmly. "This is my place—my private place—and I don't want you here."

"I don't believe you."

She smiled bitterly. "Then you're a fool."

His lips curled and she thought he might grab her and shake her, but he muttered something under his breath, snapped his jaw shut, grabbed his toolbox and strode past. The door slammed behind him with a bang that rattled the old timbers of the house and caused the suspended light fixture to swing from the ceiling.

Carlie collapsed on the couch. *Ben had thought she'd been pregnant with Kevin's child and then had aborted the baby?* She let her head fall into her hands and the tears she'd held at bay ran from her eyes. How could he have believed that she could have been that heartless? Shuddering, she drew an old afghan to her neck. God, what a mess! She wished she could stop the cold that settled deep in her soul. She'd loved Ben, believed he'd loved her and yet he could be swayed by such vicious lies. And he didn't even know the truth. She supposed that he never would.

So why would he believe such horrid lies?

Because his brother died and he felt guilty. But he didn't have the right to believe the distortions of Kevin's letters. The least he could have done was face her.

Closing her eyes, she remembered all the guilt, all the pain that had seared through her soul. She'd felt somehow responsible for Kevin's death because she hadn't loved him, because she'd never felt for him what he'd sworn he felt for her, because she'd fallen in love with his younger brother.

Though Kevin had left no suicide note, the general consensus in town was that Kevin had killed himself. He'd been unhappy and troubled for years. Some final straw had caused him to drive into the dilapidated garage of his tiny house, close the door and leave the Corvette running.

Carlie had gone to the funeral hoping to speak with Ben, but the Powells had kept their distance from the rest of the mourners and the icy glares she received from Ben's parents kept her from approaching the grieving family. Donna had returned from the Midwest to bury her son, and George, looking pale and wan, had made his wishes clear: no one was to bother the family. Especially not Carlie Surrett.

Carlie hadn't wanted to intrude; she'd just wanted to talk to Ben. She'd seen him in the funeral parlor and again at the grave site but he'd never so much as glanced her way. Standing still and straight, like the soldier he would soon become, he'd stared at a point far in the distant hills while Reverend Osgood had given a final blessing over the coffin.

The entire town had been stunned by Kevin's unfortunate death. Gold Creek was a small community and the loss of one of its young citizens was a shock. Friends, family and acquaintances had come out in droves, paying their respects and grieving. For weeks after Kevin was buried people had spoken of the Powells' "tragic loss" while shaking their heads.

Carlie had tried to see Ben, before and after the funeral, but he'd refused her calls, and sent back her letters, unopened. Desperate, she'd even plotted to go to the Powells' home on the outskirts of town where Ben was rumored to be staying with his father and demand that he see her.

Rachelle had tried to talk her out of it. Brenda had advised her to let time go by. Her parents had told her that the Powells deserved their privacy in their time of loss.

So Carlie had waited, working up her nerve, planning what she would say to Ben. By the time she'd found her courage and was ready to tell him that they were going to be parents, Ben had already taken off. She heard through the grapevine that he'd left town for the army. "That's what Patty Osgood says," her friend, Brenda, had told her three weeks after the funeral. They'd been seated at the counter in the drugstore and sipping lemonade. Brenda had swirled her ice cubes with her straw. "I usually take what Patty says as gospel, if you know what I mean. She hears all the gossip in town in church, y'know. If I were you, I'd forget him."

But he's the father of my child, Carlie had wanted to scream and had held a protective hand over her abdomen.

The rumor that Ben had joined up had proved true and Carlie had been left trying to mend her broken heart, hoping that Ben would call or write.

She'd started cramping the day after she found out that he was gone. The bleeding, just a few drops at first, followed. She'd lost the baby that one night and her romantic dreams of Ben had turned out to be the foolish wishes of a girl caught in a one-sided love affair: she'd never heard from him again.

"Oh, Lord," she whispered, refusing to shed any more tears for a past that could never be changed. "Stop it, Carlie! Get a grip, would you?" Angry with her runaway emotions, she shoved herself upright and walked to the kitchen where she found a bottle of wine and poured herself a glass of Chablis.

"Not a good sign," she told herself as she took an experimental sip and felt the cool wine slide down her throat. "Not a good sign at all. Drinking alone." But she didn't care, not tonight, and she wasn't going to sit here in the dark crying over Ben Powell or his ridiculous accusations. Let him think what he wanted. It didn't matter.

So why couldn't she convince herself?

Her stomach rumbled though it was barely five o'clock and she remembered that she'd missed lunch. The photography shop had been busy and during the noon hour, she'd driven to the hospital and visited her father. Later, there hadn't been any time to grab anything to eat.

Still, food wasn't appealing. Without a lot of enthusiasm she fixed herself a small dinner of crackers, cheese and apple slices. Sipping her wine, she ate the less-than-exciting meal and didn't taste anything, not realizing how the time was passing as she wasted the evening thinking about Ben, the man who had sworn he'd never wanted her. Not then. Not now. Not ever.

WRONG? HE'D BEEN wrong about Carlie? For long over a decade? Ben drove through the rain-washed streets and swore under his breath. He couldn't trust her, of course. She was probably lying again, but the anguish in her clear blue eyes had nearly convinced him. She might be lying but she believed her lies!

"Damn," he muttered, his eyes narrowing against the rain drizzling down his windshield. Could he have been so stupid not to realize that Carlie had given him her virginity that night so long ago? Had he been deluding himself, wasting time hating her for a decade? Not that he'd had all that much experience himself and he'd been so caught up in his own passion that he hadn't been thinking clearly. She hadn't said anything and he hadn't asked.

Later, upon finding the letters in Kevin's house and reading between the lines, thus learning of Carlie's pregnancy, Ben had felt as if a hot knife of betrayal had been twisted in his heart. The thought that she'd made love to Kevin had burned like acid in his gut and he'd thrown up. What had been so special between them suddenly seemed dirty and incestuous and ugly. His blossoming love for her had withered quickly into hatred, a hatred his family had helped nurture.

So why was he half believing her and second-guessing himself? Because he wanted her. Even though he professed to hate her, he couldn't help remembering the feel of her body against his, the way her lips rounded when she moaned, the curve of her neck when he held her close. His fingers clenched hard over the steering wheel and he nearly missed stopping for a red light. At the last minute he slammed on his brakes. A furious horn blasted from behind him.

"Damn," he said under his breath.

Another impatient honk warned him that the light had changed yet again, and he tromped on the accelerator, the back wheels spinning on the wet pavement. At the next corner, he wheeled into the parking lot of a gas station and cut the engine.

He climbed out of the cab and waved to the attendant, Joe Knapp, a man who'd gone to school with him years before. Joe had been captain of the football team way back when and after school, when he'd had his leg crushed while working in the woods for Fitzpatrick Logging, Joe's dreams of a career in football had been destroyed, as well. Kind of like Kevin. Only Joe had survived, married a hometown girl, Mary Beth Carter, and seemed happy enough with his wife and kids.

Scowling to himself, Ben shoved the nozzle of the pump into the gas tank and listened as the liquid poured into his truck.

He couldn't trust Carlie. *Couldn't!* Oh, but a part of him would love to. That same rebellious part that still wanted to kiss her senseless and make love to her forever.

That thought caused him to start and he nearly let the gas overflow.

"You're losing it, Powell," he growled to himself as he turned off the pump. With thoughts of Carlie trailing after him like a shadow, he walked inside the small Texaco station that had been on the corner of Hearst and Pine for as long as he could remember. The building had changed hands, but it still smelled of grease and stale cigarette smoke and oil.

"Good to see you around here again," Joe said as he took Ben's credit card in his grimy fingers. "I thought you'd said *adios* to Gold Creek forever."

"So did I."

Joe flashed him a toothy smile as he ran Ben's card through the verification machine. "So you feel like the prodigal son?"

"Nope. Just the black sheep."

Joe laughed and Ben signed the receipt. The conversation turned to football. The usual stuff. If the 49ers were going to the Super Bowl the following season, or if L.A. had a better chance. As if it mattered.

Later, as Ben drove away from the station and through

the heart of town, he couldn't remember any of the conversation. Retail buildings gave way to houses that bordered the eastern hills, but he didn't notice any of the landmarks that had been a part of his hometown.

Because of Carlie. Damn that woman! Why couldn't he get her out of his head?

Ben liked things cut-and-dried, clear and to the point and structured. That's why he'd felt comfortable in the army, working his way up through the rank and file, and that's why he'd planned to come back to Gold Creek, start his own business, settle down with a *sensible* small-town girl and raise his family. His future had seemed so clear.

Until he'd seen Carlie again.

And until he'd listened to her side of the story. Her lies. Or her truth?

"Hell," he growled as he turned into the drive of his little house that wasn't far from the city limits of Gold Creek. Ben had rented the place from an elderly woman, Mrs. Trover, who lived at Rosewood Terrace in an apartment just down the hall from his father. Ben promised to keep the house up, including minor and major repairs, which he could deduct from the monthly rent. It wasn't much, two bedrooms, living room, single bath, kitchen, laundry room and a basement that leaked in the winter, but it had become home and he was certain, when the time was right, he could probably buy the house, outbuildings and half acre of land from Mrs. Trover on a contract.

He turned off the ignition and sat in the pickup for a second. The cottage needed more than a little repair— "TLC" he'd heard it called, but Ben knew it was just plain hard work. Even when it was brought up to code, the house wouldn't be ritzy and Ben couldn't picture Carlie living here with a tiny bathroom and a kitchen so small, only one person could work in it. Rubbing his jaw, he wondered why he kept trying to picture her in his future. She was all wrong for him. Kevin had told him as much long ago.

He should have listened. Maybe then Kevin would still be alive and Ben wouldn't walk around with a load of guilt on his shoulders for falling for his older brother's girl.

Trying to shove Carlie and all the emotional baggage she brought with her from his mind, he grabbed the sack of dog food he'd purchased earlier in the day and hauled the bag to the back door. "Honey, I'm home," he said as he unlocked the door.

Attila growled from the darkened interior.

"Well, at least you still have your sweet disposition."

A deep-throated bark.

"Come on, get out of here and do your business," Ben said leaving the outside door open as he walked into the kitchen and found a mixing bowl. The dog padded after him, hackles raised, but not emitting a sound. "Go on. You don't have to follow me around." He sliced open the sack, poured the dry dog food into the bowl and set it on the kitchen floor.

Attila just looked at him.

"Go on. Dig in." Ben waited and the dog slowly, as if he expected to be kicked or poisoned, cautiously approached the food. "Be paranoid if you want," Ben said.

The shepherd cocked his head, then hurried outside. Within seconds he was back, his nose deep in dog food.

"That's better." Ben grabbed a beer from the refrigerator and walked into the living room. Flicking on the remote control to the television, he dropped into a chair near an old rolltop desk he'd shoved into the corner. The message light on his telephone was blinking. "Hopefully, this is about a dozen clients begging me to come work for them," he said with a glance to the dog.

Attila didn't respond.

He pressed the button, the tape rewound and a series of clicks were followed by the first message.

"This is Bill with General Drywall. We can be at the house on Bitner next week on Tuesday. I'll send a crew unless I hear from you."

The phone clicked again.

"Ben?" a female voice asked. "This is Tracy. I saw you today at the restaurant and I...we, Randy and I...were wondering if you'd like to stop by for dinner tonight. Nothing special—but we'd love to have you." She paused for a second, then said, "How about seven? And if I don't hear from you by six, I'll just figure you had other plans. It was great seeing you today. Hope you can make it."

He glanced at his watch. Five-forty-five. Why not have dinner with Tracy? A small-town girl. A woman who was content to live here with her son. Kevin's son.

Carlie's face flashed before his eyes and he felt like a Judas. But that was crazy. Even if she were telling the truth about her relationship with Kevin, she'd thrown him out of her house. Gritting his teeth, he reached for the receiver.

He owed Carlie Surrett nothing!

"THIS IS YOUR uncle Ben," Tracy said to a young red-headed freckle-faced boy. His hair was straight and fell over his forehead in a way that reminded Ben of Kevin a long, long time ago.

Randy wrinkled his nose. "Uncle Ben? You mean like the guy on the rice box?"

Ben laughed and stretched out his hand. "Not exactly," he replied, shaking Randy's hand.

"Don't give Ben a hard time," Tracy gently chastised

her son. They lived in a nice apartment in Coleville, as modern as Carlie's was rustic. White rug, white walls, white appliances and white furniture with a few throw pillows of mauve and blue.

"He's not giving me a bad time," Ben said. "What grade are you in?"

"Fourth."

"Same as Nadine's oldest boy," Tracy said, turning back to the sink. "But they don't see each other much since we don't live in Gold Creek."

"Are you talking about John Warne?" Randy asked.

"You know we are."

"He's a creep."

Tracy visibly stiffened. "That's not very nice—"

"Hey, it's the truth," Randy said. "And I don't care if he is my cousin because he's a jerk."

"You don't really know him."

"Well, I know Katie Osgood. I see her in Sunday school and she tells me all about John—like how he's the biggest dweeb in the whole school. He's always in the principal's office."

"That's enough, Randy," Tracy said, managing a forced smile. "Why don't you show Ben your baseball-card collection?"

"He won't want to see—"

"Sure, I will," Ben said, anxious to diffuse the tension between mother and son.

Hanging his head, Randy led Ben down a short hallway to a small room covered with posters of baseball players. Within minutes, he'd opened several albums and was telling Ben about all the players. He was particularly proud of a few old cards of Mickey Mantle and Whitey Ford, "you know, those old famous guys," he said to Ben, his face lighting up. "My dad had these cards when he was a kid. Grandpa kept them for me."

Ben's heart twisted. This boy was Kevin's bastard, a kid George Powell had accepted. He spent half an hour with Randy and the cards before Tracy called from the kitchen, "How about something to drink?"

"I'll have a Coke!" Randy yelled back.

"I was talking to Ben," she replied, wiping her hands as she appeared in the doorway. "But I'll get you something, too. By the way, it's seven." She glanced at Ben as Randy turned on a small black-and-white television. "There's some sports show he always watches about this time. Come on into the kitchen."

While Randy settled back on his bed, his cards spread around him, his eyes glued to the little black-and-white screen, Ben followed Tracy back to the kitchen. She was a pretty woman, but as he watched her hips sway beneath her black skirt, he felt nothing.

"Okay, the selection isn't all that great but I've got beer and wine and…a bottle of Irish whiskey, I think."

"A beer'll do," he said, feeling suddenly awkward. The apartment was clean and neat, not a magazine out of place, and on a table near the couch was a gold-framed picture of Kevin, a picture Ben recognized as having been taken only a few weeks before his brother's death. Ben stared at the photograph and felt that same mixture of pain and anger build in him as it always did when he was reminded of his older brother.

"Belly up to the bar," Tracy invited as she placed a bottle and empty glass on the counter that separated the kitchen from the eating area. She held up a frosty mug of dark soda. "I'll run this down to His Highness and be back in a flash."

He drank his beer and watched her work in the kitchen. She was efficient and smiled and laughed a lot, but there were emotions that ran deep in her brown eyes, something false, as if the layer of lightheartedness she displayed covered up other, darker feelings. Her smile seemed a little forced and there was a hardness to her that bothered him.

They ate at a little table by the sliding door and the food was delicious: steak, baked potatoes and steamed broccoli smothered in a packaged cheese sauce. She poured them each a glass of wine and made sure that Randy's manners were impeccable. Ben had the feeling that the kid had been coached for hours. "No elbows," she said when Randy set his arm on the table. "What did I say about your hat?" she asked, noticing the fact that Randy's Giants' cap was resting on his head. "Oh, Randy, you know better! Please…use the butter knife. That's what it's there for."

When Randy finally asked to be excused, Ben let out a silent sigh of relief. "He really is a good boy," she said as Randy ambled down the hall.

"Of course he is."

"Straight A's and pitcher for his Little League team. They won the pennant last year." She smiled, all filled with pride and Ben got an uneasy feeling that she was trying to sell the kid to him. "He's in the school choir, too. Last year he had the lead in their little play. It wasn't much, you understand, only third graders, but he was the one they chose. Probably because of his voice and the fact that he's smart as a whip. I've been into that school five times this year already, asking them to move him up a grade or two in math. He's bored with what they're teaching."

Ben shoved his chair from the table. "Ever thought of private school?"

She sighed. "All the time. But that takes money and, well, being a single mother, we don't have a lot of extra cash." She picked up her plate and when Ben tried to carry his to the sink, she waved him back in his chair. "Sit, sit. I can handle this."

"So can I."

"But you've been working all day."

"Haven't you?"

She smiled and seemed flustered. "Just let me do it, all right? It's been a long time since I've had a man to pamper."

Warning bells went off in his head, but he ignored them. She was just trying to be nice. Nothing to worry about. She stacked the dishes in the sink and cut him a thick slab of chocolate cake.

"Won't Randy want some of this?" he asked, when she sliced a sliver for herself and sat back down at the table.

"He's in training. No sweets."

"But—"

She shook her head and took a bite. "Baseball starts in a few weeks and tryouts are just around the corner. He's got to be in shape. He's lucky I let him have a soft drink tonight."

"He's barely ten."

"Doesn't matter," she said, that underlying hardness surfacing in her eyes. "You, of all people, should understand. It's kind of like being in the military. Randy wants to be the ace pitcher again this year and I told him that I'll support him in that goal, but only if he works hard for it. No junk food. Lots of rest. Exercise. And he's got to keep his grades up."

"And sing in the choir and do higher-level math," Ben added, unable to hide the sarcasm in his voice.

"Why not? He can do it all."

"When does he have a chance to be a little kid?"

She sat on the couch and frowned when he slid into a white chair in the corner of the living room. "He *is* a little kid. A disciplined little kid."

"But when does he build forts and play in the woods and ride his bike and swim and—"

"When he trains, he swims on the weekends in the Coleville pool and there are no woods right around here. Riding his bike is dangerous—too much traffic. Besides we have a stationary bike in my room. If he wants to work out—"

"I'm not talking about working out. I'm talking about just hanging around," Ben said, his insides clenching when he considered how much pressure the kid had to live up to.

She was about to argue, thought better of it and kicked off her high heels. Tucking her feet beneath her on the couch, she sipped her wine slowly. "I suppose it does look like Randy's on a pretty tough regimen, doesn't it?" Sighing, she ran the fingers of one hand through her hair. "And part of the reason is that it's easier for me to have him on a schedule. I work two jobs and don't have a lot of free time so I have to depend on other people to give him rides. I don't want him to spend too much time alone— that's not good—so I encourage him to participate and be with kids his own age."

"And win."

She smiled. "Because he can, Ben. He's got so much potential." Her eyes glazed for a second, she licked her lips, and she whispered, "Just like Kevin."

Ben's stomach turned to stone. He suddenly realized why Tracy had never married; no one could compare to his brother. She didn't give another man a chance. And over the years she'd created a myth about Kevin, the myth being that he was perfect.

"Kevin was an average student, Tracy."

"He had a basketball scholarship."

"That was taken away when he couldn't keep up his grades."

"He just had some bad breaks," she said quickly. "How about a cup of coffee?"

"I can't." He stood, glad for an excuse to leave. "I've got a million calls to make before it gets too late. But thanks."

"Anytime," she said as if she meant it. She walked to him and touched his arm with featherlight fingers. "The door's always open for you, Ben. It does Randy a world of good. He…he needs a…man. Just wait a minute and I'll get him. He'll want to say good-night."

She hurried down the hall and a few minutes later, she practically pushed Randy forward to shake Ben's hand.

The boy licked his lips nervously. "Glad to meet you—" he shifted his eyes to his mother, struggled for the words and added "—Uncle Ben."

"You, too, Randy. Maybe I'll see you at the ball field." Ben clasped the kid's hand.

His sullen face broke into a smile. "Would you?"

"You bet. Can I bring my dog?"

"You've got a dog?" Randy's eyes widened and all evidence of his pained expression disappeared. "What kind?"

"A mean one."

"Really."

"I call him Attila."

Tracy's lips tightened.

"He just showed up at the office with his belly sliced open."

Randy's eyes were wide. "Wow!"

"He's a German shepherd—a black long-haired one."

"Cool!" Randy said, grinning ear to ear.

"You're allergic to dogs, Randy," his mother reminded him gently as she nudged him back down the hallway. "And so am I—at least I'm allergic to big dogs that shed." She walked with Ben to the front porch and Ben felt as if she expected something from him, something he couldn't give her.

"Thanks for dinner. It was great."

"We could do it again," she suggested, her lips curved into a satisfied smile.

"I'll let you know." He felt a jab of guilt when he recognized the hope in her eyes.

"Good night, Ben," she said as he started across the parking lot. "Call me."

He didn't bother to turn around and lie to her. He wasn't about to start a romance with Tracy and he felt that whether she realized it or not, Tracy hoped to use Ben as a replacement for his dead brother.

"What a mess," he growled as he climbed into his truck and let out the clutch. He thought of Carlie again. Beautiful Carlie. Seductive Carlie. Lying Carlie.

The old Dodge leapt forward and he flicked on the windshield wipers. *Women,* he thought unkindly. *Why were they so much damned trouble?*

CHAPTER EIGHT

"WHEN YOU LEFT town, you thought Carlie was pregnant—with Kevin's baby?" Nadine was clearly astonished. Hauling a huge suitcase out of her new Mercedes, a wedding gift from her husband, she shook her head, then slammed the door shut with her hip.

"That's what the letters said."

"No way." Shaking her head in disgust, she unlocked the front door. "Sometimes, Ben, I don't understand you. Come in. I think we need to talk. But first things first. Bring in those other bags, will ya?" She tossed him her keys and he found two suitcases in the backseat. "Hayden will park it in the garage later—there's some stuff he's got to move around in there—things left over from the wedding."

Ben grabbed the other two bags, locked the sleek car and walked back into the house. The Christmas tree was still standing in the corner but some of the lights had been stripped from the stairs and all the flowers had begun to wilt.

Nadine sighed loudly as she walked to the den, dropped her large case and kicked off her shoes. "Oooh, that's better. I've been dragging my latest inventory all over the place. Heather Brooks hooked me up with some art dealers who are expanding into jewelry and jackets, you know…'wearable art.' Now I'm afraid I'm going to end up with more orders than I can fill." She led him into the kitchen where she opened the refrigerator door and peered at the contents. "How about some sparkling apple juice?"

"I don't think so," he said with more than a trace of sarcasm.

"Might brighten your mood."

"I doubt it."

"A cola?" She didn't bother waiting for an answer, just grabbed two cans and handed him one. As she sat in one of the kitchen chairs and popped the lid, she rested her heel on one of the empty chairs and said, "Now let's start over. You thought *Carlie* was pregnant—by Kevin, right?"

Was she deaf? "We already discussed this."

"But *why,* Ben?"

"Because of the letters."

"The letters?" she repeated, then caught on. "Oh, we're talking about the letters you found in Kevin's bedroom, right?"

"Yep." He didn't like talking about the subject, but knew there was no other way to get to the truth. Ben had been seated in his pickup, waiting for Nadine, brooding about Carlie for over an hour, wondering what was truth and what was fiction.

"Are you serious?" She actually had the gall to laugh.

"This isn't a joke."

"Yes, it is!" Rolling her eyes, she took a long swallow of her drink. "You really thought—"

"Yes, I did. Now what's so damned funny?"

"It's pathetic really." Her green eyes turned sober. "I think you read too much between the lines."

"What do you mean?" he asked, surprised at the hope leaping in his heart.

She massaged her foot as she shook her head. "I read those letters and yes, Kevin was in love with Carlie—

that much was obvious. He was really hurt that she was seeing you and he felt betrayed by both of you."

The old pain knotted Ben's stomach, but he'd expected as much. Nadine never pulled any punches. You asked her a question, she gave you a straight answer.

She was still talking. "...but the pregnancy he wrote about had to have been Tracy's." Nadine reached across the table and touched the back of Ben's hand. "Don't you remember? *Tracy* was pregnant. Not Carlie. And the abortion you read about was just hopeful thinking on Kevin's part," she said with a twist of the lips. "He didn't want the baby. We're talking about Randy, you know. It took a lot of guts for Tracy to have that baby and raise him on her own. Kevin was dead and the tongues in this town were wagging like crazy. But she did and Randy's a super kid. In fact," she said wryly, "with his grades and all, he certainly shows mine up, not that I'd change anything about John and Bobby. My boys are just more...trouble."

"Like their mother," Ben said, though he didn't feel much like joking. Had he been so blind? For all these years. "Those letters were addressed to Carlie."

"But never mailed. They were just a way for Kevin to let off steam, or maybe someday he would have had the nerve to send them to her, I don't know, but you turned everything around in your head." She took a long swallow of her soda and settled back in her chair.

Was that possible? Had he been so much a fool? So quick to judge? Blaming Carlie for something that wasn't her fault? He lapsed into dark silence and his thoughts were like demons in his head, poking and prodding with painful memories.

"Look, it was a rough time for all of us," she said, "but if you've been hating Carlie because of those letters, you'd better let it go. It's just not fair."

"That's what she said," he admitted, remembering her fury.

"Oh." Nadine's breath whistled through her teeth. "You didn't go charging over there half-cocked and accuse her of all sorts of vile deeds, did you?" When he didn't answer she rolled her eyes again. "Oh, Ben, why? I wanted to blame her, too. She was an easy target, but the fact of the matter is, Kevin took his own life. It's a damned shame. God, I still miss him. But that's what happened."

At that moment Hayden and the boys arrived home. The back door banged open and two dogs, muddy feet and all, bounded into the kitchen in a swirl of rain-dampened air.

"Hershel—Leo—out!" Nadine commanded, but the animals paid no heed. They raced through the kitchen and down the hallway leading to the foyer. "That's what I like about this place, the way I have absolute control," she muttered under her breath.

John and Bobby barreled in through the back door. They were hurling insults at each other at the top of their lungs.

"Nerd!"

"Baby!"

"At least I didn't kiss Katie Osgood!" Bobby said, tossing Nadine a superior glance.

"You kissed—"

"Aw, Mom, she kissed me!" John said, his face mottling red.

"So much for peace and quiet," Nadine said, reaching for Bobby as he tried to race out of the room. She captured him and planted a kiss on his cheek. He giggled loudly. "That's what you get, mister, for not even saying 'hi' to your mom."

He smiled and nuzzled her cheek. "Hi."

"And you—" She turned to John but he was back-pedaling out of the room.

"I'm too old for that sissy stuff," he said, disappearing into the hall.

"Yeah, that's because you got enough kissing for the day," Bobby crowed.

"Not me. I haven't had nearly enough sissy stuff!" Hayden leaned over and kissed his wife's crown. "The older I get the more of the 'sissy stuff' I want."

"You're incorrigible."

"And you're irresistible." He kissed her again, then glanced up at Ben. "Hi—I suppose you came with the blueprints," he said, obviously hopeful to see how the plans for Nadine's cabin were progressing.

"Nope, he just brought the blues," Nadine quipped. "But I think I can twist his arm and convince him to stay for dinner."

"With your wild bunch? No way."

"Come on—"

"Not tonight," Ben said, draining his can and shoving his chair away from the table.

"Got a lot to think about?" she asked, shooting him a knowing look.

"Too much," he admitted as he walked out the back door and cut through the breezeway to his pickup. He climbed in and fired up the old truck.

Somehow he had to figure out the truth. Had he been so naive, so insensitive that he hadn't realized that he was making love to a virgin? Had he just assumed that she'd been experienced and then ignored the signs of her own naiveté?

He felt like a fool. He remembered their night of love-making in the rain. He still felt a wonder at the thrill of it.

Never had he felt so alive and never, with the women he'd been with since that fateful night, had he ever felt so completely undone. The joining of his body and Carlie's had been unique and earth-shattering and passionate. Even Kevin's death hadn't turned that spectacular memory bitter.

He'd blamed Kevin's death for his inability to feel the same exhilaration with a woman, but now he knew differently. The reason sex had never been the same was that he'd never again allowed himself to become so emotionally attached to his partner.

Fool! he told himself as he drove home through the misting rain.

He hadn't even realized that she'd been a virgin. He'd been so caught up in his own pleasure that he hadn't noticed any sign of her discomfort, or any breakage of tissue or any pain.

"Damn it all." He felt like a complete idiot. An idiot who had falsely blamed a woman for too many years. "Hell, Powell, who did you think you were?"

Never had he considered Carlie's feelings. After Kevin's death, he'd turned her phone calls and letters callously away, never once explaining, refusing to listen to her side of the story. He'd just blamed her for Kevin's death and condemned her to his family and friends. And when he'd joined the army, he'd run as fast and as far away from her as possible.

The truck bounced along the rutted drive to his little rental house, a house he'd hoped to share with a woman someday.

He wondered if Carlie would ever be that woman and snorted at the thought. She'd be out of her mind to trust him again.

THOMAS FITZPATRICK'S OFFICE was quietly understated. Located on the third floor of one of the oldest buildings in town, the original Gold Creek Hotel, the offices of Fitzpatrick, Incorporated were plush without being ostentatious.

Carlie was seated in a chair near the window and Thomas was speaking, his even voice well modulated from years of public oration.

"...So I don't want any studio shots or pictures that are obviously posed. I want to show the men at work, doing their jobs, the American worker at his best." Thomas Fitzpatrick leaned back in his leather chair, seemingly pleased with his eloquence. His hands were tented under his chin and, from the far side of his desk, he watched Carlie over his fingertips. His gaze was speculative and thoughtful and it bothered Carlie more than it should.

She didn't know why she felt like a bird with a broken wing under the fixed stare of the neighborhood tomcat. She shook off the feeling. He was a man, a wealthy man, but he had no power over her.

Carlie hoped her smile didn't look as brittle as it felt. "No mugging for the camera?"

"Absolutely," Thomas said, a smile curving beneath his clipped mustache. "Now, mind you, I don't want anything that looks the least bit...dangerous...or uncomfortable for the men. I want to show the logging company as an exciting but safe workplace, where we, at Fitzpatrick, Incorporated are concerned with the environment and working conditions as well as the bottom line." He raised his eyebrows as if expecting her to comment.

"Is that possible?"

His lips twitched. "I think you can make it possible, Miss Surrett."

She wanted to tell him that she was a photographer, not a magician, but she decided discretion was the better part of valor in this case. "I'll give it a shot," she agreed, feeling like a traitor.

"Good. Now tell me, how is your father?" He had the decency to look genuinely concerned.

"Better. He should be going home in a couple of days."

Thomas sighed heavily. "When he's up to it, have him call me. I've already talked to the corporate attorneys and accountants about the possibility of his early retirement, but I wanted to speak to Weldon again first."

"That's a good idea," she said stiffly.

"Look, he knows that there are desk jobs available, but—"

"He doesn't want your charity, Mr. Fitzpatrick. Nor your pity." Deciding she shouldn't discuss her father's health with the man who was stripping away all of Weldon's dreams, she slung the strap of her purse over her shoulder and stood. "I can start working at the logging company offices at the beginning of next week."

"Perfect. Just check in with Marge, the secretary over there, and she'll let Brian know what's going on."

She started to turn to leave, but his voice stopped her. "There are a couple of other things."

She tensed, but willed her body to relax as she turned to face him again.

"My daughter, Toni—you know her, I believe."

"We've met."

Thomas's face clouded over. "She may be getting married soon—within the next couple of months—and we might need a photographer for the wedding. I wondered if you'd be interested."

She wanted to tell him no, that she was already regretting working for him, that she didn't want anything more to do with the Fitzpatricks and their money, but she couldn't. She was too practical and until her father was home, the hospital and doctor bills paid, and his future a little more certain, Carlie couldn't afford to turn down any offers. "I'd be very interested," she said. "Have Toni give me a call."

"I will. Now the other." He set his feet on the floor and placed his elbows on the desktop. "It's more personal. I was hoping you could find time in your busy schedule for dinner. With me."

Uncertain she'd heard correctly, she hesitated for just a heartbeat. "I don't think that would be such a good idea."

His grin was self-deprecating. "Don't get the wrong idea, Ms. Surrett. This would be strictly business. I am, after all, still married." A dark shadow passed behind his eyes for just a second, then disappeared.

"As long as we understand each other."

"Absolutely. How about a week from Friday? Seven?"

Carlie felt uncomfortable. She was used to handling passes from men of all ages; she'd had more than her share of offers when she was modeling, but she couldn't afford to offend Fitzpatrick. "Let me check my calendar."

"Fine. I'll give you a call," he said, as she made her way out of his office and into his secretary's, Melanie Patton's, sanctuary. Melanie hardly glanced up as Carlie breezed by and swept through another set of doors to the reception area where a young girl was talking on the phone. The elevator took her down three floors to the foyer of the elegant old hotel.

Thomas Fitzpatrick had done the town one good turn, she decided. Rather than call in the wrecking ball, he'd spent the money necessary to restore one of the oldest buildings in Gold Creek and returned the gold-brick building to its original charm. Thick Oriental carpets covered glossy floors and, three stories over the lobby, a skylight of stained glass allowed sunlight to pool in muted shades upon the walls and floor.

However there wasn't enough charm in the building to alleviate her distaste at dealing with the man. He was too smooth, almost oily, and she had the gut feeling that anything he did was with one sole intention: the promotion and profit of Thomas Fitzpatrick.

She had lunch with her mother at the drugstore, visited her father for the remainder of her lunch hour, then spent the rest of the day at the shop. By the time she was finished with a studio sitting with four-year-old triplets, it was nearly seven and she was exhausted.

The last person she wanted to deal with was Ben Powell, but as she pulled into the parking lot, she recognized his truck parked in between the twin spruce trees. "Great," she muttered, remembering the disaster of the night before. She was tired and cranky and didn't want to face him.

Hopefully, he was working in another apartment.

No such luck.

When she shoved the door to her unit open she found him, sprawled across her old sofa, his shoes kicked off, his head propped against the overstuffed arm. As if he belonged. As if she'd invited him. As if she wanted him.

"I'd about given up on you," he drawled.

"What're you doing here?"

His smile was slow and sexy. "Waiting for you."

"So you could come back and insult me again?" she asked, all the old anger chasing through her blood. "No way. I'm tired and I don't think I should have to make a nightly ritual of throwing you out of my apartment. So why don't you take the hint and I won't have to get rude?"

"We need to talk."

"Talk? I don't think so. We said plenty last night. More than we should have."

"That's where you're wrong." He swung his feet to the floor and stood, studying his fingernails for a second. "We've got a lot more to say to each other."

She waited.

"Okay, I'll go first. I'm sorry, Carlie," he said, though the words seemed to lodge in his throat for a second.

"You're sorry?" She couldn't believe her ears. Ben Powell was apologizing. To her? After all this time? Damn hard to believe.

"For jumping to conclusions." He glanced up at her and his expression was sober. "I made a lot of mistakes and I have no excuses. I could say that I was just a kid, that I was confused, that I was naive enough to believe lies, but the truth of the matter is I guess I wanted to believe the worst about you. You were an easy target. You made it possible for me to shrug off some of the guilt."

She felt hot tears threatening the back of her eyes again. "You believe me?" she whispered.

"I didn't want to. To tell you the truth, I wanted to go on thinking that you were a lying, callous, coldhearted woman."

"Why?"

"Because it was easier," he said. "Less complicated." He walked up to her and touched her shoulder. Quickly she drew away, crossing the room to the window and stared out at the gathering night. "I've spent the last twenty-four hours soul-searching, trying to convince myself that you're trouble, that you're the last woman in the world for me and that I'd be a fool to come back." He hesitated a minute, then let out a long sigh. "But I couldn't. Not until we straightened things out. I think there's a chance I haven't been fair to you."

"A big chance."

His jaw tightened. "As I said, I came here to apologize."

She knew she should point him in the direction of the door and shove him hard, but there was a part of her, a very small and determined part, that wanted to hear him out. For years she'd fantasized about him groveling in front of her, begging her forgiveness, but those were just girlhood dreams of vindication. "I don't want or need your apologies, Ben," she said slowly. "There's been too much time…too many years…" She lifted her hands and dropped them again. "Too much pain. I just want to be left alone."

Shaking his head slowly, never letting his gaze move from the contours of her face, he said, "I don't believe you."

"Then you're a fool."

His smile was irreverently cocky. "Been called worse."

"I'll bet." She swallowed hard and her pulse thundered in her brain as he approached her, his eyes glimmering with a silver fire. The way he was staring at her turned her blood to warm honey and she had to remind herself that he was dangerous, that spending any more time with him would only cause her more heartache than she would ever be able to bear. Until today he'd believed the most hideous lies about her. "You…you have to leave."

"Not yet."

"Please, Ben, do us both a favor."

"In a minute."

"You have to leave—" Throat so dry she could barely speak, she whispered, "Please, Ben, if you really want to make things right, just walk out the door and don't ever come back."

"If only I could," he said as his arms suddenly surrounded her and he lowered his head. For an instant he hesitated, as if he, too, were afraid to take the next step. His lips were poised over hers, bare inches from her mouth.

"Don't do this."

"I have to." Her breath caught and she thought she might die as desire and disgust warred deep within her soul. "I've wanted to do this from the minute I saw you at the lake before the wedding," he said as his lips found hers in a kiss that was hard, and hot and filled with years of repression. She told herself to squirm away, to fight, but the gentle pressure of his mouth, the sweet sensual tickle of his tongue against her teeth and lips, the hard contours of his muscles fitting perfectly against hers, kept her silently pressed against him.

She knew this was wrong, that right now she was vulnerable and that she couldn't let Ben back into her heart or her life. Yet she couldn't pull away, and the harder he kissed her, his tongue and hands becoming more demanding, the more distant the warning bells sounded.

She was wrapped in the warm, seductive haze of yesterday. The winter wind was no longer lashing at the house and rattling the windows; no, a soft summer breeze, scented with lilacs and honeysuckle played upon the air. And she was a girl again, a girl in love. Her arms wound around his neck and she didn't stop him when his hands clamped over the lowest part of her rib cage, holding her close, letting her feel the heat of desire burning through his flesh.

When at last he lifted his head, he let out a long rush of air. "It's always been like this between us," he said, as he dropped his forehead to rest against hers. "I don't understand it."

"Neither do I." Her senses began to clear and she struggled away from him. "But it's got to stop."

"Why?"

"Because it's wrong, Ben. We both know it. You use me when it's convenient and when it's not, you hurl insults at me and accuse me of things I had no part in."

She took a step backward, but his strong arms surrounded her again, more tightly this time. He yanked her back against him. "Carlie, don't—"

"You don't!" she insisted, refusing to be one of those kind of women who went weak around a man regardless of how he treated her. "A few days ago you accused me of… Oh, Lord, this isn't worth thinking about. Just let go of me!"

Ben refused. Determination and grit clamped his jaw shut. "I came here to sort things out."

"They're sorted. We both know we're wrong for each other."

"What we know is that we were young and impetuous and couldn't keep our hands off each other."

"You thought I slept with your brother," she reminded him, trying to keep her voice steady. "You thought I got pregnant by him and got rid of the baby. You thought I used him to get to you and you thought he killed himself over me. Oh, God, Ben," she whispered, blinking against the rush of unwanted tears that filled her eyes. "You blamed me for everything that went wrong in your life." She had the urge to tell him the truth, to let him know that at one time he, not Kevin, could have become a father, but she couldn't trust that very private secret to him. Not yet. Probably not ever. "I wasn't at fault and neither were you. So stop beating yourself up and while you're at it, do the same for me."

He didn't flinch, didn't move a muscle, but she could see by the hardening of his features that she'd finally gotten through to him. He looked as if he were grappling with an inner struggle, and a tiny muscle ticked above his eye. "I know I've made my share of mistakes. Big ones. But I just want a chance to start over with you, Carlie. We can't pretend that the past didn't happen, we'd be foolish to believe that it won't affect the rest of our lives, but I want to try…to find a way that we can become friends."

"Friends?" she repeated, refusing to cry though her heart was twisting painfully. "Oh, Ben, it's gone too far for that. We'll *never* be friends."

"Then lovers."

"Too late," she said, though the pulse at the base of her throat throbbed with ancient memories.

"Don't you know it's never too late, Carlie?" he said, drawing her body even closer and kissing her with lips that were demanding and hard.

She felt something uncoil within her though she fought the feeling. She could never fall for Ben again. Never! When he lifted his head, his eyes were glazed and his breath stirred her hair. "I wish I didn't feel this way," he said roughly.

"So do I."

"You can't deny it, Carlie." He kissed her again.

She wanted to stop him, to protect her heart, but all thoughts of protest fled as his fingers twined in the strands of her hair and his body, long and lean, drew her down to the couch. Her arms wound around his neck and her body molded to his, instinctively fitting intimately against the hard planes and angles. No words of love were spoken, no vows of forever passed his lips, but he kissed her with a passion that was answered only by her own hot desire.

He found the zipper on the back of her dress and it slid downward in a quiet hiss. She felt cold air on her back, but soon his hands were caressing her, bringing back the warmth, molding anxiously against her skin.

Still he kissed her, his tongue thrusting boldly through her parted lips, his mouth supple and strong. Emotions, old and new, brought a soft moan from her throat.

His weight carried them both to the floor and she closed her eyes against the protests forming in her mind as they tumbled onto her old Oriental carpet. *This is wrong,* her brain screamed, *wrong and dangerous. Stop him now, while you still can!*

But she couldn't. Or wouldn't. Instead she silenced those awful doubts and thrilled to the wonder of being with him. His hands, rough and callused, rubbed anxiously across her skin and he lowered the top of her dress slowly to reveal a lacy camisole and filmy bra.

"Oh, Carlie," he murmured as he kissed her cheek and neck, lowering himself leisurely, letting his lips and tongue trail along her collarbones before drifting lower and leaving a dewy path that chilled when the air touched that sensitive film. "You're so incredibly beautiful." His breath whispered across the dusky hollow of her breasts as he tasted of the lace that covered her nipples. "I've missed you."

She arched off the rug and he took more of her into his mouth, licking and sucking, gently teasing.

Liquid heat swirled deep inside her and her fingers delved deep into his hair, holding his head in place, offering more of herself.

Don't do this! Carlie, think! her desperate mind screamed as he lowered the straps of lace that were small protection against his seductive assault.

He doesn't love you. Doesn't even like you. You're setting yourself up for more pain than you can imagine.

Moaning, she felt her bra and camisole slip away, knew she was naked from the waist up and reveled in the feel of his hands and mouth slowly moving over her flesh, stoking the flames of desire already running rampant in her blood. "Ben," she whispered.

He slid one hand inside her dress, pushing it over her hips while he suckled at her breast.

Writhing with desire, she worked on the buttons of his shirt. Her mind was blurry with emotion, her heart pounding, the ache deep within her crying to be filled.

He's using you! He's playing you for a fool! Remember what happened before. Oh, Carlie, think! Before it's too late!

His hand slid lower, beneath the waistband of her panties.

Remember the baby! For God's sake, Carlie, remember

the baby! "Ben, no!" she said, alarm bells clanging wildly in her mind.

He froze, every muscle strident and taut.

"We...we can't. *I* can't!" Tears welled from nowhere in her eyes as he gazed down at her. "This is...this is too fast," she said, feeling like a fool as she lay, half-naked beneath him. "Way too fast." His shirt was open and his chest rose and fell with the effort of his breathing. A fine sheen of sweat glistened on his skin.

Slowly he rolled off her. She watched as he drew in long, mind-clearing breaths. "Too fast?" he said, once his voice worked again. "It's been eleven years!" With a sigh, he stared at the ceiling. "What do you want from me, Carlie? Hearts and flowers? Champagne and moonlit walks, diamonds and promises—the whole ball of wax?"

"I—" She struggled back into her clothes. "I don't want to make a mistake."

"I've got news for you, darlin'," he said, rolling onto his side and staring at her. His mouth curved into a self-deprecating smile. "We're way past making our first mistake, or our second or third. The way I figure it, we're in double-digits, maybe triple."

Carlie couldn't argue with his logic, cynical though it may be, but she wasn't a girl any longer. She was a woman determined to control her own destiny. Ben was making it difficult—damned difficult. "Okay, so I don't want to make any more, or at least I don't want to make one that will follow me for the rest of my life."

"Like sleeping with me?"

She swallowed hard against that painful lump. "Yes." Her voice was barely a whisper.

"Seems to me we already crossed that bridge," he pointed out, his hazel eyes sharpening as he stared at her.

"Not in recent history."

He snorted. "Taking it slow with you is like trying to stop a runaway train."

She had the urge to scream. It was all she could do to control her tongue. "Look, I'm not blaming you, okay? I'm here. A responsible adult. I'm supposed to know what I'm doing and so…I think we should just be careful."

He stared at her long and hard, his eyes roving over her body. She was stretched out on the thick Oriental carpet, her body only inches from his and she felt a flood of embarrassment wash up her neck. He touched her cheek and brushed her hair out of her eyes. "Okay, Carlie, you win. I didn't come over here to try and seduce you. I just wanted to apologize and get to know you again—not necessarily in the Biblical sense, although—" his eyes sparkled with a seductive gleam "—that would have been nice."

"Forget it, Powell," she said, finally able to laugh as she levered up on one elbow and tossed her hair over her shoulders. "This is probably the same old line you told every girl you met all over the world when you were in the army."

"I didn't have time for girls, or women for that matter, while I served."

She shook her head. "I've heard about soldiers and sailors and marines. You're not going to convince me that you never had a date—"

"Okay, I had a few," he conceded. "Well, more than a few, but nothing that lasted over a couple of weeks." She narrowed her eyes skeptically and he lifted a shoulder. "It's true. I was pretty dedicated and I moved around a lot and whenever a woman got too serious, I stopped seeing her."

"So you broke a million hearts all over the world."

"Not quite a million." He shoved himself upright and pulled her to her feet. "Come on. I'll buy you dinner while I tell you my life story."

"You don't have to—"

"I *want* to." His fingers closed over hers. "What will it hurt?"

She was afraid to answer that one.

HE CHOSE A restaurant in Coleville, the Blue Lobster, which specialized in seafood. Rough plank walls adorned with black-and-white photographs of fishing crews and whaling boats were complemented by fishing nets strung over individual booths. Dried starfish and sea horses were cast into the nets and colorful glass floats completed the decor.

A waitress showed them to a private booth near a fireplace. Glassed candles and fresh flowers graced a varnished table constructed from the hatch cover of a small boat.

Ben ordered a plate of seafood appetizers as well as wine for Carlie and a beer for himself.

When the drinks and hors d'oeuvres arrived, he touched the neck of his beer bottle to her glass of Chablis. "To new beginnings," he toasted.

"Here's mud in your eye," she responded, then laughed, remembering so many years ago when she'd laughed with Ben and shared her most intimate secrets with him. She'd told him her dreams, her fears and made love to him without a worry for the future.

"Nice, Carlie," he said, but laughed. The candlelight flickered, casting golden shadows on his face, and she wondered what it would be like to fall in love with him again. Gone was any trace of the boy she'd once cared for. Seated across from her was a man, one with lines around his eyes, a leg that sometimes pained him and years of military service. A man who had seen action in deserts and jungles and cities of the Third World. While she'd been in New York and Paris, he'd been in the Middle East, Africa and Central America.

Worlds apart.

She sipped her wine, studied the menu and ordered baked halibut with rice. He chose steak and prawns.

"You were telling me about your love life," she reminded him as the main course was served and the waitress disappeared.

"There was no 'love' to it," he assured her.

"No special girl?"

His head lifted and he stared at her, his hazel eyes sending her a message that caused goose bumps to rise on her arms. "No special woman," he said.

Carlie's throat nearly closed on a piece of halibut.

"What about you?" He broke off a piece of garlic bread. "You're divorced, right? Who was the lucky guy who walked you down the aisle?"

An old ache settled in her heart and the food suddenly lost its taste. She didn't like discussing her failed marriage and had barely mentioned it to anyone. Her parents knew most of the story, of course, and Rachelle, from various conversations, had pieced together the most telling details, but now, seated across from the only man she'd ever loved, she didn't know if she could face the pain. "I, um, don't talk about it much."

"Why?"

"It's…history."

Ben's lips tightened. "Does it hurt too much?"

"I suppose."

His brows lifted slowly. "You still love him."

"Oh, no! I mean…that's the problem." No time like the present to be honest. She'd convinced herself that she would be straight with any man she became involved with, that she would tell him everything that had happened in her life. But she hadn't expected to start a relationship with Ben, the very man who had caused her the greatest heartache of her life. "I didn't love Paul as much as I should have."

"Paul was your husband."

"Yes, Paul Durant. He was a struggling actor and I had just started modeling. Neither one of us had a dime to our names and we started seeing each other. I guess he caught me on the rebound from you," she admitted, and noticed Ben's mouth tighten at the corners. "He wasn't handsome, but very cute. Blond and wiry..." She smiled sadly and pushed around the uneaten portion of her fish into her rice. "Well, before I really had time to think about it, we decided to get married."

"Why?"

It seemed like a sensible question. "You know the old saying, two can live as cheaply as one? Well, we both needed roommates—Manhattan was so expensive. We, um, liked each other a lot. Even convinced each other that we were in love."

"But you weren't?"

She dropped her fork and stared at him. "I'd only been in love once before, Ben, and it hadn't worked out all that well for me." His jaw tightened perceptibly, but she plunged on. After all, he'd asked. "I don't think passion is a driving force for two people planning to spend the rest of their lives together. I just wanted to...not be alone and to spend my time with someone I liked. Someone who cared about me."

"Sounds perfect," he said sarcastically.

"It wasn't." She finished her wine in one gulp. "I started getting more jobs than he did. While he was still waiting tables in an Italian restaurant two blocks from our apartment, I was getting more work than I could handle and making a lot more money. He went to audition after audition and only landed a few parts—nothing to speak of."

"So jealousy and money drove you apart?"

She ran the tip of her finger around the rim of her glass. Somehow it seemed a violation, a betrayal of a trust to tell him any more. "That was most of it."

"And the rest?"

"He fell in love with someone else. My best—and only—friend in New York. You might have heard of her. She's starting to make a name for herself on-and-off-Broadway. Angela Rivers." She didn't add that she'd walked in on Paul and Angela, twisted in the bedsheets, making love with such passion that they hadn't heard her come into the room. She'd been horrified and embarrassed and had promptly thrown up.

Paul's biggest fear had been that Carlie might be pregnant and he would be tied to her forever, but fate had saved him that particular embarrassment. He'd told her that the marriage had been a big mistake from the get-go, that he loved Angela and that he wanted a divorce. He filed the next morning and Carlie hadn't fought him. She'd just wanted out.

Licking her wounds, she'd given up her life in Manhattan, started taking photography classes again and spent a lot of time in different cities, finally spending the last few years in Alaska where she'd taken shots of wildlife and quaint villages and natives. Her photographs had been commissioned by the state as well as bought for a book about America's rugged northern wilderness.

She'd cut all ties with Paul and knew nothing of his life. That's the way they'd both wanted it.

"I'm sorry," Ben said, though his gaze belied his words.

"I'm not. It's over. Probably never had a chance to really get started. Besides, it was all for the best."

"How so?"

"I gave up all those silly dreams about the big city," she said.

"You didn't like New York?"

"I *loved* it, but I was younger then, had different ideas about what I wanted out of life."

The waitress came with dessert and coffee and while Carlie picked at a strawberry mousse, Ben devoured a thick wedge of apple pie. He wondered about her marriage to the actor. She'd obviously glossed over her relationship and Ben sensed she wasn't being completely honest with him, but he really didn't care. Everyone was entitled to a few secrets. What bothered him was the sadness in her eyes as she'd talked of the man she'd married, and he couldn't help but feel a spurt of jealousy run hot through his blood.

At one time in his life he'd hoped to marry Carlie, dreamed of sleeping with her every night and waking with her snuggled safely in his arms. After Kevin had died, he'd convinced himself that Carlie was the wrong kind of woman for him, a schemer, a user, a woman who would stop at nothing to get what she wanted. She was too beautiful, too flighty, too interested in the bright lights of a big city.

He paid the bill and ushered her back to his pickup.

On the way home, he flipped on the radio and told himself that Carlie was still a woman to avoid. True, he'd misjudged her in the past, but although she now seemed to know what she wanted out of life, he suspected that she still flew by the seat of her pants, took chances that were unnecessary and didn't know the meaning of the words *discipline* and *structure.* Her apartment, though charming, was an eclectic blend of antiques, period pieces and modern furniture. She wore anything from high-fashion designer labels to jeans or faded "granny dresses" right out of the seventies. She was confident and secure and fascinating, but she wasn't the woman for him.

So why did you try to make love to her? his imperious mind demanded and he scowled to himself. Despite all his rational thoughts, all the reasons he should avoid her like the proverbial plague, he was entranced by her.

Shifting down, he glanced in her direction. She was certainly the most beautiful woman he'd ever met, but her looks were only a part of her allure. Sophisticated and sexy, she still smiled easily and her eyes were warm with humor and intelligence.

Boy, have you got it bad!

Swearing under his breath he wheeled into the drive of Mrs. Hunter's apartment house and let the pickup idle.

"Thanks for dinner," Carlie said, reaching for the handle of the door. She seemed anxious to escape and he had the overpowering urge to drag her into his arms and make love to her forever.

"I enjoyed it," he admitted and she offered him a fleeting smile. A darkness shadowed her eyes and he imagined that he'd hurt her more than he could remember. She was as enigmatic and mysteriously beautiful as ever.

"Next time it's on me," she said as the door opened.

"Carlie?"

"Hmm?"

He couldn't stop himself. His arms surrounded her and he drew her close. His lips found hers and though he told himself to go slow, to kiss her gently, the passion that still burned through his blood exploded and his mouth moved urgently against her lips.

She wound her arms around his neck and kissed him with the fever that seemed to have infected them both. As the windows began to steam, her tongue mated and danced with his and the swelling in his jeans ached so badly, he thought he'd go crazy.

Shifting to get closer to her, he pressed against the small of her back, urgently dragging her atop him.

Carlie lifted her head and breathing raggedly, whispered, "Slow down, soldier."

"You're going to drive me crazy," he said in frustration. With a groan he released her.

"That works two ways."

"Does it?" His hands tangled in her hair and his breath whispered across her face.

"We've got time, Ben. We're not kids anymore." Again the pained shadow appeared in her eyes. She seemed about to tell him something vital, then forced a smile and kissed him quickly and chastely on the cheek.

"How much time do we have?"

"As long as you want." She slid out of the truck and left Ben with an ache in his groin that refused to wither.

Half lying across the seat, he watched as she let herself into the building and closed the door tightly in her wake. Within a few minutes the lights of her apartment were switched on and she appeared in one of the windows of the turret.

She threw the sash open and stuck out her head. Ben rolled down his window and watched in fascination as the wind blew her hair, a black and gleaming banner, away from her face. "Go home, Ben," she said, her laughter light as a summer breeze. She'd tucked her sadness away again.

"What if I refuse?"

"You'll freeze."

It was his turn to laugh. "Not likely, lady. Not if I'm anywhere near you!"

He rolled his window back up and put the old truck into gear. All the way home he reminded himself that she wasn't the kind of woman he wanted, but by the time he opened his back door and his dog, barking and growling, raced out to the yard, he still hadn't convinced himself.

Like it or not, he wanted Carlie Surrett.

CHAPTER NINE

TRACY STARED AT her reflection in the mirror over her sink in the bathroom. She frowned at the pinch of little lines near her eyes. Whether she wanted to admit it or not, she wasn't getting any younger.

"Hey, Mom, I'm outta here!" Randy called from his bedroom.

"Got your lunch money?"

"Yeah, and my book report."

"You have a good day," she yelled at him.

"I'm gonna have a *spectacular* day," he teased, using one of the vocabulary words he'd studied the night before.

"Good." She smiled as she thought of Randy—the one joy in her miserable life. She turned that thought away; Tracy didn't like feeling sorry for herself. Both she and Randy were healthy, she made enough money that life wasn't the struggle it once was and now...Ben Powell was back in town. *And still single.*

Randy appeared in the doorway, gave her a quick kiss on the cheek, then took off with his backpack swinging from one arm. Her heart squeezed as she followed him to the front hall and watched as he hurried to the bus stop where twenty kids from the apartment complex had gathered.

Maybe she'd made a mistake in not marrying. Randy had never known his father and the men that Tracy had dated, usually men who had picked her up at the Buckeye Restaurant and Lounge, had never shown the least bit of interest in her boy. Well, there had been a couple of guys who had acted as if Randy were something special, but those men, Red Langford and Terry Knapp, weren't the marrying kind. Red was nearly fifteen years older than she was and worked as a driver for Fitzpatrick Logging. He had a steady job, but also kids from a first marriage who were nearly grown. Terry was closer to her age but spent his Friday and Saturday nights on the third stool of the Buckeye Restaurant and Lounge, sitting, watching the big screen, smoking and closing down the place. He'd been picked up by the police for driving under the influence of alcohol on more than one occasion.

Nope, not marriage material.

But things were looking up. Ever since Ben showed up again in Gold Creek. Tracy smiled to herself and closed the door. She finished with her makeup, adding extra lip gloss and heading downstairs to her job at the bank. She worked weekdays as a teller at the Bank of The Greater Bay in Coleville and a couple of nights a week in the lounge at the Buckeye. Sometimes, on Saturdays, she put in an extra shift for the lunch crowd. During her usual schedule, she was home for Randy in the morning and late afternoon and had a sitter come and watch him on the nights when she worked the late shift at the Buckeye.

She hadn't had much time for men, but she planned on making time for Ben. The only problem was that about the same time he'd landed back in Gold Creek, so had Carlie Surrett. Gossip had been spreading around town— gossip that the old romance between Carlie and Ben was heating up.

Tracy frowned as she tilted her head and slid a teardrop-shaped earring through the tiny hole in her earlobe. She didn't like thinking about Carlie, the woman who had everything that was lacking in Tracy's life. Carlie was drop-dead gorgeous, while Tracy was merely pretty. Carlie had experienced a fleeting brush with fame while Tracy, bearing her illegitimate son in a small town had been infamous for a while—the target of any jerk who had the mistaken impression that she was easy. Also, Carlie had her independence, Tracy thought with a mild twang of envy. Carlie could do what she wanted, go where she wanted and when she wanted without worrying about a child.

Tracy grabbed her purse and jacket and locked the door behind her. Years ago, Carlie had found a way to sink her claws into the Powell boys with a tenacity that was awesome. But Tracy was older and smarter than she had been then. Also, she had an ace up her sleeve: her son. Ben, with all his lofty morals, wouldn't stay clear of his brother's boy. He couldn't. His conscience would kill him if he did.

Also, Tracy had always made time for Ben's father. George adored Randy and often teased Tracy about settling down with the right man. What George didn't know was that Ben just happened to be that very man. With just a little pressure, George would be in her corner. Besides, he'd never liked Carlie and still blamed her for Kevin's death.

There was also the little secret Tracy knew about Carlie, a secret no one else in Gold Creek knew. She smiled to herself as she remembered the day she'd seen Carlie at the Coleville Women's Clinic. She'd been reading a magazine in the waiting room and had been screened from the hall by a potted palm. Carlie had rushed out of the doors leading to the examining rooms and she'd been white as a sheet. Her eyes were red and she looked scared out of her mind. A nurse had run after her. "Miss Surrett, please. The doctor thinks you should make another appointment. Next week—"

Carlie had disappeared and Tracy, acting unconcerned,

had been led into an examining room. She had a few minutes before her appointment with Dr. Dodd and so she'd casually walked to the restroom and noticed Carlie's chart obviously left on a desk near the scales when the nurse had taken off after the distressed girl.

Tracy hadn't felt a single moment's guilt as she read the report and figured out that Carlie had been pregnant but lost the baby. So far, she'd kept that information to herself. At the time she'd been worried that Carlie's baby, like her own, had been fathered by Kevin, but she'd quickly changed her mind. According to Carlie's chart, the timing wasn't right. And Kevin was dead.

So the baby had to have been Ben's.

He probably never knew how close he'd come to being a father. Tracy wondered how he would feel if, and when, he ever found out. She smiled a little wickedly and was grateful that Carlie hadn't been able to carry the kid to term.

So, now, Tracy wasn't really too worried about Carlie Surrett. Concerned, but not worried. She climbed into her little Pontiac. Humming to herself, she started the ignition. If Ben didn't call tonight, well, she'd just have to drum up a reason to contact him. It was as simple as that.

CARLIE BRACED HERSELF. Her father had been moved home and, according to her mother, was cranky and irritable, tired of being cooped up. Opening the door, she heard the argument drifting from the dining room.

"I'll talk to him myself!" her father bellowed. "Fitzpatrick can't pull the rug out from under me. Not after all the years I've put in with the company! Damn it all, where are my cigarettes?"

Carlie started through the living room.

"The doctor told you—"

"I know what he told me and I said I'd cut down. But I'm not about to stop cold turkey."

"Weldon, it's been nearly two weeks and you haven't had one. Why start now and—"

"Hi!" Carlie interrupted brightly as she breezed into the room. The dining room table had been shoved against the wall and a hospital bed had been set under the window.

Her father, half reclining, was glowering at his wife.

"You don't really want to smoke, do you?" Carlie's mom asked anxiously.

"Damn straight I want a smoke."

"Dad—"

"Don't you get on me, too. You women!" Muttering under his breath Weldon reached into the drawer of the night table that had been placed near his bed, but came up empty. As he scowled angrily, he slammed the drawer shut and muttered under his breath. "And where the hell's my chew?"

"Weldon—" Thelma said.

"Hell!"

Carlie sat on the foot of the bed. "Hey, Dad, give it a rest, will ya?"

"Take it easy. Give it a rest. A lot you know," he grumbled. His color was back to normal and he was talking much more clearly. His face, too, had improved, though there was a little droop at one corner of his mouth.

"Let me handle Fitzpatrick," Carlie said, smoothing the folds of the old quilt.

"This is my fight, kid."

"I know, but I'm out there anyway, taking pictures."

"You stay out of it." His tone brooked no argument and his eyes, sunken farther into his head than they should have been, sent her a glare that could have cut through steel. "I mean it."

"Don't worry about Thomas Fitzpatrick."

"I'm not concerned about that old buzzard, but I sure as hell want my job back!" He let out an angry puff of indignation. "And now the bastard has the gall to invite us to an engagement party for his daughter!" Weldon glared at his wife. "We're not going. Not unless I get my job back!"

Thelma's lips pursed. "Don't be rash."

"I'll be anything I damned well please, and I sure would like a smoke!" He started coughing then settled back on the pillows. "It's hell to get old, Carlie-girl."

"You're not that old, Dad."

He smiled. "What's that they say—it's not the years, it's the miles? Damn it all anyway."

Carlie sat down and held her father's work-roughened hand. She wanted to set him straight about his job and his health, to beg him to take care of himself, to ease his mind about his finances, but the arguments forming on her tongue went silent when she saw the nearly imperceptible wag of her mother's head, cautioning her that it would be best to let the subject drop.

"What've you been doing?" Thelma asked, turning the conversation in a new direction.

Carlie spent the next hour talking about her job, avoiding mention of the logging company and keeping Ben's name from the discussion. The less her family knew about her tenuous relationship with Ben, the better. She stayed another forty-five minutes with her folks, but felt more than a little depressed when she was leaving. Her father had refused to be jollied into a good humor and her mother was obviously worried about him.

"He'll be better in a few days," Thelma said, hope in her voice as she held open the screen door for her daughter. "The physical therapist says he's improving much faster than they'd expected."

"It's his will of iron," Carlie replied.

"We'll just have to give him time to get used to all this. It's new to him, you know. And he's worried that we might have to move into something a little cheaper, something with only one level." Thelma sighed and leaned on the door. "It's not as bad as he makes out. We've saved all our lives, and we have a little nest egg. Unfortunately, your father thinks it's the size of a hummingbird egg and he thinks we need an ostrich egg." Thelma managed a thin smile. "Things'll get better."

"I'll stop by tomorrow," Carlie promised as she dashed through the rain, sidestepping puddles on the way to her Jeep. She rammed the rig into reverse, turned around and tried not to let her father's depression settle on her shoulders. It was times like these when she wished she had a sister or a brother to share the load. She envied Rachelle and Heather. Even though they'd fought like cats and dogs while growing up, the bond between them was deep and when the family had split up, the two sisters had rallied together.

Carlie stared through the raindrops gathering on the windshield and flipped on the wipers. Even Ben had Nadine, a sister who was as stubborn as he was bullheaded. Though Kevin was dead and their family had been ripped to shreds, brother and sister were still friends, still staunch allies.

Nadine's marriage to Hayden Monroe had been a strain on the relationship, but it seemed as if Ben was now grudgingly accepting his new brother-in-law.

Carlie blew her bangs out of her eyes as she thought of Ben. Despite everything she'd told herself about protecting her heart, about avoiding him because he was trouble with a capital *T,* about staying away from a man who was as dangerous as a loaded gun, she still found excuses to be with him.

He'd called and invited her to a movie. She'd accepted and though the picture had been dull, they'd laughed about it together. They'd met for lunch in Coleville twice in the past week and they'd even bumped into each other at Fitzpatrick Logging where Ben had been contracted to restore some of the company buildings that needed work. Thomas had told her not to take any photographs of the buildings until Ben's crew had given the offices a "face-lift."

They hadn't so much as kissed since the night she'd found him in her apartment, hadn't even touched. Nor had he surprised her again in her own home. She'd met a couple members of his crew, subcontractors hired to update the plumbing and wiring, others who were scheduled to paint and refinish the floors, but Ben himself hadn't been around and she was surprised at the disappointment she'd felt that he hadn't bothered to stop by.

"That's the way you wanted it," she told herself as she got home and unlocked the door of her apartment. Shrugging out of her coat, she dropped her purse on the floor before sifting through her mail. Bills. Receipts. Advertisements. Investment opportunities. And one handwritten envelope with the return address of Fitzpatrick.

Her own personal invitation to Toni Fitzpatrick's engagement party, which was slated for the weekend of February fourteenth, near Valentine's Day.

Wonderful. Another way to remember romance and the celebration of love. She tossed the invitation onto the counter and watched the raindrops sheet down the window over the sink. Would Ben be invited? If so, would he bother to attend a formal party? Even though he worked for Fitzpatrick, there was no love lost between

Ben Powell and Thomas Fitzpatrick, the man who had a stranglehold on the town of Gold Creek.

Time would tell.

BEN SLID THE finished blueprints across the kitchen table. "Voilà."

While his crews were out hauling debris and preparing the site for Nadine's cabin, or scraping the peeling paint off the old Hunter house or checking the wiring, insulation and roofing at Fitzpatrick Logging, he'd put in hour after hour at the computer. Finally, after his rough draft was complete, he'd met with an architect-friend again, made sure that the building was as sound as it was eye appealing, then made the final revisions to his plans.

Nadine, her green eyes twinkling, slowly unrolled the plans. As she looked at the front elevation of her new cabin, she shook her head. "This is a little more elaborate than I had in mind."

"Hayden insisted on his input, as well."

She sighed, but smiled at the drawings as she flipped through the oversize pages. "Three bedrooms, *and* a loft, plus a den with sewing alcove. And what's this—four— no, three bathrooms."

"A concession to you."

"The original cabin only had one."

"Resale value."

Her lips compressed. "I'm not reselling. Not ever."

Ben laughed. "Why do you want it, Nadine? You're married now. You live in a damned mansion—" He swung his arm around the kitchen of the Monroe Manor, trying to impress upon her the width and breadth of the house. "And you're rebuilding right across the lake? I hate to be the one to tell you this, sister, but it doesn't make a whole lotta sense."

She bristled slightly, her pencil wiggling in agitation

between her fingers. "That cabin was the only security my boys had, and now, with Sam still out of work..." She frowned at the thought of her ex-husband who was still recovering from the burns that covered his hands and upper arms, burns that were the result of the fire he'd inadvertently started, the fire that had destroyed Nadine's house. "I want to make sure John and Bobby and whoever—" she said, patting her still-flat tummy, as if she were caressing the baby growing therein "—aren't robbed of their education."

"Hayden would never do that," Ben said, standing up for the brother-in-law he'd sworn to hate.

"I don't think so, either, but I hate to be dependent."

"The man's a multimillionaire, Nadine, and unless you signed some god-awful prenuptial agreement, I don't see how you're ever going to end up destitute!"

"I didn't sign anything."

"There you go."

Nadine's green eyes darkened with memories. "I just don't want what happened to Kevin and you and me to happen to the boys."

"It won't," Ben said and though there had been a time when he hadn't trusted Hayden Monroe, he knew that the man adored Nadine and the boys. He hated to admit it, but Monroe seemed to be one helluva good husband and stepfather. The kids, and Nadine, couldn't have asked for more. Though it galled Ben to concede that Hayden had proved himself to be a stellar kind of guy, he couldn't deny what was so damned obvious. "Besides, I heard somewhere that your little jewelry and clothing business is really picking up."

"I guess I'd better remind you that it's not a 'little business' or a hobby or something to fill my hours. I've got more orders than I can handle and have thought about hiring someone to help."

"Really?"

"Really." With a cat-that-ate-the-canary smile, Nadine studied the blueprints as Ben poured himself a cup of coffee from the pot simmering on the coffeemaker. She made a few notes with a red pencil, chewed on the inside of her lip and finally said, "You know, you really are brilliant. I can't find much wrong with these."

Ben nearly choked on his coffee. Praise from his kid sister was unusual. "Good."

"Just put in another dormer in the loft and add a ceiling fan, shore out the back porch two feet and change the bath tub to a shower for the boys."

"Anything else?"

"That's it for now."

"Thank God."

She started to roll up the plans, but he said, "Keep 'em. I've got copies. I'll make your changes, file one with the county, make sure the permits are all in order and then we'll start excavation, so—"

"I know. If there are any more changes, I should let you know yesterday."

"You got it." Ben swallowed the rest of his coffee and set his empty cup in the sink. He then moved to leave.

Nadine shooed her black-and-white shepherd off the rug near the front door. "Move, Hershel," she commanded and the dog cocked his ears without budging. She opened the door and finally Hershel got the message. He bounded outside to join the grizzled yellow Lab who was standing guard near the rhododendrons. "Did you get an invitation to the big party?" Nadine asked.

"If you're talking about the Fitzpatrick extravaganza, the answer is yes, but I don't know that I have the stomach to go."

"Come on, Ben. Be a sport. He's practically family

now," Nadine said with a gleam in her eyes. "Besides, you can take Carlie. I heard you were seeing her again."

"This damned town."

"Is it a secret?"

He studied his sister intently. "I just like to keep things private."

She laughed and waved as he climbed into the truck. "Then you shouldn't have moved back to Gold Creek."

"You're telling me," Ben grumbled, stepping on the throttle a little harder than he'd planned. Just the mention of Carlie set his teeth on edge. It was true, he'd been seeing her and he'd tried like hell to keep his hands off her. But it had been a losing proposition because it was driving him out of his mind.

He told himself that he was going straight home, but then he conjured up an excuse to stop by the Hunter house to see if the electrical crew had shown up.

As he walked up the front steps he caught sight of Mrs. Hunter peeking through her curtains. She met him in the vestibule, her eyes shining.

"Good news. I won't have to rent the studio to you."

"You must've heard I inherited a dog," he said with a wink.

"Oh, my, no. I love animals, but you haven't even finished your work around here and it looks like I might have a buyer for the house," she said, beaming brightly. She was wearing a pair of her deceased husband's overalls, a faded red flannel shirt and a smile that wouldn't quit.

"Looks like all this remodeling worked."

"Well, the deal isn't signed yet, but when Thomas Fitzpatrick says he's going to do something, he usually does."

"Fitzpatrick?" Ben said, his guts clenching. "He's the buyer?"

"If things go as planned." She picked up a pair of rubber boots she'd left by her door. "Wish me luck."

"You got it." Ben climbed the stairs and told himself it didn't matter who was buying the place. Mrs. Hunter wanted to sell the old house and Fitzpatrick had the money. They were working on a deal. So what if Fitzpatrick's name was on everything in town? Who cared if he was going to be Carlie's new landlord?

Nonetheless his good mood was destroyed, and when he rapped on Carlie's door, he fidgeted, anxious to be away from the cloying grasp of Fitzpatrick. His feelings were irrational he realized. Just because Fitzpatrick had been part of the scheme with H. G. Monroe III that had forced the Powell family into near bankruptcy didn't mean that Ben should hold a grudge. Oh, hell, why not?

Carlie opened the door and smiled at the sight of him. "I didn't know you were coming over."

"I'm not. I thought we'd go out."

"Are you sure? I could cook—"

"I'll cook," he said, anxious to leave. He wondered if Fitzpatrick had a key. Surely not yet. Nonetheless he wanted Carlie out of there.

She was laughing, staring at him as if he'd said he was going to fly to Jupiter. "Ben Powell, chef extraordinaire?" she teased.

"You'll be surprised."

"It won't be any of that army stuff, will it? You know… what do they call it…something on shingles?" Her blue-green eyes twinkled and he was reminded of sunlight refracting on a tropical sea.

He laughed despite himself. "Believe me, you'll love it."

"Just let me get my jacket."

He followed her into the apartment and wondered why it seemed like home. He looked around at the smattering of antiques, modern pieces of art and the cork bulletin board with notes pinned haphazardly on it. And everywhere, on the walls, propped against the floor, stacked on an old bookcase, were her photographs. All different. They hadn't been here before. "What are these?"

"My work. I had them stored at the studio, but I decided I needed a few pieces around here. You know, to show off a little."

As she walked to the closet near the daybed, he looked through a stack of black-and-white pictures of Native Americans in Alaska. A kayak with a single oarsman on a vast sea, whales breaching...

"Ready?" she asked.

"Not quite." He was fascinated with the pictures. "I don't know much about photography, but I like these."

"Do you?"

He saw the hint of her smile and his gut tightened. "Maybe we should go—"

The phone jangled and Carlie ignored it. "The machine'll pick up," she explained as she slid her arms into the sleeves of her jacket. After a few rings and a slight pause, a woman's shrill voice rang from the speaker.

"Carlie? Are you there? It's Constance. Come on, I know you're probably working in that damned darkroom or something.... Look, I know you're not all that interested in trying to reestablish yourself, but Cosmos Jeans is doing a retrospective, wants all the women who have posed for their 'out of this world' commercials. They're willing to pay and...if you want to launch that career again, this would be the perfect time. Well, think about it. You know my number. Can't wait to hear from you."

There was a loud click and Ben watched Carlie's face as it lost all of its animation. "Let's go before she calls back." Grabbing her purse, she opened the door.

"Your agent?" he asked.

"Owner of the agency I worked for." She locked the door behind them and hurried down the stairs.

"In New York?"

"She's there, but there are offices in L.A. and London and Paris."

"Big time," he said.

"I'm not going."

"Sounds like quite an opportunity." He couldn't hide a trace of mockery in his voice.

"It is. I just don't want it."

"You did once."

"A long time ago." She shoved open the door and stepped outside. The night was clear and cool and a soft breeze tugged at Carlie's hair. She didn't want to think about Constance, or New York, or the fact that she could really use the extra money modeling could provide. She was getting older; not too many more opportunities would come knocking on her door. And yet…she'd come back home because she was through with the fast lane.

Wasn't she?

As Ben started the truck, she stared out the window. He was suddenly silent, wrapped in his own thoughts as he drove into the heart of town. She didn't know what to expect from this night, but she didn't really care. She slid a glance at him from the corner of her eye. Despite the call from Constance, being with Ben gave the evening a tingle of excitement and she let herself think about falling in love with him again.

Don't! She couldn't let herself start thinking about anything so foolish as falling in love. Especially not with Ben.

"This is cheating," she said as she struggled with her chopsticks. They sat at a small table in the kitchen of his house. White cartons and sacks from a local Chinese restaurant littered the tabletop.

"Why?"

"I definitely heard you say 'I'll cook,' not 'I'll order out.' Big difference, Powell." She wagged a chopstick at his nose.

"Next time," he promised.

"I'll hold you to it." She started to shove her plate aside but his black shepherd, seated next to her, barked and wagged his tail, hoping for a tidbit. "He likes chop suey?" she asked.

"He likes anything but me."

The dog, as if on cue, placed his head in her lap. She ruffled him behind the ears and he yawned, displaying pink gums and sharp white teeth. "I think he knows a sucker when he sees one," she said, giving the beast a piece of ginger chicken.

Ben grinned. It was funny how comfortable he felt with Carlie in his home, almost as if she belonged. He'd expected her to wrinkle her nose in distaste at the furnishings in his austere house: a single leather couch that he'd bought secondhand, desk, table and chairs from garage sales. No warm, soft rug, no throw pillows, not an afghan in sight and not one picture on the walls.

But she didn't seem to mind and he was surprised. Although she'd grown up with humble roots, she'd always dreamed of escaping Gold Creek to the fame and glitter of Manhattan. She'd planned to model, had even considered acting and felt that she might end up in L.A., so it amused him to see her sit, jean-clad legs tucked beneath her on his couch. She swirled a glass of wine as he built a fire and he imagined how easily she could fit into his life, into his routine.

"So why'd you quit the army?" she asked, when he

settled back on his heels and watched the mossy logs ignite. The fire crackled and spit.

"It was time."

"Because you were wounded."

He sighed and rubbed the wood dust from his palms. "I joined to get out of town, just like you took off for New York. Kevin was dead, my family was splitting up—I just needed time away. I wanted order and discipline and...adventure, I guess." His eyes darkened. "I liked it at first. I felt duty-bound and patriotic and felt that I was important, but... Oh, hell, I don't know, I just got older. I saw some of my friends get killed and it all seemed so useless. When I was wounded I was offered a discharge. I took it. Seemed like it was time for something else." He snorted. "Time to grow up, I suppose."

"And that something else was Gold Creek?"

"It's home, Carlie." He stood and reached for his beer on the mantel. "And you can't run away forever."

"Are you talking about yourself or giving me advice?"

"A little of both, I suppose." He drained the beer and walked over to her. She wasn't a tiny person, but she was thin, and curled up on the couch, her eyes wide and luminous, her hair gleaming black, he found her irresistible. He'd kept his hands off her for a couple of weeks, ever since their passion had exploded in her apartment, but now seeing her beautiful face tipped up to his, her lips parted in an inviting smile, he couldn't stop himself.

In two swift strides he closed the distance between them and took her into his arms. His mouth covered hers and he tasted the wine on her lips, heard the weak little moan from the back of her throat. Her skin smelled of lavender and felt like warm silk against his fingertips. Heat pulsed through his body and his mind shut off any protests. He didn't care about the past, didn't want to remember that he'd told himself for years he couldn't trust her, wouldn't think of the ramifications of making love to her. All he knew was the want that started hot and hard in his loins and swept upward through his body.

Carlie closed her eyes and concentrated on the feel of him. His lips, his hands, his tongue. Liquid fire swept through her veins as he began to unbutton her blouse. She knew she should stop, that making love to him was dangerous, but her heart persuaded her to take a chance. The smell of burning wood, the feel of his hands against her flesh, the musky flavor of the wine, the intoxicating feel of him shoved aside all her doubts.

She wound her arms around his neck, kissing him hungrily, her tongue anxiously mating with his. Her blouse parted and he nuzzled her neck, dipping low in the dusky hollow between her breasts, trailing his wet tongue over the silky lace of her bra.

Arching upward, she felt his hands span her waist, holding her against him, making her aware of the hardness swelling against his jeans.

"You make me crazy," he whispered as he breathed across her nipple.

She could barely speak and when she did, her voice was unrecognizable. "Please," she begged, "please, Ben, don't stop."

"Never." He shoved her blouse from her shoulders and stripped her of her bra, until the firelight played upon her naked torso and he stared down at her nipples. "So incredible," he murmured, running a work-roughened thumb across one dark peak. He lowered his head and sucked gently and she wound her fingers in the thick strands of his hair.

His fingers found the waistband of her jeans and dipped low over her buttocks.

Like lava, liquid fire swirled deep within Carlie and

she found the buttons of his shirt. Her blood pounded in her ears as he stripped her of her clothes and he kicked off his jeans, pausing only long enough to reach into his pocket for a plastic-wrapped packet of protection.

"I've dreamed of being with you again," he admitted, holding himself above her, lowering his head to kiss her lips lightly, or brush his tongue across her nipples.

"So have I," she said over a suddenly thick throat.

"You're sure?"

"Absolutely," she cried.

His lips clamped over hers and after a moment's hesitation, he entered her. Not the high-speed, quick thrill of a teenager, but slowly and surely with long strokes that took her breath away.

Carlie clung to him, moved with his intimate rhythm and stared into the magnetic beauty of his hazel eyes. The pupils were dilated, his dark skin shiny with sweat as he moved more quickly, taking Carlie on a roller-coaster ride that soared upward, faster and faster.

"Carlie!" he cried, as if he'd found something he'd lost for so long a time. "Oh, Carlie."

In a flash of brilliance, the world exploded behind her eyes. Her body convulsed and he shuddered against her. The world seemed to tilt a little as his weight settled comfortably over her and she wrapped her arms around his muscular back. *I love you,* she thought miserably, knowing that loving him was her burden in life. *God forgive me, Ben, but I love you!*

She would never tell him, of course. But as she clung to him and the fire hissed softly, she realized that she would never love another man.

CHAPTER TEN

AN AFFAIR. SHE rolled the thought around in her head and stretched, the back of her calves rustling the cotton sheets. She'd never believed in affairs; she preferred being single or the permanence of marriage.

Ben was already up. She heard him rattling around in the kitchen and smelled the rich scent of brewing coffee. Stretching, she relived their night of lovemaking that had taken place first, in the living room in front of the fire and later, in here, this tiny bedroom that was large enough for only a double bed and a chest of drawers. Sparse. Utilitarian. Perfect.

She looked out the window and saw ice collecting on the thin panes. Frost covered the grass in the yard and a wintry sun was just peaking over the eastern hills. She found Ben's dark blue terry-cloth bathrobe and wrapped it around her middle, cinched the waist and rolled up the sleeves. Barefoot, she padded into the living area.

"Good morning, Sleeping Beauty," he said.

He looked so good. His hair was still damp from the shower and a knowing smile played upon his thin lips. Yes, she could fall in love with him too easily. "I don't feel very beautiful."

"Take my word for it. Coffee?"

"How about a shower first?"

"All yours," he said, and she made her way to the bathroom.

She'd just ducked her head under the hot spray when

she heard the door open and the curtain was thrown back. "I lied," he said, grinning devilishly as he stood stark naked on the tile floor. "The shower isn't all yours. You'll have to share." He stepped inside and took her into his arms and while the sharp needles of water sprayed her back and mist rose around them, he made love to her again.

He touched her water-slickened breasts, kissed her sleepy eyes and opened up that special part of her, touching her with strong fingers, forcing her to moan and gasp until at last he became one with her.

She clung to his slippery body as wave after wave of hot desire caused her to cry out. When he finally finished, he held her close, the water beginning to turn cold as it ran down their bodies.

He kissed her until her teeth began to chatter, then shoved the curtain back. "How about coffee now?" he asked, his eyes twinkling.

"Sounds like heaven."

Within minutes she'd towel-dried and dressed and was cradling a cup of coffee as she sat in front of the fire warming her feet. They ate toast and scrambled eggs and, since it was the weekend, didn't worry about work.

"Rory works Saturdays," she explained when he asked.

"Unfortunately I've got a seven-day-a-week job." But he didn't rush out the door. Instead, he rubbed a kink from his back and asked, "What about that call from the modeling agency?"

"What about it?"

"Aren't you tempted to go back, make a big splash, prove that you've still got what it takes?"

She shook her head. "I don't think so."

"But you're not sure?"

"I think I am, but I've thought that before." She stared

deep into his eyes. "I don't have any plans to go back to New York, Ben, but I can't predict the future."

They sat together on the couch and the phone began to ring. Ben didn't bother answering, but listened to the messages as they were recorded. His foreman, Ralph Katcher, called and his sister, Nadine, left a message about a few last-minute changes to her plans, but Ben didn't move. They sat side by side on the couch, sipping coffee, talking and laughing and tossing a tennis ball to the dog.

Carlie told herself to stop dreaming, but she felt as if she'd finally quit running and come home. She let herself think that maybe they had a chance of a future together— if not marriage then a long-term affair.

The word that she'd avoided for so long didn't seem so wrong when she considered that the affair would be with Ben. *One day at a time, girl,* she cautioned herself. *Don't get ahead of yourself. Remember what you just told him. Who knows what the future may bring?*

The phone rang again and Ben nuzzled her ear. "Maybe we should get out of here. Go on a picnic."

"It's February."

"So what?"

"We'd freeze."

"I can think of ways to keep warm."

The answering machine picked up the call and after the tape of Ben's voice instructed the caller to leave a message, a woman's voice filled the room.

"Ben? It's Tracy—"

Carlie's heart slid to the floor and beside her, Ben tensed.

"I was hoping to catch you at home."

She sounded vastly disappointed.

"Anyway, I left a message yesterday.... Maybe you didn't get it, but I was hoping that we could do something together. Randy has been talking nonstop about you since the last time you came over and I could make us lunch… or whatever. He's, um, got Little League tryouts this morning at the park in just a few minutes.… Oh, well, don't worry about it." There was a weighty pause and Ben shifted restlessly on the couch. Tracy added, "Randy misses you," before hanging up with a click that seemed to echo through the cozy little house.

Carlie glanced at Ben and noticed that the fun-loving glint in his eyes had disappeared. His mouth curved into a frown and he shoved an impatient hand through his hair.

"Tracy Niday," Carlie guessed.

"Damn."

A deafening roar seemed to fill her ears. "You're… seeing her?" All Carlie's dreams shattered in that second when she saw the answer in his eyes. Her heart cracked. Good Lord, what had she expected? That he was in love with her? That because they'd made love, he wasn't involved with anyone else? Her world tilting wildly, she set her empty coffee cup on a table and stood. "I…I think I'd better go," she whispered, hearing her voice as if from a distance. Bitter disappointment flooded through her.

Strong fingers clamped around her wrist. "Let me explain."

"You don't have to."

"Of course I do." He pulled her down to sit next to him. "I'm not dating Tracy, if that's what you're thinking. I only saw her a couple of times."

Oh, Lord!

"She waited on me when I had lunch at the Buckeye and then she invited me over to dinner. That was a couple of weeks ago."

"And you haven't seen her since?"

He rubbed his jaw, as if guilt were eating him up. "No," he admitted, "but I plan to." He looked at her and must have seen the disappointment in her eyes. "For Randy. Kevin's boy. He…uh…he needs a man. You know, to toss a football, to talk about baseball with, to fix his bike, to—"

"To be a father," she said and hated the dead sound in her voice. *Randy is Ben's nephew. The poor kid doesn't have a dad. He just needs a man. But, why, oh, why does Tracy have to enter into it?* She hated her jealousy. It made her feel so small. Tracy was a struggling single mother, for crying out loud, and yet Carlie felt this overwhelming need to hold on to Ben with all her might—to possess him! But he wasn't a man who could be possessed. That's why she loved him. Oh, God, she'd never admitted that horrible fact to herself before!

"I'm not Randy's father," Ben said as his gaze searched her face.

"But Kevin was," Carlie whispered and everything became clear to her. She could never have Ben, not while Tracy was interested in him. Maybe Tracy only wanted to see him for the boy's sake, but Carlie had a gut instinct, feminine intuition, that Tracy wanted Ben for herself. Carlie couldn't blame her for that. Didn't she feel the same?

"Yes, Kevin was."

"So you need to see him."

"I think so," he admitted, still scowling into the fire.

Carlie didn't have the heart to tell him to stay away from his nephew. She didn't doubt that the boy needed a father figure in his life and Ben was the most likely choice. She saw Ben as Tracy saw him: strong, good-looking, responsible and sexy. Fresh out of the army, starting a new business and a new life, he'd be the perfect catch.

Carlie's heart squeezed. "Look," she said, suddenly

yanking her hand away from him as she scrambled to her feet, "I really have to go."

"You're angry."

"Just confused."

He stood and wrapped his arms around her, holding her close, as if afraid she might disappear. "I don't feel anything for Tracy, you know that. She just happens to be Randy's mother."

Her voice failed her for a moment and tears burned at the back of her eyes. "I understand," she whispered, though her voice threatened to crack.

"Do you?"

"Mmm. We're not teenagers any longer. A lot has happened. I have to share you."

He held her at arm's length and shook his head. "No way," he said before dragging her close again and kissing her long and hard. Tears, unbidden, streamed from Carlie's eyes. He didn't understand—not the way she did. He was naive enough to think that they could still be lovers while he had dinner at Tracy's and played ball with her son. Thoughts she'd never before experienced raced through her mind and she felt guilty for her need to have him to herself. She had to let Ben go. Kevin's boy needed him. Probably more than Carlie did.

Slowly she disentangled herself and started for the door before she heard the jangle of his keys. "I'll drive you," he said, "unless you were planning on hitchhiking back to town."

She managed a short, bittersweet laugh and Ben whistled to the dog. Attila raced to the door and as it was open, bounded outside to leap at the sides of the cab.

"He's crazy about taking a drive," Ben explained. "Hope you don't mind."

"Never," Carlie replied, hoping that her broken heart didn't show in her eyes. She scratched the dog behind his ears and held open the door for him. Attila wanted the window seat so he could stick his head through the opening and Carlie ended up pressed tightly against Ben. She stared through the windshield and felt cold inside though the sun was shining brightly enough for Ben to reach in the glove compartment for his dark glasses.

They passed the park and Ben glanced at the baseball field. "Randy's already here," he said with a frown. "I really should stop—" Without waiting for her response, he turned onto a side street near the baseball diamonds and guided the truck to a stop near the curb. "It'll only take a minute."

"It's okay," she said, forcing a smile.

"You sure?"

"Absolutely. Take your time. I'll wait."

Ben didn't look convinced, but pocketed his keys and climbed quickly out of the cab. Attila, ready for adventure, leapt to the ground and took off at a sprint. Hands in his back pockets, Ben strode across the dewy grass to join a huddle of men and boys, some of whom were already tossing a ball around. Carlie's heart twisted as she watched the sunlight gleam against his dark hair and his face break into a smile as he spied his nephew.

Ben was irrevocably tied to Randy, whether he knew it or not, and therefore tied to Tracy, as well. Carlie felt like a selfish fool for the jealousy that balled in her stomach. Randy needed him. More than she did.

Swallowing back a lump in her throat, she watched. Ben stood out in the crowd of men wearing warm-up suits, baseball hats and league jackets. In his faded jeans, rumpled leather jacket, T-shirt and aviator glasses, he looked more like a stuntman for a Hollywood film than a father.

Carlie couldn't help but watch. A skinny kid with brown hair and an Oakland A's cap ran up to Ben. Ben teased the boy and yanked off his hat to rumple his hair. The kid danced around him and made a big fuss over Attila, who barked and jumped like a puppy. Carlie's heart cracked as she realized this should be her son—she and Ben should have had a child—a son or daughter—this very age.

Other kids raced over to check out the dog. Bundled in sweatpants and sweatshirts, with major league caps on their heads and huge fielding gloves on their hands, the boys were laughing and talking and shoving each other, their faces red, their eyes sparkling with anticipation.

One big lanky kid threw the dog a ball and the anxious shepherd took off at a sprint. Excited voices and peals of laughter floated on the morning breeze.

Carlie felt numb inside. This was where Ben belonged. He glanced to the pickup and waved as he extracted himself from the group. She lifted her hand but he'd already turned away and helped sign the boy up at a table where mothers were sipping coffee while guarding application forms.

One mom offered him coffee and a smile; another was all business, pointing to the registration forms. Other boys had already batted and pitched while judges in windbreakers and baseball caps watched their performance from bleachers that needed a new coat of paint.

Tracy was there, too, wearing a baseball cap and hovering nearby and smiling up at Ben. It hit Carlie like a ton of bricks: *she* was the outsider, the one who didn't belong. That thought made her stomach clench into a painful ball. Why wouldn't she ever learn?

Ben said something to Tracy and she laughed. Then Randy handed his uncle a ball and they started playing catch, Ben squatting like a catcher, Randy winding up to pitch.

If only their own child had lived! Knowing that she had to leave before her raw emotions started to strangle her, Carlie hopped out of the truck and trudged across the wet grass. She would explain to Ben that she could walk back to the apartment. The hike was less than a mile and the exercise would do her some good. She could leave him here with his nephew—where he belonged—and she wouldn't have to torture herself any longer.

Randy was just getting ready to bat for the judges. Carlie was close enough to hear Ben talking to the boy.

"Remember—eye on the ball," Ben encouraged, his face as intense as if his own son were trying out. "Address the plate and don't let that pitcher scare you." Ben took off his glasses and gave the boy a wink.

"I won't."

"You can do it," Tracy encouraged, straightening the boy's sweatshirt. "You're the best, honey."

Was it her imagination, or did Carlie see Randy's back stiffen a little as he walked to the short line near the on-deck circle.

"He's just got to do well," Tracy confided in Ben. She was so nervous, she was chewing on her polished nails. "Jerry Tienman is here and he's the coach I want for Randy."

"Is he who Randy wants?"

"Of course. Tienman is the best coach in the league and last year, over half his team became all-stars...." Her voice drifted off as she noticed Carlie approaching. A web of tiny lines formed between her eyebrows.

"I didn't mean to interrupt," Carlie said, forcing a smile as she caught Ben's attention. "But I've got to go."

Ben glanced from Carlie to the plate. "This'll only be a few minutes."

"Randy would really be disappointed if you left," Tracy cut in, and Carlie felt like a heel.

"Really. You stay here. It's okay. I'll just cut through the park. It's only a few blocks."

Ben's lips tightened. "Just hang in here, okay?"

"Really—"

His eyes found hers and for a moment the crowd of boys, Tracy, the dog and all the action at the plate seemed to stop. "Please, just a couple of minutes."

"Sure," Carlie said, rather than cause a scene, and she knew in that instant that if she and Ben were to have any relationship at all, she would have to settle for coming in second. Whether he knew it or not, he was committed to his nephew. She saw it in his eyes.

Tracy's eyes narrowed a fraction before she turned and leaned against the wire backdrop. "Come on, slugger!" she yelled and again, Randy's back tightened.

The pitcher, a big, rangy boy, wound up and let loose. The ball streaked across the plate. Randy swung and fouled the ball over the backstop.

"That's good," Ben encouraged. "You got a piece of it."

"Come on, honey!"

Randy threw his mother a hard look over his shoulder. He twisted his feet, adjusting his stance, and stared back at the pitcher.

The boy wound up. Another pitch. This one, right down the middle, hit the catcher's glove with a thud. Randy hadn't moved, not even swung.

"Come on," Ben said under his breath.

"That one was good as gold," Tracy said, with more than a trace of irritation. "You can do it, Randy!"

The next pitch was high, clear over Randy's head, and he swung wildly.

"No!" Tracy yelled.

"Hey, lady, put a lid on it," one of the coaches said. "Let the kid do his thing."

"He's my son."

"So lighten up."

Tracy looked as if she wanted to tear into the guy, but Ben grabbed her arm. "He's right, Tracy."

Three more balls and three more misses. Carlie wished she could disappear.

"I can't believe it," Tracy said, shaking her head. "I don't know what's wrong! He's usually so good."

"He is good," Ben assured her. "His timing's just a little off."

"But we've been to the batting cages, I've worked with him. Oh, God, if he doesn't make Tienman's team, he'll be so disappointed."

"Will he?" Ben asked. "Or will you?"

"He will! He wants to be the best!"

"Next! Number eighty-seven!" the coach yelled and Randy threw off his batting helmet and dropped his bat. His face was contorted and he was swearing under his breath.

"Honey, what happened?" Tracy asked.

"I screwed up!" He kicked at a clod of dirt with the toe of his baseball shoe and battled the urge to break down and cry.

"You did fine," Ben said, clapping him on the back. "That pitcher was really on. His curveball—"

"—sucked! And so did I!"

"Don't talk that way, Randall," Tracy said, her face flushing with color. "Pull yourself together. You've got to pitch next."

"Don't want to."

"Oh, come on, honey. You know you love this."

"No, you love it!" He threw his mitt to the ground and stalked away, Tracy chasing after him, Attila romping as if it were all a game. Several kids watched him leave. "What a jerk," one boy said around a wad of bubble gum.

"Crybaby."

"He's just having a rough day," Ben told the kids.

"Yeah, so what's it to you?"

"He's my nephew."

"Well, then, your nephew is a jerk."

"Shut up, Billy!" a big, unshaven man said. "Warm up. You're after this guy."

Grumbling, Billy and his friends wandered away.

"I think I'd better stay," Ben said to Carlie, casting a look behind the bleachers where it looked as if Tracy were reading her son the riot act.

"I know," she said. The boy needed him. It was as simple as that.

"Tracy's got some crazy notion that Randy's got to be the best at everything he does."

Carlie managed a smile, though she felt like breaking down and crying. "You'll fix things, Ben. I'll walk home." When he started to protest, she placed her palm against his face. "Go on, I'll be fine. I'll see you later."

"At least take Attila with you. I'll pick him up in a little while." He whistled for the dog, kissed her lightly on the cheek then took off at a jog, catching up with Randy and tossing his arm around the boy's slim shoulders. Randy tried to pull away, but Ben kept up with him and Tracy managed to throw one look over her shoulder—a smug look of victory.

Carlie's blood began to boil, but she gritted her teeth as she started across the park. Attila bounded ahead, scaring birds and chasing runaway balls. Carlie barely noticed because she was thinking of Ben and their one night together. It would have to be their last. Just like before. She was too damned selfish to share him with Tracy and her son, and Ben belonged with the boy.

She'd just crossed Main when she heard a horn blast behind her. Ben's pickup cruised up to the curb and he leaned over the seat and shoved open the door. "The least I can do is drive you the rest of the way."

She didn't argue and both she and Attila climbed into the cab. "How'd Randy do?"

"He didn't."

"No?"

"No one, not even God himself, could have talked that kid into finishing tryouts. If you ask me, it was a case of flat-out rebellion. He's tired of his mom pushing him so hard."

"So what're you going to do about it?"

"Nothing I can do. This is Randy's call."

"What about Tracy?"

"She's fit to be tied," he admitted as he slowed for a corner, "but then she's got to remember that Randy's just a kid—no special hero and certainly not his father."

"She wants you to be his father."

"I can't, Carlie." Ben stared out the window. "I'll be his uncle. Hell, I'll be the best damned uncle in the world. He can call me anytime and I'll do whatever I can to help out. But I can't be the kid's dad."

He pulled into a parking spot beneath a spruce tree and walked her upstairs. "Can I see you tonight? As much as I detest the idea, I think I should put in an appearance at Toni Fitzpatrick's engagement party."

"I, um, I'll have to meet you there. I promised my mother I'd take her and Dad, and since she had to twist Dad's arm to go, I don't want to change plans."

He hesitated. "Hey, look, I'm sorry about Randy—"

"Don't be," she said. "Life's just a lot more complicated than it used to be."

He offered her a smile that lifted one side of his mouth. "Then I'll see you there."

"I'd...I'd like that."

He hesitated. "I think the whole damned town will

be there. People at tryouts were talking about it. Even Tracy."

Carlie's muscles tightened. "She was invited?"

"Her father worked for Fitzpatrick for forty years. Seems as if she knows him and Toni."

Carlie felt a huge sense of disappointment, but Ben reached for her and drew her into the circle of his arms. "I guess I'll have to wait until tomorrow to be alone with you." His smile was sexy.

"Yes." She knew she should tell him no, but couldn't, not while he was touching her. Then she remembered. "Oh, no, that doesn't work, either. Believe it or not, I've got a dinner meeting with Thomas Fitzpatrick."

He didn't move, just stood there stunned, as if she'd slapped him. "A dinner date?" he repeated, his eyes slitting suspiciously.

"Yes. He asked me a few weeks ago and I turned him down, even canceling once, but he insists that we have to talk about the photographs for the company brochure—"

"Over dinner?"

"Hey, it wasn't my idea."

"But you went along with it."

"That's right, Ben, I did," she said, suddenly angry. All her coiled emotions released in a burst of fury. "Just like you might have lunch or dinner with a potential client. It's no big deal."

"With Fitzpatrick, everything's a big deal! Do you know that he's planning to buy this house?"

"This house?" she whispered, glancing around her apartment. "*This* house."

"Yep. All of a sudden it seems as if old Tom has an interest in the property." He clamped his hands under his arms. "I wondered if it had anything to do with you."

"Of course not!"

His skeptical look said he didn't believe her.

"What is this phobia you've got against the man?"

"He's slimy and two-faced and out for number one."

"I know that. Don't worry about me, Ben. I can take care of myself."

"Maybe I don't want that," he said, his eyes growing dark. "Maybe I want to take care of you."

Her throat closed for an instant and her anger melted away. It was so easy, so damned easy, to trust him. "I don't want someone to take care of me. I'm not a child. I make my own decisions, one of which is to go out to dinner with Fitzpatrick and hear what he has to say."

The skin tightened over his cheekbones and he looked as if he wanted to spit out a string of blue oaths, but he held his tongue, turned on his heel and headed down the stairs.

"Great," Carlie mumbled to herself. "Just great." She slammed the door behind her and wondered why she bothered with Ben. His moods were mercurial and now he wanted to control her.

You bother with Ben because you love him.

"Then you're a fool, Carlie Surrett," she told herself as she flopped down on the couch and wondered if she'd made a mistake returning to Gold Creek. Maybe she would have been better off staying away.

You can't run forever. And she wouldn't. Ben Powell or no Ben Powell.

TONI FITZPATRICK'S ENGAGEMENT party was the social event of the year. Miniature lights twinkled from a forest of potted trees and red, white and silver ribbons looped from the chandeliers, which were suspended above the main dining room at the Coleville Country Club. Silver balloons floated lazily to the two-storied ceiling. An ice sculpture of twin swans rose from a table laden with platters of fruit, caviar and hors d'oeuvres. Champagne bubbled from a three-tiered fountain and chefs stood at attention behind serving trays of roast beef, turkey and ham. Lobster, prawns and salmon were served at yet another table and a dessert cart offered chocolates, truffle cake and raspberry mousse.

"How's he gonna beat this?" Weldon asked as he, with his cane, hobbled across the upper balcony and stared down at the party below. A curved staircase swept from one floor to the next and a string quartet played love songs while waiters scurried back and forth to the kitchen. "When the girl gets married, I mean. How can he top this spread?"

"He'll find a way," Carlie predicted. She let her gaze wander through the bejeweled guests, searching for Ben.

"Always does," Thelma agreed as they used the elevator and rode down to the festivities.

"He'll have to rent the damned Ritz," Weldon grumbled. The elevator doors opened. Her father, moving stiffly with his "damned walking stick," headed toward the open bar.

"Should he drink?" Carlie asked.

"I don't know." Thelma threw up her hands. "But he's been such a bear to live with since he gave up cigarettes and chewing tobacco, I'm not going to be the one to tell him to lay off the drinks. At least not tonight."

"All right. We'll let him cut loose a little," Carlie said with a smile.

Even though she'd spent two hours in the beauty shop and was wearing a shimmery new green dress, Thelma looked tired. Her days of working at the soda counter and evenings of taking care of her husband were starting to tell. Between her shifts she'd had to run Weldon back and forth to the hospital for physical therapy and even though Carlie helped out when she could, the strain was beginning to show on Thelma's pretty face.

"Come on. You, too. Have a glass of champagne," Carlie encouraged her mother. "I'm driving, so you can have all the fun you want. Come on. All your friends are here. It's a party."

"Fun—" her mother started to complain, but changed her mind. "All right. Don't mind if I do." Her lips twitched and she headed off to the champagne fountain.

Carlie saw people she'd known all her life and stopped to speak to old classmates and friends, but she couldn't help searching the crowd, hoping to find Ben. She allowed herself one fluted glass of champagne and mingled with the other guests.

"Glad you could make it." Thomas Fitzpatrick's voice was a gentle whisper behind her.

"Wouldn't miss the social event of the season," she said, turning to face him. His wife, June, stood fifty feet away, her inflexible back turned toward her husband as she chatted with a wasp-thin woman in purple and an elderly man. The woman was a reporter for the *Gold Creek Clarion*. The man with her owned the newspaper.

"Oh, this isn't the event of the season," Thomas said proudly. "Just you wait until the wedding. *That* will be something. Oh, here they come now." He touched Carlie lightly on her upper arm and pointed to the top of the stairs where Toni, in a shimmering silver dress, was speaking with a tall blond man of around thirty. An engagement ring with a huge, sparkling diamond graced Toni's hand.

"That's Phil," Thomas said as he gazed at his future son-in-law. "Phil Larkin, attorney, stockbroker and financial whiz kid."

"You like him?"

"Couldn't be more pleased if I'd handpicked him myself, which, come to think of it, I did. Introduced the two of them last year. Phil's father—you remember Kent

Larkin—was a state senator in the sixties, and Phil's ambitious. He could follow in Kent's footsteps."

"I suppose," she said, shifting to put a little distance between her body and his. Thomas dropped his hand from her arm as casually as if he hadn't known he was still touching her.

Thomas had always been interested in politics. Just before Roy was killed, Thomas had considered running for office himself. Now, if his future son-in-law's dreams were realized, Thomas would have an ear to the state legislature and a doorway open to push in his ideas. It all depended upon Phil and how much he wanted to please his soon-to-be father-in-law.

"When's the wedding?" Carlie asked, trying to make small talk.

"Around Christmas, if all goes as planned." His lips tightened a bit as he watched his daughter. Toni flung her blond curls over her shoulder rebelliously and with a pout, started down the stairs without Phil. He scurried to catch up to her, his face red in embarrassment. Toni didn't seem to care. She mingled with the crowd, smiled and seemed to ignore the man of her dreams.

A blast of February wind seeped inside and Carlie glanced behind her as one of the pairs of French doors opened. Ben, dressed in a black tuxedo, walked into the room and Carlie's heart kicked. His hair was slightly mussed from the wind, his cheeks dark, his expression thunderous. As if he knew exactly where she was, he glared in her direction, grabbed a drink off the tray near the door and took a long swallow. His gaze shifted for a second on her companion and his scowl deepened as he began threading his way through the crowd.

So he was jealous. Carlie didn't know whether to be angry or flattered. She started to excuse herself from Thomas and meet Ben, but Ben was intercepted by a petite woman with straight brown hair and a skin-tight white dress. *Tracy.* Carlie's face seemed suddenly tight. Thomas whispered something to her, but she missed it.

Tracy wound her arm through Ben's and beamed up at him.

Ben leaned over to whisper in Tracy's ear. She tossed back her head and laughed lightly, as if she adored him.

Carlie's heart seemed to turn to stone. She told herself to relax, Ben was only talking to Tracy. She had no rational reason to feel the jealousy that coiled around her insides. Besides, if anything, she should admire Tracy. She'd overcome the stigma of being an unwed parent and was struggling to raise her child and all Carlie could think about was the fact that she was already irrevocably tied to Ben. Somehow, some way, Carlie had to learn to deal with Tracy or else she had to accept the fact that she had no future with Ben.

Rather than watch Tracy beam raptly up at Ben another second, Carlie turned her attention back to Thomas. There was a change in his tone and she wondered if he noticed that she hadn't been listening. He touched her again, lightly on the hand and she managed a tight smile.

"Friend of yours?" he asked when she glanced back to find Ben still in conversation with Tracy.

"I've known Ben a long time," she hedged.

"I was talking about Tracy."

"Oh." She felt her cheeks grow warm. "I hardly know her."

"Good woman. Responsible. Takes care of her boy and holds down two jobs." There was genuine admiration in Thomas's voice.

"She's…industrious."

"Hmm. Like her father. One of my best employees. I've known Tracy since she was a little girl." He smiled again. "As I've known you." He sipped from his drink.

"I think I'd better go check on my mom and dad," Carlie said as an excuse to break free of Fitzpatrick when a group of men approached him.

As she walked past one of the huge pillars supporting the roof, a strong male hand clamped over her arm.

"Carlie." Ben's voice was a harsh whisper. She turned and found him glaring at her, the back of his neck a deep shade of red, his lips white and thin. "Having a good time?"

"Good enough," she replied, bristling a little at his anger.

"With Fitzpatrick?"

"He cornered me."

"And you ate it up."

"Are you crazy?" she demanded, keeping her voice low. "I was just being polite."

His eyes narrowed on her and, as if realizing that they might be overheard, he took her hand and led her quickly through a knot of men who had clustered near a baby grand piano positioned near the front doors. The men were in a heated discussion of taxes and politics and were raising their voices over the mellow notes of "I Will Always Love You" being played by the band.

Ben shoved on the handle, opening the door, and drew her outside where the chilly February wind cut through her dress and brushed her face.

The door clicked shut. "I don't know how many times I have to warn you about him!" he growled through clenched teeth.

"Get over it, Ben," she shot back. "I'm not a sixteen-year-old virgin who can be manipulated and taken advantage of."

His shoulder muscles bunched beneath his jacket. "Fitzpatrick wants something from you."

"Like what?"

"Take a guess." When she didn't answer, he said, "Fitzpatrick's looking for a mistress. You seem to be top on the list."

"Give me a break!" she said, but remembered the lingering touches and the dark glances that Thomas had cast in her direction.

"The man's had affairs all his life. You don't need to be a genius to figure that out. Jackson Moore is proof enough. And now Fitzpatrick's wife has filed for divorce, or at least that's the rumor going about the logging company, so guess what? Good ol' Tom is going to have his freedom."

"I'm not interested."

"He's a wealthy man, Carlie."

"I should slap you for that one."

"A powerful man."

"Oh, come on—"

"He could give you everything you'd ever want."

Stung, she turned on her heel. "I don't have to listen to these insults!" She tried to push past him and reached for the brass lever of the doors, but Ben grabbed her again. Before she could say anything, he yanked her roughly to him, slanted his lips over hers and kissed her with all the passion and anger that stormed through his blood. His lips were hot and hard and demanding, his body lean and firm.

She jerked away, anger still coursing through her blood. "Don't drag me out here, insult me and then think you can make it all better by kissing me!" she said.

"Nothing's better."

"You're damned right. I don't like being manhandled, Ben. Not by you. Not by anyone. So cut out the Neanderthal macho routine!"

His eyes flashed fire, but he released her. "Oh, hell, Carlie, I didn't mean to insult you." He drew in a deep breath of the wintry air. "I'm just warning you about Fitzpatrick."

"I don't need a mother."

"I'm not—"

"Or a babysitter."

"Carlie—"

"Shh. I don't even need an older brother, Ben. I can take care of myself."

"Can you?" His voice was suddenly low and sexy. "Maybe I don't want to think that you're so damned independent. Maybe I want to think that you need a man."

"Are you applying for the job?" she asked, her anger beginning to fade.

"I'd like to."

She stood on her tiptoes and brushed her lips gently across his. "I'm a big girl now."

His grin, a slash of white in the darkness, was wicked and sensual. "I've noticed." His lips found hers and his hands spanned her waist. "Let's ditch this party."

"Mmm, I can't," she said with genuine reluctance. "I promised Mom and Dad I'd drive them home."

"Later?"

She wanted to say yes, to beg him to meet her at her apartment, but she held her tongue. She remembered their argument about Tracy, about the past, about Thomas Fitzpatrick. "Soon," she promised, closing her eyes and drinking in the smell of him—of soap and champagne and some musky cologne.

His lips found hers again and her head began to swim. Her eyes closed and desire pumped through her blood. She wondered what the future would bring, but steadfastly shoved all her cloying doubts into a dark corner of her mind. She was caught in the wonder and magic of loving him.

Slowly she opened her eyes and saw, through the

steamy glass of the French doors, a woman in white. Tracy Niday, her eyes squinting through the glass, her jaw set in renewed determination was staring at them. A chill, deep as the February night, passed through Carlie's bones.

Carlie drew back from Ben's embrace, but he groaned and pulled her close again, his lips hot and wet against her own. She fell willingly against him and when she looked back to the glass, Tracy had disappeared.

"We can't do this all night?"

"Not here."

"Come home with me."

"I will, but not tonight," she said, regret heavy in her voice.

"I'll hold you to it."

"You'd better."

Ben took Carlie's hand as they walked back into the dining room. Though Tracy was drinking champagne and flirting with several of the men collecting near the open bar, Carlie was certain that Tracy knew the exact moment they'd walked inside.

Telling herself she was being petty, Carlie turned her attention back to the party. She talked to some friends, avoided any more champagne and held Ben's hand. His eyes sparkled when he asked her to dance and she couldn't say no. Other couples, including Hayden and Nadine, swept around the floor. Nadine looked radiant. Her red hair was piled in loose curls on her head and her dress, black silk with rhinestones, caught in the light. The newlyweds laughed and talked as they danced, and when they passed Ben and Carlie, Nadine winked, as if at a private joke.

"What was that all about?" Carlie demanded.

"Just my sister's perverse sense of humor."

"Meaning—"

"Meaning nothing." He held Carlie tighter and gazed into her eyes. "Just dance with me, lady. Forget about everything else."

She did. Snuggled in the warmth of Ben's embrace, she listened to the music and the beating of his heart and the muted sounds of conversation and tinkling glass. It was all so perfect, so romantic…

"I never want to see you again!" Toni Fitzpatrick's voice rang through the dining room.

The band stopped playing, instrument by instrument. Conversation lapsed. Carlie and Ben froze on the dance floor and turned, with the rest of the crowd, toward the ice-sculpture and the couple standing next to it: Toni and Phil, for whom this lavish party was thrown.

So furious she was shaking, Toni yanked off her diamond ring and hurled it across the room. "Never!" she repeated amid gasps and whispers and shocked expressions.

"Toni, please—" Phil said, his face as red as the lobster tails being served on the opposite side of the room.

"Get out! Just get the hell out!" Toni screamed, then realizing where she was, ran up the stairs. Tears streamed from her eyes and Thomas, lithe as a jungle cat, took off after her.

"I'm sorry," Phil said to the crowd as a whole and June Fitzpatrick, who was suddenly white as a sheet, waved impatiently to the bandleader, who cleared his throat and began playing a love ballad. The rest of the band joined in, adding a soft harmony to the hushed speculation that buzzed through the guests.

"I wonder what that was all about," Carlie whispered as Phil collected the ring and hurried up the steps.

"Looks like Toni got cold feet." Ben took her into his arms again. "I'm not surprised. She's a rebel and

Phil Larkin is too buttoned-down for her. A lawyer and stockbroker? Boring combination."

"Jackson's a lawyer."

"Jackson deals with interesting cases. I read where he just got some oil heiress off the hook. The D.A. backed off."

"Alexandra Stillwell," Carlie said, remembering an earlier conversation with Rachelle. "The D.A. had originally thought she'd killed her father. Turns out Jackson found evidence proving she couldn't have done it." She arched an eyebrow at him. "Sound familiar?"

"Too familiar."

Her mother found her. "Can you believe that?" Thelma asked, motioning to the stairs. "Walking out on your own engagement party? That Toni always was a wild one. I know, too. Saw her cutting school and hanging around the drugstore, smoking cigarettes when she should have been in class." Thelma clucked her tongue. "Look, I think your father's about all in—" She glanced at Ben and her spine stiffened slightly.

"The party's about over anyway," Carlie said. "Mom, you remember Ben."

"I've heard that Carlie's been seeing you again," she said, her words clipped with old resentment. "I'd like to tell you that I approve because I believe that bygones should be bygones, but I remember—"

"Mom, please," Carlie cut in, realizing too late that her mother's tongue had been loosened by the champagne.

Thelma's face clouded over. "I just don't want to see you hurt again," she said, and Ben shoved his hands in his pockets.

"Look, Mrs. Surrett," he said, his features sober, his gaze sincere as he met Thelma's, "I know I made some mistakes, some big ones where Carlie is concerned. I won't insult you with excuses. I can only tell you that I won't be making the same mistakes twice."

"I hope not," Thelma replied and walked to the elevator where her husband was waiting for her.

"I've got to go," Carlie said.

"Me, too." Ben squared his shoulders. "While I'm mending fences, I may as well fix them all." He walked with her to the elevator and met Weldon's harsh glare with his steady gaze. He looked like a captured soldier walking into an enemy headquarters, Carlie thought as she noticed the tension in all of Ben's muscles. He extended his hand to her father who, after a second's hesitation, clasped it. "Mr. Surrett."

"Powell." Weldon's mouth tightened.

After a few minutes of small talk as Ben inquired into Carlie's father's health, Weldon said, "You may as well know, I told Carlie she should stop seein' you. It's the same advice I gave her ten years ago, and I think it still stands."

"I hope to prove you wrong."

"You can't, boy," he said, shaking his head and motioning for his wife to hit the elevator call button. "It's not in your nature."

"I might surprise you."

"I hope so." The elevator landed and a bell chimed softly. As the doors whispered open, Thelma pushed her husband into the waiting car.

"I'll see you later," Carlie said to Ben.

"When?" Ben held on to Carlie's arm while her mother impatiently pressed the door open button and waited.

"Call me."

Ben let her go and Carlie slipped into the waiting car. The doors began to close and Carlie watched as Ben walked toward the stairs only to be caught in midstride by Tracy Niday. The doors closed, blocking her view.

Carlie's heart squeezed.

"I saw him with her earlier," Thelma said as the elevator began moving upward.

Weldon agreed. "So did I. She'll always be a part of his life, honey." He reached for his daughter's hand. "Because of that boy of hers."

The elevator stopped on the main floor and Carlie was left with the sinking sensation that her father was right. As long as Randy needed a father, Tracy's sights would be set on Ben.

CHAPTER ELEVEN

BEN WATCHED THE backhoe gouging out huge chunks of mud from the excavation site. He'd been lucky. The weather had broken and it looked as if the concrete foundation for Nadine's cabin could be poured in the next couple of weeks.

All in all, things were going well. Work on the Hunter apartment house would be finished by the middle of March, this cabin would take him through part of the summer and the projects at the logging company would keep his subcontractors busy throughout the spring.

So why was he so restless? The answer was obvious. *Carlie.* The woman he didn't know whether to love or hate. When she'd first returned to Gold Creek, he'd been certain that she was a user, a gold digger, a callous woman who stepped on men's souls. Then, as the weeks had passed and they argued about the past he'd seen a new side to Carlie—a side that beguiled him and told him that he'd made a mistake about her in the past. Then he'd made love to her and that lovemaking had been as soul-wrenching and earth-shattering as it had been eleven years ago. He'd thought he'd lost his ability to become so involved in a woman, but he'd been wrong. He could feel that same exhilaration. But only with Carlie.

Damn it all anyway! He kicked a stone with the toe of his work boot and wondered what the hell he was going to do about her.

He should trust her, get over the past, start fresh.

That's what he wanted to do, and last night, when he held her in his arms and kissed her on the veranda of the country club, it had been all he could do not to pull her into the shadows beyond the interior lights and make love to her over and over again. She was in his blood, in his mind, and…it seemed, in his heart.

He was about to make the same mistake with her as he had in the past. His destiny, it seemed.

So why was she having dinner with Thomas Fitzpatrick?

Because Fitzpatrick was interested in her, and had been from the moment she set foot back in Gold Creek. Ben had noticed the way Fitzpatrick had watched Carlie on the dance floor, his old eyes following her every move as he'd pretended interest in another conversation.

He clenched his jaw so hard that it began to ache. "Son of a bitch!"

"Ben! Hey, Ben!" Ralph Katcher slogged through the mud. "Lookin' good here, eh?" He stopped to stuff some tobacco behind his gum.

"Better," Ben allowed.

"Hell, yes, better. A damned sight better. You know, I think you might just end up a solid citizen of Gold Creek. End up on the board of the chamber of commerce. You and Thomas Fitzpatrick!"

"That'll be the day," he said. They shared a cup of coffee from his thermos, then Ben drove off to check the other jobs he'd contracted.

All the work looked good at the Hunter house. He hung out for a while, spending more time than necessary checking the finishing touches, hoping that Carlie would show up. When she didn't arrive, he headed out to the logging company offices and told himself over and over that Thomas Fitzpatrick's money was the same color as anyone else's. However, dealing with Fitzpatrick burned a hole in his gut. He'd never forgiven him for being part of the scheme that had fleeced his father out of his life savings—and he didn't trust him now. With Carlie.

It was probably just his imagination, but he'd seen how Thomas had looked at her at Nadine's wedding, read the unspoken messages in his eyes. Again, last night, in front of his family and all the guests at the engagement party, Thomas had made a beeline to Carlie and hovered around her. Later, as she and Ben had danced, Fitzpatrick had eyed them. Then there was the sudden interest in the apartment house where Carlie lived. Why would Fitzpatrick want the old building?

Fitzpatrick was also throwing a lot of work Carlie's way, which wasn't a big deal in and of itself, but the fact that there were so many other strings that tied Carlie to him made Ben sweat. There was also the business with her dad. Fitzpatrick was playing God on that one, teasing a sick old man with his pension and retirement benefits.

Ben didn't like it. It smelled bad. But his hands were tied. Carlie, damn her, insisted upon being her own woman and she'd have to learn about Fitzpatrick on her own.

His teeth gritted and he told himself to forget it, but a black mood settled over him.

He drove home, changed quickly and after feeding Attila and skimming a Frisbee through the air for fifteen minutes, he left the dog in the yard and climbed into his truck again. But he hesitated before switching on the ignition. He wasn't looking forward to the evening in front of him. Tracy had called him on the car phone and invited him over and Ben hadn't found the spite in him to refuse. She'd wheedled and explained that Randy would really like to see him again after the disaster of Little League tryouts, so Ben had bowed to his own guilt and agreed to take them both to a restaurant and a movie.

Tracy hadn't been able to hide the smile in her voice and Ben felt trapped.

He picked them up at six and they drove to the outskirts of town where they stopped at the Burger Den for triple-decker cheeseburgers and spicy fries. Randy ordered a large root beer milk shake and though his mother teased him about breaking training, she let him have the drink anyway and Ben was relieved. He didn't want to get into another discussion about child rearing. Randy was her kid and she had the right to raise him as she saw fit, as long as she didn't harm the boy.

They laughed and talked and Ben wondered why he'd felt so ill at ease earlier. Tracy was her most charming and she smiled at him often, her brown eyes twinkling, her full lips stretching into a sexy grin.

But Ben couldn't stop thinking about Carlie. Through-out the evening, no matter what direction the conversation took, his mind wandered and he wondered where she was. Tonight she was supposed to be meeting Fitzpatrick for a business dinner. Just the thought of it curled Ben's insides.

"Is something wrong?" Tracy asked, snapping him back to the present.

"Nothing."

She stared pointedly at his half-eaten cheeseburger. "Nothing?"

"Nothing that matters." He grinned at Randy. "Hurry up, sport. The movie starts in twenty minutes."

The film was an action/adventure film that featured teenaged stars Randy recognized from television. Randy ate popcorn from a tub and watched raptly and Ben tried to show some interest in the thin plot, but his mind continued to wander to Carlie. Always to Carlie. He felt like a traitor being here with Kevin's family, and yet there was no way out of this particular emotional entanglement—at least no easy way. He slid a glance at Randy and the kid looked at him and smiled—Kevin's smile.

Tracy touched him on the arm and he nearly jumped out of his skin.

"Where are you?" she whispered.

"Here."

"More like a million miles away."

"Got a lot on my mind."

"The business?" she asked hopefully.

"That's a big part of it."

"And the rest?"

Even in the darkness he could see the worry and sadness in her eyes. "Nothing important," he lied and glanced at his watch.

When he dropped them off at their apartment, Randy grinned at Ben and thanked him for the "good time."

"My pleasure."

Randy glanced at his mom. "Aren't you coming in?" he asked Ben.

"Not now."

"But…you'll be back?"

Ben felt as if Randy had been coached, but smiled and ruffled the kid's hair anyway. "Sure I will."

"When?" Tracy asked.

"I'm not sure."

"We're free tomorrow," she said lightly though Ben thought he detected a hint of desperation in her voice.

"Tomorrow doesn't work for me."

She waited hopefully.

"I'll call." He felt like a heel as he read the skepticism that flickered in her eyes.

"Good. Now, Randy, you go on inside and I'll be there in a minute," she said. "I need to talk to Uncle Ben alone."

She handed her son her keys and Ben tensed, watching as the boy slipped through the door.

"He's a good boy, Tracy," he said. "I guess I already told you that."

"He thinks a lot of you."

"Not too much, I hope."

She ran a finger along the truck's fender. "You're the best thing that's happened to Randy...and to me...in a long, long while."

"I don't think so."

"Oh, yes. He lights up like a Christmas tree around you, Ben, and I know why." Before he knew what she was doing, she placed her hands on his shoulders, stood on her tiptoes and brushed his lips seductively with her own. Ben tried to step away just as her tongue pressed against his teeth.

"Tracy, don't—" His fingers curled over her waist but not before she traced the edge of his lips with her tongue.

"Why not, Ben?" she asked petulantly, her smile taking on a feline curve. "We could be good together, you and I."

"I can't."

"Sure you can."

"I'm already involved with someone," he said, firmly shoving her away from him.

She looked stunned, but just for a second. She would have had to have been blind at the engagement party not to have seen him with Carlie. Besides, Carlie had been with him at Randy's Little League tryouts. Surely she understood.

"I...I...guess I made a fool of myself."

"No—"

"It's just that I've been so lonely," she said suddenly as if a dam of emotions had cracked and burst. She blinked against a rush of tears. "I've dated a lot of men, but they...

Well, they never seemed to measure up to Kevin and then you come back to Gold Creek and you're so… Oh, damn, look, I'm sorry." She sniffed loudly. "But, please, don't blame Randy for this. He really does like you, and just because his mother had the uncanny ability to make an ass of herself…"

"You didn't," Ben said and reluctantly folded her into his arms. "It was a mistake. I should have told you."

"No, it's all right. Really. Just…just don't stop seeing Randy." She took in a deep breath and her gaze shifted away from his for just a second. "I've seen you with Carlie and I, um, hope that you don't end up getting hurt."

"You don't have to worry about that."

"But I do. I care about you, Ben," she said blinking rapidly as if she were going to break down and cry. "You see, I, uh, know some things about Carlie that you might not."

"I'm not interested in gossip," he said defensively, but he felt more than a little worry. The look on Tracy's face convinced him that whatever her little secret about Carlie was, it was ugly.

"It's not gossip."

"Really. I'm not interested." Tracy was staring at him and measuring his reaction. Ben felt as if a thick hemp rope had been cinched around his neck. She was smiling, but it wasn't a kind smile. He stepped away from her and turned toward the truck. Fast. Before he heard something he didn't want to know.

"It's kind of private," she said but added quickly, "but I thought you should know since it involves you."

The noose tightened another notch. He grabbed the handle of the door.

"Did you know that when Kevin died she was pregnant?"

Ben froze. He could barely breathe.

"That's impossible," he heard himself saying, remembering Carlie's desperate eyes when she'd told him she'd been a virgin when they'd first made love.

"I saw her medical chart. At the Coleville Women's Clinic," Tracy said as he turned and saw a glimmer of a smile flit through her eyes. She was enjoying this! "Yep. Carlie was definitely with child."

Ben whirled, grabbed her by the arms and gave her a quick little shake. His fingers dug into her flesh. "You're lying. I don't know why, but—"

"It's not a lie, Ben. Think about it! What would I have to gain by lying to you? I'm not a nurse or a doctor, but I can read a medical chart if it's spelled out to me, and she was pregnant."

"What happened?" he demanded, not releasing her.

"She lost the baby. Miscarried, I guess. Maybe had an abortion. As I said, I didn't have a lot of time and—"

"You lying bitch—!" He dropped her as if her skin burned his hands.

"Oh, no, honey, you've got the wrong woman. You should be saying things like that to Carlie. After all, you had the right to know about your kid."

"My kid?" he said, his voice barely a whisper. "My kid?"

"Sure." She lifted her shoulders. "Whose do you think it was?" she asked lightly, then blanched when she saw the answer in his eyes. "Oh, God, not Kevin's…"

He didn't wait to say goodbye, just spun on his heel, yanked open the truck door and jumped in behind the wheel. *His baby? His? Carlie was pregnant with his baby?* A thousand thoughts raced through his suddenly throbbing head. But she'd sworn she'd never been pregnant! Who was lying? Tracy or Carlie?

He shoved the truck into gear and took off with a squeal of tires. Tracy was left standing in the parking lot of her apartment building and from the corner of his eye Ben noticed a curtain move in Randy's bedroom. The kid had probably witnessed the entire scene between Ben and his mother. What would he think? Ben couldn't begin to guess. He slowed for the street, then gunned the engine. He couldn't feel responsible for Tracy and Randy...well, not too responsible. They'd gotten along all right without him for all of Randy's life; they certainly didn't need him now.

He drove to Carlie's house like a man possessed, but when he arrived, he had to wait. She was out with Thomas Fitzpatrick. Impatiently Ben jammed his own key into the lock and climbed the staircase to her apartment. It was time they had it out.

CARLIE KNEW SHE'D made a vast mistake when Thomas insisted that they go to dinner in the company helicopter.

"You're not serious," she'd said, as he'd driven her to the offices of the logging company and the flat stretch of ground where a chopper sat, pilot ready, to speed them to a hotel in San Francisco.

"I'm very serious," he said and her heart sank as she stepped aboard and saw two bottles of champagne chilling in a bucket. Once they were airborne, he offered her champagne, but she declined. Ben had been right, she realized, and wished she could change plans that had been set for nearly a week.

The view from the craft was beautiful. A full moon added luster to the dark skies and the lights of the city brightened the horizon. They landed gently and Thomas helped her through the doors of the hotel and down to a private dining room that overlooked the Golden Gate Bridge.

The linen on the table was a rich mulberry color, the napkins snow white. A bud vase held a single rose.

"What exactly do you want me to do?" she asked when he presumed to order for them both.

"I told you. The pictures for the company—I've seen the first proofs and they're very good—and then there's the matter of Toni's wedding, if it's still on. After last night, who knows?" He sighed heavily and shook his head.

"We didn't have to come all this way to discuss wedding photographs," she said, taking a sip of wine.

His blue eyes caught in the reflection. "Well, I have a confession to make," he admitted, looking somewhat sheepish. "I wanted to be alone with you."

"With me?"

"My wife's divorcing me," he said flatly.

"So—"

"So I thought I could spend an evening with a beautiful woman without feeling guilty."

"Mr. Fitzpatrick—"

"Thomas, please." He reached across the table and took her hand in his smooth fingers. She thought then how unlike Ben he was.

"Just as long as we understand each other, *Thomas,* I don't like being manipulated."

"Did I manipulate you?"

"Not if this is strictly a business meeting, and if it is, I see no reason to discuss your marriage."

"The divorce will be final within the month."

"I'm sorry," she said as the waiter brought hot rolls and delicate salads garnished with tiny sprigs of asparagus. The waiter disappeared.

"No reason to be sorry. It's probably for the best. We started drifting apart years ago...when Roy was killed. Everything came to a head a few months ago when Jackson found out I was his father." Thomas frowned thoughtfully as if rolling old reels of memories over in

his mind and for a second Carlie felt a jab of sympathy
for a man who had tried so desperately to control and
exploit the destiny of others only to lose sight of his own
happiness. "June couldn't handle that. The scandal, you
know. Things have gone downhill since then. Last night
wasn't completely unexpected. Toni's going through a
lot right now. Just when she's hoping to get married, her
parents are throwing in the matrimonial towel."

She didn't know what to say and picked at her salad.

"So, let's talk about you. You've grown up, Carlie. I
have to admit that years ago I was angry with you."

"Because you wanted Jackson to be blamed for Roy's
murder."

Thomas sighed. "I didn't *want* it, Carlie. I thought it
was what had happened. I would have supplied money
for the best lawyers in town to see that he got a lenient
sentence, but I truly believed that he'd killed Roy, either
accidentally or intentionally. Whether he was my son or
not, he had to face justice."

"But he was innocent."

"Thankfully," Thomas said, though the lines around
his eyes deepened and Carlie remembered the fact that
Brian's wife, Laura, had accidentally killed Roy.

The waiter cleared the salad plates and returned with
the main course: a brace of quail on a bed of wild rice.
Carlie said little and ate even less. Coming here had been
a mistake. She should have listened to Ben.

Ben. Just the thought of him made her heart turn over.

"I'm thinking of buying Mrs. Hunter's apartment
house."

"Is that so?" she said, trying to sound surprised.

"I like to preserve some of the unique architecture of
Gold Creek."

"It's a beautiful house."

"I thought maybe you'd like to manage it for me."

"Pardon me?"

He smiled then, a practiced, patrician smile that had no warmth. "If you would manage the units—there're five of them with the studio, isn't that right?"

"Yes."

"I could give you a break on the rent. Perhaps your folks would like to move into Mrs. Hunter's place."

"Wait a minute—" Things were moving much too quickly.

"I'm just trying to help your father. I've talked to the attorneys and the accountants and the financial advisers and think that there's a way your father can collect disability for a little while, retrain for office work, at which time he'll be retirement age and be able to collect his full pension and benefits."

Carlie waited for the catch. "Have…have you talked this over with him?"

"Just this afternoon."

"And?" She held her breath.

"He seemed pleased. Even considered moving into the apartment house to be closer to you."

"If I stay," she said, setting down her fork. "Look, Mr.—Thomas, I appreciate everything you're trying to do for my family and I know you probably think you're doing me a favor by making plans for me, but I can't accept your offer."

"You haven't even heard it yet."

"I've heard enough. I have to live my life my way."

"Of course." He looked slightly offended. "I was only trying to help."

"Thanks, but I don't think I need any."

His nostrils flared slightly and if the waiter hadn't come to remove their dishes, she was certain he would have said something not particularly kind. They finished dessert in relative silence and afterward he helped her with her coat and his fingers trailed along her arm. She shrugged him off, told herself that she was imagining things, but when he brushed his lips to her nape, she whirled on him. "I'm not interested, Mr. Fitzpatrick."

Fortunately, he didn't press the issue but the helicopter ride back to Gold Creek seemed to take forever. She didn't notice the moon or the stars or the lights of the city. When they finally touched down it was all she could do not to bolt from the chopper.

He helped her into his white Cadillac and she sat stiffly on the leather seats.

Ben had been right. She should never have accepted anything that seemed to remotely resemble a date with Fitzpatrick. She stared out the window, listening to the radio and was thankful Thomas didn't want to make small talk. All she wanted was to get home.

Home. How would she feel when the old house where she lived was owned by Thomas Fitzpatrick? One more way to be indebted to the man. Would she ever feel safe, knowing that he had a key to the house as well as her apartment?

She slid a glance in his direction. She wasn't afraid of him, at least not physically. But powerful men could exert their force in other, more subtle ways. Her father's job had already become an issue. Her work, now that she'd done a photographic layout for him, if he didn't like it, could suffer. He had the means and the power in a town the size of Gold Creek to ruin her reputation and to make her work dry up.

There was still the studio, of course. Loyal customers wouldn't be aware that Fitzpatrick was unhappy with her work, but the larger clients, the CEOs of corporations who might want a photographer could be swayed if the word was out that Fitzpatrick, Incorporated was unhappy with her work.

Too bad. She wasn't going to back down or be afraid of anyone, including Thomas Fitzpatrick. If she had to, she could call Constance about that modeling assignment with Cosmos Jeans.

At her apartment, he started to get out of the car, but Carlie said, "Don't bother. I've been thinking, and I've decided that it's probably not a good idea to work with you."

"But—"

"This evening proved one thing to me. I don't need you, Mr. Fitzpatrick, and I won't be manipulated into doing everything you want."

"I didn't mean to imply—"

"You did. You have, since I returned. I'm sorry your personal life is a mess, but there's nothing I can do about it and I'm tired of veiled threats or promises or whatever you want to call them, about my dad. Do what you have to do. Take it up with him. As for me, I'm through with you. This wasn't a business dinner tonight, it was a planned seduction."

She thought he'd argue, but he didn't. "If you're offended—"

"I am, Mr. Fitzpatrick, but if you want to know the truth, I'm more disgusted with myself than with you. I should have known better. Good night!" Before he could say anything, she slid out of the car, slammed the door and marched up the steps to her house. As far as she was concerned, Thomas Fitzpatrick was out of her life.

She'd call Constance in the morning and take the Cosmos job, and maybe she'd move back to New York once her father was well.

You'd be running away. From your family. From Fitzpatrick. From Ben. So what? It was her life. She wasn't forced to spend the rest of her years in Gold Creek.

As for Ben. He was better off without her! Her heart

squeezed painfully, but she fought the urge to break down and cry. No more tears. She was in charge of her life now and she didn't have time for any more pain and broken promises.

BEN WAS WAITING for her. Shoulder propped against the window, arms folded over his chest, eyes narrowed suspiciously, he waited, like a tiger ready to spring as she stepped into her apartment.

"What're you—"

"Close the door, Carlie," he commanded, his voice firm.

She kicked the door shut but didn't move. "What's this all about?"

"First of all, you just got a call."

She glanced to the answering machine and saw the red light blinking.

"Your friend Constance. Seems she thinks you might be going back to New York for a commercial."

So this was how it was going to be. She noticed his jaded gaze and the cynicism etched in the lines of his face. So he'd come spoiling for a fight. "You aren't here because you decided to be my answering service."

"No." He studied her face for a long moment. "Running back to the big city?"

"It's business. That's all."

His lips curved into a smile that was as cold as the bottom of the lake.

"What is it, Ben? What happened that made you think you should let yourself into *my* house and start making insinuations again? For your information—I don't need it. Not tonight. Not ever."

"There is another reason." The light in his eyes was deadly.

Carlie swallowed hard. "What?" she asked, though

part of her didn't want to know. He was too cold, too calmly angry.

Shoving himself upright, he walked across the short space that separated them and stared down at her. His skin was tight, the muscles in his face so tense, they stretched rigidly across the angles of his face. "Tell me about the baby."

"What baby? I already told you—"

"You lied!" he said. "I want to know about *our* baby."

"Oh, God," she whispered, swallowing hard. *Our baby.* "How—how did you find out?"

"So it's true." The sound of his voice seemed to echo in the small room and through her heart.

She nodded, unable to trust her voice. The pain and disappointment in his eyes cut her to the quick.

"And you didn't tell me," he said. "Didn't you think I'd want to know? Didn't you think I had that right?"

"I did try! Over and over again!"

"Did you? Or did you get rid of it and hoped that I never found out."

"No!"

"You lying—"

"No! Oh, God, no!" she cried, anger mixed with her grief. "I wanted that baby more than I wanted anything in my life! And do you know why? Because that baby was a part of you. The only part I had left."

His eyes accused her of lying, but she didn't care. "I found out I was pregnant just before you left for the army. I tried to tell you, to phone you or write you or let you know, but you wouldn't take my calls and you sent my letters back unopened. I didn't know who to tell, who I could trust. Don't you remember, Ben? Kevin had just died and everything was such a mess."

She was shaking with the old memories, her heart

turned to stone. "Then you were gone…and so was the baby."

He didn't move, just stood in silent judgment.

"So you did have an—"

"No! I miscarried!" She could feel his breath in two hot streams against her cheeks. "Damn it, Ben, I would have done anything, *anything* to keep that baby. To keep a part of you! But I failed," she said, her voice cracking. "I barely knew I was pregnant when you left, not much more than a suspicion. Then the doctor confirmed it and the next week…well, it was over."

"You should have let me know—"

"You wouldn't let me. And then it was too late."

A muscle worked in his jaw. "Was it too late the other night?"

"Yes!" she said vehemently. "After all the accusations you leveled at me when I first got back into town, I didn't think it would be such a good idea."

"So you were never going to tell me?"

"I hoped to, but not until I thought we both could handle it." Tears were hot against the back of her eyes. "I'm not sure that would have ever happened."

"Neither am I," he said, and without another word he stalked through the door and out of her life.

CHAPTER TWELVE

CARLIE STARED DOWN at the bustling street below. Cars, trucks and cabs jammed the intersection. Pedestrians, heads bent against the sleet, umbrellas vying for space, scurried along the sidewalk and spilled between parked vehicles. The noise of the city never quit. Horns blared, people yelled, engines thrummed, twenty stories below.

New York. So far removed from Gold Creek.

"Okay, that's it!" Constance said as she hung up the phone. A tiny woman with a big voice, she snapped the file on her desk shut with manicured hands and swiveled her chair to face Carlie. "The photographer is happy with the shots—well, as happy as Dino ever is—and it looks like the Cosmos campaign is rolling."

"Good," Carlie said, forcing some enthusiasm into her voice.

"So—can I start shopping you around again?"

Carlie had anticipated the question. Constance had been after her for years to resume her career. "I don't think so."

"For God's sake, why not? You're through with your soul-searching in Alaska, aren't you?"

"Yes."

"About time." Constance leaned back in her desk chair until the leather creaked. "So you're going back to that little town in California."

"I have to. Even if it's just to tie up a few loose ends...."

she said, thinking of her father. Thinking of the studio in Coleville. Thinking of Ben.

"There's a man out there, isn't there?" Constance shook her head from side to side and didn't wait for an answer. "It's always a man."

"I just think it's time to stop wandering all over the planet."

"Sure you do, honey, sure you do."

The intercom buzzed and Constance picked up the phone. After a one-sided conversation, she set the receiver in the cradle and cast Carlie an I-told-you-so look. "That man who doesn't exist?" she said picking up the conversation as if they'd never been interrupted. "He's outside in the reception area, making a big scene, scaring poor Nina half out of her mind."

Ben? Ben was here? In New York City?

"You'd better go on out there because as angry as he is, he's still interesting. Nina mentioned something about signing him up as a male model."

"I wouldn't suggest it," Carlie said, grabbing her purse and throwing her coat over her arm. She hurried out the door and had started down the short corridor to the reception area, when she saw Ben, arguing with the petite strawberry-blond receptionist as he turned the corner.

Her heart caught at the sight of him.

Ben hesitated when he saw her, then continued down the hallway and took hold of her arm. "We're getting out of here."

"Wait a minute—"

"Now, Carlie."

She stopped dead in her tracks. "You can't push me around, Ben. Haven't you learned that yet? I don't know why you're here or what you want, but you can't come barging into my place of business, or my house for that matter, and start ordering me around like I'm some damned private in the army!"

By this time Nina and two leggy models sitting in the reception area were staring at them. The models had dropped their magazines and Nina was ignoring the phone that jangled incessantly.

Even Constance was watching from her office doorway.

"I just thought we could use some privacy."

"Why?"

His gaze slid to the other women in the room, then landed with full force on Carlie's face. "Because, damn it, I was going to ask you to marry me."

The women behind her gasped and even the phone stopped ringing for a few heart-stopping seconds. "What?"

"You heard me. Now, let's go."

"You...you want to get married?"

"Yeah. Right now, if we can."

"Oh, Ben, we can't—"

"Carlie, I'm sorry. For everything. I was wrong."

"But—"

"And I want to marry you."

By this time the phone had started up again but all eyes were still trained on her. She felt embarrassment wash up her neck. "But just last week—"

"I was a fool." He stared straight into her eyes. "A lot has happened since last week and the upshot is that I know that I don't want to spend the rest of my life without you."

"Are you out of your mind? I don't think—"

"Don't think," he whispered, grabbing her suddenly, his lips crashing down on hers, his arms surrounding her. He smelled of brandy and rain and musk and he held her as if he'd never let go. His kiss was filled with the same bone-melting passion that always existed between them, and when he finally let her go, she could barely breathe.

"Go on. Get out of here," Constance said from somewhere down the hall. "This man means business. And the rest of you, back to work."

Carlie hardly remembered the elevator ride down to the lobby of the office building. Somehow, with Ben's hand clamped on her elbow, he guided her outside and they braved the icy sleet and wind. Two blocks and around a corner, he held open the door to a crowded bar. They found a small table near the back and Ben ordered Irish coffees for them both.

"Okay," Carlie said, her heart still pumping, her ears still ringing with his proposal. "Start over. Why'd you come here?"

"For you."

"The last I heard you never wanted to see me again."

"I sorted some things out."

"Maybe you should sort them out for me," she said, trying to stay calm. She couldn't marry Ben. His temper was too mercurial, his mood swings too violent. True, she loved him, but that didn't mean she could live with him. Or did it?

"I was upset the last time I saw you," Ben admitted. "Tracy had told me about the baby—"

"Tracy?" Carlie whispered, aghast.

The waiter brought their drinks and disappeared.

"Seems she saw you at the Coleville Women's Clinic once and figured out about the baby."

"Oh, God," she whispered. "Look, Ben, I know I should have told you but there never seemed to be the right time."

"It's all right." He grabbed her hand and held it between his. "I, um, have done a lot of soul-searching the last week. I talked to Nadine and we found all Kevin's old letters up in a trunk she'd stored in the attic. I read them again, made a little more sense out of the past and realized that Kevin did kill himself over a woman, but the woman wasn't you. It was Tracy."

"You know this?"

"I had it out with her," he admitted, his face creasing into a frown. "She admitted that when she found out she was pregnant, he'd wanted her to get an abortion. She'd refused and pressured him to marry her. Also, he was having trouble at the mill, more trouble than we knew about. He was probably going to be fired or laid off. All that, along with the fact that he wasn't completely over you and I was seeing you, pushed him over the edge. He did kill himself, Carlie, but it wasn't our fault."

"But what about Randy?" she asked, her throat closing.

"Randy will always be a part of my life. I told Tracy the same thing. If the kid needs me, I'll be there. Even when he doesn't think he needs me, I'll be in his face. The one thing that Tracy was right about was that the kid needs a father figure." He sipped his coffee. "And I'm going to be it."

Her heart swelled in her chest.

"But that doesn't mean I don't want kids—our kids. I do. Three of them."

"Three?"

"Well, four. That way two won't gang up on one."

"You've got it all figured out, don't you?" she whispered.

"Nope. Just a couple of ideas. I think we should figure it out together."

"You're serious about us getting married?" she said, still unbelieving.

With a half smile, he reached into the inside pocket of his jacket and withdrew a tiny box.

"What—?"

He handed her the box and she opened it. A single clear diamond winked up at her. "I'd like to say that I bought this eleven years ago and kept it all the time, 'cause I'd planned to go out and buy you a ring the night Kevin… Well, anyway, I didn't get around to it."

Her hands were shaking so he slipped the ring out of the velvet liner and slid it over her finger. "Will you marry me?" he asked and her throat was so full, she could barely answer.

"Of course I'll marry you, Ben. I've been waiting to hear you ask me for as long as I can remember…."

EPILOGUE

December

CARLIE HEARD A soft cry and burrowed deeper under the covers before she was suddenly awake.

"Want me to get her?" Ben's voice was groggy.

"I'm up." She leaned over, kissed her husband and felt the milk in her breasts start to let down. "Coming," she whispered, nearly tripping over Attila who lay at the foot of the bed.

The cabin still smelled new, the scents of wood and paint lingering as Carlie picked up her baby and cuddled the warm little body to hers. She crept downstairs, turned on a switch that caused the tiny winking lights on the Christmas tree to sparkle to life.

In an old rocker, near the window, she held her daughter to her breast and smiled at the tiny face with sky-blue eyes and a cap of dark curls.

"Here you go," she whispered and kissed Mary on her downy head. From the window, she could look across the lake and see the mist rising over the water as dawn approached. She felt an incredible calm.

Nadine had insisted on giving them this cabin as a wedding present. Ben had declined of course, but worked out some deal with his sister so that they could afford to live here. Nadine, caught up with twin girls and preadolescent boys, had finally realized that she didn't need a second home.

It was satisfying, Carlie thought, smoothing one of Mary's downy curls with her finger. They were all parents now. Turner and Heather had a second little boy, the spitting image of his older brother, Adam, and Rachelle and Jackson were the proud parents of a son. A new generation for Gold Creek.

And though some couples had divorced, others had married. Ben's father, George, had married Ellen Tremont Little, and wonder of wonder, Thomas Fitzpatrick was squiring Tracy Niday around, though Carlie had little hope that their affair would blossom into anything other than what it was.

"Hey, you two, how about a walk?"

"Now? I'm in my robe," Carlie protested as she gazed up the stairs. Ben was dressed in jeans and his leather jacket and he was carrying a snowsuit for Mary and Carlie's long black coat. "It's freezing."

"We'll be fine."

Wondering what he was up to, Carlie finished feeding and changing her daughter, then put the infant into the heavy snowsuit. Ben and Attila were waiting outside on the porch. "I'll carry her," he said, taking the baby from his wife's arms and walking toward the lake.

The sun was rising over the mountains to the east and mist danced upon the smooth water. "What's going on?"

"Just honoring a time-honored tradition." At the shore, he bent down and scooped some water into his hand.

"You're not serious."

"Absolutely." He pulled a champagne glass from the pocket of his jacket, bent down and scooped some of the water from the lake, then held the glass to Carlie's lips. "I think we've been blessed by the God of the moon—"

"Sun," she corrected.

"Whatever. Drink. But not too much."

She sipped and then Ben took a swallow before

dunking his finger and spilling a few tiny drops on his daughter's forehead.

"Hey—wait—"

"Christening her."

"I don't think Reverend Osgood would approve."

"I'm sure he wouldn't," Ben agreed, kissing his daughter on her cheek. "But we have a lot to be thankful for. This pip-squeak of a daughter, your father's new job at the Bait and Fish, the house—"

"Each other."

He smiled and sighed. "Each other." Slinging an arm around Carlie's shoulder, he held her close. Little Mary yawned and closed her eyes again.

Carlie rested her head against his shoulder and watched as the sun rose in the sky, turning the mist on the water's surface to a glorious white cloud—the ghosts of Whitefire Lake.

She closed her eyes and imagined she heard the sounds of native drums but realized it was only the steady, constant beating of Ben's heart.

* * * * *

AUTHOR'S NOTE

A short history of
Gold Creek, California

THE NATIVE AMERICAN legend of Whitefire Lake was whispered to the white men who came from the East in search of gold in the mountains. Even in the missions, there was talk of the legend, though men of the Christian God professed to disbelieve any pagan myths.

None was less believing than Kelvin Fitzpatrick, a brawny Irishman who was rumored to have killed a man before he first thrust his pickax into the hills surrounding the lake. No body was ever found, and the claim jumper vanished, so murder couldn't be proved. But the rumors around Fitzpatrick didn't disappear.

He found the first gold in the hills on a morning when the lake was still shrouded in the white mist that was as beautiful as it was deceptive. Fitzpatrick staked his claim and drank lustily from the water. He'd found his home and his fortune in these hills.

He named the creek near his claim Gold Creek and decided to become the first founding father of a town by the same name. He took his pebbles southwest to the city of San Francisco, where he transformed gold to money and a scrubby forty-niner into what appeared to be a wealthy gentleman. With his money and looks, Kelvin wooed and married a socialite from the city, Marian Dubois.

News of Fitzpatrick's gold strike traveled fast, and soon Gold Creek had grown into a small shantytown. With the prospectors came the merchants, the gamblers, the saloon keepers, the clergy and the whores. The Silver Horseshoe Saloon stood on the west end of town and the Presbyterian church was built on the east, and Gold Creek soon earned a reputation for fistfights, barroom brawls and hangings.

Kelvin's wealth increased and he fathered four children—all girls. Two were from Marian, the third from a town whore and the fourth by a Native American woman. All the children were disappointments as Kelvin Fitzpatrick needed an heir for his empire.

The community was growing from a boisterous mining camp to a full-fledged town, with Kelvin Fitzpatrick as Gold Creek's first mayor and most prominent citizen. The persecuted Native Americans with their legends and pagan ways were soon forced into servitude or thrown off their land. They made their way into the hills, away from the white man's town and the white man's troubles.

In 1860, when Kelvin was forty-three, his wife finally bore him a son, Rodwell Kelvin Fitzpatrick. Roddy, handsome and precocious, quickly became the apple of his father's eye. Though considered a "bad seed" and a hellion by most of the churchgoing citizens of Gold Creek, Roddy Fitzpatrick was the crown prince to the Fitzpatrick fortune, and when his father could no longer mine gold from the earth's crust, he discovered a new mode of wealth, and perhaps, more sacred: the forest.

Roddy Fitzpatrick started the first logging operation and opened the first sawmill. All competitors were quickly bought or forced out of business. But other men, bankers and smiths, carpenters and doctors, settled down to stay and hopefully smooth out the rough edges of the town. Men with names of Kendrick, Monroe and Powell made Gold Creek their home and brought their wives in homespun and woolens, women who baked pies, planned fairs and corralled their wayward Saturday night drinking men into church each Sunday morning.

Roddy Fitzpatrick, who grew into a handsome but cruel man, ran the family businesses when the older Fitzpatrick retired. In a few short years, Roddy had gambled or squandered most of the family fortune. Competitors had finally gotten a toehold in the lumber-rich mountains surrounding Gold Creek and new businesses were sprouting along the muddy streets of the town.

The railroad arrived, bringing with its coal-spewing engines much wealth and commerce. The railway station was situated on the west end of town, not too far from the Silver Horseshoe Saloon, and a skeletal trestle bridged the gorge of the creek. Ranchers and farmers brought their produce into town for the market and more people stayed on, settling in the growing community, though Gold Creek was still known for the bullet holes above the bar in the saloon.

And still there was the rumor of some Indian curse that occasionally was whispered by the older people of the town.

Roddy Fitzpatrick married a woman of breeding, a woman who was as quick with a gun as she was to quote a verse. Belinda Surrett became his wife and bore him three sons.

Roddy, always a hothead and frustrated at his shrinking empire, was involved in more than his share of brawls. Knives flashed, guns smoked and threats and curses were spit around wads of tobacco and shots of whiskey.

When a man tried to cheat him at cards, Roddy plunged

a knife into the blackguard's heart and killed him before a packed house of gamblers, drinkers, barkeeps and whores. After a night in jail, Roddy was set free with no charges leveled against him by the sheriff, who was a fast friend of the elder Fitzpatrick.

But Roddy's life was not to be the same. One night he didn't return home to his wife. She located Kelvin and they formed a search party. Two days later, Roddy's body washed up on the shores of Whitefire Lake. There was a bullet in his chest and his wallet was empty.

Some people thought he was killed by a thief; still others decided Roddy had been shot by a jealous husband, but some, those who still believed in the legend, knew that the God of the Sun had taken Roddy's life to punish Kelvin Fitzpatrick by not only taking away his wealth, but the only thing Kelvin had loved: his son.

The older Fitzpatrick, hovering on the brink of bankruptcy, took his own life after learning that his son was dead. Kelvin's daughters, those legitimate, and those who were born out of wedlock, each began their own lives.

The town survived the dwindling empire of the Fitzpatricks and new people arrived at the turn of the century. New names were added to the town records. Industry and commerce brought the flagging community into the twentieth century, though the great earthquake of 1906 did much damage. Many buildings toppled, but the Silver Horseshoe Saloon and the Presbyterian church and the railroad trestle bridge survived.

Monroe Sawmill, a new company owned and operated by Hayden Garreth Monroe, bought some of the dwindling Fitzpatrick forests and mills, and during the twenties, thirties and forties, Gold Creek became a company town. The people were spared destitution during the depression as the company kept the workers employed, even when they were forced to pay in company cash that could only be spent on goods at the company store. But no family employed by Monroe Sawmill went hungry; therefore, the community, who had hated Fitzpatrick's empire, paid homage to Hayden Garreth Monroe, even when the forests dwindled, logging prices dropped and the mills were shut down.

In the early 1960s, the largest sawmill burned to the ground. The police suspected arson. As the night sky turned orange by the flames licking toward the black heavens, and the volunteer firemen fought the blaze, the townspeople stood and watched. Some thought the fire was a random act of violence, others believed that Hayden Garreth Monroe III, grandson of the well-loved old man, had lost favor and developed more than his share of enemies when the company cash became worthless and the townspeople, other than those who were already wealthy, began to go bankrupt. They thought the fire was personal revenge. Names of those he'd harmed were murmured. Fitzpatrick came to mind, though by now, the families had been bonded by marriage and the timber empire of the Fitzpatricks had experienced another boom.

Some of the townspeople, the very old with long memories, thought of the legend that had nearly been forgotten. Hayden Garreth Monroe III had drunk like a glutton from Whitefire Lake and he, too, would lose all that he held dear—first his wealth and eventually his wife.

As time passed, other firms found toeholds in Gold Creek, and in the seventies and eighties technology crept over the hills. From the ashes of Kelvin Fitzpatrick's gold and timber empire rose the new wealth of other families.

The Fitzpatricks still rule the town, and Thomas Fitzpatrick, patriarch of the family, intends one day to turn to state politics. However, scandal has tarnished his name and as his political aspiration turns to ashes and his once-envied life crumbles, he will have to give way to new rulers—young men who are willing to fight for what they want. Men like Jackson Moore, Turner Brooks, Hayden Garreth Monroe IV and Ben Powell. With strong women at their sides, these men are destined to rule.

In Gold Creek, old names mingle and marry with new, but the town and its legend continue to exist. And, to this day, the people of Gold Creek cannot shake the gold dust of those California hills from their feet. Though they walk many paths away from the shores of the lake, the men and women of Gold Creek—the boys and the girls— can never forget their hometown. Nor can they forget the legend and curse of Whitefire Lake.